Bloodstone
Regenesis.

.

A Novel by

D.W.Mace.

To Gary.
Good Luck with the
New Job!

D.W.Mace

Published in 2013 by FeedARead.com Publishing – Arts Council funded.

First Edition

A CIP catalogue record for this title is available from the British Library.

Also by the Author.

The Eternal Watchtower Trilogy:

Book One: A Bright, and Shining Land.
Book Two: The Riddle of Storien-Rhudd.
Book Three: The Hand of Baelar.

~ ~ ~ ~ ~ ~ ~ ~ ~ ~

The Vanavara Protocol.

~ ~ ~ ~ ~ ~ ~ ~ ~ ~

The Abaddon Stone.

~ ~ ~ ~ ~ ~ ~ ~ ~ ~

Transliteration is used throughout the novel for Russian and Korean language words and expressions used in the text.

North Korea. Highway One.

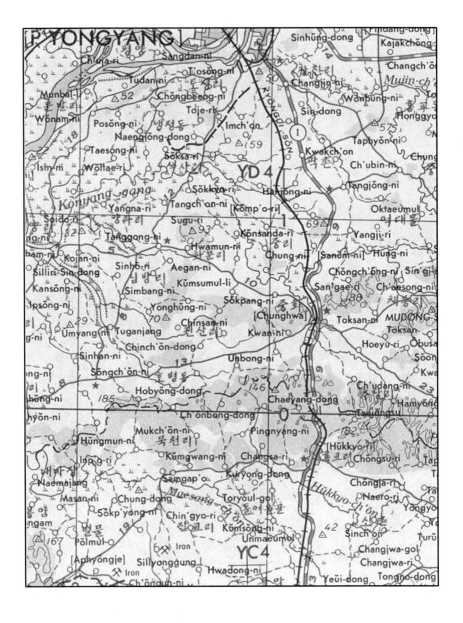

Eastern and Western sectors of Berlin. 1960.

Introduction.

"Abaddon"...

The New Testament Book of Revelation makes reference to a male angel called Abaddon. His name is commonly used in the context of being Hell personified; the Prince of the Underworld... The Angel of the Bottomless pit. The name is also found in Hebrew teachings; and his name is first transcribed in Greek as "whose name in Hebrew is Abaddon."

In *Revelation 9:7-11*, Abaddon is described as *"The Destroyer," "The Angel of The Abyss."*

Or, to be more specific...

Revelation 9:11 (Quote):
"And they had a king over them, which is the angel of the bottomless pit, whose name in the Hebrew tongue is Abaddon, but in the Greek tongue hath his name Apollyon."

This study of the history of words, their origins, and how their form and meaning have changed over time may be of interest to those of a Theological persuasion; and the Entity may even exist for those who hold faith in the doctrines and teachings of their Religion; but, in the real world there is another Abaddon.

It is a Garnet gemstone that is the absolute antithesis of all of the beliefs surrounding the many benevolent myths and legends concerning this particular gemstone. The Garnet in question is a large, seventy-carat, blood-red stone that has become known as "The Abaddon Stone."

The first intimation of this malignant gem came from the pages of an ancient volume discovered in 1936, in the icy wastelands of Siberia, in the area of the great 1908 Tunguska explosion. It was unknowingly retrieved by a young, female German archaeologist as a consequence of her deciphering the ancient script contained within the pages of the ancient volume.

The ancient volume told that the gem was said to have been mounted in the sword pommel of an unspeakably evil Entity who was called by name: "Baelar... Lord of The Underdark." According to the ancient volume; the broken sword-hilt, complete with the Abaddon Stone still mounted in its setting, and still clutched in the claw-like severed hand of the Dark Lord, himself; had been sealed by a sword-maker in a seamless block of metal inscribed with a monitory inscription which she had succeeded in deciphering. The inscription warned...

"Behold. Herein, is trammelled The Evil of all time.
Seek not its deliverance, for there is none.
Meddle not with this Abomination,
For it is The Destroyer of Worlds."

The volume told, that, as the sword-maker had poured the last of the metal into the mould to encase this monstrosity; he had glimpsed, deep within the heart of the Garnet, the flare of a tiny, blood-red spark of light.

Resolved not to let this appalling artefact fall into Soviet hands; the young archaeologist had brought it back to Germany; having destroyed her translation notes to prevent the Nazi hierarchy... and Reichsführer-SS Heinrich Himmler in particular, from ever discovering the secret of the metal block. Himmler, fascinated as he was, by mysticism, accepted that it was no more than an interesting Untermensch curiosity. He had not seen this type of metal before, and decided to have it analysed in order to establish if it might be useful as a weapons-grade material.

The block was dissected on the evening of Thursday, 31st August, 1939 in a Krupp's machine-shop in Essen, Germany. As it was exposed by the cutting away of a section of the block; the Garnet flared again with a tiny blood-red spark of light deep within its heart.

At the very moment that the Garnet flared; the clock on the workshop wall in Essen struck eight o'clock. Five hundred kilometres away to the east, at 20.00 hrs precisely; the local audience was listening to Gleiwitzer Sender... a German long-wave radio transmitter

8

seven kilometres from the Polish border of the German-Polish frontier. The popular music programme was suddenly interrupted, and excited German voices announced that the town of Gleiwitz had been invaded by Polish irregular formations marching towards the emitting station. Then the station broadcast went dead. When the broadcast resumed, Polish was being spoken.

German army intelligence... the Abwehr; together with the SS, had put into action the first stage of "Unternehmen Himmler"... Operation Himmler; the first of twenty-one orchestrated incidents along the Germano-Polish border intended to give the appearance of Polish aggression against Germany.

All along the Polish border, units of the German Wehrmacht were taking their final positions for the launch of "Fall Weiss"... "Case White"... the German strategic plan for the Invasion of Poland, which would be the catalyst that unleashed The Second World War. Thus, was the malignant influence of the terrible Abaddon Stone loosed upon humanity.

The gemstone was first named "The Abaddon Stone" by no less a personage than Reichsmarschall Hermann Göring; who was presented with this malignant gemstone by Reichsführer-SS Heinrich Himmler as yet one more trinket for Göring's extensive collection. With the defeat of Nazi Germany, the gemstone had disappeared; and the young archaeologist; now recruited by the American Intelligence organisation, and a naturalised American citizen, with a new identity... Charlotte Mckenna; had eventually been posted back to Berlin. Whilst there; she decided that she must try to track down this gemstone to prevent it from inflicting its malignant influence any further. Wherever it went, it seemed to inflict mayhem and death.

The trail led her to Hamburg, and then out to the Far East... firstly, to Hong Kong; and then, on to Korea... just as the Korean War broke out. A coincidence?... Or the Abaddon Stone's malignant influence once again?

Charlotte Mckenna was eventually deployed on a dangerous espionage mission in the heart of the North Korean capital; P'yŏngyang. Whilst there, she also attempted to discover the fate of her lover, another Intelligence officer who had previously been sent into the enemy capital on another covert mission.

With the stone still unaccounted for; she focussed her energy on locating her lover. She eventually found him, but discovered that as a result of an automobile accident, he had no memory of her, or of their previous life together.

Undeterred, she decided to bring him out of North Korea to the relative safety of the Embassy in Seoul, from where they would be flown out of the country back to the United States.

Meanwhile, the Abaddon Stone had fallen into the hands of the Hong Kong and Macau Triads and was leaving a trail of death across the Korean peninsula; the Sino-Portuguese territory of Macau, and the British colony of Hong Kong. It would eventually travel west, and Charlotte Mckenna would follow it.

Chapter One.

Wednesday, 25th May. 1960.
P'yŏngyang. North Korea.

CIA deep cover agent Captain Charlotte Mckenna sat in her office in the austere surroundings of the T17 sniper academy in P'yŏngyang and studied, perhaps for the hundredth time, the thick dossier containing the files of all the Soviet officers posted as missing in North Korea during the war. She sighed. So far, through months of searching she had not found even the most inconsequential reference to a *"Polkovnik"*... Colonel, Konstantin Sharansky of the Soviet Administration troops... the *"Sovetskaia Voennaia Administratsia."*

Colonel Konstantin Sharansky was the cover identity that had been allocated to her lover, Max Segal, when he went into North. His legend had been that he was a Soviet Military Attaché on rotation from the Russian Legation in Seoul to the Number 2 KPA Officers School. Nothing had been heard of him since. There was simply no way of establishing if he was still alive. There was no indication that he had ever been discovered... the North Koreans would have seized on the opportunity to mount a show trial for an exposed Imperialist spy in their midst, and, with the suspicion that the captured spy was CIA; the Soviets would have moved him swiftly to the Lubyanka prison back in Moscow for extensive interrogation.

Charlotte had now been in deep cover in P'yŏngyang for almost two years; fully accepted as an accredited member of the Soviet Embassy on Somun Street, and attached as an advanced marksmanship Instructor/Advisor at the sniper academy. When her daughter Stacey was eight, Charlotte had been called into the CIA Chief of Station's office on the U.S. Naval air station, Atsugi, Japan and instructed that she was being made operational once again. An Intelligence Information cable had been received from William Colby, the Chief of

11

Station in Saigon, and Chief of the CIA's Far East Division, requiring that an agent was to be placed in the very heart of North Korea's Military environment. The obvious choice would be P'yŏngyang... the Kim Il Sung Military University on the western side of the city, which had been virtually obliterated by American bombing raids and rebuilt.

Relations with the Soviet Union had soured as the USSR de-Stalinised and sought better relations with the West. North Korea was caught in the middle of the Sino-Soviet split. Although Kim Il-sung hoped to remain neutral and play the two larger powers off against each other, the Soviets concluded that he favoured the Chinese, and cut off all support. North Korean troops were taking a much more aggressive stance toward U.S. forces in and around South Korea, engaging U.S. Army troops in fire-fights along the Demilitarized Zone. North Korea had all but re-ignited the Korean War.

Believing that America would be slow to respond due to its increasing presence in Vietnam, North Korea had also initiated its infiltration campaign. Specially trained commandos were sent across the DMZ. Several commandos made it to the capital where they intended to assassinate the South Korean President. The plot failed however when the Commandos were killed in a shoot out with the Seoul police. As the Great Cultural revolution in China began to gather momentum, Chinese Red Guards hurled insults at Kim through wall posters and blasted tirades from loudspeakers on the border, accusing North Koreans as being revisionist like Khrushchev; refusing to aid North Vietnam, and ignoring the Cultural Revolution.

Something was about to happen. Washington was edgy. Would Kim make a move against the south as an appeasement to the Communist Chinese? Colby wanted someone on the inside of the North Korean communist national organisation. Head of Station had decided that Charlotte, because of her multi-lingual skills, would be chosen for this assignment. Her legend would be that she was a Soviet advisor. The Soviet embassy in P'yŏngyang had been observing the rise of Kim Il Sung's political process of the "Cult of Personality in the DPRK" with unease and alarm. Their misgiving had been revealed in a cable intercepted by the CIA Station in Seoul.

Colby had decided that an agent should be place in deep cover inside the Soviet Embassy in P'yŏngyang. The old landline from the Seoul telephone exchange that had been used during the war to connect between the Bureau and Kim Il Sung's intelligence headquarters in P'yŏngyang's former No. 2 KPA Officers School was still serviceable. Seoul knew that it had been tapped by the Soviets when it was discovered during the post war reconstruction by Soviet engineers in the Government quarter of P'yŏngyang. A message would be sent notifying the North Korean Intelligence headquarters of the imminent arrival of a new Soviet advisor. The Embassy would intercept this message and, in view of the deteriorating relations between them and the North Koreans, would almost certainly extract the new "Advisor" before the Korean intelligence staff arrived to meet him or her. At least, that was the most likely scenario according to the available intelligence.

Charlotte studied Head of Station.

'You really think that I'm the one for this assignment? Don't forget, I'm no spring chicken... I am forty-six, and I have an eight-year old daughter.'

Head of Station nodded.

'Yeah, Charlotte, I know; but you don't look a day over thirty-five and your blonde hair is typical of a Belorussian girl. You speak fluent Russian and know their customs and behaviours from your Pre-war Siberian assignment. You really are the best bet for this deployment. Stacey will be OK with us. Josie Pullen will look after her, and we'll see to it that she has the best education money can buy.'

Charlotte nodded.

'So what's the legend you're putting together for me?'

Head of Station pushed a slim folder across the desk.

'It's all in here. You are now *"Polkovnik"*... Colonel Nadia Tolenkanovna. You were born on March 18th, 1912, in a small rural farming community outside Smolensk. At the age of sixteen, your family moved to Moscow, and there you joined a youth marksman club. You excelled as a markswoman.

You were twenty-nine and a civilian firearms instructor when Germany invaded Russia in the June of 1941. You were allowed by the military commissariat to enrol in the Central Women's School for Snipers at Veshnyaki near Moscow. Its graduates completed a regimented eight month training program of tactics, camouflage, field craft, and marksmanship, and were then posted to specific rifle regiments. You were selected for the *Rezerv Verkhovnogo Glavnokomandovaniya...* the Reserves of the Supreme High Command, and went operational in the Autumn of 1943 with the 3rd Shock Army, 1st Belorussian Front with the rank of Guards senior sergeant in the Nevel'-Gorodok offensive operation.

Through the Winter-Spring Campaign of 43-44, the Starorussa-Novorzhev offensive operation, and the Summer-Autumn Campaign of 1944, your score rapidly mounted, until, during the Riga Offensive and the Kurland peninsula blockade between September 1944 and May 1945, your score of confirmed kills topped one hundred, and you had been awarded the Order of the Red Star.

You then moved west, and by the time you arrived in Berlin, you had increased your score to one hundred and fifty-two, of which twelve were German snipers. You were one of only six of your original class at Veshnyaki who survived. You returned to the Central Female Sniper Academy, which, in the autumn of 1943 had been relocated to Podolsk, as an instructor with the rank of Major in 1946. Whilst there, you were again promoted and awarded the Order of The Great Patriotic War (1st Class.)

In 1952, the Soviet Union closed its national system of sniper schools, and most women were demobilized and banned from attending military schools and academies. A common belief reasserted itself among the Politburo of the Central Committee that women should serve only when the country was endangered. Those who remained in the army were posted to women's traditional military occupations such as nursing, political work, communications, and administration.'

Charlotte studied him.

'So, what happened to Colonel Tolenkanovna?'

Head of Station smiled.

'She was transferred to the Administration Directorate… which, as we all know, is actually Russian Military Intelligence. The Soviet Union and China trained and equipped North Korea's snipers. The Communist regime went on to utilise snipers during the Korean War very effectively. A sniper was actually chosen to be a member of a sniper team. The many tunnels that North Korea had dug through to South Korean territory allowed their snipers to reach prime locations. Consequently, that, in addition to sniping skills led to the success of North Korean snipers, who eventually were reorganised into the DPRK Special Operations Forces Reconnaissance sniper brigades.

They were intensively trained at the T17 sniper academy in P'yŏngyang, which is where Major… now promoted to Colonel Tolenkanovna, and awarded the Order of Lenin for her services to the Motherland, was to be seconded as an advanced marksmanship Instructor/Advisor.'

Charlotte raised an eyebrow. Head of Station gave a cold smile and continued.

'Colonel Tolenkanovna is permanently out of the picture. The car bringing her to P'yŏngyang was targeted by a North Korean patrol by mistake last month, and shot up. There were no survivors. P'yŏngyang was never told of the incident; in fact, it was never reported at all. It was all hushed up because of the ongoing disintegration of the anti-Soviet pro-Maoist bloc, which has been gathering pace. This has been due to the Cultural Revolution. The internal propaganda of North Korea has begun to criticize "dogmatism" and "superpower chauvinism," clearly directed at China. Relations have now reached their lowest ebb, and the patrol commander would rather not admit that they'd accidentally popped a heroine of Russia's Great Patriotic War for fear of terminal reprisals from his superiors. Consequently, the blame was laid squarely at the door of some anonymous air attack. The bodies were never identified; and the whole thing was written off as "Fortunes of War." We discovered the truth, almost by accident when an unimportant North Korean officer who had been with the patrol was captured and routinely interrogated.

Colonel Nadia Tolenkanovna was the same age as you appear to be, and our intelligence sources in Russia say that she was very similar to you in her appearance. The Embassy officials in P'yŏngyang have never seen her, so you should fit in without any problem, with your reputation for tradecraft and security.'

Charlotte nodded.

'Impressive. So how do you propose to insert me into North Korea?'

Head of Station studied her briefly, and then drew another slim file from his desk drawer.

'The Seoul Bureau has utilised the old landline we had covertly re-routed from the Seoul telephone exchange during the War to connect between the Bureau and Kim Il Sung's Intelligence Headquarters in the old P'yŏngyang Number 2 KPA Officers School... now renamed the Korea Central Intelligence Agency. (KCIA.) We used it very effectively for disinformation, and it was never discovered as being our "Trojan Horse."

A signal purporting to be from Moscow Central has been transmitted along this clandestine route informing them of the imminent arrival of a certain Colonel Nadia Tolenkanovna of the Administration Directorate, who has been appointed by Moscow as an advanced marksmanship Instructor/Advisor, seconded to the T17 sniper academy in P'yŏngyang. This information will have been forwarded by the Koreans to the Soviet Embassy in P'yŏngyang as a matter of diplomatic protocol, and thus, they will be expecting you.'

He placed the sheet of paper to one side and removed another. This one bore the Seoul U.S. Consulate crest and was marked "Secret." He glanced up at Charlotte.

'We have arranged to use the same method that the Bureau used to

15

insert Max Segal. We'll sail the Yangtze River-type coal barge along the Taedong River to the old wharves at Sep'o, where they will off-load a Soviet staff car which you will use to drive into P'yŏngyang along the main P'yŏngyang-Chinnamp'o highway. Once in the city, you are to report to the Soviet Embassy in Somun Street. They will make all the subsequent arrangements.'

Charlotte studied him solemnly.

'The same route? Will we get away with it twice?'

Head of Station nodded.

'Yes. They're far too busy rebuilding their country to worry too much about a grimy old Chinese coal barge... and besides which; it's the same crew: Chief Warrant Officer Jimmylee Chung and his men... the same guys who successfully inserted Max.'

He closed the file and studied Charlotte.

'OK. Here's the deal. You fly out from Tokyo International at the end of the week for Seoul. This time, you'll be flying on an ordinary Japan Airlines, civilian scheduled flight to Gimpo International Airport... that's the old K14 Kimpo Air Base which they've renamed this year by Presidential Order, and is being given a full-scale upgrade to international airport status.

We're doing it this way so that you will appear to be just another passenger in case one of the many North Korean spies who are roaming the city is keeping watch on the airport.'

The Japan Airlines DC 7 circled low over the city as the pilot joined the landing circuit to Gimpo International Airport. Gazing down from the cabin window, Charlotte was surprised how different it appeared to what she remembered of Seoul from her time at the Bureau. Following the war, Seoul had undergone an immense reconstruction and modernization effort due mainly to necessity, but also due in part to the symbolic nature of Seoul as the political and economic centre of Korea.

During the Korean War, the city had changed hands between the Chinese-backed North Korean forces and the UN-backed South Korean forces several times, leaving vast tracts of Seoul in ruins after the War ended in 1953, with at least half of the city laid to waste by the fighting and bombing. In addition, a flood of refugees had entered the city during the war, swelling the population of Seoul and its metropolitan area to more than two million; more than half of them homeless. The formerly bustling East Gate Market had become an empty wilderness of rubble, rusty galvanized iron, and silence. The stark ruins scattering across the once great city she remembered were still in plain view, seven years after the guns had fallen silent... gutted buildings, jagged walls without ceilings, acres of desolation through which the breeze moaned and whimpered from off the Han River.

As the DC7 turned west to line up on its final approach, she noticed that the old, six-kilometre-long Cheonggyecheon stream, which cut east to west across the city, effectively bisecting the northern and southern districts, was finally being covered over. She smiled to herself. Not before time! Neglected and highly polluted, it had been an eyesore for years... lined with a multitude of shabby, makeshift, shanty huts built by refugees, and the stench emitting from its dirty waters could be savoured across the entire city when the wind was in the right direction.

During her time at the Seoul Bureau, the Cheonggyecheon was considered a symbol of the poverty and filth that were the legacy of a half-century of colonialism and war. The open sewer in the centre of the city was also a major obstacle to the redevelopment of Seoul. The war had sorted some of that problem out, but, somehow, Seoul would never be the same without the lingering aroma of the festering waterway that the Colonial Japanese occupational forces had christened the *"Takgyecheon,"* which meant "dirty water stream." This was supremely ironic, because "Cheonggyecheon" had originally been known as the "clean stream," but, following liberation in 1945 and the Korean War the area had become a large, seething slum. Soon, the "clean stream" was filled with human waste, rubbish, and rising sediment, until, as Seoul began its rapid industrialization, the stream was finally paved over, and the slums were destroyed. An elevated highway was now being constructed over the old stream bed.

The DC7 began its descent. She heard the familiar shrill hydraulic whine of the flaps and the landing-wheels being lowered, as they were crossing the Han River below, obscured by a candescent haze that hung over the flat, sluggish, eddying grey waters. She felt her ears began to block with the slow descent towards the pale concrete ribbon that was the main runway at Gimpo International. Then there came the hiss and sickly smell of the insecticide bomb being deployed, and the dip of the plane's nose; followed by the sharp squeal and the tearing bump of the tyres meeting the runway.

The cabin was suddenly filled with an ugly roar as the pilot pulled the propeller pitch levers back through the reverse pitch "gate" and into reverse to slow the plane for the turn-off taxiway, before the rumbling progress over the grass towards the tarmac apron as the big airliner slowed with squealing brakes and came to a standstill in front of the flight terminal which still showed the marks of war, with machine gun bullet holes in the walls. The roar of the engines faded as the pilot closed the throttles, and with a weary mechanical wheezing from the power recovery turbines, the propellers slowed and finally came to rest, with a faint haze of blueish smoke puffing fitfully from the exhaust stacks.

The stewardess opened the passenger door with a soft thud, and the passengers began disembarking down the passenger stairs which had been towed up to the port side of the airplane, just aft of the wing. Charlotte was about half-way back in the queue that formed as the passengers left their seats in the cabin. As she stepped out into the daylight, the old, familiar, hot, damp heat hit her. A young man in a civilian suit was waiting with the flight attendants at the foot of the passenger stairs. His whole appearance screamed "Spook"... even down to the obligatory quasi-military sunglasses.

As she stepped onto the tarmac, he moved forward, hesitated, and spoke.

'Captain Mckenna? Welcome to Seoul, Ma'am. I am Bradley Snyder...Brad, for short; under secretary at the Chancery. I have a car waiting for you.'

Charlotte studied him discreetly. Under-secretary indeed! He couldn't have broadcast the fact that he was a rooky agent any plainer than if he had the letters "CIA" stencilled in big red letters across his forehead. She sighed under her breath. It wasn't really his fault... he had just read too many Matt Helm novels... and all the experienced agents were deployed in Vietnam and Laos. Best to get him out of the public view. Smoothly, she took charge of the situation.

'OK, Brad. Pleased to meet you. Now, let's go get out of this damned heat.'

Together, they walked across the tarmac to where a plain black Pontiac sedan that he had pointed out was waiting. The driver opened the rear door for her, whilst Snyder took the front passenger seat. Checking that she was comfortably settled, the man climbed into the driving seat, engaged gear, and swept away from the terminal building towards the main road. The driver turned left onto the road that led from the airfield down towards Yŏngdungp'o and accelerated up to sixty mph. Brad Snyder turned in his seat and spoke.

'We're taking you down to K-55 Osan Air base on the orders of Head of station, Seoul. It's about sixty-five klicks down MSR1.The insertion will take place from there. The old coal barge trick is out, I'm afraid. The gooks sank her last month. You'll be flying into P'yŏngyang this time.'

Charlotte gave him a quizzical glance.

'MSR1? What's that?'

He grinned.

'Army slang... it's short for Military Supply Route One... the main road south to Pusan.'

Yŏngdungp'o had undergone extensive rebuilding since Charlotte was last there. Most of the dingy shops and Chi-Chi clubs had long since vanished... either by war damage or urban clearance. At the intersection at the end of the main street of the Itaewono District, the driver turned left into what appeared to be a tree-lined, dusty dirt road heading south towards Anyang and Suwon. The trees were incongruous. Since she had returned to Korea, Charlotte had perceived that there were practically no trees left anywhere in South Korea. Snyder explained that the U.S. had given Korea millions to pave MSR1. Instead they bought trees to "keep the pedestrians cool" and pocketed most of the money. Snyder added that the extensive road works along this route were the initial construction stages of what would become the Kyŏngbu Expressway, which was scheduled for completion from Seoul via Suwon to Osan by the end of the year.

Osan Air base was not quite what she had expected. Immediately outside the perimeter fence, rice paddies were still being carefully tended as they had been for countless generations. Once through the main gate the base still retained its Korean War-vintage facilities and infrastructure and looked as though little had been spent to improve them. This was understandable considering Washington's focus on Cuba with the Missile Crisis and Europe in the new Cold War flare up. Korea... or at least, this part of it looked as though it had been quietly forgotten. On base the barracks were still the corrugated iron Quonset huts of the Korean War period, and the base appeared to have simply stagnated. However; the flying infrastructure appeared sound. The nine thousand feet runway and the hardstandings... which were occupied by a handful of apparently unmarked F4 Phantom jets appeared to be in good repair. The main structures looked sound, and well maintained, but it was a far cry from the other Military bases with which she was familiar.

The car crossed the base to a remote *Choga-chi*... a traditional Korean country house with white-painted mud-wattle walls and a rice-thatch roof, and stopped in the open courtyard in front of the building. The entrance was guarded by two mean-looking MPs, each, with an even meaner-looking German shepherd guard dog on a chain leash. Snyder escorted her inside where she was introduced to a youngish Lieutenant-colonel, the base's Director of intelligence. He smiled.

19

'Pleased to meet you Captain. No names here if you please. What you don't know can't hurt you.'

He waited until Snyder had left the room and invited her to sit.

'Your papers and uniform are in the next room. We're only about seventy klicks south of the DMZ, so we'll fly you out over the Sea of Japan at low level in one of our covert ships, then turn, climb to altitude, and come in over the North Korean coast on a heading that will lead them to believe the airplane is approaching from the general area of Vladivostok.'

He then said that Operations base in Seoul had sent the signal up the clandestine landline to P'yŏngyang that Colonel Tolenkanovna would be arriving by airplane at a military airfield at Mirim, sited on the southern side of the Taedong River on the eastern edge of the city. The U.S. had used it as a base for P-51 Mustang fighters of the 18th U.S. Bomber Wing during the Korean War but it was little-used these days according to the available intelligence. As such, it would be the destination of choice by the North Koreans for the confidential arrival of a high-profile Soviet Advisor... there would be minimal security risk.

Having fully briefed Charlotte, the Director of intelligence invited her to avail herself of his private suite where she could change into her uniform that had been provided by his department. He rose from behind his desk and escorted her to the far side of the *Choga-chi*. She entered a comfortable-looking bedroom suite and he closed the door firmly behind her. The venetian blinds at the windows were closed, and the uniform was laid out on the single bed.

She undressed and put on the uniform. It fitted perfectly. This was no great surprise. The Bureau was very efficient in these matters... and her measurements were in her personal file, after all. She studied herself in the mirror on the dresser. Not bad... not bad at all. Her Prussian good looks... blonde, and high cheek-boned, had served her well. She smiled quietly. Forty-six years old, and she could still get away with people thinking she was in her late thirties.

She had been afraid that the stern elegance of the Soviet uniform would cause her to end up resembling the repulsive Colonel Rosa Klebb; the character in the recently published James Bond spy novel by the English author, Ian Fleming, titled *"From Russia, with Love"*... but the olive green wool tunic jacket with matching red piped shoulder boards bearing two red stripes and three stars, and gold-coloured metal oak leaf collar tabs; the dove-green shirt, olive tie, and Military black skirt for female Officers actually flattered her still-trim figure.

By the side of the bed was a well-travelled, mushroom-brown leather suitcase with white metal locks and corners and a leather handle. Opening it, she saw that it contained a dress uniform and greatcoat, spare shirts and underclothes. Next to it was a pair of high, black chrome leather Officer's boots. As she sat on the bed and pulled the boots on, there was a soft tapping on the door. She walked across the room and opened it to be faced by the Director of intelligence who held out a light olive, trenchcoat-style, U.S. Army issue raincoat to her. The larger of the two mean-looking MPs stood behind him.

The Director nodded.

'Every inch a Russian Officer. Time to go, "Comrade Colonel." You'd better slip this on… just in case.'

She nodded, put on the raincoat, and followed him out to the courtyard in front of the building where an MP jeep was waiting with its engine idling. The large MP followed them, carrying the suitcase, which he put on the rear seat. Climbing aboard he checked his passengers were safely seated, banged the jeep into gear, and accelerated away out to the parallel concrete track that ran the length of the runway. At a fairly high speed the jeep travelled the length of the airfield to the far western end of the runway where there stood two large and secluded, curved-roof hangars. The MP brought the jeep to a squealing halt on the wide concrete hardstanding in front of the most westerly of the pair of hangars. The front of the hangar was shrouded in a substantial weather curtain that obscured whatever lurked within, and was guarded by two more heavily-armed MPs.

Getting out of the jeep, the party walked towards the front of the hangar. One of the MPs pulled the edge of the weather curtain to one side in order that they might enter. The interior was brightly lit from overhead sodium lamps; from which the light glittered on the large silver, twin-engined airplane that sat in menacing isolation under the wide arched roof. The Red Star glared down impassively from its wings and tail fin. The only other markings it bore was a large red "42" painted on the either side of the rear fuselage.

Director of intelligence gave Charlotte a wry grin.

'Your magic carpet. She's the real deal… A Lisunov Li-2, compliments of the Korean People's Army Air Force. She's a Russian license-built version of the DC-3 Skytrain. She was captured after her crew had engine trouble, strayed over the DMZ, and force-landed at Kimpo. We flew her down here; re-engined and repainted her for covert operations.'

He turned and beckoned to the MP who held out a brown leather belt and holster to Charlotte. The Director smiled.

'Your weapon. A Makarov semi-automatic pistol. It's been the Soviet standard military side arm since 1951. Basically, it's a scaled-up Walther PP, with a straight blowback action. It fires a 9x18mm cartridge which is incompatible with all other NATO 9mm rounds, so you'd better take these...'

He held out a box of ammunition and continued.

'This weapon is widely regarded as being particularly well balanced in spite of its weight, and is easy to field strip and reassemble... including removing the firing pin... without any tools.'

Charlotte took the holster belt and box of ammunition and the Director walked her to the boarding steps at the rear port side of the airplane. The whine of the inverters winding up broke the silence. The Director shook her hand.

'Good luck, "Colonel." See you around.'

He stepped back and saluted her as she climbed the access ladder and entered the fuselage. The MP placed her suitcase on board as she made her way forward to one of the seats in the cabin. The flight attendant... a young man wearing a Soviet Air Force uniform, pulled the passenger door shut as the pilot pressed the start button and the starboard engine began running up... followed by the port engine. The weather curtains were pulled back by the ground crew, and with a slight jolt, the brakes were released and the airplane rolled gently out into the sunlight. The pilot held on the brakes while the pressures and temperatures built up on his instruments, then eased the throttles forward, released the brakes, and, with another slight jolt, taxied out to the active runway.

Turning into the wind, he waited for clearance from the tower, and ran up the engines. Charlotte saw a green lamp flash from the observation windows of the control tower. The engine noise rose to a crescendo, and with yet one more jolt, the airplane began to move. She watched the scorched grass at the edge of the runway begin to flatten as it sped past below the wing; the tail lifted, and the shadow of the wing began falling away as the airplane rose into the sky.

The perimeter fence and main road passed beneath them, then they were out over the paddy fields and scattered villages, heading east towards the Han River, and on towards the coast and the Sea of Japan.

Friday, June 30th, 1950.11.45.am.
Highway One, Twenty-two kilometres south of P'yŏngyang.
North Korea.

Nineteen-year-old Jo Mi Ryung had been working in the rice fields when she heard the rising howl of a diving airplane, out of sight, but coming from the general direction of the main Highway One that led out towards Kaesŏng. As she stared out across the tree line bordering the rice field she heard the deep, staccato clatter of its guns as it opened fire at something... or someone.

Jo Mi Ryung dropped her basket of rice seedlings and ran towards the bund on the south side of the paddy. Was it someone from her village? The South Korean pilots were notorious for shooting up anything that moved on the roads... villagers, water buffalo, farm carts; and especially military vehicles. As she ran through the trees towards the road, she felt the apprehension of what she might find out there on the road rising around her like a shroud.

The GAZ saloon lay on its side in the ditch, with smoke and fumes rising from its engine. Jo Mi Ryung stared at the bullet-riddled vehicle with wide, frightened eyes, not knowing quite what she should do. It was painted olive green... a military vehicle...a Russian military vehicle. Gathering her courage, she approached. The car was empty. Biting her lip, she looked around. There was no sign of a body anywhere near to the wreck. Then she saw the smears of blood on the long grasses. The tell-tale trail led off into the woods. Cautiously, she began to follow the sprinkles of blood shining brightly against the deep green of the blades of grass.

She found him twenty metres in from the tree line. He lay sprawled on the pathway, face-down and unmoving. Timidly, she approached. He wore a khaki-coloured military uniform and high black boots. Nervously, she reached down and turned him over, wincing at the sight of the great tear in his right temple and the bloodstained rents in the right side of the waist and shoulder of his uniform tunic. He was still breathing, and looked to be in his mid-thirties. He was a Russian officer.

Jo Mi Ryung stared down at him. Although his face was covered in blood from the head wound, she could easily discern that he was very handsome. What should she do? They would be bound to come searching for him when he failed to arrive at wherever he was going. If he died here, there would be reprisals on her village of Kwan-ni. It was the nearest one to the scene of the wreck, and the Ministry of Public Security investigators from P'yŏngyang would automatically assume that her villagers were responsible.

The safest thing to do would to be to get him back to the village where the local doctor could attend to him. But how? She couldn't carry him bodily... he was at least, one-point-eight metres tall and must have weighed at least seventy-five kilogrammes. She was slender, just one-point-five metres tall; and weighed a mere forty-five kilogrammes. She would have to find some way to try to waken him. She knelt beside him and fretted for a while. Then, she had an idea. Rising to her feet, she hurried into the woods.

She searched for ten minutes, and eventually found what she was looking for. In the shade of a large Daimyo Oak tree grew a cluster of fungus with reddish, cylindrical fluted stems capped with several "arms" that formed a spire with an olive-green slimy spore mass covering the outer surface of the arms... a fungus that she knew of as being called the "Ribbed lizard claw." She could smell it from almost a metre's distance... the smell of rotting flesh. Pulling a face, she carefully plucked two of the disgusting-smelling fungi and turned back towards the pathway. If the stench of these didn't waken him... nothing would.

He was still lying where she had found him. Bending down, she squeezed the slimy fungi close to his nose. The stench was overpowering. As the foul smell assailed his nostrils, he convulsed and regained consciousness. He retched, and vomited into the grass, then gazed blankly at her with the glazed eyes of a sleepwalker. She helped him to sit up. He turned vaguely towards her and spoke.

'Who are you? How did I get here? What is this place?'

His Korean was halting and awkward. Jo Mi Ryung studied him; a gentle expression on her pretty face.

'You cannot remember anything? You do not remember who you are and where you came from?'

He touched his forehead, wiped away some blood, and squeezed his eyes.

'Nothing; nothing at all.'

He said wearily;

'Nothing, except the world turning upside down and the smell of smoke and cordite.'

He struggled to get to his feet, staggered and nearly lost his balance. The pain in his head and side almost caused him to lose consciousness again. Her arms were around him, holding him steady. She spoke again. Her voice was soft and comforting.

'You have been in a car accident. Can you walk a little? I must take you to my village and get you some food and a doctor to see you. You have a terrible wound on the side of your head and there are deep wounds in your right side and shoulder.'

She held him firmly, and gently guided him along the pathway through the woods towards the village.

24

Zhang Jae-Sun had been the physician in the village of Kwan-ni for many years. He had delivered Jo Mi Ryung, and had tended to her childhood illnesses. Now, she stood before him in his "L"-shaped *Hanok* which also served as his surgery and operating theatre and begged him to apply his skills to this *"waegookin"*... this foreigner that she had found in the woods. He studied Jo Mi Ryung who returned his gaze with large, beseeching eyes.

Zhang Jae-Sun spoke gently, but firmly to her.

'Why should you care for this Russian, child? He is gravely wounded, but he will eventually recover. It is certain that he is one of the Eternal President's advisers, and as such, has no time for a simple country girl... save perhaps, to take you as a concubine.'

Jo Mi Ryung lowered her eyes, and blushed scarlet.

'Zhang-Ssi; I wish to keep him here and care for him. He remembers nothing of the past. I wish it to remain so, so that he can stay here and stay in Kwan-ni with me.'

Zhang Jae-Sun smiled gently.

'That will not be possible Jo Mi Ryung. In due course he will recover and go off across the world to where he came from. And there will certainly be official inquiries for him, from P'yŏngyang, perhaps even from his Russian homeland; for he is an officer, and most certainly a man of substance in his own country.'

She raised her eyes to his.

'But, Zhang-Ssi; if you advise the elders of Kwan-ni, they will show these people the blank face. They will say they know nothing, and then the people will go away.'

Zhang Jae-Sun studied her pleading face.

'Very well, Jo Mi Ryung; I will speak with the elders. But for many weeks you-must be very discreet and the *waegookin* must be kept hidden. Now, let us mend his wounds.'

He knelt beside the Russian and spread out a large, ancient vellum map of the human head with sections divided up and marked with figures and ideograms. He gently probed the Russian's head wound for signs of fracture, then bent and lifted the eyelids one by one, gazing deeply into the glazed eyes through a large magnifying glass. Jo Mi Ryung brought boiling water and Zhang Jae-Sun proceeded to clean the head wound. Then he tapped finely ground garlic powder into the wound and bound up the head neatly and expertly.

He then began cleaning the deep gashes in the Russian's side and shoulder; tapped more garlic powder over the wounds, and, having established that there were no broken ribs or bones other than a cracked collar bone; bandaged the waist and shoulder area firmly. He studied Jo Mi Ryung thoughtfully, and then spoke.

'He will live, but it may be months, perhaps even years before he regains his memory. The injury has probably damaged the part of his brain where his memory is stored. It is what we physicians call a temporal lesion, but the damage is not severe, seeing as how he can speak and understand what you say to him. However; much education will be necessary. You must endeavour all the time to remind him about past things and places. If you are resolute in this undertaking... which will be no easy matter... then isolated facts that he will recognise may become chains of association and his memory may well return. On the other hand, it is entirely possible that he will never regain any memory of his past life.'

Zhang Jae-Sun's diagnosis was entirely accurate. Over the next three months, under the gentle care of Jo Mi Ryung, the Russian officer regained his health, but his memory remained blank. He occasionally experienced flashbacks, but these were vague and incohesive. As time progressed, Jo Mi Ryung taught him the practicalities of rice cultivation and the traditions and customs of rural Korean life in her tiny community. He was diligent and hard-working and was eventually accepted into the community by the village elders. The first indication of this was when they began addressing him as "*Ku-da Chingu*"..."tall friend;" and not the usual "*Waegookin*"... "Foreigner."

As the days passed and turned into weeks, and the weeks turned into months; Jo Mi Ryung held a secret wish that, one day, he would take her as his "*anae*"... his wife; but he showed no interest in this. His relationship with her was more akin to sister and brother. Jo Mi Ryung remained philosophical. Perhaps, one day it would happen. The men from the Ministry of Public Security in P'yŏngyang came to the village in search of him... just as Zhang Jae-Sun had predicted, but the elders had shown them the blank face and denied all knowledge of the occupants of the wrecked car out on the highway. They said that some villagers had heard gunfire and seen a fighter airplane low in the skies, but no trace had ever been found of the car's occupants. The men from the Ministry of Public Security had searched the village, but found no trace of anything that might disprove the elders' story.

"*Ku-da Chingu*" was out in the north paddy with two of the villagers shoring up a slump in the far bund. All that the men from the Ministry of Public Security saw were three workers in the paddy wearing traditional conical hats... the "*satgat*," and light-coloured smocks. The men were too far away to recognise and were bent over the damaged bund with their backs towards the officials... a stance which gave no clue to their individual heights. The men from the Ministry of Public Security didn't relish trudging a thousand metres through muddy rice fields on the off-chance that one of the peasants might be their unaccounted-for Russian officer. They shrugged and turned back towards the village. The Russian, Colonel Konstantin Sharansky was not here. They would have to widen the search.

Taewi... Captain Kim Hyang-soon, ranking officer of the search party retained an impassive face, but cursed vehemently under his breath. This missing Russian was rapidly becoming a real pain in the ass. His superiors in P'yŏngyang had made it perfectly clear that, unless the Russian was found... or substantive evidence was found that he had been killed; the next assignment that Kim Hyang-soon could be looking forward to would be in a bunker in the Joint Security Area of the North Korean DMZ border. Yelling to his men to get a move on, he stomped irritably back down the woodland path towards the highway, whilst the village elders bowed respectfully with the merest hint of wry smiles on their otherwise impassive faces.

Chapter Two.

Monday, 25th September, 1950. 2.50pm,
Highway One, Toksan.
North Korea.

Jo Mi Ryung had spent the morning planting rice seedlings in the east paddy with *"Ku-da Chingu"*..."tall friend;" as the villagers now called the Russian she had rescued from Highway One. The Russian had still not regained his memory after three months in her care, and the village physician, Zhang Jae-Sun was now resigned to the fact that he probably never would. Jo Mi Ryung still hoped that her Russian would eventually become interested in her and develop something more intimate that the brother-sister relationship they had shared up until now, but there were no promising signs so far.

The Russian had settled down quite happily to the rural existence in the tiny settlement of Kwan-ni. He was showing great promise as a farmer, and the village elders were pleased to have an extra strong pair of hands. Jo Mi Ryung had left him in the village and was walking back along Highway One from the little town of Toksan, some two kilometres north, where she had been to collect a fresh supply of rice seedlings for the south paddy of the village. She suddenly became aware of a distant, deep droning coming from the south-east. Gazing up; she could just see the stream of silver bombers glittering like so many minnows in the little brook that ran through her village. They were heading for P'yŏngyang. More tiny silver shapes were dashing around them and the faint thudding of gunfire drifted down. As she gazed, wide-eyed at the spectacle high above; suddenly, one of the big silver bombers began to trail smoke and drift away from its companions.

As it began to spiral down, white puffs came from it. They looked like dandelion seeds drifting in the bright blue sky. Some of the crew

28

had parachuted out! She watched in fascination as they drifted away and down. Then a sound came from behind her... a rising scream. She turned, and saw a little silver jet plane with steeply swept-back wings skidding around the sky and heading towards her. It was followed by another one; slightly bigger, with bright yellow stripes on its wings and body. The first jet plane, now very low, suddenly veered to the right... towards her village as yellowy-orange flames erupted from the nose of the following jet. The burst of gunfire missed the first little silver plane and tore up the asphalt of Highway One towards her. She dropped her basket of rice seedlings and turned to run... as the concentrated fire of the American F86 Sabre jet's six, fifty-caliber machine-guns which had missed the jinking North Korean MiG-15 struck her squarely in the back and tore her to pieces.

Major Leroy "Cookie" Cipriano... so-called because his family ran a popular Italian restaurant in Brooklyn, New York, was concentrating too hard to see where his last burst of gunfire had gone. You just didn't goof around at an altitude of fifty feet when you were doing over five hundred knots on the tail of a twisting, jinking bogey. The MiG was two hundred yards ahead and being flown by a real hot-shot. Cipriano was convinced that this guy was one of the Russian Honchos who were rumoured to be fighting in Korea; he was just too good to be a Dink or a Chink.

He pulled another tight turn and felt his G-suit inflating. Glancing at the accelerometer at top left of the instrument panel he saw the pointer teetering on the red mark indicating maximum safe at eight-point-five G's positive. Any more of this and he'd pull the goddamned wings off! As he hauled the Sabre out of the vicious port bank, the range limiter on his radar gun sight activated. The "Pipper" centred in his screen and Cipriano punched the firing button on his control column.

The three second burst from his six, fifty-caliber machine-guns tore into the fleeing MiG; pieces flew off, and it spun in... straight into the middle of a small rural ville where it exploded in a huge chrysanthemum of flaring jet fuel. Cipriano hauled back on the control column and shoved the throttle wide open, soaring up and away from the fiery devastation that had once been the tiny community of Kwan-ni.

Kwan-ni's old physician, Zhang Jae-Sun was walking through the east side of the village when the MiG hit the ground. All he remembered was an enormous shock wave picking him up bodily and hurling him into the border of the north paddy. He lay there in the muddy water, stunned by the explosion; with the stink of burning jet fuel in his nostrils and throat. He gazed groggily out over the berm of the paddy that had protected him from the burgeoning wall of fire which had incinerated the centre of the village and every living soul contained within it; then everything began to turn black.

He vaguely felt the muddy water surge up his nostrils. He tried to lift his head, but couldn't find the strength to do so. Suddenly, he felt strong hands pulling him out of the water. He looked up into the face of *"Ku-da Chingu"*...the tall Russian. Confused and disoriented, Zhang Jae-Sun tried to pull away. The Russian waved his arm in the direction of the inferno that had once been the MiG. Its ammunition was starting to explode sending cannon shells whining haphazardly around what remained of the village. He yelled at Zhang Jae-Sun in terrible Korean...

'Di jillae?... U ri neun ji geum tteo nap ni da!'... 'You want to die?... We leave now!' *'Ttara oseyo!'*... 'Come with me!'

He picked up the old physician and carried him bodily away towards the far berm-line of the north paddy.

Thursday, 21st December, 1950.
Chosin Valley; South Hamgyong Province.
North Korea.

The malignant Garnet gemstone that Charlotte had been pursuing for the last thirteen years... from the frozen wastes of Siberia, through War-torn Europe, and on out to the Far East, was about to be re-discovered and unleashed upon Mankind once again.

Shang Shi... Senior NCO Huang Zheheng of the 89th Division, IX Army Group, Peoples Liberation Army cautiously made his way across the nightmare, frozen landscape of the destroyed US Marine positions on Hill 1403 northwest of Yudam-ni, and west of the Chosin Reservoir. The slaughter around here had been unimaginable. Frozen corpses lay thick upon the ground. Determined to break through the Marine lines at any cost, the Chinese attackers had advanced in waves, with unarmed soldiers in the rear ranks picking up weapons from the dead who had fallen in front of them and the fighting had descended into hand-to-hand savagery.

Casualties on both sides had been crippling. The slopes of the hill were covered with the human wreckage; both American and Chinese. It was estimated that the Chinese forces alone, had lost in excess of twenty-five thousand men. As for the Americans; at least nine hundred had perished. Few American bodies remained on the hill and surrounding area. The Americans evacuated their dead and dying, whereas the Chinese forces had left their dead where they had fallen. The Chinese had not been able to prevent the Americans' withdrawal, as ordered, and the main body of the Marine forces at Yudam-ni had fought their way south and east to Hagaru-ri.

Huang Zheheng was out foraging for American maps and documents... anything that would be of use to Chinese Intelligence who had set up a command post in the evacuated village of Yudam-ni. Moving up the slope of hill 1403, he came across a defensive position where the Marines had dug in and built machine-gun posts out of blocks of snow. A few bodies and parts of bodies remained, frozen solid. Depleted first-aid packs and broken weapons lay scattered about. These Marines had obviously fought hard, judging by the number of Chinese corpses strewn around the ramparts. He checked the scattered American bodies and equipment. There was nothing of any interest remaining in this lower defensive position. A little farther up the slope was what appeared to be a dug-out; perhaps it could be the Command post. Picking his way carefully amongst the debris, he reached the entrance and cautiously peered inside. He reached up and lit a blood-spattered hurricane lamp hanging precariously from the roof. By its flickering red-tinged light he saw that the interior of the bunker resembled a slaughterhouse in which the resident butchers had run amok.

The rough floor was a sticky mass of crushed bone, blood, and shredded flesh. Great patches of blood were splattered across the corrugated iron ceiling, and torn-off limbs, bloody chunks of human flesh, and shattered bodies were scattered everywhere. Huang Zheheng forced back a retch. He had seen this sort of thing before. Last time; it had been the result of a suicide attack by a PLA soldier who had rushed into a similar command post and detonated a satchel charge slung on his chest.

He glanced around There were no map cases or documents. The place had been thoroughly stripped of all strategic material before it had been abandoned. His eyes fell upon the shattered body of a Marine propped up against the far wall in a large pool of congealed blood. Most of the man was still intact, except, that where his legs had once been, were no more than a few shards of bone and some long strings of flesh and sinew. Propped against the wall by his side was a Thompson submachine gun. Huang Zheheng smiled. He had always wanted one of those. A few of the higher-echelon ranking officers possessed one that had been captured from the Nationalist Chinese Military; but most line troops... if they had an automatic weapon at all... used the Soviet PPSh-41 submachine gun. The Thompson was

31

favoured over this weapon because of its capability to deliver large quantities of short-range automatic assault fire which had proved very useful in both defence and assault.

Huang Zheheng reached down and checked the dead Marine's pockets and equipment for spare ammunition, although the slopes outside were strewn with discarded ordnance. It was easier to check out the weapon's previous owner than go foraging out on the frozen ground. The corpse had a blood-spattered three-pouch rig for thirty round magazines attached to its webbing, as well as two smaller ammo pouches. Huang Zheheng popped the "Lift-the-Dot" fasteners of the three-pouch rig and withdrew the magazines. All three were fully loaded. He smiled with satisfaction and removed the pouch rig from the Marine's equipment belt suspenders. Then, he turned his attention to the smaller pouches. The first one contained loose, point forty-five rounds. The second contained personal effects... a Zippo lighter, a neat little metal can opener; a small crumpled pack of four "Camel" cigarettes, and two small bars of "Hershey's" sweet chocolate. His fingers touched something smooth at the bottom of the pouch. He pulled it out and his eyes widened in surprise. Resting in his palm was a deep red, pigeon-egg-sized Garnet gemstone.

As he stared; a tiny pinprick of light flickering briefly in the depths of its blood-red heart as it nestled in his hand. It was probably just a reflection from the hurricane lamp, but suddenly, and for no logical reason; Huang Zheheng shivered. Quickly, he pocketed the contents of the small pouch, gathered up the spare magazines and weapon, and almost ran out of the dug-out.

Outside in the cold air, he stopped and looked at the gemstone again. It was a beautiful thing, and would most probably be much sought-after back home... if he ever managed to get back home. It would probably fetch enough to provide his family with a new plough... or maybe, even a tractor. In China they called this gem a "Blood Stone." It was much prized for its magical properties. As well as being used for jewellery, it was used to alternatively cure severe melancholy and depression. Little pieces of Garnet were traditionally given to Chinese pregnant women to help them with their pregnancy. An ancient Chinese legend told that if you tied a piece of Garnet in your front door it would protect your house against thieves.

Huang Zheheng looked around. There was nothing else of any strategic value on this forlorn hill that had cost so many lives over the past few days. Shouldering the Thompson, he began the arduous walk back down to Yudam-ni.

Friday, 16th September, 1960.
P'yŏngyang. North Korea.

Charlotte Mckenna was sitting at the desk in her office of the T17 sniper academy in P'yŏngyang, grading her latest batch of trainees, when the harsh jangle of the telephone disturbed her concentration. Pushing the thick file aside, she picked up the receiver and spoke.

'*Polkovnik*... Colonel Nadia Tolenkanovna. How may I help you?'

The voice on the other end of the telephone was apologetic.

'Nadia? I'm so sorry to have to disturb you, but we have a situation on our hands.'

It was Viktor Malinovskii, Second secretary at the Soviet Embassy in Somun Street. He had established a relationship with Charlotte some time ago... and occasionally she allowed him to make love to her... but this was merely to manipulate him; and through him, the Embassy, in order to retain a cast-iron cover. He was, after all, fairly attractive; a placid and undemanding lover, and he suited her purpose perfectly.

She lowered her voice a little.

'Yes Viktor; how may I be of assistance?'

His voice was anxious.

'We have received a report that one of our North Korean associates' MiG fighters was discovered yesterday. It was shot down by the Americans to the south of Toksan on Highway One, almost ten years ago. It seems that the pilot was one of our covert Soviet pilots who were rotated in and out of Manchuria. As you are aware; there has always been a political denial of any such involvement in the Korean conflict.

This has the potential to create a diplomatic embarrassment for Moscow if the truth ever comes out. Considering your status as Advisor to the North Korean Military; the Embassy would like you to travel down there to establish that there is nothing remaining that might reveal this state of affairs to the U.S. government.'

She paused.

'Very well, Viktor. I will arrange to travel down to the site. Where exactly did the fighter crash?'

The voice on the telephone lost its anxious tone.

Our sources state that it crashed on a little peasant village named Kwan-ni... about two kilometres south-west of Toksan... that's about twenty-two kilometres to the south. The village is about a kilometre to the west of Highway One.'

Charlotte replied.

'Very well, Viktor; I have that. I'll leave directly, and see if there is any evidence remaining that could be embarrassing; but ten years is an awfully long time for anything to still be there.'

'Thank you, Nadia; I know, but we just can't take any chance that there might be. Incidentally; we have a reception at the Embassy this evening. It would be nice if you could come.'

She smiled to herself. That was his way of hinting that he was hoping to have sex with her again.

'Thank you, Viktor. I shall be there if I manage to get back to P'yŏngyang in good time.'

His voice was soft and hopeful

'Oh, I do hope you can get back in time. Until then, Goodbye.'

She smiled again

'Goodbye Viktor.'

And replaced the telephone receiver. She leaned back in her chair, and smiled softly to herself. Viktor Malinovskii was so transparent… like a little boy peering into a sweetshop window. Oh, what the hell? Why not?

Her Korean driver made good time down Highway One. Traffic was light, and there were no condensation trails in the skies. A little to the south of Toksan was the rusting hulk of a Soviet Military Staff car slewed into the ditch at the side of the highway. Her driver stopped the four-wheel drive GAZ M-72 saloon for Charlotte to examine the wreck. She noted the bullet holes in the rear bodywork and roof and the dark stains on the upholstery. This vehicle had obviously been strafed from the air. Then she noticed the stained and mouldering green visor cap with a red band. This cap had belonged to an officer of the Soviet Administration troops.

Her heart missed a beat. Max had been given the cover of a member of that corps… and he had been inserted into the Military Establishment at P'yŏngyang. She stared at the old, grubby cap, her heart racing. Was this the answer to his disappearance? She took a deep breath. No; this was just a coincidence. It had to be. Nonetheless, she took a note of the wreck's licence plate. She would search the records properly when she returned to P'yŏngyang. Her driver was standing patiently by the staff car. She turned, and began walking back across the highway. The young Korean pointed deferentially to a track that led into the wood. This was the path to the village. He pointed to the tops of the trees. Several of the topmost branches were much lower than the surrounding woodland. Something had sliced straight through them. The re-growth suggested that this had not been

34

a recent occurrence.

They began walking down the path. The broken trees became more frequent, until, the very trunks had been shattered in a great descending swathe, until there! A broad, weed-strewn gouge ploughed into in the earth with shards of shiny metal showing signs of white powdery corrosion scattered all around... a gouge that suddenly turned into a scorched pathway leading straight into the little ville... or what had once been a ville. Even now, all these years later there was still the faint, acrid smell of jet fuel clinging to the rotting and charred remains of what had once been fifteen or so *Hanoks*... the traditional Korean peasant houses. The ground was thick with the decomposing ash of their *choga*... roofs plaited by rice straw, and in the middle of this desolation lay strewn the burned and corroding wreckage of the MiG fighter. It lay, a jumble of blackened scrap metal; minus its wings which had sheared off as it had hit the ground, and whirled into more *Hanoks* farther to the west; slicing through their walls like a draw-knife.

The remains of the fuselage were laying upside-down. The pilot's canopy had melted in the heat; and the charred and rotting remains of the pilot was still strapped into the seat. The only things that moved in the village were sickly looking weeds and grasses, and a mangy, half-starved-looking dog that slunk across the path some fifteen metres in front of them.

There wasn't anything left unburnt that could possibly be used to identify the charred mummy. Charlotte turned to walk back towards the car, when her driver, who had been poking about in the wreckage suddenly shouted. He delved into the cockpit and she heard a sharp snap... almost like a dry twig being broken. He emerged triumphantly with a claw-like, blackened talon that had once been a living finger... and on that finger was an engraved gold signet ring. He removed the ring, threw down the calcined digit, and respectfully offered the ring to her, holding it out in both hands. In keeping with the Korean convoluted code of behaviour; she politely declined his offering of the ring three times, and then accepted it.

She carefully lifted the ring from his outstretched hand. It was heavy, and looked to be very old. She studied it, turning it in her hand. The hallmark identified it as being twenty-one carat....a rare and expensive piece. The ring was engraved with the Cyrillic letters "В" and "С"... which, in the common Latin alphabet, denoted the letters "V" and "S." The table setting appeared to be in two parts; much like one would expect to find on a locket. Charlotte carefully inserted her thumbnail into the joint and twisted. The cover flipped up to reveal a tiny, discoloured, and scorched photograph of a pretty, dark-haired girl with pronounced Slavic features. The inner surface of the ring's shank was stamped with the normal Russian Assay marks and the maker's mark: *"Klingert"* in Latin script.

She nodded her approval to her driver.

'Well done, Kwon; your diligence is noted. Now, let us return to. P'yŏngyang.'

Kwon bowed.

'Thank you honourable Colonel; I am pleased to have been of service.'

As he dutifully followed her out to the car, he smiled… a contented smile. His sharp eyes may well have secured him a permanent position as her driver. This could be his ticket away from the distinct possibility of following in the footsteps of the rest of his class from the Academy, who had been transferred to the Joint Security Area in the south. Kwon really didn't relish the idea of sitting in some shithole of a bunker somewhere down towards the DMZ; freezing his nuts off whilst those round-eyed bastards on the opposite side of the line tried to blow his head off.

As she settled herself into the rear seat of the car, she glanced back across the shattered swathe of woodland towards the destroyed village. On the overgrown berm line of the neglected far paddy she noticed a solitary figure wearing the traditional conical hat… the *"satgat,"* and a light-coloured smock. The figure stood motionless, as though he was watching her. He; for it had to be a man, judging by his height; was taller than most Korean peasants. She suddenly had a strange feeling as she watched him; but then, the moment passed and the figure turned away; stooping to continue whatever he had been doing. At that moment Kwon shifted into gear and drove away, and the figure was lost from sight.

Back in her office in P'yŏngyang; Charlotte made a telephone call to Viktor Malinovskii at the Embassy. She told him that there was nothing remaining of the crashed MiG that could be remotely connected with the Soviet air regiments flying from Chinese bases in Manchuria. There may have been the odd data label inscribed with Cyrillic characters attached to various components; but seeing as how the airplane was Russian-built; that was tenuous evidence, to say the least. The wreckage was so badly burned and corroded that no National markings were distinguishable. The incinerated remains of the pilot were still in the aircraft, but his nationality had been impossible to establish. The burning jet fuel had shrunk his remains to such an extent that he might easily have been Chinese or Korean. Without dental records it would be impossible to tell.

Viktor Malinovskii breathed a sigh of relief.

'You are certain there is nothing there?'

'Nothing at all. Viktor. The only thing that might have identified the pilot was a gold signet ring, and I have that in front of me on my desk as we speak. It's very old; with a St Petersburg hallmark; is engraved with the initials "V" and "S," and opens to reveal a photograph of a woman.'

The telephone went quiet for a moment, and then Malinovskii replied.

'A "V" and an "S" you say? I'll obtain what records I can through Diplomatic channels. Very well done, Nadia; you have averted the likelihood of an embarrassing predicament for Moscow. Now, am I likely to be privileged with your company at the Embassy reception this evening?'

Charlotte smiled to herself... Oh, why not?... and replied in her best sultry voice...

'Viktor; I think that is a distinct possibility.'

Two days later, Charlotte sat behind her desk, staring out of the window across the northern suburbs of P'yŏngyang; thoughtfully twisting the engraved gold signet around her right ring finger. Her visit to the MiG crash site troubled her. It was not so much the desolation of the little rural ville that the fighter had crashed onto; it was more the tall, solitary figure she had seen across in the far paddy field. She had checked the archives for the licence plate of the wrecked staff car on Highway One, south of Toksan and discovered that it was a motor pool car that had once belonged to the No.2 KPA Officers School in P'yŏngyang. Its last allocation had been to a certain Colonel Konstantin Sharansky of the Soviet Administration troops. It had been signed out by Sharansky's adjutant, as being required for an inspection of the Kaesŏng area command. Highway One ran between P'yŏngyang and Kaesŏng; and the wreck was in the ditch at the side of Highway One.

She had been gripped by a cold shudder as she read the motor pool register. Colonel Konstantin Sharansky had been the Firm's legend identity of Max Segal... Charlotte's lover and father of her daughter. She knew that he had been sent into the north under deep cover... and that extensive enquires had been made by P'yŏngyang investigators as to his disappearance; but no trace of his fate had ever been established.

Could it possibly be that Max had survived, and perhaps gone native? There was something about the distant solitary figure; it was no more than her intuition, but she felt compelled to check again. If it was indeed Max... and it was a big "if"... she would extract him out of the north through her covert escape route. Consequently, she had telephoned Viktor Malinovskii at the Embassy, and suggested that she return the ring to the airbase at Andung in Manchuria. She would then send confirmation in her role as intelligence liaison, to VVR Command in Moscow.

At first Viktor Malinovskii was ambivalent. It should be the Embassy that contacted Command. She smiled to herself. He was always the cautious one, but she knew how to manipulate him. She suggested that they meet for drinks to discuss the matter. Viktor Malinovskii brightened considerably at her suggestion, anticipating another night of passion with her. An evening of vodka and then, the promise of her warm, perfumed charms was irresistible.

The following morning, Charlotte signed out a vehicle from the motor pool at the sniper academy on the premise that she was going to further investigate the wreckage of the MiG fighter down at Toksan. In her position as Instructor/Adviser, no questions were asked. Living in the capital was an important privilege and one had to be a politically reliable and/or well-connected person... and a "Soviet Adviser" was as well-connected as it was possible to be. She was allocated a GAZ four-wheel drive vehicle of indeterminate vintage that was effectively the Soviet equivalent of the ubiquitous Willys jeep.

She drove down through the city and crossed to the eastern bank of the Taedonggang River by way of the Taedonggyo Bridge; then drove down to Senkyori Station, turning right and following the lines of warehouses and the compound of the huge Kanegafuchi spinning mill, where she turned left across the railway tracks and headed out to Highway One. The first checkpoint she reached was situated at Kwakch'on, some eight kilometres south of the Capital. She was waved through with a smart salute from the North Korean guards. As she drove south she was formulating her plan.

The landline that the Seoul Bureau had covertly re-routed from the Seoul telephone exchange early in the Korean War to connect between the Bureau and the North Korean intelligence headquarters in P'yŏngyang's former No. 2 KPA Officers School had been tapped by the Soviets when it was discovered during post-war reconstruction by Soviet engineers in the Government quarter of P'yŏngyang. A covert connection was made to the Soviet Embassy switchboard for future intelligence gathering use. She could easily gain access to it through Viktor Malinovskii. Arrangements could then be made with the Bureau for a suitably covert extraction.

Toksan was quiet. She passed two North Korean army trucks parked at the side of Highway One, but other than that, there was nothing on the road. A little farther south and she came upon the rusting hulk of the Soviet Military Staff car. Braking to a halt behind it, she climbed out of the GAZ jeep and made her way along the track that led into the wood. The desolated ville was silent as the grave. Any surviving inhabitants had obviously moved elsewhere. The charred and twisted, corroding remains of the MiG lay undisturbed in the desolated centre area of the settlement which was now beginning to become overgrown with a thick carpet of weeds. The incinerated pilot however, was no longer in the cockpit.

Charlotte gazed around. There were no workers in the paddies; no livestock in the surrounding fields… nothing but a sullen silence. She stood, hands on hips surveying this panorama of the desultory obliteration of an entire rural community. They wouldn't even have had time to look up before the monstrously swelling blossom of exploding jet fuel enveloped them. She shrugged and began to turn away, and then a movement in the trees attracted her attention. She turned back and was confronted by an old Korean man who limped painfully towards her. He stopped, a respectful distance from her and bowed. His right leg was heavily bandaged, and he stood awkwardly; seemingly to relieve the leg of his weight. Keeping his hands together in the symbolic gesture of *Añjali Mudrā,* he spoke,

'Honoured Colonel; I am Zhang Jae-Sun, once physician in this place. May I ask if you are here to seek out your countryman?'

Charlotte hesitated.

'My countryman? To whom do you refer?'

Zhang Jae-Sun studied her for a few moments.

'Why, I speak of the Russian officer whom we call *"Ku-da Chingu"*…"tall friend"; he who was driving the motor car which you see wrecked out on the Highway. He was gravely injured and had no memory of his past existence, but we cared for him and returned him to good health, although his memory has never returned to any real degree. He has lived among us and worked our fields, these ten years since passed.'

Charlotte nodded.

'How was he injured, and what were his injuries?'

Zhang Jae-Sun smiled gently.

'It seems his motor car was attacked by a South Korean fighter plane. His injuries were deep gashes to shoulder and side; and a serious contused cut to his left temple. It was this contusion that caused his memory loss, even though there was no skull fracture.'

Charlotte nodded gravely.

'Your diligence is appreciated. Where is he now?'

Zhang Jae-Sun motioned with his hand.

'He is with those of our village who prevailed after the catastrophe befell us. They are in our new village in the Chunghwa hills to the north of the paddies. If I may, I shall guide you there; although it may well be a time-consuming enterprise. My leg is unfortunately weak from the kiss of the flames. It has never healed properly.'

He smiled stoically.

'I fear that age is a great leveller. When the flames came I was not as nimble as I might have been. *"Ku-da Chingu"* pulled me from the paddy into which the explosion had hurled me, and where I might well have drowned, had he not dragged me into the shelter of the berm.'

She smiled.

'Time is of no essence, venerable Sir. We shall proceed at a pace that is comfortable to you.'

Charlotte and the old village physician, Zhang Jae-Sun made slow progress across the treacherously unstable berm banks surrounding the neglected paddies of his desolated ville of *Kwan-ni*. As they trudged across the slippery berms, Charlotte strove to contain her almost palpable sense of rising excitement and anticipation. She hadn't seen or heard from Max for almost ten years; if this *"Ku-da Chingu"* was indeed, him… what would he now be like? Would he even remember her? Would he remember their adventures… their love? How would he react to the knowledge that he had a daughter?

Once clear of the neglected and stagnant paddy fields, the ground began to rise as they started to ascend the lower slopes of the Chunghwa hills. Zhang Jae-Sun was beginning to find the climb difficult. Charlotte took his arm and supported him in order that he could relieve a little of his weight from his damaged right leg. He nodded his appreciation.

'Thank you Comrade Colonel. I must apologise for my infirmity, but the new village is only a little farther along this track; and then, we shall see if *"Ku-da Chingu"* is the one whom you seek.'

In a short while, they approached the new village that had been built in a small valley surrounded by the Chunghwa hills to the north of the ruins of what was once the original settlement of Kwan-ni. It wasn't much… just a cluster of hurriedly built *Hanoks,* and a few terraces scraped out from the gentler slopes of the surrounding hills.

Zhang Jae-Sun motioned towards a *Hanok* on the western edge of the settlement.

Honourable Colonel; that is the dwelling of the one we call *"Ku-da Chingu"*… "Tall friend"; but I doubt that he is there. He is probably out levelling the new rice terraces beyond the western slopes of that distant hill.'

As he spoke; a figure appeared over the crest of the hill he had pointed to. Zhang Jae-Sun smiled.

'Comrade Colonel, he must have heard us. That is *"Ku-da Chingu"* himself.'

Charlotte studied the distant figure. The man was about the correct height; but his gait was unfamiliar. He seemed to walk with a slight limp, and his whole bearing was not that of Max as she remembered him. Her heart sank… but then, it was almost ten years since she had said goodbye to him in the Embassy at Seoul. As he came closer, she scrutinised him closely. He bore a passing resemblance to Max, but she saw no spark of recognition in his eyes as he studied this female Russian colonel standing with his old friend at the foot of the pathway.

He stopped, and put his hands together in the symbolic gesture of *Añjali Mudrā* with his eyes lowered respectfully. Charlotte studied him. His face was lined and sunburned from years of working in the paddies; his hands were strong and calloused. He may well have once been Max Segal, but now bore little resemblance to her lover.

She spoke, in Russian…

"Kak Vas zovut?"… 'What is your name?'

He looked blankly at her, and replied in halting Russian;

'My Russian is not good. My name is Ku-da Chingu. This is my village. I tend the paddies. Who are you? And what do you want of me?'

Charlotte's heart sank. There was not the slightest hint of recognition in his eyes as he gazed blankly at her. There was no purpose in continuing in this manner. Impassively, although her disappointment was hard to bear; she became once again, the Russian colonel.

'I am here to try to establish what became of the Soviet officer who was driving that motor car that lies wrecked out on the highway. Do you know anything about what happened to him?'

Ku-da Chingu shook his head. His gaze was distant and apathetic.

'I know nothing of this man. The motor car has been there for as long as I can remember.'

He then excused himself and continued his limping walk down the pathway towards the village.

Zhang Jae-Sun touched Charlotte's arm.

'It is as I said, Honourable Colonel; he has no practical memory of his past life. His thoughts have remained remote and faraway; and every night he tells me of curious dreams of a quite different world of white people and big cities and half-remembered faces. Perhaps, in time, some of these scattered memories will take shape, and lead him to remember his past; but, I fear it is not for now.'

Charlotte nodded.

'Thank you, Comrade Zhang Jae-Sun. It seems that he is not the officer for whom I was searching. However; if any indication as to who he was, returns; I would be obliged if you could get a message to me. My name is Nadia Tolenkanovna, and my office is at the T17 sniper academy in P'yŏngyang.'

Zhang Jae-Sun bowed.

'Certainly, Honourable colonel. I still have items that were on his person when he was discovered. He has never shown any interest in seeing them, but it is my thinking that I shall introduce them to him gradually, and see if there is anything amongst them that he remembers.'

Charlotte paused.

'Might I see them, Comrade? They might hold some clue to his identity.'

The old physician nodded.

'You are most welcome, Honourable colonel. I have them in my dwelling.'

In his *Hanok;* Zhang Jae-Sun invited Charlotte to sit at the rough wooden table and brought out an old tin box; the faded printing upon which, declared that it had once held wax candles. Placing it in front of her, he invited her to examine the contents. There wasn't much. All the identity documents had been destroyed on the instructions of the village elders to prevent the P'yŏngyang investigators from finding Max in the old ville when they had come searching for the Russian who had been driving the wrecked car out on Highway One. The box contained a few papers, a couple of ticket stubs; and two faded, creased, and dog-eared photographs.

One photograph was of a young and pretty, blonde-haired girl in a white, halter-necked swimsuit, wearing aviator's sunglasses and a big, floppy-brimmed woven sun hat; reclining on a wicker chaise longue overlooking a sunny expanse of water. She recognised it immediately. It was a photograph of her... taken by Max in the early autumn of 1949, at Strandbad Wannsee, Berlin. The second photograph was of the little white house at Number Three, Alsbacher Weg, in the old Nazi SS Veterans Settlement at Krumme Lanke in the Berlin Grunewald... the safe house that she and Max had shared during those last days before they were extracted from Berlin... the little house in which they had made love for the first time.

Her heart skipped a beat. This "Ku-da Chingu" had to be Max. There could be no other explanation. Zhang Jae-Sun was studying her intently. His wise eyes had interpreted her reaction. He smiled gently.

'Honourable colonel; these pictures have a profound depth of meaning for you. I can read it in your eyes. What would you like me to do? Shall I go and bring Ku-da Chingu to you so that he might recognise something in them?'

She nodded; forcing herself not to reveal the emotional turmoil that was rising to engulf her implied authoritarian persona.

Zhang Jae-Sun returned in a little while with Ku-da Chingu and sat him at the table opposite Charlotte. She placed the photographs in front of him, and gazed steadily at his weather-beaten face. Holding him in eye to eye contact, she spoke quietly in Russian...

'You recognise these photographs? Do they mean anything to you?'

He gazed at the photographs of a while, and then looked up. His eyes were puzzled and his whole demeanour suggested that he seemed to be preoccupied with some inner mental struggle. He looked back down at the photograph of the little white house, then, in halting Russian, he spoke...

'What is this place?'

She looked steadily at him.

'It is a house in Berlin... in Germany.'

He stared at her, and murmured,

'Berlin... Germany.'

Then, he dropped his eyes back to the photographs. He ran his fingertips over the photograph of her at Strandbad Wannsee. He glanced up at her face... his expression was that of a child who had just woken from a deep sleep. He bit his lip, and then said, hesitantly...

'I remember this girl ... this girl is... You?'

She nodded. He continued.

'And this house... we stayed there together?'

She nodded again; struggling to keep her composure. Reaching across the table, she took hold of his hands; hard and calloused from

43

years of labour, working the paddies.

'Your name is Konstantin Sharansky; Colonel of the Soviet Administration troops.'

He stared at her in disbelief.

She continued; struggling to hold back her tears.

'We have searched for you for ten years and now, I have come to take you home.'

Chapter Three

Zhang Jae-Sun rose from his chair in the corner of the room and approached the table. He smiled gently at Charlotte.

'I am so pleased that Ku-da Chingu has, at last begun to have perhaps, found himself. You must take him home to where, hopefully, he will be able to take up his true identity, and no longer be the lost soul that he has become since his misfortune. We shall regret his departure, for he has been a stalwart member of our community during his stay here. He must, however, return to his own world. Thank you, Comrade Colonel; may you and Ku-da Chingu go in peace, and prosper.'

He then turned to Ku-da Chingu.

'Go and gather your possessions, my friend. The colonel will take you to start your journey of exploration to find yourself once more.'

Ku-da Chingu gave them a puzzled look, then nodded silently and left Zhang Jae-Sun's *Hanok*. Turning to Charlotte, the old physician gazed at her steadily, and then spoke quietly.

'As you have seen, his memory of his past life is so vague as to be almost as though it never existed. Much education will be necessary. You must endeavour to remind him about past things and places. This will undoubtedly take much time and patience, but if you persevere, it is entirely likely that his full memory will, in time, return.'

Having bid farewell to Zhang Jae-Sun; Charlotte accompanied the silent Ku-da Chingu back down the path through the woods to where her vehicle was parked up on the side of Highway One. As they came out of the tree-line, they saw that a North Korean Army motorcyclist was rummaging about inside the parked-up GAZ jeep. Ku-da Chingu froze at the sight of the soldier and made to run back into the woods. Charlotte caught his arm, and silently shook her head. She straightened her uniform jacket and strode towards the unwary soldier who was preoccupied with searching the rear of the jeep. She stopped, a couple of metres behind him, and snapped, in Korean,

'Attention! Why are you searching my vehicle?'

The man jumped back and spun around. His face froze at the sight of this Russian colonel. She repeated her question, and there was no mistaking the cold authority in her voice. Standing rigidly to attention, with fear written all over his face, the soldier reported that he had come upon the apparently abandoned vehicle and was conducting a search to try to establish the reason why it was parked up out here in the middle of nowhere.

Charlotte looked him up and down.

'Very well. You may continue with your patrol. I shall now return to P'yŏngyang to interview this peasant.'

She motioned with a disdainful hand towards Ku-da Chingu, who was standing with his head bowed, and his eyes fixed firmly on a patch of grass a little way in front of him. The soldier nodded eagerly.

'Thank you, Honourable colonel. My profound apologies for my impertinence in examining your vehicle.'

He turned, and almost ran back to where his motorcycle was parked; vaulted into the saddle, kicked the engine into life and roared off along Highway One in a southerly direction.

Charlotte beckoned to Ku-da Chingu and asked him to get into the front passenger seat. Climbing into the driving seat, and starting the engine; she told him to take off the traditional conical hat... the "*satgat*"; and toss it into the back seat. She looked at him. He still had a good head of hair, albeit, turning silver at the sides; and his profile was still tight. Yes, it was Max. Pulling out onto the highway, she turned the GAZ around, and accelerated away towards Toksan.

No one took any notice of the military jeep as it drove through the little town. The two North Korean army trucks were still parked at the side of Highway One, with soldiers lounging around smoking; but they paid little attention to the Russian jeep... why should they? The Russian woman officer who was driving didn't even glance in their direction... although, had they been a little more observant, they would have perhaps noticed that she kept her eye on the jeep's rear-view mirror until she was safely out of their sight. Beyond Toksan, Highway One was deserted. She turned to Max.

'I'm sorry, but I had to lie to you back at the village. Your real name is not Konstantin Sharansky; and neither are you a colonel of the Soviet Administration troops.'

He stared at her. She continued.

46

'Nor am I a Russian colonel. My name is Charlotte Mckenna, and I am an American Officer with the Central Intelligence Agency. Your true name is Max Segal; and you are also a CIA officer. You were sent into North Korea during the early days of the Korean War under deep cover as this Russian colonel, Konstantin Sharansky. As far as we can guess, you were driving south to a rendezvous point for extraction back to South Korea when whatever caused you to crash your car took place. By the look of the wreck it was some sort of air attack. Since then, having lost your memory; you have lived in the village. It is now my job to get you out of North Korea to safety.'

He stared at her in disbelief.

'But, I am Ku-da Chingu. I have always been Ku-da Chingu. Zhang Jae-Sun has told me this.'

She shook her head.

'No. You are Max Segal. I can prove this to you. You have a deep, crescent-shaped scar just below your navel.'

He stared harder at her.

'How could you possibly know that? I have never met you...'

She smiled.

'You told me that you got it in a bar brawl in Berlin. I saw it when we sun-bathed at Strandbad Wannsee... the place in the photograph, with me wearing the white swim suit; and later, at the little white house in the other photograph, when we made love for the first time.'

He dropped his eyes and touched his hand to his stomach.

'For the first time? Then, we were together before...?'

She nodded.

'Yes; at first, in Berlin, then in America; and finally, in the Seoul Embassy. We were together for four years before you were sent into the North on your mission.'

She paused. Should she tell him that he had a daughter? No. It would be too much, too soon. Better to let him come to terms that they were a couple; disunited by ten long years separation, before she spread his whole previous existence out before him.

She studied him. He sat there silently, a look of dumbfounded shock on his face. He looked across at her and laid his hand gently over her's as she gripped the steering wheel. He spoke softly in his terrible Russian accent,

'I'm so sorry. I cannot remember anything about you.'

She smiled gently.

'You will, Max. You will.'

Eight hundred kilometres to the north-west; in Beijing, the Capital city of The People's Republic of China; Huang Zheheng... former *Shang Shi*... Senior NCO Huang Zheheng of the 89th Division, IX Army Group, Peoples Liberation Army, and now, an officer in the Central Investigation Department, otherwise known as the Chinese Intelligence Service, opened the top drawer of his desk in his office and studied the large, blood-red Garnet that he had taken from the dead US Marine in the devastated bunker on Hill 1403 north-west of Yudam-ni, and west of the Chosin Reservoir during the Korean war, back in 1950.

He had thought to sell the gem when he returned to civilian life, to finance a new plough for his family farm; but, in the ensuing three years of war, he had accumulated a considerable amount of booty by way of relieving the enemy dead of their gold rings and teeth. This, in itself, had been grounds for summary execution, but Huang Zheheng had now risen from lowly *Shang Shi*... Senior NCO, to the staff rank of *"Zhong Xiao"*... Lieutenant Colonel, and thus, was effectively not subject to investigation. This was, for the most part, due to a fortuitous event for him, at least; during the bloody attrition in what had come to be known as the Battle of Heartbreak Ridge, which had taken place in Yanggu County in the Kangwon Province of North Korea, during September and October of 1951.

Attached to the Intelligence Command post in the Mundung-ni Valley; Huang Zheheng had been out scouting to the north of the area the combatants had nicknamed 'The Punchbowl", when the American combat engineers finally breached the six-foot-high rock barrier built by the North Koreans to protect the valley, and allowed the American armour to punch through. Caught in the open, the defending Chinese division suffered heavy casualties from the American tanks. For the next five days the Shermans had roared up and down the Mundung-ni Valley, over-running supply dumps, mauling troop concentrations, and destroying bunkers on Heartbreak and in the surrounding hills and valleys. Out of the thirty Intelligence personnel attached to the sector; ranging in rank from *Xia Shi*... Junior NCO, to *Zhong Jiang*... Lieutenant General; Huang Zheheng had been the sole survivor. After that, as the war ground down to a tentative stalemate, his rise through the ranks had been rapid... there were simply not enough experienced officers left. During the battle of Heartbreak Ridge alone; the Chinese and North Koreans lost twenty-five thousand men.

He glanced at the Bulova Navigator's watch on his wrist. This was also part of his war booty; the sum total of which... not including whatever anybody would pay for the Garnet gemstone; was in excess of two hundred thousand Silver Yuan; the equivalent of about fifteen thousand American Dollars. The Director had allocated Huang Zheheng a post in Shanghai. Consequently he had decided that it was time to liquefy his assets. A meeting with the buyer had been arranged for this afternoon in the plush Beijing Hotel, formerly known as the Grand Hotel on East Chang An Avenue.

His contact was a shifty-looking Chinese in an expensive suit who, according to Huang Zheheng's information, was one of the enforcers of the notorious Macau-based Triad: *"Dai Huen Jai";* otherwise known as the "Big Circle Boys."

In the expansive lounge of the hotel, the man apprised him with cold, black, expressionless eyes.

'You have the agreed merchandise?'

Huang Zheheng nodded.

'What sum has your Mountain Master authorised you to offer?'

The Dai Huen Jai enforcer smiled; a cold, mirthless smile.

'Five thousand Dollars, American.'

Huang Zheheng smiled again.

'You imagine I am a fool from the Golden Mountain? You would not have travelled so far unless your Mountain Master had authorised you to spend the worth of this gemstone.'

The Dai Huen Jai enforcer's eyes narrowed to black, unfathomable slits.

'It is not the wise man who chooses negotiation with the Dai Huen Jai brotherhood rather than compliance.'

Huang Zheheng laid his Type 59 pistol carefully on the table and studied the man.

'It is also not the wise man who chooses to attempt to intimidate a member of the Central Investigation Department.'

The intimation was not lost on the Dai Huen Jai enforcer. His eyes glittered. He was obviously not a man who was familiar with making concessions.

'Very well. The limit of my authority is eight thousand, American. Let us complete the transaction amicably.'

Huang Zheheng handed over the little velvet pouch containing the gemstone as the Dai Huen Jai enforcer slipped a thick manila envelope across the surface of the table. Both men checked the contents of their respective items and nodded. The enforcer slipped the pouch into his pocket and rose from the table. His expression was impassive, but his eyes were deadly.

'You would be well advised never to set foot in Macao.'

Huang Zheheng watched the enforcer leave and relaxed. He had no intention of ever setting foot in the shit-hole that was Macao. His intention was to retire to Hong Kong; purchase a decent property on the Island and enjoy a good capitalist life-style filled with wine and women. He peered into the manila envelope. It was stuffed with a thick wad of one-hundred Dollar bills. He smiled and ordered a whisky. It was American Rye... more war booty. As the golden liquid slid down, warming his stomach, he idly mused as to which of the many desirable locations in Hong Kong he would settle in, now that he could afford to do so.

They found his body the next morning, floating face-down in the southern lake in Beihai Park; less than one and a half kilometres west of the hotel. When they pulled the corpse out of the water they discovered that he had endured a particularly gruesome death. He had been impaled with a metre-long metal spike that had been rammed up between his buttocks into his rectum; the pointed end of which, had torn up through his entrails and now protruded from his belly exactly mid-way between his pubic bone and his navel. Both his index fingers had also been chopped off... the classic Triad calling card.

The Dai Huen Jai enforcer had long gone. He had boarded the late express on the Jinghu Railway... the main line from Beijing to Shanghai, the previous night; and was now approaching the Yangtze River south of Pukou, almost seven hundred kilometres south of Beijing. As the express pulled out of Beijing station, he had opened the little pouch and examined the Garnet gemstone. He smiled to himself. The gemstone certainly met all the aspirations of his Triad Mountain Master... and he still had the American currency which he had recovered from that dumb Chinese Intelligence bastard before he had disposed of his body in the lake at Beihai Park. A self-satisfied smile spread across his brutal face as he carefully replaced the little pouch in his inside jacket pocket and shifted to a more comfortable position in his seat as the express sped on into the south.

Monday, 19th September, 1960.
Shanghai.
People's Republic of China.

Meng Hanyong... the Dai Huen Jai Triad Enforcer came out of the large arched entrance of Shanghai North Railway Station, on East Tianmu Road in the Zhabei District, slightly north of the city centre; paused, and lit a cigarette.

The journey down from Beijing had been long and tedious, and now he was faced with another irksome trip by train or bus to Guangzhou;

and then, by bus from Guangzhou to Zhuhai. It would take at least another full day before he reached Macao. It was no use looking for a pretty, little Shanghainese girl to help pass the time before his next train. The countrywide, radical Maoist re-education programs had been undertaken on the largest scale in Shanghai since the beginning of the year, and such measures had basically wiped all visible forms of prostitution from the city's streets. The only thing left to do would be to find a suitable teahouse in the old city; have a few drinks and see if he got lucky.

He found one that looked suitably seedy on the Xue Yuan Road. He sat in a wicker chair facing the door, sipping tea and surveying the other customers. In a darker corner of the room he noticed a corpulent, middle-aged Chinese fondling a young girl. She appeared to be Korean, judging by her facial features... her face was flatter than most Chinese; with higher and squarer cheek bones, and she possessed smaller eyes with single eyelids. She was very pretty, with her glossy blue-black hair cut into a short-bob. She looked to be about fifteen. Meng Hanyong surveyed the room. The girl was the only one worth having; except perhaps, for the waitress who had brought his tea. He turned his gaze back to the fat Chinese. He was beginning to get more insistent in his attentions towards the girl. She appeared to be trying vainly to ward off his more licentious approaches.

Meng Hanyong watched this unfolding molestation with cold, detached interest. The girl would be an attractive distraction to while away an hour or so before he caught the train south. He watched, as the fat Chinese thrust his hand up under the girl's skirt and she recoiled from his groping hand. Scraping his chair back; the Dai Huen Jai Triad Enforcer strode across to the table, reached out, and closed his vice-like grip on the fat Chinese's arm.

The Chinese glanced up, startled. Meng Hanyong hissed,

'Stop that, you fat pig. Leave the girl alone.'

The fat Chinese's eyes narrowed as he spat out the words, in Cantonese...

'Gwan lei lun see ah, sou hai'... 'None of your fucking business, dumbass.'

Meng Hanyong only hit him once. The fat Chinese collapsed, scattering the delicate tea bowls as the enforcer grabbed the girl and hurried out of the tea room whilst pandemonium broke out amongst the other patrons. The ensuing Shanghai police report stated that witnesses saw the stranger hit the fat man just once. He seemed to deliver the phenomenally rapid blow not with his fist, but with the side of his left hand, and the fat man fell straight across the table, then collapsed onto the floor and lay as still as a rock.

The girl and Meng Hanyong hurried away along the Xue Yuan Road as the distant wail of police sirens began to echo through the warren of convoluted, cobbled streets. She pulled him into a narrow, dingy alleyway and guided him away from the main thoroughfare and prying eyes. In a deep doorway, she turned to him, and slipped a knowing hand down to stroke his crotch. She smiled up at him innocently.

'Thank you, honourable sir for saving me from that Cantonese pig. How may I repay you?'

Meng Hanyong grinned and fondled her pert little breasts through the thin material of her silk top. A quick "up against the wall" was just what he had been hoping for. He turned her into the doorway and pushed her back against the stained, paint-peeling brickwork; feeling her hands deftly undoing his trouser fly buttons. She slipped her delicate fingers inside; encircling him with firm, long strokes, gently caressing and kneading his rapidly tumescing member. Breathing hard, he ran his hands up under her skirt to her hips; groping for the waist-band of her cotton pants, intent on dragging them down around her ankles.

He heard nothing of the stealthy approach behind him; so engrossed was he with his exploration of the girl's soft, warm young flesh. A hand snatched a handful of his hair and viciously jerked his head back... he scarcely felt the cold, impersonal kiss of the cut-throat razor's keen edge that his assailant slashed across his throat from ear to ear.

The girl darted to one side as the blood sprayed from Meng Hanyong's severed jugular veins. He was dead long before he even began to sway. His assailant released his grip and the Enforcer's body slumped face-first against the decaying brickwork then slid to the ground. With a speed and deftness that belied his corpulence; the fat Chinese expertly frisked the twitching corpse, removing the thick manila envelope containing several thousand American Dollars and the little pouch that held the large, flawless Garnet gemstone; both of which disappeared into his voluminous pockets. He smiled contentedly to the girl and stroked her hair.

'A fine day's work, little flower.'

She smiled back.

'Yes, Uncle.'

He took her hand, and they hurried away out towards the Renmin Lu ring road that circled the old town, where they flagged down a cruising taxi and travelled north across the city to Shanghai North Railway Station. They boarded a train for the thirty-six-hour journey to Hong Kong. With his newly acquired wealth; the fat Chinese took a two-berth "deluxe soft sleeper" with private toilet, where he could "relax" undisturbed in the company of his "niece."

Wednesday, 21st September, 1960.
Central Kowloon District.
Hong Kong.

Sheih Shou Rong; the fat Chinese, stepped down onto the platform of Kowloon station from the night sleeper and turned to assist his "niece" down the steps of the sleeper coach. The journey down from Shanghai had been uneventful, and he had spent several hours relaxing and sampling her versatile delights in the privacy of the "deluxe soft sleeper" which he had taken for their journey.

He smiled to himself. She was certainly a desirable liquid asset, and one that could easily be used to generate a considerable working capital, if delivered into the right hands... as could the Garnet gemstone. He led her off the platform out to the station forecourt, where he hailed a cab. He knew exactly where to take both her, and the gemstone to secure the best deal... The Walled City... the wickedest place on earth. It was the centre of the Hong Kong narcotics trade, of the sex trade, of the Chinese criminal gangs.

The City of Darkness was a festering, monolithic labyrinth of anarchy and lawlessness rearing up abruptly in the heart of urban Hong Kong, between ten and fourteen storeys high; inhabited by tens of thousands of people living in small rooms stacked on top of each other; ruled by the Triads, and out of bounds to the British Hong Kong police force. A man could be murdered here without the British Colonial authorities ever hearing about it. Crime flourished in this Triad stronghold which measured a mere two hundred metres by one hundred metres, and covered little more than five acres. Prostitution was rife in the twisting *hutongs*... the cramped corridors and alleys winding maze-like, amongst the illegal businesses, unlicensed dentists, doctors, and opium parlours. Sweat shops had been set up in the area to avoid labour laws, and electricity was illegally tapped off the Hong Kong grid to feed the area. There was no sewage system, and the water supply was a solitary standpipe supplied by the Hong Kong government, as well as several self-dug wells. The alleys were lit by fluorescent bulbs twenty-four hours a day. The ground level rarely received sunlight because of the density and height of the buildings that were haphazardly constructed as every available space within its tiny acreage was expanded out, and crammed into, until its contorted labyrinth of thoroughfares and pathways became festooned with a tangled overhead network of pipes and wiring, dripping and hissing above the city's dark, dank walkways. The maze of staircases and alleys was so extensive that one could actually walk around the city without ever touching the ground. It was a perfect criminal hide-out; and it was here that Sheih Shou Rong intended to dispose of his "niece," Mei Hua. Some Triad whoremaster would pay good money for her.

The fat Chinese had found her on a sleazy street in Macao when she was twelve, and had groomed her to perfection. Some girls you could teach; but Mei-Hua possessed a natural instinct for carnal virtuosity. That was rare... and expensive. The Triads, who rigidly controlled all the brothels, opium dens, and gambling parlours in the City of Darkness, would pay highly for control of her. She might even end up installed in one of the better, Triad-owned apartments on the Mei Tung estate across the road to the north, servicing Hong Kong's Society Elite who came in for the sex, drugs, and gambling.

The Garnet Gemstone was an easy sell. The Garnet carried significant reverence in Chinese beliefs as bestowing immunity to injury upon its wearer. It was also believed to attract the energy and influence of the Sun. The larger the gem, the greater the attraction; and a Triad Dragon Lord would bestow great favour upon one of his lieutenants offering such a prize.

As he settled into the rear seat of the cab and slipped his hand up under Mei-Hua's skirt for possibly the last time; he smiled complacently to himself. He would accrue a considerable sum of money for these two assets... and he still had the envelope of American dollars. His smile became even more complacent as Mei-Hua delicately unbuttoned his fly, slipped her hand within; wrapping her little fingers around his swollen, aroused member, and began to fondle and squeeze. She gently eased it out; delicately moistened her lips with her tongue, and bent her pretty head down towards him.

The cab stopped a little way back from Carpenter Road... far enough away to be out of the shadow cast by the overcrowded, rat-breeding cauldron of iniquity they called *"Hak Nam"*... the City of Darkness. Sheih Shou Rong paid off the cab driver and, taking Mei-Hua by the hand, crossed Carpenter Road, and stood on the garbage-strewn, broken pavement. He studied the towering, ramshackle tenement buildings, looking for a narrow passage about two thirds of

54

the way along the south frontage, named Tai Chang Street. He knew that the contact he had arranged to meet would be in a *Dim Sum* shop somewhere along its murky depths.

The passage stank. It was no more than four feet wide; dipping and twisting along its dark and dank length into the dingy, deep green light that suffused the lower levels of this cesspool of garbage, dark wet corridors, rats, and disease. He led the girl farther into the semi-darkness that echoed to the endless splatter and drip of water leaking onto the stone-flagged pathway; whose centre had been worn down into a shallow depression, and was running with filthy water. The smell of rot and decay permeated the very air. The slimy walls were mildewed and water-stained black and green from the tangle of overhead leaking pipes.

The dark shadows crept across everything, smothering the passageway's furthest reaches as, holding Mei-Hua's hand firmly, he moved forward deeper into this bizarre, squalid warren of dark and brooding half-light, suffused with the overwhelming, sweet-rank smell of opium, cooking oil and frying fish-balls, interspersed with the smells of wood smoke, joss-sticks, and boiling rice; and the ever-pervading stench of human excrement and rotting garbage lingering in the stale, humid air.

Glancing up, he could see nothing but crisscrossing clothes lines and electrical wires spider-webbing up to a sky made only of rooftops, and of wire mesh stretched across from building to building in order to prevent too much garbage and sewage thrown over the side from the hundreds of people living in tents of cloth or cardboard erected on the tops of the buildings, from falling down and blocking the passageway. Cockroaches crackled under his feet, and, gripping his hand tighter, Mei-Hue stepped gingerly over a large, dead rat lying in the stream of oily, fetid water running along the middle of the worn stone path. Rats were a common sight in this part of Hong Kong. They outnumbered people two to one.

Sheih Shou Rong walked slowly whilst his eyes became accustomed to the gloomy darkness. The narrow passage was inky-black in places, with only thin strands of weak sunlight penetrating from high above. Every few hundred feet a naked light bulb cast a faint, yellowish light, creating strange shadows that flickered across the dripping walls. He began to wish that he hadn't agreed to traffick the girl within the enclave of this teeming, nightmarish, twilight world; but his source had insisted that the transaction was completed inside the city, where no outside law enforcement dared to interfere.

As it was; there was little to fear from the authorities. Girls as young as twelve plied their trade under the watchful eye of the Triad whoremasters; and Mei-Hua was almost sixteen. Such was the moral code of The City of Darkness, which in reality, could be better called The City of Victims… living in perpetual twilight whilst under the iron rule of the Triads.

The *Dim Sum* shop halfway along the fifth alley on the right, off Lung Chun Back Street, was crammed in between an unlicensed Dentist's parlour on the one side, and a Mah-jong-cum-opium parlour on the other. The shabby interior was lit by a single grimy, fly-specked fluorescent tube that flickered fitfully; casting an unpleasant strobing effect across the surfaces of the chipped and stained tables. Sheih Shou Rong ordered a beer and a bowl of minced shrimp *Dim Sum…* bite-sized dough envelopes; steamed or deep-fried, and eaten with a touch of soya, and saucers of chicken and other meats in various sauces; whilst Mei-Hua said she would prefer noodles and soup. As they were waiting for the old proprietor to cook their order, a man stepped in from the shadowy alley and sat at their table. He introduced himself as the *423… "Straw Sandal"* of the Sun Yee On Brotherhood.

He smiled graciously, but his eyes were cold.

'I am Chang Lok, the Liaison officer of the Brotherhood, and have come to close the transaction as arranged.'

He studied Mei-Hua, and nodded; then held out his hand to Sheih Shou Rong, who brought out the little pouch and tipped the Garnet gemstone into the man's palm. Chang Lok held the stone up and turned it in the light. The stone refracted blood-red flashes of light around the shabby walls as its facets caught the reflections from the flickering fluorescent tube. It was a beautiful gem; but the thing that intrigued him was the tiny spark that seemed to shimmer deep in its heart. He nodded. Yes, the girl and the stone were well worth the negotiated price. He carefully slipped the gem back into its little pouch, and laid it on the surface of the grimy tabletop.

Leaning back in his chair, he spoke.

'The transaction is satisfactory. I shall take the girl, but the gemstone can remain in your possession until my associate brother, *"Red Pole"* comes to bring you the agreed capital; whereupon, the transaction will be completed by the exchange of assets. Agreed?'

Sheih Shou Rong nodded. He didn't have any choice, seeing as how he was isolated in bandit country… and besides which; he needed someone to show him a safe way out of this dank and mysterious no-man's land in one piece. Chang Lok rose from the table and held out his hand to Mei-Hua. She stood up, and clasping her hands together,

bowed to Sheih Shou Rong. She raised her eyes, and murmured,
'Farewell, Uncle.'

Then, she took Chang Lok's hand and walked out of the shop with
him without a backwards glance.

The fat Chinese shrugged and turned his attention to the bowl of
Dim Sum that the proprietor brought and placed in front of him.

He had eaten about half the portion when he sensed a presence
behind him. Looking up over his shoulder, he saw a powerful-looking
man. The man bowed briefly and spoke.

'You are Sheih Shou Rong? I am *426... "Red Pole"*... The Enforcer.
My name is Shen Ming-húa. I have come on the instructions of my
"Straw Sandal" of the Sun Yee On Brotherhood to close the
transaction and escort you out of *Hak Nam*.'

He sat at the table and held out his hand. Sheih Shou Rong passed
over the little pouch containing the garnet gemstone, and the Enforcer
pulled out a thick manila envelope and laid it softly on the table. He
then opened the pouch and glanced inside. He looked up and nodded.
Sheih Shou Rong lifted the envelope flap and looked inside. It was
stuffed with American Dollar bills. He also looked up and nodded.
The Enforcer smiled… a cold, humourless smile.

'Then our transaction is complete. Come. I will guide you out of
Hak Nam.'

They both rose and stepped out into the alley. The Enforcer turned
to the right and led the way into the dim half-light. They walked
through a series of dank, shadowy corridors; across stairwells and
cross alleys until Sheih Shou Rong was completely disorientated. The
Enforcer strode on, with the fat Chinese struggling to keep up with
him. At last, the alley widened. It was still shadowy, but at least the
big man in the lead was visible. A narrow open space dominated by a
water standpipe appeared. The big man stopped; as though he was
waiting for Sheih Shou Rong to catch up.

The Enforcer waited… Sheih Shou Rong was almost within
touching distance of the big man's back. Suddenly, the Enforcer
turned and struck. The razor-sharp blade of the throwing hatchet he
had drawn from its concealment under his jacket caught the fat
Chinese dead-centre of his forehead; cleaving his skull as though it
was a watermelon. Sheih Shou Rong was dead before he hit the
ground. Stooping, the Enforcer removed the two envelopes containing
the cash and the little pouch containing the Garnet gemstone. He then
prised the hatchet out of the corpse's skull and turned to the standpipe
to wash the blood and brain matter from the blade. Stepping back, he
turned and walked away to be swallowed up by the shadowy half-

light, as the oily, filthy water running down the deep hollow worn in middle of the stone walkway slowly turned red as the bloody tendrils seeping from the corpse ran into, and gently swirled on its surface.

Friday, 23rd September, 1960.
Central Kowloon District.
Hong Kong.

Shen Ming-húa; the *426... "Red Pole"...* the Enforcer of the Hong Kong Sun Yee On Triad, came out of the Walled city and walked purposefully along Carpenter Road towards its junction with Tung Tau Tsuen Road. In his jacket pockets he carried the two envelopes containing the cash and the little pouch containing the Garnet gemstone he had taken from the body of the Fat Chinese whom he had coldly executed in the dank, shadowy alleyways of the City of Darkness on the instructions of his Triad Master. At the junction, a black Mercedes-Benz 300D limousine waited, with its engine whispering. The Enforcer opened the rear door and climbed in. He nodded to the driver, who engaged gear, pulled out smoothly into the traffic, and sped away towards downtown Kowloon.

The Mercedes purred down Salisbury Road and stopped in front of the Star Ferry Terminal. The hour hand of the clock in the low tower over the entrance read eleven o'clock. Two tough-looking Chinese dressed in similar dark suits to the driver approached and opened the rear door for the Enforcer to alight. As he stepped out of the Mercedes, both men bowed, and escorted him down the covered pier to where a Chriscraft Corsair motorboat... a sleek twenty-two feet of stainless steel and varnished teak, with white pleated leather seats, waited with its V-six-cylinder engine quietly burbling away. The Enforcer stepped down into the launch's cockpit; settled himself on the rear seats, as the two heavies pushed off from the pier and the boat headed out across Victoria Harbour towards the waterfront of Hong Kong Island.

Ten minutes later, the motorboat came alongside the pier to the west of the elegant renaissance-style Hong Kong Club building. Another black Mercedes-Benz limousine was waiting in front of the imposing façade of the Central pier. As they approached, the driver opened the rear door for the Enforcer and bowed. As he settled himself on the spacious, dark blue Bedford cloth upholstery of the deep rear seat, the two escorts slid into the front seat beside the driver, who pressed the engine self-starter, engaged gear, and swept out into Queen's Road Central, with the Mercedes-Benz limousine's tyres whimpering on the asphalt; past the monolithic Hong Kong and Shanghai Bank, said to be "the tallest building between Cairo and San Francisco;" and headed out of Victoria City in the direction of Magazine Gap and its junction with Peak Road that led up to Victoria Peak.

As the limousine wound its way up the sinuous Peak Road towards its destination, the Enforcer switched on the car interior light and tipped the contents of the little velvet pouch into his lap, appreciatively studying the gems. The big, pigeon egg-sized Garnet was beautiful. The tiny blood-red spark in its heart twinkled seductively. Yes, he could see why his *489... "Mountain Master"...* the head of the Triad, coveted this gem, and why so much time and expense had been invested in tracking it through its journey from mainland China. He allowed himself a self-satisfied smile as he replaced the gem in the little pouch.

The limousine turned onto Barker Road and drove in through the imposing gates of one of the large white mansions on The Peak... the best locality in Hong Kong; the exclusive residential area formerly reserved for non-Chinese. The driver proceeded up the sweeping drive and stopped outside the Colonial-pillared entrance. A servant ran to open the rear door; the Enforcer alighted and entered the building followed by the two escorts. Another servant deferentially conducted him to the drawing room, opened the door, and bowing deeply; backed away as he entered.

The Enforcer walked across the vast expanse of finest English Wilton carpet to the figure seated behind the massive camphor-wood desk that dominated the huge drawing room. Heung Wah-yim, Master of the Sun Yee On Triad, gently pushed away the head of his newest concubine, the sixteen-year-old Mei-Hua who had been delivered to him less than two ago from the City of Darkness, and had been delicately, and expertly fellating him from within her concealed position under the central kneehole of the desk. As she settled back on her heels, and continued to delicately stroke his engorged member and tease his scrotum; he placed his elbows on the finely tooled leather surface of the desk and rested his chin on his hands. His face was impassive.

The Enforcer stood before him and bowed deeply. He brought out the two manila envelopes and the little pouch and carefully placed them on the surface of the desk. Heung Wah-yim ignored the envelopes and loosened the drawstring of the little pouch; tipping its contents onto the leather surface. The pigeon egg-sized Garnet glowed in the light of the ornate Tiffany desk lamp. Heung Wah-yim picked it up and turned it in his fingers, admiring the tiny blood-red spark in its heart. He nodded.

'You are to be congratulated, Shen Ming-húa. It is everything we were led to believe.'

He pushed the envelope containing the eight thousand American Dollars that had been the original payment for the transaction back in Beijing between the Chinese Intelligence Service Officer, Huang Zheheng, and the Macau-based Dai Huen Jai Triad enforcer, Meng Hanyong.

'You may retain this envelope as a reward for your diligence.'

Shen Ming-húa bowed deeply.

'Thank you Master. Your benevolence is munificent.'

Heung Wah-yim nodded, and dismissed the Enforcer with a languid flourish of his hand. As the Enforcer left the drawing room, he reached forward under the desk, and, placing his hands either side of Mei-Hua's face, gently drew her head down towards him again; gasping as she gently caressed his scrotum with her fingertips and slowly slipped her lips over the head of his penis.

Chapter Four.

Saturday, 8th October 1960.
Ch'angwang-san District,
P'yŏngyang. North Korea.

Charlotte had installed Max... or, to use the name he responded to... Ku-da Chingu, in her apartment just off the Chŏnggŏ Jangjŏn-t'ong Highway in downtown P'yŏngyang for a little over three weeks since she had brought him up from the south. She had spent the time slowly introducing him to memories of his previous life, but as yet, he had grasped little recollection of his previous life. She had provided him with city clothes and took him on frequent walks around the bustling city. No one ever stopped them and demanded identity papers... why should they?... this tall European was accompanied by a Russian colonel. There would be no suggestion that anything was other than it appeared to be... two Russian officials taking a leisurely stroll in the autumn sunshine.

Although she always called him Max, he seemed to exhibit little response to this name, and the thing that saddened her most, was that, because her apartment was tiny; from the first night, she had shared her bed with him. She had waited every night for him to show some inclination to make love to her. But, other than an occasional kiss and cuddle, his body seemed totally unaware of her soft, naked warmth however much she pressed against him and even caressed him.

This state of affairs continued for several weeks, until early November. One morning, Charlotte was walking with him past the Government residence quarter towards the centre of the city, when Max suddenly stopped. He stared across the busy thoroughfare to where a pre-war, maroon BMW four-door saloon was parked at the kerbside. His face creased into a troubled frown, and he glanced at Charlotte, and then looked back to the car.

She touched his arm.

'What is it, Max? What's the matter?'

His face held a puzzled expression... which slowly changed to recognition.

'That car... it reminds me of a place. A street in a big city... I think it was named Joachim Strasse... in... Berlin; and again, a place out of the city, in the woods... a place with a woman's name.'

Charlotte felt her throat tighten. She squeezed his arm.

'Yes, Max. That place was called Carinhall. It was the country estate of an important Nazi... Reichsmarschall Hermann Göring; the second-in-command in Hitler's Nazi Germany. We drove out there to look for any clue as to the whereabouts of an artefact that I have been searching for since before the war. That's not important for now. What is important is that you are beginning to remember things from your past.'

He nodded dumbly.

'Do you think so? All I really remember is my life in the village. All the rest is either blank, fuzzy, or flashbacks that don't connect to anything.'

She smiled.

'Don't worry, Max. The car reminded you of past events. We can work on that, and then other pieces might begin to connect.'

She linked her arm with his and continued their stroll along the wide boulevard. As they walked, he played back this memory which blazed in his head. Faces and names were slowly beginning to return without any conscious thought. This was very strange. He studied his companion. She was so familiar. There were times when old dreams had caught him unawares, sending pictures of once-loved girls and women swirling through his mind. Usually, the picture was faint, but this woman... this Charlotte was different. He was beginning to feel a vague, half-remembered state of a true obligation to her; it was as if they were joined by an invisible but inescapable bond of love and duty, one to the other. She was in her mid-to late forties... the same age as him. Her golden-blonde hair was so familiar, as were her forget-me-not blue eyes. If only he could remember more.

Thirteen-hundred miles to the west, on The Peak district, Hong Kong Island; Brotherhood foot-soldier-cum-chauffeur, Zang Yun-fat was sitting in the black Mercedes-Benz limousine waiting for his bosses to complete whatever business they were conducting inside the imposing Colonial pillared, white mansion belonging to his Triad boss, Heung Wah-yim. He was admiring the centerfold of Playboy magazine's Playmate of the Month for October. He grinned, and ran his tongue across his lips. She was ripe and ready... an eighteen-year-old, American brunette model named Kathy Douglas. Nice tight body, pretty little breasts, and puffy nipples.

His lascivious thoughts were interrupted by the appearance of his passengers. He quickly stepped out of the limousine and opened the rear door for the two men. Shen Ming-húa, the Enforcer; and Chang Lok, the Liaison officer of the Brotherhood of the Hong Kong Sun Yee On Triad settled themselves in the plush rear seat as Zang Yun-fat turned the key in the ignition, and died, together with his two bosses and three innocent servants. The stupendous explosion was heard over four miles away in Kowloon city itself, as it ripped through the car, hurling shards of metal and fragments of its unfortunate occupants in every direction, and partially demolishing the frontage of Heung Wah-yim's elegant white mansion.

Later evidence painstakingly collected by the Hong Kong Police forensic squad established that the bomb had probably been attached to the Mercedes-Benz for almost seventy-two hours, and had been detonated by an ingenious electronic timing device which had allowed the vehicle to be started and driven several times before the critical "ball-bearing in a tube" tilt switch was activated to detonate the ten pounds of C3 plastic explosive moulded into a neat package and concealed behind the Mercedes-Benz's dashboard.

Tell-tale residual traces established that the source of the explosive was probably Korea. This type of explosive had been found to have marginal plasticity at the very low temperatures encountered during Korean winters, and was significantly toxic, including by vapour and skin absorption. As a consequence, considerable quantities had been disposed of by the South Korean Military, and it was not beyond the realms of possibility that some had found its way into the hands of Korean criminal gangs.

Heung Wah-yim survived, although it was assumed that he had been the target of an assassination attempt. The Police were concerned that perhaps, this was the opening gambit of in inter-Triad war. The truth was; that the Kim Jonghyun, boss of the Seoul Yangeundongpa mob, had been tracking the Garnet gemstone for years, and had finally discovered that it was in Heung Wah-yim's possession. He reasoned that, since he had originally made a gift of the Garnet to the North Korean leader, Kim Il Sung; and therefore there had been an inferred obligation, which had not been honoured by reason that the South had not fallen during the war; it was his right to repossess the gemstone.

Unbeknown to the investigating police; Kim Jonghyun had ordered that the mansion be kept under surveillance since the time at which the bomb was planted. When it finally detonated, Heung Wah-yim... its intended target, had been out on the terrace at the rear of the property enjoying a cigarette after little Mei-Hua's oral virtuosity had drawn to a gratifying conclusion. He immediately fled the scene without concerning himself about what might have happened to her; in another of his fleet of cars.

At the top of the hill that led down to the mansion; two of Kim Jonghyun's trigger men were waiting. As the driver of Heung Wah-yim's silver Mercedes-Benz 220SB slowed to negotiate the sharp bend at the T-junction with Barker Road proper; the two trigger men stepped out from the cover of the heavily wooded roadsides and opened up with their Russian-made PPSh-41 submachine guns on full automatic fire.

With a dead driver at the wheel, the Mercedes-Benz ploughed straight on through the low guard railings and over the edge of the steep precipice. As it careened down towards Severn road, two hundred feet farther down the slope; smashing and tumbling through the trees, the two trigger men walked nonchalantly back to their little Simca saloon parked a few hundred yards back along Barker Road; climbed in, and drove down the winding roadways to finish the job.

The Mercedes-Benz had come to rest about ten feet up from the road, jammed between two large pine trees. One of the trigger men stepped out of the little Simca and clambered up the steep slope to the wrecked car. As he approached, he pulled out a silenced Beretta pistol, and ignoring the driver who was slumped across the steering wheel with half his head shot away; cautiously studied the bloodied body of Heung Wah-yim slumped across the back seat.

The other trigger man waiting in the Simca heard the silenced shots..."Phft!... Phft!" as his colleague fired into the back of the motionless Triad boss's head. He smiled grimly to himself as the other man scrambled back down the slope and climbed into the passenger seat; then the two men drove away down towards Peak Road and the main Highway One which led to the Causeway Bay waterfront where they would catch the Star ferry back to Kowloon.

Two days later; a Hong Kong and China Gas Company van arrived at the damaged mansion. Two men in company overalls left the van and approached the solitary policeman guarding the property. They explained that they had to check the building to establish that the gas supply was safe and undamaged. Was the building still occupied? The policeman assured them that it was empty. All remaining staff had been evacuated immediately after the explosion. The men nodded and suggested that the lone policeman position himself at a safe distance… just in case. They then proceeded to erect a tape cordon around the damaged frontage of the building.

With the policeman at a suitably safe distance, they entered the building; having instructed him to stay well back, whilst they checked the place out. Once inside, they systematically searched the building, and eventually found the Garnet gemstone that their boss, Kim Jonghyun had ordered them to find; hidden in a secret compartment in Heung Wah-yim's massive camphor-wood desk in the mansion's badly damaged drawing room. They also helped themselves to several hundred American Dollars stuffed into a manila envelope from the same secret compartment.

They then waited for a suitable period of time before emerging and removing the tape cordon. Informing the apprehensive policeman that all was safe, and the gas supply was disconnected; they climbed into their van and drove away, leaving the policeman relieved, and unaware of how close he had come to meeting his ancestors, had he decided to ask the wrong questions or check up on what they were doing inside the building.

Wednesday, 12th October 1960.
Soviet Embassy Compound. Somun Street,
P'yŏngyang. North Korea.

Charlotte walked purposefully down the long, echoing corridor that led to Second secretary Viktor Malinovskii's office in the sepulchral interior of the Soviet Embassy. Her uniform, denoting her rank of Colonel ensured that no questions would have been asked, and certainly, no challenges would have been made as she entered the heavily guarded compound. Quite the opposite, in fact; the guards literally fell over themselves to adhere to the correct Military etiquette.

Viktor Malinovskii rose from his desk as she entered his office; a bright, anticipatory smile on his face.

'Nadia; how good to see you. How may I be of assistance?'

She smiled.

'Viktor, I'm sorry to bother you, but I have to make a secure call to Moscow. Could you arrange for me to use the telephone room alone for ten minutes or so?'

He nodded.

'That should be no problem. I'll arrange for you to be taken down immediately.'

He picked up the telephone and instructed that the telephone operators were to leave the room when the Colonel arrived. This was Presidium business and she was not to be interrupted.

Charlotte smiled.

'Thank you, Viktor. I owe you a favour.'

His smile broadened at the thought of another night of passion with her. She smiled back, thinking; Sorry Viktor, you're going to be disappointed, this time.

She and Max would have disappeared before the opportunity presented itself.

The niceties were interrupted by a knock on the door. A guard entered to escort her down to the telephone room. She smiled again at Viktor and left the room. The telephone room was in the basement. As she entered, the guard shouted *"Uydi otsyuda!"*... 'Get out from here!' to the telephone operators, who scrambled for the door. He saluted, and closed the door of the soundproofed room with a hollow thud.

Charlotte walked across to the switchboard and scanned the connection sockets. One of them was the covert old landline from the Seoul telephone exchange that had been used during the war to connect between the Bureau and Kim Il Sung's intelligence headquarters in P'yŏngyang's former No. 2 KPA Officers School. It had been tapped by the Soviets when it was discovered by them during the post war reconstruction by Soviet engineers in the Government quarter of P'yŏngyang, and was hopefully, still serviceable. She carefully studied the rows of sockets to see which one appeared odd or different to the rest. There! That one was slightly tarnished, and didn't show any signs of shiny brass caused by friction wear from frequent insertion of the mating plug. She put on a switchboard operator's headset, and plugged into the socket. She took a deep breath... here goes nothing... and dialled. A thin, crackly voice answered.

'United States Chancery. How may I help you?'

Charlotte paused momentarily, unable to actually grasp that the line still functioned. Would they remember the old code word that the Bureau had used for extracting agents? Well here goes nothing... again.

She spoke the code word she had been issued with, almost three years previously... *"Bomzj"*... 'Homeless.'

She thought she heard a sharp intake of breath on the other end of the line. Then a barely audible voice... 'Mckenna?'

She glanced around the room. The door was still closed. She spoke swiftly into the mouthpiece.

'Affirmative. I repeat *"Bomzj"*... 'Homeless.'

There followed a long pause. Then the voice came back.

'Expedite Mike Four-eight. *"Bomzj."*

The line went dead. Swiftly, Charlotte unplugged the connection and walked to the door. She knocked twice, and the door opened. She nodded to the guard, who escorted her back to Viktor Malinovskii's office.

As she entered his office Viktor looked up from the pile of folders on his desk. He smiled.

'Everything satisfactory?'

She nodded.

'Yes, thank you Viktor. The communication was successfully completed.'

He smiled again.

'Good. Shall I see you again, this evening?'

She smiled, ruefully.

'I'm afraid I can't at the moment, Viktor. There's too much going on at the Academy.'

Seeing his crestfallen expression; she quickly added,

'I'll give you a call when things settle down and I can concentrate on us.'

His face brightened considerably.

'Oh, yes. That would be nice.'

She nodded.

'Well, it's a date then. I must go. Thank you Viktor. You have been most helpful to me today.'

Outside his office in the corridor as the guard was escorting her to the Embassy staircase; her mind was working coldly and calculatingly. According to the coded message, the Bureau was sending an airplane to Mirim airfield... sited along the opposite side of the Taedong River, and about eight kilometres east of the city, in forty-eight hours. It was where Charlotte had been inserted more than two and a half years previously.

The place had been run-down, back then. By now it was probably overgrown and deserted. The actual departure from P'yŏngyang would not be a problem as such. It was a straightforward drive up to the Taedong Bridge by way of Chŏnggŏ jangjŏn-t'ong to its junction with Soje-t'ong; then on across the bridge. The only possible problem would be the check-point at the Customs House on the western approach to the bridge.

Two days later, Private Maeng Ho-jung was standing guard on the western approach to the Taedong bridge when he heard the unmistakeably ominous howl of a Soviet Military GAZ jeep approaching from the direction of Downtown P'yŏngyang. Quickly, he stubbed out his cigarette and pulled himself up to attention as the vehicle appeared on Soje-t'ong and approached his position. He stepped out into the middle of the road and waved down the oncoming vehicle. As it pulled up beside him with an ugly squeal of brakes, he saw that the driver was a female Soviet Colonel. He tentatively held out his hand for her papers, and then chose not to, as she locked her cold, blue eyes upon him. She spoke quietly and in perfect Korean...

'I am transporting this prisoner from P'yŏnysang Prison...'

She jerked her thumb at the shackled European man slumped in the back seat...

'... To the Heijo steam power plant to complete his sentence to the benefit of the Motherland.'

Private Maeng Ho-jung nodded enthusiastically.

'Thank you, Comrade Colonel. You may proceed.'

He stepped back and ordered arms smartly with his Kalashnikov AKM Assault rifle as the Soviet Colonel crashed in the gears of the jeep and drove out across the Taedong Bridge.

Once beyond the bridge and into Saesallim Street, the main thoroughfare of East P'yŏngyang, connecting the centre with the eastern suburbs, it was almost impossible to find any buildings which predated the Korean War. Old P'yŏngyang had been literally wiped off the map by the American bombing campaign of 1950-1953, and rebuilding had been invariably carried out in the Stalinist Neo-classical style. Massive, heavy and pompous buildings reminiscent of the Soviet post-war style dominated the western part of the city; but out here, on the other side of the river, it was a very different story.

Along tree-lined streets were rows of basically similar, if somewhat more modest, apartment blocks which gave the impression of a modern city However, it was just an illusion. The modern buildings had been constructed along the streets to shield from view the slums located inside the blocks. These slums consisting of small huts filling the entire space within each block, and safely guarded from outsiders' eyes by the high-rise buildings surrounding them. In addition to the apartment complexes, there were also high concrete walls around each quarter, which also served to render the interior spaces invisible.

Farther out from the city centre, less effort had been taken to hide the slums. This eastern part of P'yŏngyang was particularly poor. Modern buildings formed a narrow line along several streets running parallel to the left bank of the Taedonggang, as well as along the

Saesallim and Taedongwon Prospects towards the eastern edge of the city. The rest of eastern P'yŏngyang was a sea of small brick-and-clay huts built very close to each other. Between the houses there were few streets; just paths... unpaved and often very dirty after rain.

Charlotte accelerated away down towards the eastern edge of the city. There wasn't much traffic in this poorer area of P'yŏngyang. She headed on down towards the Songsin flyover, and then turned left out through the Sadong District towards Mirim. A little way down the road, she pulled over and removed Max's shackles. If there was any presence at Mirim airfield, a Soviet Colonel accompanied by a plain-clothes companion would not raise much suspicion, whereas, a Soviet Colonel with a shackled prisoner most certainly would. She glanced at her wristwatch... two kilometres to go and twenty minutes to wait until the arranged extraction rendezvous time.

Turning the GAZ into the airfield; as she had suspected, Mirim was not deserted. It was rumoured that the area was used as a practice parade ground to rehearse the grand military parades which were frequently held in the city. There appeared to be a battalion-strength contingent of the Worker-Peasant Red Guard and a detachment of Korean People's Army Ground Force drawn up in parade order and equipped with the latest-model tanks, and armoured cars.

Charlotte drove the GAZ across the western end of the concrete runway and stopped on the western parking pad. She and Max got out of the Jeep and leaned against the hood, as though they were idly watching the parade rehearsal. The actual airstrip appeared to be disused. There was no sign of life in either the dilapidated control tower or the rusting maintenance hangars. She glanced again at her wristwatch. Those troops had better be ready to move off the runway before too long. She scanned the skies out to the east. Was that a tiny black dot far away out there? The extraction was scheduled within the next ten minutes.

Slowly, the dot grew in size, and a distant deep drone of engines became more distinct. Yes! It was the Seoul Bureau's covert Li-2; the Soviet, license-built version of the Douglas DC-3 in which she had originally been flown into North Korea. It was getting much lower and approaching rather more quickly than anyone out on the runway might have anticipated. The troops out on the runway broke ranks and doubled back to the relative safety of the centre taxiway as the Li-2 made a low pass down the centre-line of the runway, with the Red Stars on her fuselage and wings shining balefully in the bright afternoon sunlight, then banked around to join what, had the airstrip been active, would have been the landing circuit. As they watched her progress; a solitary figure left the ranks of parade troops and began marching officiously across the airfield in their direction. The silver Li-2 turned in on finals; the wheels came down, and she began to sink towards the eastern end of the runway with her wing landing lights blazing; so that there could be no mistaking the pilot's intention to land. The figure quickened its pace.

The Li-2 touched down with a squeal and puffs of blue tire smoke, and rumbled down the concrete with flaps fully extended and propellers windmilling. The pilot began braking, and a teeth-gritting shriek of brakes echoed across the grass. At the end of the runway, the pilot turned onto the western taxiway and brought the big airplane to a standstill. The fuselage door banged open and a set of metal steps were shoved out.

The KPA Major, who had been pompously approaching Charlotte and Max, stopped dead. Six tough-looking troopers piled out of the airplane fuselage door and doubled across the singed brown grass to form two flanking ranks either side of the path between the Russian Colonel and her companion, and the airplane. Even from this distance, he saw that the troopers were wearing the distinctive light-blue-and-white-striped "*Spetsnaz*" "*telnyashka*" undershirts beneath their camo uniforms and were carrying Kalashnikov AKMS assault rifles... the folding-stock variants. Even more alarming was the fact that the weapons appeared to be fitted with the ominous Russian PBS1 silencers. He suppressed a shiver. They could only be Russian Special Forces!

They were going to be either VDV... the Soviet Airborne Troops or, more ominously, GRU... the Soviet Main Intelligence Directorate troops... neither of whom was in the business of being fucked about with by a lowly KPA Major. Deciding that prudence was most definitely the better part of valour concerning these dangerous bastards; he stopped dead, turned on his heel, and hurried back to his parade.

As Charlotte and Max moved away from the jeep towards the airplane, the *Spetsnaz* troopers ordered arms and snapped to attention. They then formed up around Charlotte and Max in what was effectively a protection squad; and the group moved to the airplane. Charlotte climbed the ladder into the fuselage, followed by Max, to be met by a man in the uniform of a VDV Captain. He grinned; and said, in a broad, New England accent...

'Hi! I'm Scott Ferrell; Osan Station co-ordinator... Welcome home, Captain Mckenna. Now let's get the hell out of here.'

Turning; he yelled back along the fuselage to the pilot, who raised a thumb and began to run up the idling engines as one of the troopers hauled up the ladder and banged the fuselage door shut. The pilot released the brakes with a slight jolt; the airplane began turning and taxied out to the runway. At the threshold, the pilot held on the brakes while the pressures and temperatures built up on his instruments, then eased the throttles forward, turned into the wind and released the brakes.

The engine noise rose to a crescendo, and the airplane began to move. Charlotte watched the scorched grass at the edge of the runway begin to flatten as it sped past below the wing; the tail lifted, and the shadow of the wing began falling away as the airplane rose into the sky. The troopers were relaxing and talking quietly. She recognised several distinct accents... a Texas drawl here... a Midwestern accent there... a couple of Southern boys... Scott Ferrell grinned.

'Good guys. Our paramilitary operatives. They all volunteered to come and bring you and the Colonel out.'

Max was studying the troopers with suspicion. Their uniforms were familiar. Somewhere far away… somewhere long ago. He recognised the style; but where?... And when? A place name seemed to have some significance with those uniforms. What was it? And where was it? Charlotte noticed his puzzled frown. She squeezed his hand.

'What is it, *Milaya Moya?*'

She deliberately used the Russian endearment they had always used for each other.

He shook his head.

'I don't know. I can't remember. Those uniforms; I know them from somewhere.'

She studied him. Fragments of his lost memory were beginning to surface. She smiled.

'Perhaps it was in Berlin, when you were at Karlshorst.'

Scott Ferrell's ears pricked up. The term "Karlshorst" had long since become synonymous with the KGB *Rezidentura* on Zwieseler Strasse in Berlin; the Soviet intelligence's largest Cold War foreign post. So the intelligence he had been given on Max Segal; formerly Lieutenant-Colonel Maksim Siegel of the Berlin-Karlshorst Headquarters, Soviet Military Administration was accurate. Segal had been given full clearance from Washington. He had been granted permanent residence under the "PL-110" clause of the CIA Act, and was a fully accredited deep cover operative carrying Diplomatic Status. How the hell he had managed to remain undiscovered inside the very heart of the Military in this Commie shithole for ten years was astonishing. He studied Max with a newly-found deference. This guy; even in his slightly debilitated state; was a goddamned Hero... as was this still-attractive blonde Captain.

Up in the cockpit, Captain Ricardo Flores hit the landing gear lever and began to milk up the flaps as the Li-2 clambered away into the eastern skies, painfully aware of the thousands of Commie eyes watching from the ground. He nodded to his copilot, Brody Callahan.

'OK set a course on Zero-Four-Five, point Eight. Let's sucker the little bastards into thinking we're heading home to Vladivostok.'

Callahan nodded and set the radio compass.'

'That's a Rog, Boss. Let's hope they don't decide to send up any bogies to eyeball us.'

Flores grinned and eased back on the throttle levers.

'Just keep 'em crossed for the next five hundred klicks to our turning point out over the Ocean!'

Friday, 14th October 1960.
Osan Air Force Base, Songtan District.
Forty miles south of Seoul, South Korea.

As the Li-2 transport airplane began to descend; gazing out of the cabin window, Charlotte could plainly see the workers in the paddy fields below, pause and peer up from under the floppy brims of their wide straw hats as the big airplane thundered overhead. Almost all the scattered villages on the flight path were the same... closely packed dwellings with earthen walls and thatched roofs; the dwellings bisected by narrow lanes leading out to the surrounding paddy fields and vegetable patches... a simple, if austere, utopian existence.

Her thoughts were interrupted by the familiar hiss and whine of the landing flaps and undercarriage actuators operating as the pilot committed the Li-2 to her final approach. The racing shadow on the paddy fields grew darker and larger as the airplane descended, until with a bump and squeal of tortured rubber, the main wheels made contact with the concrete of Osan runway. Curiously, as the Li-2 rolled down the runway, there were few aircraft to be seen, other than a couple of C-47s parked up by the scattering of buildings on the northern edge of the airfield. Other than what looked like a major reconstruction of the runway; the base still retained most of its Korean War-vintage facilities and infrastructure... just as Charlotte remembered.

The Li-2 turned and came back along the runway, turning off onto the eastern taxiway, and stopped on the edge of the concrete in front of the buildings. The young airman-steward opened the passenger door and invited Charlotte and Max to leave their seats. A rudimentary set of loading stairs had been brought up, down which he helped Charlotte and Max.

They were met by a tall, crew-cut civilian wearing casual tropical clothing, who had appeared from an anonymous looking black Mercury sedan parked at the edge of the parking apron. He introduced himself as Jerrod Carbone, Assistant Case Officer of the Seoul Bureau. He settled Charlotte and Max in the rear seat of the Mercury; had the young airman load their luggage, then, without another word, drove quickly away out to Highway One that led from the Air Base up to Seoul, and accelerated the Mercury sedan up to sixty.

Charlotte glanced at Max. This crew-cut American, Jerrod Carbone, gave the impression of being something considerably more ominous than an "Assistant Case Officer." Max gave her a puzzled glance and squeezed her hand. With luck, they wouldn't have to spend too much time in his company. He smelled of Secret Service... or something even scarier.

Turning off highway One; Carbone drove into the Yongdungp'o district of the city. The streets were fairly quiet... this area was one of the better known red-light districts of Seoul and didn't really come alive until after dark. Cordone slowed the black Mercury at the intersection at the end of the main street of the Itaewono, and turned left on to the approach road which led down to the six Iron-truss arched, Han River Bridge.

Once across the bridge, it was a lengthy drive north, past Seoul station with its Byzantine-style central dome and adjacent goods yards, and on along Taipyung Road, then turning right, opposite the Museum, into Euljiro Street in the Kyongsong District. Cordone stopped outside the wide street canopy of the eight-storey Hotel Bando, which vaguely resembled the architectural style of The Peninsula Hotel in Hong Kong... although its "U" shaped frontage was much shallower, and there was no forecourt to speak of. It did have a quasi-Colonial-Era style, but was much starker than its Hong Kong counterpart.

Leaving the car engine idling, he guided Charlotte and Max to the hotel entrance where another crew-cut man wearing sunglasses met them. Cordone then returned to the car; cut out into the traffic, and drove away towards the centre of the city.

The marble reception area of the Hotel Bando was deserted except for the Marine Corps Staff Sergeant at the reception desk. The young, crew-cut American escorted Charlotte and Max across the checkerboard marble floor to the desk and introduced them. The Marine Corps Sergeant logged their arrival, saluted, and directed them to the three elevators at the far end of the reception hall. The crew-cut young man pressed the call button of the central elevator. Entering, Charlotte noticed it was still the one-floor-only button and an emergency button in the flush control panel. Nothing much had changed here!

The elevator hummed to a stop. The doors slid open to reveal a brightly lit corridor occupied by two Marine Corps corporals sitting opposite the elevator entrance. They were both armed. As the party stepped out into the long, quiet, neutral-smelling corridor, they both stood and presented arms. Their escort nodded, and led Charlotte and Max along the corridor to the familiar anonymous-looking solid teak door. The young man knocked, and opened the door; stepped back, and invited them to enter. They entered a spacious office which appeared to be exactly the same as the last time Charlotte had stood here. The room was dominated by a large desk, behind which, sat an unfamiliar man in an expensive linen suit. Behind him, the corner was still occupied by an artistically draped Stars and Stripes flag.

The man studied them for a few moments, and then gave them a thin smile.

'Pleased to see you again, Mckenna. This must be Segal.'

She nodded.

'Yes, I found him in a rural village. He sustained a head injury at some point in his mission and has lost most of his previous memory. I have been trying to get him to remember people and places; incidents and experiences. We have made some progress, but it will take more skill than I possess to completely unlock his memories.'

The man nodded.

'So I understand. You'll be with us for a few days while we arrange for you to be extracted for de-briefing. We still use the hotel for our staff quarters; it's a damn sight more secure than out there in Seoul. I'll have Hilburn show you your quarters.'

He pressed a bell-push under the edge of the desk which summoned the young, crew-cut man who had brought them up from the lobby. Hilburn led them through the main lateral corridor to the right wing of the building, and along the corridor to the end door on the left. Opening the door, he said that their few possessions had already been brought up, and they should settle themselves in. He smiled, and handed Charlotte the key.

The room had originally been one of the hotel's suites. It was divided into two separate main areas; the main living accommodation which contained four comfortable-looking armchairs placed around a small occasional table; lamp standards, potted plants and all the other accoutrements one would expect in a top hotel suite. The sleeping area was divided from the main room by sliding full-width doors, and contained a substantial Colonial-style double bed, bedside cabinets, wardrobes and a dressing table. Another door led to a small, but well-appointed bathroom and toilet.

Charlotte smiled at Max.

'Well, we might as well make ourselves comfortable.'

Max sat on the edge of the bed and looked at her blankly.

'De-briefing us? How can they de-brief me when I can't remember anything?... And where will they take us?'

She came and sat beside him. Taking his hand in hers; she looked at him.

'I don't know where we will go, Max... but wherever it is, I'm sure there will be people there who will help you to remember.'

He gave a sad, apprehensive smile.

'Oh, I do hope so. I really want to remember what it was like sharing my life with you. All the rest really doesn't matter.'

Wednesday, 12th October 1960.
Hong Kong Island.

Sheren Chung walked nervously along the Gloucester Road heading for the Chater Road pier where she would take the Star ferry across the harbour to Kowloon. She had good reason to be nervous; she carried in her purse an item which she was to deliver to one of the most dangerous factions in the entire Colony.

Twenty-two year-old Sheren Chung; daughter of an English Ex-pat mother, and a Chinese *Tai-pan*... businessman; was a courier for the Seoul Yangeundongpa mob boss, Kim Jonghyun. The previous evening, she had been summoned by telephone to an innocuous-looking house in the Wan Chi District of Hong Kong Island, and given a package which she was instructed to deliver to an address on the corner of Forfar Road and Argyll Street in the Ho Man Tin area of Kowloon.

She had become involved, much to her regret, in this shadowy world as a result of the malign influence of an ex-boyfriend. In this world, once you were in... you were in; and there was no easy way of getting out. There were benefits... protection; the money financed a comfortable life-style; but, any deviation from the rigid protocols; and the penalty that the miscreant invariably paid was becoming part of the foundations for the new Kai Tak airport passenger terminal, or, failing that; part of the foundations for any one of the multitude of new buildings being erected in downtown Kowloon.

The package that she was carrying contained the large Garnet gemstone that the two fake gas company men had recovered from the wreckage of the Colonial-style mansion out on The Peak district of Hong Kong Island that had belonged to the recently assassinated Heung Wah-yim; Master of the Sun Yee On Triad of Hong Kong. She had been chosen for this assignment because the Hong Kong Police Force were pulling in anyone who had the slightest known connection to the Yangeundongpa mob's offshoot based in the Colony. They were zealously enforcing a Stop and Search policy on the flimsy premise of slightest suspicion. The official reason for this was that the assassination of the Triad Boss, Heung Wah-yim, out on the side of Severn road up on The Peak could be the precursor of an all-out Triad War... the manner of Heung Wah-yim's execution... two bullets in the back of the Triad boss's head was a typical signature killing. Another scurrilous rumour suggested that the Triad boss had powerful friends in the Colony's Executive Council, who were, themselves, clandestine Triad members.

Whatever the truth of it; the Yangeundongpa mob boss, Kim Jonghyun had commanded that the artefact that Sheren Chung now carried be returned to him in Seoul at the earliest opportunity.

Number 157, Argyle Street, on the corner of Forfar Road and Argyll Street was a shabby, three-storey, Art-Deco-style house that had certainly seen better days. Apprehensively, she opened the eight-feet-high; double gates decorated in the fashion of an open fan, and walked up the asphalt drive to the front door, which was set back from the front wall in a large alcoved area beneath an open, second-floor balcony supported by a single tapering concrete pillar. Ringing the doorbell, she stepped back and waited.

After a few moments the door opened, and a young man appeared. He scrutinised her suspiciously; saying nothing. His features suggested that he was Korean... flat face; higher and squarer cheek bones. She smiled timidly and uttered the secret word that they had given her; holding out the parcel to him. He accepted it with a slight bow and spoke a single word: *"Kamsahamnida"* ... 'Thank You'... in Korean.

He then stepped back and closed the door on her. Sheren Chung breathed a sigh of relief. So, was that was all there was to it? They had warned her that the foot soldiers of the Yangeundongpa mob were unpredictable and dangerous. Under no circumstances was she to accept an invitation to enter the house. If she did; it was more than likely that she would be drugged and eventually find herself incarcerated in some squalid brothel in Seoul's red light district. Many affluent Koreans had a taste for Eurasian girls; and the best she could ever hope for in such a circumstance would be being taken as a sex-slave concubine by some paunchy Korean businessman. Rebuttal would result in severe and methodical beatings; perhaps, even death. Her Triad handler had pulled no punches in his warning. He despised all Korean mobsters as being uncultured barbarians.

Nervously, Sheren Chung walked to the gate and stepped out into Forfar Road. She walked along the pavement to the corner, and checking for traffic, began to cross Argyll Street; hastening her pace as one of the Kowloon Motor Bus Company's red and cream Daimler double-deck buses came rumbling up Argyll Street from the direction of the city centre. Passers-by saw her stumble and fall directly in front of the oncoming bus, whose driver slammed on the brakes, but could not avoid running over her. They did not, however hear the single, sharp "Phft!" which was no louder than a bubble of air escaping from a tube of toothpaste; or witness the barrel of the silenced sniper's rifle being stealthily withdrawn from the parapet of the flat roof of Number 157, Argyle Street.

When they reversed the bus from the girl there was no possible way that they could establish that she had indeed been shot. The front wheel had crushed her head; and that was where the marksman had aimed, and where his single round had struck. The Police wrote it off as another sad, but unfortunate traffic accident; and one more loose end to the Yangeundongpa mob boss, Kim Jonghyun's carefully planned strategy to regain the gemstone had been neatly tied up.

Chapter Five.

The journey from Forfar Road and along Prince Edward Road to the bridge crossing the infamous Kai Tak nullah, which was still little more than an open sewer, in spite of major reconstruction; and then, into the airport took no more than ten minutes by car. Outside the terminal building, the two Yangeundongpa mob thugs dropped off the next courier... twenty-eight year-old Choi Yong-Jin, and waited patiently until he had boarded the Korean National Airlines Lockheed Constellation, and, with a burst of oil and methanol smoke, she had fired up her engines in sequence.

The big airliner slowly taxied out to the long runway that thrust out into the placid blue waters of Kowloon bay, stopped, and trembled against its brakes as the Captain revved the four engines up to take-off speed and tested the wing flaps. Then the big airliner turned slowly towards the wide expanse of Kowloon Bay; the Captain released the brakes, and gathering speed, the Constellation accelerated down the one and a half miles of blinding white, stressed concrete and rose into the east, aiming ultimately for another little strip of concrete ribbon thirteen hundred miles away.

The driver started the car's engine and drove smoothly out of the airport towards Kowloon Walled City. One job successfully completed and now for the day's entertainment... a little visit into the City of Darkness to bust a cap... as the Yankee gangsters said... into the nuts of a 14K Brotherhood *Tong kumong*... asshole, who had been sniffing around the mob's girls. Then, when the job was done; perhaps a celebration by forcefully fucking a couple of the 14K-controlled whores after the killing... just to put the emphasis on who were the meanest sons of bitches in the Colony.

Choi Yong-Jin settled in his seat in the Constellation as she droned out over Joss House Bay, skirted the northern tip of Tung Lung Island, and gently banked around to the east for the thirteen-hundred miles flight to Seoul. In his briefcase he carried the artefact supposedly destined for the Seoul Yangeundongpa mob boss, Kim Jonghyun. This would not be the case… this trip. Choi Yong-Jin was the illegitimate son of a U.S. Army Nurse Corps Major and a Japanese navy surgeon. He was also a field agent for the Seoul Bureau, and had been working under deep cover in the very heart of the Yangeundongpa mob for the past two years.

He knew exactly what he was carrying, and was aware that one of his Bureau staff officers… a certain Captain Mckenna, had been searching for an artefact… which might well be this one; since her days with the Berlin Bureau. Why?... He had no idea; but it was common knowledge in the Bureau that this had been some sort of personal quest which was fully condoned by whomever she knew back in Washington.

He also knew the risk he was taking by double-crossing the Seoul mob. He would automatically become a marked man and would have to be posted elsewhere… probably with a new identity. Even then; it was quite possible that he would be tracked down and killed. The sinister reach of Kim Jonghyun spanned Continents. He shrugged. Mom had always said that he had to be true to himself and to his Country. He would just have to be extra-vigilant from the moment he set foot on Korean soil.

The flight was uneventful. There was nothing to see from the cabin windows; nothing but seemingly endless miles of Ocean interspersed with occasional glimpses of the Chinese Mainland out on the distant horizon. The closest that the airliner came to land was when the flight path left the South China Sea and followed the Taiwan Strait. Here, the Chinese mainland was only sixty miles to the left, and the Island of Taiwan was a mere thirty miles to the right. This vaguely interesting distraction only lasted for an hour or so, however; then it was on out over the East China Sea for another hour of endless Ocean to the final course-change point some two hundred miles east of Shanghai, where the airliner would gently turn for the final ninety-or-so miles last leg into Kimpo International Airport outside Seoul. From up here at four and a quarter miles high, the Ocean appeared to be a shimmering blue carpet that touched and merged with the cloudless azure sky. Choi Yong-Jin settled more comfortably into his seat and began to doze.

He was awakened by the mild sensation of falling. His ears began to block with the long descent over the tapestry of wooded mountains and paddy fields towards the racing shadow of the airliner that grew darker and larger as she descended on her final approach. The patrolling stewardess prompted him to fasten his seat belt, and as he did so, there was a faint, abrupt hiss, and a sickly smell as the pilot fired the insecticide bomb; followed by the shrill hydraulic whine of the air-brakes and the landing-wheels being lowered.

The nose of the airliner dipped, and the tearing bump of the tyres touching the concrete runway shuddered through the cabin; followed by the ugly roar of the propellers being reversed to slow the plane as it rushed down the rubber-streaked concrete ribbon. With squealing brakes, the Constellation turned off the main runway and rumbled around the taxiway to the east apron in front of the terminal building.

Having passed through Immigration and Customs without any hold-ups; Choi Yong-Jin hailed a taxicab to take him into Seoul. As the cab pulled away from the terminal building and headed out towards the road that led down to little town of Yongdungp'o; he didn't notice the small black Renault Dauphine sedan that pulled out from behind the row of parked-up cabs in the cab rank and began to unobtrusively follow his cab at a discreet distance.

The battered Ford Consul taxicab turned right off the Taipyung Road opposite the Museum into Euljiro Street, and stopped outside the wide, street canopy of the eight-storey Hotel Bando. The small black Renault Dauphine sedan stopped on the opposite side of the avenue, a little way back from the American Embassy housed in the old Mitsui Building which stood almost opposite the hotel. Choi Yong-Jin alighted from the cab, paid the driver, and walked across the pavement to the hotel entrance. The two men in the unobtrusive black car watched, with cold, vigilant eyes as he entered the hotel; and then settled down for a waiting game to see what he did next.

Choi Yong-Jin walked purposefully across the marble reception area of the Hotel Bando to the reception desk. Producing his pass he identified himself to the Marine Corps Master Sergeant at the reception desk. The master sergeant logged his arrival, and directed him to the three elevators at the far end of the reception hall. Choi Yong-Jin pressed the call button of the central elevator. Entering, he pressed to solitary floor button in the flush control panel. There were no other controls apart from an emergency button. This elevator only served the bureau floor. All the other floor accesses were sealed off.

The elevator hummed to a stop. The doors slid open to reveal a brightly lit corridor occupied by two Marine Corps corporals sitting opposite the elevator entrance. They were both armed. As Choi Yong-Jin stepped out into the long, quiet, neutral-smelling corridor, they both stood and presented arms. Choi Yong-Jin nodded, and walked along the corridor to an anonymous-looking door. He knocked, and opened the door; entering a spacious office. The room was dominated by a large desk, behind which, sat a middle-aged man wearing a elegantly tailored white cotton shirt, and a U.S. Marine Corps navy-blue silk tie embellished with the with Eagle, Globe and Anchor insignia in gold. This was Gus Hartigan... allegedly, a senior case officer... but in reality, Deputy Head of Station. Behind him, in the corner was placed the omnipresent, artistically draped Stars and Stripes flag.

Hartigan smiled thinly.

'Good afternoon, Choi Yong-Jin. To what do we owe this pleasure?'

Choi Yong-Jin placed his briefcase on the carpet, opened it, and withdrew the little velvet pouch.

'This is just a flying visit, Hartigan. I'm supposed to be on a courier run for Kim Jonghyun, the Yangeundongpa gang mob boss. This is the package. It will be of great interest to Captain Mckenna.'

Hartigan nodded.

'She's not here; and won't be for another forty-eight hours. She's still in P'yŏngyang .We're running an extraction mission for her as we speak.'

Choi Yong-Jin bit his lip.

'I can't wait that long for her. That'll blow my cover. Can I leave the package with you until she arrives?'

Hartigan nodded again.

'OK I'll have them put it in the secure room. Now that you've double-crossed the Yangeundongpa gang mob boss, we'll have to relocate you. You are now a potential security risk in this Bureau. There's no telling what you might reveal if the mob catches you. Go to the safe house on Choong Moo Ro and we'll contact you when we've placed a new legend for you. Good luck and Goodbye, Choi Yong-Jin.'

Choi Yong-Jin was feeling slightly more relaxed as he walked down the web of neutral corridors of the Hotel Bando. The Bureau was going to repost him somewhere well away from the clutches of the Yangeundongpa gang.

He was smiling as he came out of the hotel and turned right to walk the half-mile or so, to the safe house. He didn't notice that, as he began to walk away along Euljiro, the little black Renault Dauphine pulled out from the kerb, and began to slowly follow him; keeping pace, some fifteen metres behind him. They followed him into Sup'yodar-gil; the first main intersection on the right, and unobtrusively closed the distance.

The little Renault paused momentarily, and one of the men got out, and began to shadow Choi Yong-Jin. Outside the Catholic Cathedral, he struck. A pillowcase was wrenched down over the head, and the hypodermic needle stabbed into the neck of his target. Bundling the semi-conscious Choi Yong-Jin into the back of the car, he jumped back into the passenger seat, and the little black Renault Dauphine sedan sped away to be lost in the throng of traffic around Namdaemun market. The whole abduction had taken less than two minutes.

Choi Yong-Jin came to in a large, echoing, dark place. He was strapped stark-naked to some kind of metal bench or table. A disembodied voice, out of view, cut across his fearfully apprehensive thoughts.

'You are helpless, and totally in my power. You have a choice. You either tell me now, where you have secreted the package you were entrusted to deliver to me; and you will die swiftly and painlessly; or, the information will be extracted from you... in which case, you will die extremely slowly and in excruciating pain.'

A figure appeared just within his peripheral vision. A tall, middle-aged man wearing an elegantly-tailored suit moved into Choi Yong-Jin's line of sight, and gazed impassively down at him. The man gave the merest hint of a smile and spoke.

'I am Kim Jonghyun. I do urge you to tell me what I want to know whilst you still have the strength and opportunity so to do.'

Choi Yong-Jin remained silent.

Kim Jonghyun's face assumed an almost sad expression. His voice had an almost resigned tone to it.

'Very well. Prepare yourself for a journey into the Abyss of unimaginable agony.'

He snapped his fingers at someone out of Choi Yong-Jin's line of sight, and stepped back; lighting a cigarette as he did so. Another figure appeared beside Choi Yong-Jin. He strained his head around and looked straight into the cold, black eyes of one of the most beautiful Asian women he had ever seen. She was tall and slender. Her bell of blue-black hair framed her flawless, porcelain complexion; and the curve of her perfect lips held a tiny hint of a smile... just enough to slightly turn up the corners of her exquisitely kissable mouth. His skin tensed and fluttered as she laid the long, scarlet fingernails of her left hand on his chest, and then slowly and delicately dragged them down his body... across his stomach...

He felt her slip something cold and smooth into his urethra and shivered with the disturbingly pleasurable sensation of her gently easing it up the length of his rapidly stiffening member; followed by a slight movement deep inside, as she did something to the instrument... or whatever it was that she was holding. Then she pulled it very slightly, but somewhat sharply.

A terrible, shrieking, burning pain tore through his genitals, building to an excruciating crescendo of stabbing agony deep into his belly as she jerked the device out a few millimetres. Kim Jonghyun's face swam into view. He smiled benignly.

'That was the effect of Miss Soo-Yun moving the device a mere five millimetres. There are one hundred and forty millimetres still embedded in your joy stick. She is a virtuoso with these toys. She can make this infliction of intense pain last for at least two hours before she moves on to more sophisticated devices. It really would be in your best interest to tell me what I want to know now; or the last few hours of your miserable and dishonourable existence will be spent in indescribable, shrieking agony.'

He waited patiently. The only sound was the stilted, gasping breath of Choi Yong-Ji.

Kim Jonghyun's expression was inscrutable. He shrugged and shook his head sadly.

'Your decision. So now, I'm afraid Miss Soo-Yun is going to get very medieval in her choice of tongue-loosening initiatives.'

He turned and walked quietly away; his footsteps receding in the gloom of the deserted slaughterhouse. As he reached the door, the first of many terrible, squealing shrieks ripped through the shadowy gloom of the sprawling, abandoned building.

Choi Yong-Jin's tenuous reality had existed as a world of screaming, shrieking agony at the slender hands of the beautiful Soo-Yun Kaneko for three hours before he finally cracked, and whimpered to her the information that Kim Jonghyun required.

The corners of her perfectly formed lips turned upwards in a tiny, gentle smile as she brushed his sweat-soaked hair out of his eyes with her immaculately manicured fingers. She murmured huskily...

'Good boy. Now you can sleep.'

She gently flicked the slender metal object that was still inserted some twenty millimetres into his urethra with the tip of one of her long, slender fingers. He flinched; his stomach muscles spasmed and he gave a small whimper. Smiling serenely, she delicately grasped the end of the instrument... then suddenly yanked it fully out. He didn't even have a chance to form the scream in his throat. His eyes bulged, and then he went limp. The shrieking, burning agony of her last action caused him to instantly lose consciousness.

Laying aside the little instrument... which now revealed that, as she had initially twisted its end when it had been fully inserted; tiny barbs had been extended along its circumference and length; and, as she had manipulated the device, these had torn and shredded the internal walls of his urethra. She glanced down. The only sign on his entire body of the previous three hours of unendurably excruciating pain was a tiny, bright dribble of blood welling up through the urethral orifice of his internally lacerated penis. She smiled softly. He had been a tough one. She had used more than her normal selection of agony-inducing devices on this one. It had been difficult not to leave any tell-tale marks. She could easily have employed her father's methods that she had learned from the dog-eared Kempeitai interrogator's handbook that had belonged to him.

These methods included burning and electric shocks with 'Live' electric wires, candles, lighted cigarettes, boiling oil or water which were applied to sensitive parts of the victim's body; Sticks placed between the victim's fingers and squeezed, fracturing the bones; the tearing out of fingernails and toenails; with slivers of bamboo or toothpicks inserted under the nails before they were torn out by pliers.

All of these; no matter how carefully applied, would have left traces. Kim Jonghyun mob boss of the Yangeundongpa gang had specified that she could employ any means at her disposal to loosen the tongue of this Imperialist lackey, Choi Yong-Jin. He deserved nothing less than an agonising departure from his miserable existence... but, she must not leave any marks on the body. He was to be found face-down in the Han River with all the indications that it had been an accidental death... or suicide. Kim Jonghyun didn't want the American Secret Service community in Seoul sniffing around his business concerns. Consequently, she had employed invasive techniques on all his bodily orifices. He had resisted the urethral torture for quite some time, and also the sharp ends of pencils being inserted into his ears until they slowly pierced his eardrums. He had finally cracked when she applied the flame of her cigarette lighter to the end of the slender metal instrument embedded in his penis.

Soo-Yun Kaneko gazed down at the almost peaceful expression on Choi Yong-Jin's face. She smiled and spoke softly to the unconscious figure.

'Time to take the final trip, darling. *"Annyonghi kasayo"*... Goodbye.'

She raised her slender right hand; straightened and locked her fingers, and brought its rigid edge sharply down in a swooping chop into his throat just above his prominent "Adam's apple." She heard a distinct crunch as the blow broke the hyoid bone at the top of his larynx. She then leaned over and positioned her forearm across his throat; resting her full upper-body weight on that arm. His face slowly contused; his breathing became laboured and stilted, and imperceptibly lessened; becoming shallower and shallower until it had stopped completely.

She stepped back. Damn! She'd chipped the scarlet polish on one of her fingernails. She shrugged. Well; Kim Jonghyun could just treat her to another expensive manicure. She left the corpse where it was; tidied away her devices; turned, and walked quickly towards the exit door; her high heels' tap-tapping echoing hollowly through the deserted slaughterhouse.

Soo-Yun Kaneko had attained a notorious reputation in the Seoul criminal underworld as a contract assassin-cum-enforcer. Only eighteen years old; she was already feared throughout the city. If Soo-Yun Kaneko came after you; you were as good as dead... and invariably, you begged her to put you out of your misery, so that her elegantly depraved and fastidious torture techniques would cease.

Soo-Yun Kaneko was a beautiful, psychopathic killer; a sadomasochist's wet dream. Even by the standards of the east with regard to the cheapness of life; she really was something else. Her Korean mother had been kidnapped, aged sixteen, by Japanese soldiers in Seoul to serve as a "Comfort woman" in the military brothels. Her father was a *"Jotohei"*... a Superior Private in the Kempeitai... the feared Japanese Military Secret Police, attending the Koho Kimmu Yoin Yoseijo... the Rear Service Personal Training Centre at Kudan, in Tokyo.

Unusually, he had committed to a permanent relationship with her mother... which was virtually unheard of with regard to the usual fate of a mere "Comfort woman" of the Japanese troops. Their normal fate was to be forced into so-called comfort houses to sexually please their captors, sometimes several at a time, up to several times a day. To resist, invited beatings, torture and even death. Three quarters of all comfort women died, and most survivors were left infertile due to sexual trauma or sexually transmitted disease. The girls were raped and beaten day and night, with those who became pregnant being forced to have abortions. Soo-Yun Kaneko and her mother were amongst the fortunate ones. They survived, under the protection of the Kempeitai in Tokyo.

Her father had been tried by the Americans during the Tokyo War Crimes Trials and had been executed in 1946; when Soo-Yun Kaneko was just four years old. Her mother had returned to Seoul with her daughter and had attempted to rebuild her life there.

Soo-Yun Kaneko grew up with a healthy loathing of all things Caucasian, and all Americans in particular, because of her father's fate. One day, she found his Kempeitai interrogator's handbook. It made fascinating reading to the disturbed child.

Later, she became involved with the Seoul gangs and was taken under the wing of Kim Jonghyun and the Yangeundongpa gang. She learned her trade in the backstreets of Seoul, and developed a particularly inventive imagination for devising techniques with which to inflict unbearable pain upon her victims.

Kim Jonghyun recognised her potential, and installed her in her own apartment in a classy district of Seoul. Here, he could pay her frequent visits, and eventually, she became one of his many mistresses. Her position in the mob hierarchy was now assured. She rarely accepted contracts for less than a thousand American Dollars. Sometimes, depending on the level of her virtuosity for loosening tongues that would be required, and the status of the subject of the contract; her fee would be considerably more. Consequently, she had become an extremely affluent young lady by the age of. Eighteen.

Stepping through the rusty door into the darkened street lined with grimy warehouses; she nodded to the two men in the shabby, parked-up Peugeot estate car and walked quickly to the sleek, pearl-grey, Jaguar XK150 drop-head coupé parked a little farther down the street. Slipping into the driving seat, she started the engine and drove away; the deep boom of the Jaguar's exhaust echoing back from the shadowy brick canyon as she headed back towards Seoul to make her report to Kim Jonghyun. As her exhaust note diminished, the two men disappeared into the building, and reappeared a little later, carrying the corpse of Choi Yong-Jin wrapped in a soiled dust sheet. They dumped it unceremoniously into the back of the Peugeot, climbed in, and drove away; heading north towards the Gwangjin Bridge where they would heave the body over the bridge parapet into the river.

In Kim Jonghyun's luxurious apartment, Soo-Yun Kaneko relaxed in one of the deep leather club chairs and sipped her crystal flute of imported champagne. She crossed her long shapely legs, allowing her skirt to ride a little higher for the benefit of Kim Jonghyun who was sitting opposite her. He smiled benignly.

'So, the little swine talked?'

She nodded.

'Yes; *Kim-sshi* The artefact is at present in the Americans' possession at the Bando Hotel; but it has been left there for a woman Captain who is supposed to be arriving in a few days.'

He raised an eyebrow.

'Why should she seek possession?'

She shrugged.

'I have absolutely no idea, *Kim-sshi*... but her name is Charlotte Mckenna. She's blonde, in her late forties... and she works for the CIA.'

Monday, 17th October 1960.
Euljiro Street. Seoul.
South Korea.

Kim Jin Ho... "Nine fingers" Kim; so called because of his lack of a right index finger... a memento of an old altercation with a rival mob; sat in the passenger seat of the decrepit old split-screen Chevrolet panel van parked up outside City Hall, keeping watch on the Hotel Bando. A little farther along from the hotel, a scruffy road sweeper was lethargically leaning on his broom... or rather that was what the passers-by were meant to think. In reality, he was Kang Dong Hoon; one of the Seoul Yangeundongpa mob's lieutenants, who went by the nickname: Kang "The Claw."

Their mob-boss, Kim Jonghyun had ordered them to keep watch on the Bando for any sign of this CIA woman, Mckenna. Kang had been scrutinising the occupants of every vehicle that left the compound next to the hotel for half the morning. As yet, there had been no sign of any female occupant who might feasibly be his target. This was the third day of their surveillance. Was the woman actually in the hotel? There was no way of knowing... it wasn't as if they could just march into the place and ask.

Hilburn knocked on the door of Charlotte's and Max's room at eight-o'clock, Monday morning. He informed them that it had been arranged to fly them out that morning from Osan air base to the Naval Hospital at Pearl Harbor with a stop-over at Wake Island. It was hoped that the neurologists at Pearl could properly assess the extent of Max's memory loss.

He escorted them to Hartigan's office ushered them in and left the room. Hartigan invited them to sit and reached into the drawer of his desk. Taking out a small velvet pouch, he placed it in front of Charlotte.

'Captain Mckenna; one of our field-agents brought this to me five days ago. He said that you would be interested in it.'

He pushed the little pouch across to her. She picked it up and loosened the drawstring as she looked into its depths, her face froze, and she almost dropped the pouch. The two men stared at her; startled by her reaction. Hartigan studied her for a few moments, and then spoke.

'I guess what's in there has some meaning to you?'

'She stared at him. Her eyes were cold, and her lips tightly pressed together in an expression of trepidation. She nodded; her voice tight and controlled.

'You could say that, Hartigan. I am almost certain that this is what is known as "The Abaddon Stone." I've been chasing this evil relic since the last days of the war in Berlin. This Garnet gemstone was once set into the hilt of a broken sword that was grasped by a severed, skeletal hand, and was encased in a block of metal. It was retrieved from the site of the huge explosion at Tunguska, in Central Siberia. I was chosen... because of my gift for deciphering ancient languages... for the expedition arranged by Himmler with the Russians, to establish if the explosion had any significance of Military value. The metal block was inscribed with the words...'

"Behold. Herein, is trammelled The Evil of all time.
Seek not its deliverance, for there is none.
Meddle not with this Abomination,
For it is The Destroyer of Worlds."

As far as I was able to establish; it was presented to Göring as a trinket. When I went to his villa in Leipziger Platz, his old butler told me that Göring had departed to his estate at Carinhall, and had taken the stone... which he had decided to name "The Abaddon Stone," with him. Max and I checked out the site of Carinhall, but there was nothing to be found there. We picked up a lead in the area and traced the stone to Hamburg where we discovered that it had been sold on to a Chinese seaman whose ship had sailed for Hong Kong. To cut a long story short, it has been moving around in this part of the world ever since. It seems to bring catastrophe wherever it goes. I want no further part of it. It is far too dangerous. You should send it to

Washington so that they can bury it away in some secure vault somewhere where it will never be able to wreak its havoc ever again.'

Hartigan studied her silently for a while.

'It's really that bad? OK, Mckenna; I'll have it shipped out. Now, it's time to get you moving. Have a safe flight.'

Kang saw the anonymous dark blue Ford sedan pulling out of the parking slot in the gated compound beside the hotel and casually wandered across the entrance sweeping the roadway, causing the sedan to slow. He glanced, with seeming disinterest at the occupants; observing that a blonde woman and a man were sitting in the rear passenger seats, and then slowly moved on out of the sedan's path. As the Ford accelerated away up towards the Taipyung Road; Kang signalled to "Nine fingers" Kim, who pulled out from the kerb and accelerated towards him. The old Chevrolet panel van made a rapid "U"-turn in the midst of the traffic and Kang jumped in. They then set off in hot pursuit of the disappearing Ford.

The Ford sedan driver, Jack Stauffer was half a kilometre or so along Taipyung Road heading towards the station, when the old Chevrolet panel van appeared in his mirror. At first, he didn't take too much notice of it; there was no reason to do so. He began to get suspicious when it held pace with him all the way down through the Okazakicho district. There was little traffic as he slid neatly in and out of the stray cars and lorries. The Chevrolet panel van held back, but even at speed, he could not throw it off his tail. He glanced at his passengers.

'I think we're being tailed, Ma'am.'

Charlotte turned and glanced out of the rear window. The old Chevrolet panel van was about two hundred yards behind. It had two occupants. She turned back and drew her Colt automatic from her purse; chambered a round, and flicked off the safety.

'Ok, Jack; let's see if we can shake them.'

Stauffer nodded and floored the gas pedal. The car surged forward, gathering pace, the speedometer rising to sixty then eighty miles per hour as they sped down through the military warehouses and barracks area and turned onto the long, three-kilometre straight of the Han'gang-tong that led down to the Han river bridge. The Chevrolet panel van stayed with them through the narrow twisting streets of Yongdungp'o; but as they left the outskirts and approached Highway One, it seemed to have disappeared. Maybe they'd gotten tangled up in the traffic. Stauffer breathed a sigh of relief as he settled down for the drive down to Osan. Highway One was relatively empty… just a few heavy lorries trundling south. He glanced into the rear-view mirror... nothing. All seemed normal. He passed a Mercedes-Benz sedan at the side of the highway with its hood up and the driver rummaging about in the engine compartment. He grinned. So much for German engineering. He'd stick with good 'ole Detroit Iron! The next time he looked in the rear-view mirror the Mercedes had hooked itself on to his tail, and the Chevrolet panel van had appeared again; about two hundred metres farther back. Stauffer accelerated again; the Mercedes dropped back. The road was beginning to develop curves. As he rounded the next bend, Stauffer caught a flash of the Mercedes-Benz's headlights blinking on and off. He drew his point-forty-five Colt and laid it on the seat beside him. Keeping his eyes on the road, he spoke over his shoulder, asking Charlotte to cock the weapon for him. She reached over, picked up the big automatic and chambered a round; then placed it back on the front passenger seat beside him.

Charlotte spoke. Her voice was cold and assertive.

'What's wrong, Jack?'

Flicking his eyes from the road to the rearview mirror and back again he answered her.

'There's a Mercedes tailing us, Ma'am. He's just blinked his headlights. That damn Chevy panel van is there as well. I think we've got an ambush somewhere up ahead.'

Max; who up to now, had said nothing; suddenly spoke. His voice was terse. The tone reminded Charlotte of the old Max she had known in Berlin.

'Have you any other weapons in the car?'

Stauffer nodded again.

'Yes, Sir. If you pull down the centre armrest of the rear seats, there's a compartment holding a shotgun.'

Max turned in his seat, and pulled out the armrest. From a narrow, deep recess in the car's trunk he withdrew an Ithaca 37, pump-action shotgun. He smiled... the old, familiar Max smile that she hadn't seen for years... and cycled the slide with a mean, ominous "Ka-chack" sound.

'What's the load, Jack?'

Stauffer gave a thin smile.

'Double-zero Buckshot, Sir.'

Max smiled.

'Good!'

The road was straightening out again. About half a mile ahead, was a small, wooded area. The Mercedes began closing up behind them;

the Chevy panel van dropped back to block the road to the rear. Suddenly, two other cars emerged from the trees, and pulled across the road ahead, completely blocking the Ford's path. Stauffer hit the brakes and slewed the car off the road in a vain attempt to try to go around them. The Ford was still doing fifty as it left the road, zigzagging wildly as he fought to avoid hitting any trees. It tore through the undergrowth among the trees with Stauffer fighting to control it, and Charlotte and Max braced against the backs of the front seats with their weapons ready. The first burst of gunfire stitched along the left side of the Ford. Stauffer grunted and lurched sideways across the front seats. With no-one at the wheel, the Ford slammed sideways on into one of the trees, and Charlotte was thrown out into a tangle of bushes. Lying there, half-stunned, she vaguely heard the deep boom of the shotgun again and again; then blackness smothered everything.

It seemed like half a lifetime later, she felt a hand on her shoulder, gently shaking her. Go away!... let her sleep! The hand became more compelling. A muffled, repetitious voice...

"Ma'am, are you OK?"

Painfully, she forced her eyes open. An earnest, and worried young face beneath a white helmet swam into view; the face of a young, Air Police lieutenant. He carefully helped her to her feet and she leaned unsteadily against him. Out on the road an Air Police jeep and a Dodge ambulance were parked up. A military Dodge tow truck was dragging one of the roadblock cars to the side of the road. She found her voice.

'What about the two guys with me?'

The young lieutenant shook his head.

'The driver was killed at the wheel of your car. The other guy didn't make it either. Looks like he made a last stand where we found him; surrounded by spent shotgun shell cases, and shot through the chest. He took eight of those dinks who jumped you with him.'

She nodded dumbly. Yes; that was the Max she had longed for him to be... not the one that she had found in the little rural village just a few weeks ago.

The young lieutenant helped her to the jeep. She was in shock, and the fact that Max was dead hadn't really sunk in. The only lucid thought that she could hold was that Stacey would now never be able to meet her father. The young lieutenant was at a loss as to how to best handle this situation. The first course of action was to get her back to the medical facility at Osan Air Base. Making sure she was safely seated in the jeep, he started the engine, banged it into gear, and, making a tight turn in the road, headed back towards Suwon as quickly as it was safe to do, with the condition that his passenger was in.

Charlotte knew she was about to wake from a dream filled with ghostly images of violent deaths; but she was dreaming that she was dreaming about waking up. No! It was safer in the darkness, despite the ghosts; and she wrapped the velvet nothingness tighter around herself. She was lying in a soft, warm place that occasionally faded to a sort of twilight in which she thought she could hear people and movement around her. She wanted to stay in this place and made no effort to open her eyes and come back to the real world.

A man's voice was speaking; it was indistinct and seemed to be far away, but the words gradually became clearer. It seemed to be a kind voice... a friendly voice; but she wished it would go away; so she ignored it and sank back into her dreams which gradually became a bloody nightmare of gunshots, tearing metal and pain that inexorably dragged her back to a trembling reality.

She felt a hand on her forehead that had nothing to do with her dream. She slowly opened her eyes. Sun was streaming into the bright, white room. As she moved her head on the pillow she heard a rustle, and an Air Force Medical Service nurse wearing First-lieutenant bars on the collar of her pristine white duty uniform, who had been sitting beside the bed, rose and moved into her line of vision. She smiled as she put her hand on Charlotte's wrist to check her pulse, and spoke softly.

'Just lie quiet Ma'am, and don't try to move. I'll go and tell the doctor you're awake. You've been unconscious since they brought you in and we've been real worried about you.'

Charlotte closed her eyes and mentally checked out her body. She ached all over, but the worst pain was in her right side. She tried to move and the sudden, sharp, stabbing pain almost took her breath away. She gingerly lay back and decided to wait for the doctor.

The door opened and the doctor came in followed by the nurse. He looked very young. He walked across the room and stood beside the bed. Reaching down, he put a cool hand on Charlotte's forehead and studied the temperature chart behind the bed. He nodded and looked back at her.

'Your injuries are not serious, but you have lost a quite a lot of blood due to internal bleeding caused by one of your three broken ribs lacerating the lower pleura on your right side. This was most probably caused by blunt abdominal trauma from being thrown violently from the vehicle. We have now successfully arrested the haemorrhaging, and if all goes well, you will recover completely, but I fear that you will continue to be in pain for several days and we will endeavour to keep you as comfortable as possible.

You must not move your body excessively or suddenly, and it is most important that you rest and regain your strength. At the moment you are suffering from a serious condition of mental and physical shock and I would prefer a natural, rather than an induced recovery which would be dependent upon intravenous use of amphetamines.'

Charlotte remained confined to bed for another three days. Her ribs hurt, but the First lieutenant Nurse carefully re-strapped her ribcage with fresh bandages each morning as the existing ones became sweaty and uncomfortable. On the fourth day, the young doctor appeared. He smiled.

'Good morning, Captain Mckenna. Today, we can discharge you. They have arranged to fly you out this afternoon. I'll have a nurse bring you your clothes, and I'll prescribe you some Demerol tablets in case the rib fracture causes you some trouble.'

His face became serious.

'You must not take Demerol in larger amounts than I shall prescribe, or for longer than I recommend. Do not stop using Demerol suddenly, or you could have unpleasant withdrawal symptoms. It is a powerful analgesic, and you must be careful in its usage.'

She nodded.

'Thank you, doctor; I understand.'

She paused.

'Could you tell me what has happened to my colleagues?'

His face became solemn.

'They have already been flown back to The Zone of Interior…'

He glanced at his wristwatch.

'They should be arriving at Andrews in about three hours.'

She nodded.

'Thank you, doctor.'

He smiled grimly.

'You were lucky, this time, Captain; try to stay out of trouble until those ribs are mended.'

As she dressed, she wondered where Max would be buried. They were flying him into Andrews Air Force Base, so it was obvious that Foggy Bottom… the familiar name for CIA Headquarters in Washington, would be dealing with his interment. She smiled sadly. His name would never appear in any memorial book in the

Headquarters building, although they might well bury him in Arlington if there was Presidential agreement. He was, after all, a naturalised American citizen... albeit one arranged under the old "PL-110" clause of the CIA Act; and had been killed whilst serving as an active CIA officer on deployment for the Firm.

The Duty Medical Officer handed Charlotte her itinerary as he carried her meagre hand luggage to the waiting airplane. The roster listed her route back to the Zone of Interior... the American Mainland. The first leg of her journey would be aboard the C117A Skytrooper waiting on the parking ramp. This was a conversion of the faithful old C47 Skytrain, but was fitted out with a twenty-four seat, airline-type interior, and was used for Staff transport purposes. The first stop would be Yokoto Air Force Base in Japan; a flight lasting about four and a half hours. Boarding the airplane, she was surprised to find that she was the only passenger. A young WAF Staff Sergeant came down the cabin aisle and welcomed her aboard. She smiled, and moved her arm in an elegant gesture to the empty cabin.

'It's all yours, Ma'am. Take your choice of seats. I'll bring coffee when we're airborne.'

Charlotte thanked her and chose a seat on the port side just aft of the wing.

As she fastened her seat belt the whistle of the engine starter penetrated the cabin, and the starboard prop began turning. With a belch of smoke the engine fired and clattered roughly until it settled down to a steady rhythm. The port prop began to slowly turn, until again, with a belch of blue smoke it also fired up. The pilot ran the engines up carefully, until his gauges were reading correctly, then, with a gentle jolt, he released the brakes and the Skytrooper began to move.

The pilot taxied to the threshold of the runway and held on the brakes as he ran up the engines. When he was satisfied with the instrument readings, he released the brakes, and pushed the throttles to full power. With a rising roar, the airplane began to accelerate down the runway; the tail lifted, and the concrete dropped away as she lifted off and set her nose for another strip of concrete six hundred miles to the south-east.

Chapter Seven.

At Yokota; after a meal in the Officer's Club and a chance to have a shower and freshen up; Charlotte was escorted to the airplane in which she would make the next leg of the flight home. She hadn't quite known what to expect; perhaps, another long-range MATS transport... noisy and uncomfortable. What she saw waiting on the ramp was a complete surprise. It was a big, four-engined Boeing Stratocruiser airliner painted in Pan American Airways livery that had been one of Pan Am's signature craft; the last word in airborne opulence during the luxury era of the fifties. Her escort said that it had been impressed by the military after it had force-landed in Northern Japan with engine failure. The military had rectified and re-engined her and then made Pan Am an offer they couldn't refuse... settle the bill for four brand-new Pratt and Whitney Wasp major engines... or strike her off their books and let the military have her. Now, she was being flown back to America to be converted into a C-97 Stratofreighter at the Boeing Field plant in Seattle.

If truth be told, Pan Am was not particularly dismayed at this little exercise in arm-twisting. Piston-engined airliners were coming to the end of the road, and being superseded by the first jets. There would be a measure of compensation from the Government, and there would be no corporate aggravation involved in disposing of the old lady on the commercial market. The new Boeing 707 jetliners were the rising stars, and the earlier Stratocruisers' niche as glamorous and luxurious, post-war long-range airliners was being pre-empted by the newcomers as far as Pan Am was concerned.

Out on the ramp at the airplane the Flight Engineer was performing his walk around inspection before entering the flight deck and getting ready for the prestart checklist, after which he would give the "Ready to Start Engines" report. At the same time, such passengers as there were, stood in a group at the foot of the two-flight airstair ready to board. A young airman wearing Staff Sergeant's insignia appeared at the top of the airstair and motioned them to board the airplane. Charlotte's escort handed her a thick manila envelope and bid her farewell. She climbed the stairs and paused at the top for one last look at Japan. Then she stepped inside the fuselage and the Staff Sergeant closed the door behind her.

The Stratocruiser was unusual in that it had two decks. Its "double-bubble" fuselage... shaped in cross-section like an upside-down figure eight, enabled a downstairs bar and lounge to be fitted. This was reached by a circular stairway just aft of the main passenger loading door in the centre left side of the fuselage. The main, upper passenger cabin was divided into six sections - a forward passenger section seating eight, the two dressing rooms, the forward main cabin, the galley, the rear main cabin and the stateroom.

The young Staff Sergeant invited her to go forward and take one of the seats in what would, in airline service, have been the first-class luxury compartment. He said that the advantage was that the exclusive, First-class reclining seats allotted enough space to allow a six-foot man to completely lie out without disturbing anyone around him. The two facing pairs could be converted to a lounge bed by means of a simple adjustment whereby the foam rubber seat backs lowered to a nearly horizontal position, whilst the comfortable leg rests pulled out full length; and the movable centre arm-rests adjusted to seat level. With this arrangement, all she had to do was call him, using the call button mounted in the seat armrest and he could convert the seat for her to sleep. Alternatively, she could use one of the bunks on the opposite side of the compartment. Either choice would ensure her comfort and privacy. The Ladies' dressing room was in the compartment immediately aft. She thanked him and went forward. Why the VIP treatment? The Bureau had made the arrangements for her flight itinerary... but Company officers normally travelled on a "need to know" basis. Perhaps the young Staff Sergeant was not just a "Staff Sergeant."

Her thoughts were interrupted by the whine of the engine starter. She glanced out of the compartment window. The big propellers on the two left engines were stationary. The procedure must be to start up the engines on the right wing first. Sure enough; faint engine noises and vibration were beginning to penetrate the compartment... not much; the soundproofing was impressive. The starter motor on another engine whined. The noise and vibration increased slightly. Charlotte chose the almost club-like, luxurious seat by the window and fastened her lap belt. The starter whine came again, and the inner left engine propeller began to turn, increasing speed as the engine exhaust belched a cloud of bluish-white smoke. The engine fired up and the propeller blades became a blur. As the smoke cleared; the starter whine came again for the last time, and the outer left engine propeller blade began to turn lazily. With another cloud of smoke, the last engine fired up and the vibration settled. She glanced at the wall at the front of the compartment. Beyond that was the flight deck with the crew busying themselves with their final checks.

After starting, the engines would be run until the oil temperature warmed. Then they would open up the engines and check the propeller controls. Then would come the magneto checks, and the crew would go over the printed check list before taking off. After getting tower clearance and taxiing to the runway, the pilot would hold the airplane on the brakes and open the throttles. Once he released the brakes, the take-off run would commence, and Japan, Korea, and all the danger and subterfuge would become just a memory.

The Stratocruiser lifted off from Yokota Air Base at 11.26am precisely, for the seventeen hundred and fifty mile leg to Wake Atoll airfield, just under half-way across the Pacific Ocean to Hickam Field on Oahu, in the Hawaiian Islands.; a flying time for the Stratocruiser at cruise speed of six and three-quarter hours. As she settled more comfortably in her luxurious seat and watched the Japanese coastline disappear beneath the port wing, Charlotte wondered if indeed, with the removal of the malignant artefact they called "The Abaddon Stone" to some covert and impenetrable U.S. government warehouse; that this was the end of the trail of death and destruction that it had wrought across the span of the last twenty years. Even so, the very thought of the blood-red monstrosity suddenly gave her a fleeting shiver of the sort they say you feel when a grey goose flies over your grave.

Thursday, 20th October 1960.
Hotel Bando.
Euljiro Street. Seoul.
South Korea.

Gus Hartigan, Deputy Head of Station, Seoul; pressed the bell under his desk to summon his assistant support officer. After a few minutes, a fresh-faced young man entered the office. Hartigan handed him a small package.

'Get this down to the post room and tell them to get it on a flight

Stateside.'

The young man nodded, picked up the package, and left the office. Hartigan turned his attention to the files on his desk. He wasn't really convinced of Charlotte Mckenna's concerns about the contents of the package. He didn't believe in "evil" artefacts... there were a damn sight more evil things just over the border to the north; which was why he hadn't bothered about it until now. It was the report of the ambush of Charlotte's car out on the road to Osan, and the deaths of Max Segal and Jack Stauffer that had made him decide to do something about it. He shrugged. Mckenna had been discharged from hospital and was on her way back to Washington. If the package wasn't on its way by the time she reported in; then all manner of shit might well hit the fan, and there was no way he was about to let any of it stick to him.

In the basement post room of the Hotel Bando; Jang Soon-Chun reached for the small package that had just come down from upstairs and tentatively shook it. He smiled. The rattle suggested that the package contained a single object. This was probably the item that he had been instructed to locate on the instructions of Kim Jonghyun, mob boss of Seoul's notorious Yangeundongpa gang, who had arranged for him to be placed in the post room specifically for that purpose. He glanced around. Too many people. He couldn't open the package without being observed.

He thought quickly. The best course of action would be to note the address and report back so that the package could be intercepted after he had processed it. That way, there would be no suspicion; and his presence in the post room would not be compromised. The package had no indications that it should be included in the Diplomatic pouch. Jang Soon-Chun nodded to himself. This would be simple. He merely had to copy the information from the address label that he would affix to the package, and report back when his shift was finished. He removed the printed address label from the folder that had accompanied the package. Attached to it was a Korean Airlines freight label. The address label was for somewhere in Virginia, U.S.A. He grinned. This was better than easy! They were sending this package by a commercial carrier to Japan, and then, on across the Pacific. It could easily be intercepted at any one of half a dozen places on its journey.

Jang Soon-Chun carefully affixed the Korean Air freight label to the package and smiled quietly to himself. There would be no need to inform Kim Jonghyun of the situation. This was an opportunity to for him to gain much face in his boss's estimation. Jang Soon-Chun had a contact in the Korean Air staff... an air hostess named Chang Su-Dae. She had reported that she would be on the Japanese route for the entire week. He would contact her and instruct her to intercept the package en-route, to be passed to a subsequent contact when the flight landed in Japan. He completed the processing of the package and tossed it into the commercial certified mail bin. Glancing at his cheap, Chinese wristwatch, he called to the post room supervisor that he was taking an early meal break. The supervisor nodded his agreement, and turned back to his task as Jang Soon-Chun strolled unhurriedly from the room.

Outside the Hotel Bando; having passed through the security screening that was obligatory for all civilian employees; Jang Soon-Chun quickened his pace as he crossed Euljiro street and hurried down to the small restaurant on the corner of Cho Dong Ro.

He ordered *Sam-gyup-sal* with *Kimchi*... grilled pork strips served with fermented chilli peppers and vegetables, and moved to the public telephone. He dialled the number for the Gimpo Airport reception and asked for the call to be transferred to the Korean Air flight-ready room.

A man's voice answered;

'This is Captain Jeung Yong-Jo speaking. How may I help you?'

Jang Soon-Chun paused. This was the flight Captain of Chang Su-Dae; his air hostess contact. It was against airline protocols to try to contact a flight crew immediately prior to their flight. He decided to press ahead.

'Would it be possible to speak with Chang Su-Dae please? It is a matter of family importance.'

Jeung Yong-Jo smiled quietly. Although against all the rules; if he permitted this call, he would be seen by her as an altruistic and kindly father figure. He had lusted for her since she had joined the airline. Chang Su-Da was twenty-three; her skin held the soft, flawless, honey-gold sheen that is common in Korean women; and her figure was slender and lithe. Her hair was as black as a raven's wing, and was cut in a stylish bob, and there was no doubt in his mind that she was in awe of him; he had, after all, been one of the heroic, hot-shot South Korean Air Force Mustang jockeys during the war. If he treated her well, she might just let him fuck her in the hotel on their overnight stop in Japan.

Unfortunately, for Jeung Yong-Jo, what he didn't know was, that Su-Dae was closely related to the notorious, Korean Chang crime syndicate family of San Francisco; and if he had attempted anything with her whilst in Japan, he would have ended up face-down in the

Sumida river, minus at least, both index fingers, and probably several more rather personal and delicate appendages. Chang Su-Dae was a beautiful, deadly enigma... to both men; not only was she protected by the Seoul crime syndicate... but, unbeknown to Jang Soon-Chun, who believed that she was one of Kim Jonghyun's foot soldiers; in fact, Chang Su-Dae was the granddaughter of the Chang criminal family patriarch, Chang Ho-Pyong.

The Chang family was affiliated to several powerful Korean-American mobs in the United States. Some of these mobs were also connected to the Japanese Yakuza and to Chinese Triads. The Chang family effectively controlled Chinatown in San Francisco, and had important links to Korean crime syndicates in South Korea. They all involved themselves in extortion, property invasions, gambling, drug trafficking and prostitution. If Kim Jonghyun was prepared to go to such lengths as to attempt to divert mail from under the very noses of the American CIA... and from inside their own headquarters in Seoul; Su-Dae reasoned that the package must contain something that was extremely important. It might well be of significant advantage to the family if this package were to be diverted into their possession.

She smiled briefly to herself. Her contact in the Japanese Customs Service could initiate the diversion. This decision irrevocably sealed the fate of Jang Soon-Chun. Kim Jonghyun had expended considerable funds to secure the contents of the package and would not tolerate failure by his man to intercept it as instructed... which, of course, would now be, for him, totally impossible. There would be only one punishment for this failure to carry out his Master's command.

Four days later, Jang Soon-Chun's gruesomely tortured corpse was found in the Han River. The rotting carcass was still identifiable as being one of the lesser members of one of the Seoul mobs... the extensive tattoo across its shoulders attested to this fact; but, the corpse bore all the signature marks of Soo-Yun Kaneko; Kim Jonghyun's beautiful Contract assassin. The Seoul police dragged the ruined corpse from the river, and began taking photographs. The Precinct Police Chief suddenly arrived unexpectedly, and issued a direct order to his men that the incident should be recorded as "Accidental death." It was obvious that the body had been struck by some vessel's propeller as it floated in the river.

Although the evidence as to Soo-Yun Kaneko's involvement was as glaringly obvious as though she had signed her name across the corpse; the order had been given. The police officers dumped the

100

corpse into a panel van as the Precinct Police Chief drove away; satisfied that he had successfully defused an embarrassing situation, and that Kim Jonghyun would now permit him to retain his genitalia intact for the foreseeable future. Consequently, Jang Soon-Chun's corpse was deposited in the city morgue and quietly forgotten about.

Thursday, 20th October 1960.
Haneda Airport.
Ōta, Tokyo.
Japan.

Chang Su-Dae's flight landed at Haneda at 2.30pm after a three and a half hour journey. With the passengers disembarked and the mail cargo being unloaded; Su-Dae excused herself from the crew room on the pretext that she needed to go to the powder room. She made a discreet telephone call in the terminal lobby to her contact in Customs control and advised him of what he should look for and what he should do.

Ten minutes later; Customs officer Kenichi Saito intercepted the small package. He carefully removed the Virginia address label and replaced it with one printed with an address at Montgomery Street in the Telegraph Hill district of San Francisco...the heart of Chinatown. He then made to customary blue chalk scribble across the package denoting that it had passed through Customs checking and tossed it into the outbound mail hopper.

Twenty minutes later, it was loaded into the cargo hold of the San Francisco-bound Northwest Orient Airlines Constellation for its destination on the far side of the Pacific Ocean.

Friday, 21st October 1960.
North Pacific Ocean.

Charlotte glanced at her wristwatch... almost eight o'clock in the evening. They should be approaching Wake Island soon. She looked out of the compartment window down towards the seemingly endless ocean. Far ahead, on the edge of the horizon there appeared a horseshoe of bright turquoise framed in flashing white; standing out against the indigo-blue carpet below. As she watched, the turquoise blob slid slowly to the right and disappeared as the pilot made a slight course change to port. The unobtrusive engine noise changed pitch as the pilot brought the power setting slightly back whilst manoeuvring onto the upwind leg of his approach pattern. The young Staff Sergeant came forward into the compartment.

He smiled.

'We're twenty minutes out, Ma'am. Just time for a coffee if you would like one.'

Charlotte returned his smile.

'No thank you; I'm fine.'

He nodded.

'Yes, Ma'am. If you could please fasten your seat belt when you see Toki Point on the easterly island. We're only stopping for a minimum time to refuel; then it's on to Hickam field on Oahu, Hawaii. I'll come and set your sleeping arrangements when we're airborne again. The flight should take about seven and a half hours, which means we'll be landing at Hickam at about 0.600, tomorrow morning.'

Gazing down out of the window, Charlotte watched the Atoll drift into view. Wake comprised three islets; Wake islet, the largest, on the southwest, was shaped roughly in the form of a "V," the arms of which appeared to be about two and three-quarters miles long. Each arm was continued as a separate islet, each with a narrow channel between it and the end of the arms of the V. The western ends of the two islets were connected by a sweep of flat reef, which continued as a narrow border around the three islets. In the middle of this enclosing reef was a rectangular lagoon. There appeared to be few buildings and sparse vegetation except for palm trees. As the Stratocruiser overflew the island and turned into its landing circuit, Charlotte noticed that the western end of Wake Island was devoted to the docks and landing area, as well as to warehouse facilities gathered around the end of the single runway.

The Island seemed to begin spinning slowly clockwise as the pilot banked around and committed to his down leg and began to lose height. Then came the final turn, and she heard the shrill hydraulic whine of the air-brakes and the landing-wheels being lowered as the airplane's nose dipped and the hum of the engines settled to a whistling purr as the scrubby vegetation at the edge of the runway rushed towards her. Suddenly she heard the welcome screech of the airplane's tires as they touched the runway; the ugly roar of the propellers being reversed to slow the headlong rush down the length of the asphalt ribbon that ran the length of the southern leg of the "V" towards the ocean, and felt the noticeable deceleration pushing her hips into her seat belt.

The big airplane coasted along; losing speed smoothly and progressively as the pilot applied gentle braking. Charlotte looked out across the tranquil turquoise lagoon... yes; it was easy to see why Pan

American had chosen this place as a staging post for their Trans-Pacific Clipper flying boats. They had built a facility that had been named "PAAville" complete with a forty-eight room hotel with port stewards, chefs, and attendants, on Peale Island, to maintain a high standard of service for the overnight guests. Wake had been used as a refuelling and rest stop on their then-new "China Clipper" passenger and mail route between San Francisco and Hong Kong. Unfortunately, most of the Pan Am facility had been destroyed during the Japanese attacks of 1941.

At the southern end of the runway, the Stratocruiser slowed to a standstill. As Charlotte watched, fascinated; the slowly rotating propeller blades began to move smoothly in their hubs as the pilot disengaged thrust reverse. The two inner engines revved up and the propellers increased in speed as he began turning the big airplane and taxied off the runway towards the waiting ramp. With a thin squeal of brakes, the airplane came to a halt and the engine noise diminished as the pilot closed the throttles. As the propellers windmilled to a standstill, the Staff Sergeant came forward and asked Charlotte to follow him back along the fuselage. The passengers would be disembarking while the refuelling was taking place. They would use the lower deck passenger door, because Wake did not possess the luxury of an airline airstair, which meant that she should follow him down the spiral staircase to the lower lounge, and then out to the apron by way of the steps that were built into the inner face of the door which was hinged at its lower edge. As she stepped down onto the concrete, the ground engineers were already clambering up on the wing from the trestles that had been brought up, and a big USAF semi-trailer tank truck refueller was parked up close to the airplane with the fat black fuel hoses already connected and snaking up onto the wing upper surface to be manually connected to the fuel tank filler valves by the waiting engineers.

The Staff Sergeant smiled.

'The stop-over and fuelling will take about twenty minutes. With the underwing pressure refuelling system it would take less time, but again, Wake just hasn't got the equipment. Perhaps you'd like to go and grab a cold soda in the PX club?'

He pointed to a low building just off the edge of the apron and grinned.

'Whatever you do, Ma'am; don't drink any of the water.'

At about 9.15pm, the Staff Sergeant returned to the PX and informed everyone that the airplane was ready and they should now resume their seats. Outside, the temperature was still warm... almost balmy. Charlotte smiled. Romantic tropical nights... if only!

The Stratocruiser sat with its gleaming aluminium lower fuselage reflecting the ramp lights and the white-painted upper deck glowing pink in the soft rays of the setting sun. The engines on the starboard side of the airplane on the opposite side of the fuselage from the entry door were already running. Charlotte returned to her seat. Glancing out of the window, she saw one of the ground crew raise his hand with three fingers extended in the direction of the cockpit. The whine of a starter motor penetrated the compartment and the inboard left propeller began to turn lethargically and slowly speed up its revolutions. A huge billow of bluish-grey smoke belched forth from the exhaust stacks and the engine fired, and the propeller blades became a blur. The crewman raised his hand again, but with four fingers extended. Again, the whine penetrated the muted roar of the freshly started engine and the outer left propeller began to turn. Nothing happened for something like a minute or so... just the propeller grinding round and round. Suddenly, a tongue of flame burst from the exhaust stacks, followed by an even huger billow of the same bluish-grey smoke. The staff sergeant had returned to check that she was comfortable. He saw the apprehensive look on her face and smiled.

'Nothing to worry about, Ma'am; that was just a "Hot Start." It happens sometimes when the engine hasn't cooled down enough, and is nothing to worry about. All it means is that the fuel ignited before enough air had been drawn into the mix.'

He glanced at his watch.

'It's 21.40pm. I'll come back to see if you want your berth set out, or your seat converted in about thirty minutes. OK?'

Charlotte nodded, as the Stratocruiser began to turn on the apron and taxi out to the runway. With a thin squeal of brakes, the airplane turned onto the runway and began to back-track to the northern end of the asphalt strip. She looked out of the window towards the horizon. The golden and scarlet sky was beginning to darken to a soft indigo as twilight began creeping in from the east; then as the airplane turned at the north end, the compartment was washed golden by the rays of the evening sun lowering in the west.

The pilot revved the four engines up to take-off speed, one by one; and she heard the thin hydraulic whine of the wing flaps being extended. Then the big airplane turned slowly away from the setting sun. There was a jerk as the brakes were released and she began to roll down the runway. In the cockpit, the pilot and copilot watched the speed climb... seventy... eighty... at ninety, the pilot eased the control wheel back and the nose wheel lifted. Power settings, OK... and the Stratocruiser flew herself off as the airspeed indicator pointer touched one hundred and ten. The copilot applied the brakes to stop the rotation of the wheels and retracted the landing gear as the pilot eased her over into a gentle port bank and set her course for the two thousand nautical mile leg to Hickam Air Force Base on Oahu in the Hawaiian Islands.

The Stratocruiser was still climbing to its cruising height, with the Pacific Ocean all but lost in the inky void three miles below, when the Staff Sergeant returned to convert her luxurious seat into a bed, or prepare a berth. She said that she had decided on one of the berths. He nodded. She rose and went to the dressing room aft, to change into her night attire. She had just finished removing her make-up when he tapped discreetly on the door, said that her berth was ready, and wished her Goodnight. She returned to the compartment and snuggled down between the crisp white sheets. Turning out the wall light, she gazed out of the little round compartment porthole at the stars. How bright they were up here in the clear cold air.

Looking out across the wing, she watched the engine turbo superchargers' ghostly, icy-blue flames streaming back from the exhausts whilst the propeller blades catching the brilliant moonlight and the glow from the green navigation light on the far tip of the wing glistened and splintered into the night. The blue flames brought back the memory of her flight out of Nazi Germany, all those years ago. They were the same intense, icy-blue flicker that she had seen coming from the exhausts of the big, black American night-fighter that had escorted her airplane as it flew across the North Sea to England.

She watched the almost hypnotic shimmer of the silvery-green glow on the propellers for a while; then pulled the beige window curtain closed and was slowly lulled to sleep by the muted hum of the engines and the air conditioning/pressurisation system.

Charlotte woke early the next morning. Stretching luxuriantly, she pulled the window curtain back and gazed out across the pale saffron sky tinged with vanilla and silver streaks as the sun came up over the rim of the world, glazing the sky with subtle hues of orange and red; and painting the clouds to resemble a sea of pink cotton candy. As she lay there, marvelling at the sight, there was a gentle tap on the door. Pulling the sheets up to her chin, she called out,

'Come in.'

The Staff Sergeant entered and smiled.

'Good morning, Ma'am. I hope you slept well. Would you care for breakfast?'

She nodded. He smiled and brought out a note pad.

'Might I suggest eggs, sunny-side up with bacon or sausage, with country ham; pancakes with syrup; and maybe French toast... and, of course, juice and coffee?'

Charlotte raised an eyebrow.

'Just coffee, eggs and bacon, and a small portion of pancakes, please.'

He nodded.

'Yes, Ma'am. I'll bring them directly, on a tray. Breakfast in bed is a nice way to start the day.'

He turned, and then spoke again.

'We're about one and a half hours out of Oahu, Ma'am; so there's no rush.'

'He returned in ten minutes with her breakfast. It was served on a silver bed tray covered with a white linen napkin, upon which were arranged original Pan American Airways white china plates, with silver cutlery; and a black coffee cup on a white saucer. Also on the tray was placed a silver coffee pot and milk pitcher; together with a silver sugar bowl containing both brown and white sugar cubes. The Staff Sergeant carefully placed the tray over Charlotte's lap and poured her a cup of coffee. He then smiled, said "Enjoy"; and left the compartment.

The breakfast was delicious. This must be how the pampered Pan American First Class customers were cosseted on the "President's Special" service flying to Europe a few years previously. Charlotte smiled ruefully. So now this majestic old lady of the skies was fated to be converted into a military freighter. Somehow the name "Stratofreighter" just didn't have the same ring to it as the names that the various airlines had christened their First Class Stratocruiser flights... Pan American's "President Clippers" and BOAC's "Monarchs." It may have taken more than thirteen hours to get from New York, to Europe, but they certainly did it in impeccable style and comfort.

She finished breakfast and carefully got out of the berth. Stepping across the compartment, she pressed the call button on the armrest of her luxurious seat. The Staff Sergeant appeared to remove the tray. He smiled.

'I hope the breakfast was to your satisfaction, Ma'am.'

She nodded.

'It was wonderful. Thank you so much.'

He smiled again.

'Thank you, Ma'am; you're welcome. Now, if you would care to use the Ladies' dressing room, I shall re-make the berth and tidy everything for you. We are due to land in approximately thirty minutes.'

She nodded, and made to move aft towards the dressing room, but paused, and turned to him.

'You're not just a Staff Sergeant, are you?'

His smile broadened, and he shook his head imperceptibly.

'No, Ma'am. I'm Gil Callaghan; your support officer.'

She nodded. So Callaghan was with "The Company"... she should have guessed.

Having dressed, freshened herself up, and gargled away the taste of a night of pressurised air, Charlotte returned to her seat. Callaghan had made up the bunk and removed the breakfast tray. She made herself comfortable and gazed out of the window. The pristine blue of the Pacific Ocean stretched to the horizon, and there! Just coming into view; the Hawaiian Island chain, stretching away like a sumptuous necklace of jade beads. Slowly, they slipped from her view as the pilot made a gentle turn to port and began his descent.

With only the Ocean below, the impression was that the airplane was hanging dead-steady in the middle of a blue nothingness; the only clues as to any movement were the glittering discs of the propeller blades. This curious impression lasted for something like ten minutes, and then, the most northerly of the islands... Kauai, drifted into view; lush and green... so different from the sandy coral atoll of Wake. The Stratocruiser was much lower now. Kauai slipped out of sight and they were out over open water again, on the last sixty-mile leg to Oahu.

Callaghan returned with a coffee pot. She declined his offer. He smiled.

'OK, Ma'am. We're ten minutes to final approach. Please fasten your lap strap when the sign illuminates.'

She nodded.

'Thank you, Mr Callaghan.'

He smiled again.

'Please call me Gil, Ma'am.'

Ten minutes later, Charlotte felt the airplane begin to turn again. The sign on the front wall of her compartment illuminated... "Fasten Seat Belts." As she clicked the catch together, the Stratocruiser swept in over the coast. The hum of the engines softened, and a faint, sickly odour of the insecticide bomb being fired in the baggage hold crept through the air-conditioning system, followed by the shrill hydraulic whine of the air-brakes and the landing-wheels being lowered. The big airplane slowed noticeably, and the nose dipped. An industrial area dotted with what appeared to be many fuel storage tanks slid past under the wing, followed by a small airfield, then a wooded area which gave way to a jumble of houses. Immediately beyond that was a river estuary. As the airplane crossed it; power was slowly throttled back, and she watched the belching gouts of flame from the engine exhausts, as what must have been the turbo superchargers wound down. Out to the right, a long runway and clusters of buildings and hangars appeared. That was probably Hickam Air Force Base, if the layout was anything to go by.

She watched the shadow of the Stratocruiser getting larger as it descended, but was still unprepared for the pained squeal from the tyres of the main undercarriage as they touched the tarmac. The engine hum increased to an ugly roar as the pilot selected reverse pitch, and the big airplane began to slow as it rolled down the long, wide runway. The engine roar settled to a hum once again as the propellers were returned to their normal pitch and the Stratocruiser coasted along smoothly until, with what seemed to be only a light brake application; it turned, and taxied off the runway at the mid-intersection point, continuing to roll past the civilian terminal building towards Hickam Air Force Base.

Crossing the Hickam main runway, the Stratocruiser taxied up to a large hardstanding and stopped with a slight jerk. The engine hum diminished as the pilot shut down the engines in sequence. As she was unbuckling her lap strap, and watching the big, four-bladed propellers windmilling down to a standstill, Callaghan appeared.

He grinned.

'Here we are, Ma'am. End of the line with this old lady. You're booked into the officer's quarters for the night, and then you'll be riding a MATS C-121 Super Connie to Travis Air Force Base just outside Fairfield, California... about forty miles south-west from Sacramento. That'll take something like eight hours. From there, it's another eight-hour flight cross-country to Andrews.'

Charlotte nodded.

'Will you be coming with me all the way?'

He nodded.

'All the way to Foggy Bottom, Ma'am.'

Saturday evening, 22nd October 1960.
Hickam Air Force Base. Honolulu.
Oahu.
The Hawaiian Islands.
North Pacific Ocean.

The Officers Club at Hickam was elegant and pristine. After an impressive evening meal, Charlotte relaxed comfortably in a plush deep brown leather chair gazing out of the window across the mouth of Pearl Harbor towards the Waianae Mountains as she waited for Gil Callaghan to return with another round of drinks. Her room was two doors down from Callaghan; arrangements had been made through Foggy Bottom for them to stop over in the Officers Club, although this arrangement was normally reserved for Hickam's serving officers.

Callaghan returned with two highball glasses containing a blue concoction. These were "Blue Hawaiians"... one of the latest drink crazes on the Islands. A mixture of Blue Curaçao and light rum, blended with cream of coconut and pineapple juice over ice; they were very refreshing but had a kick like a mule. As she sipped her drink, Charlotte gazed at Callaghan over the rim of her glass. He was very handsome in a rugged sort of way; built like an All-American quarterback, and close on six feet, two inches tall. He had serious, blue-grey eyes and short, dark hair. He was obviously interested in her... she had seen the sidelong glances throughout the trip from Japan. She smiled softly to herself. Dammit! Here she was... forty-eight years old; and he couldn't have been much more than thirty-two, perhaps, thirty-three. This really was stupid.

They sat and drank, making small talk. He didn't ask her any questions about what she had been engaged in during her time in the Korean Peninsula... he was too well-trained for that; but he certainly gave the impression that he was slightly in awe of her. It was obvious to her that he was not a field agent... more likely; he was one of Foggy Bottom's administration staff.

They sat for a while, drinking and watching the huge Navy ships and submarines pass by on their way out to sea. As the sun began to sink into a beautiful Hawaiian sunset over the Waianae Mountains, she put down her glass and smiled across at him.

'I think I'll turn in now, Gil. It's been a long day.'

With impeccable manners, he stood up as she rose. She smiled.

'Stay here and finish your drink. I'll look in and say goodnight before I go to bed.'

As she walked along the long, impersonal corridor to her room,

Charlotte came to a decision. She thought,

'Hell. Why not? He's young and handsome and he obviously wants me. Max has gone. I'm still in fairly good shape; and I do so want to feel someone's arms around me again, before it's too late.'

Half an hour later Callaghan heard the door to his room open, and heard a whisper of silk. He saw Charlotte, framed in the doorway. She wore nothing but a filmy négligée of silk and lace, her bell of blonde hair gleamed, and her blue eyes held him transfixed. She smiled softly, and he knew, in that instant that she had the ability to drown him with nothing more than a look. He dragged his eyes away from her gaze and allowed them to slide down her body; devouring her almost alabaster-white skin; her luscious breasts straining against the translucent bodice of the négligée. He sat up and made to get out of the bed, but she came towards him, and pushed him back; sliding in beside him and pressing her body against his. She slipped her hand around the back of his neck and pulled his lips on to hers.

'It's been so long,'

She murmured.

'I need some comfort tonight.'

Slipping out of her négligée, she pulled him to her. Her skin was soft and warm, and perfumed; her hair smelt of summer meadows. Her body was toned and tight from years of existing on the utilitarian diet of North Korea. He caught his breath. God! She was beautiful.

He gasped as her hand slipped down to caress him. He slid quietly on top of her, taking his weight on his forearms, as she wrapped her fingers around him; pulling his mouth to her lips and kissing him. As their tongues danced with each other, she gently pushed him back so that his stiffening manhood lay hot across her stomach. He reached out his hand, moving her hair aside and kissing her throat, running his lips over her shoulder, sucking at her flesh gently. She felt his hands slide under her buttocks, pressing, stroking, and kneading them as he bent his mouth to kiss first one breast and then the other; teasing her nipples with his tongue and lips. Her hands guided him as he lifted her buttocks in his hands, and slowly slid into her.

She let out a tiny mew of pleasure as she felt his long, thick, hardness slowly easing deeper into her; and for a fleeting moment, he imagined that he was looking into the face of someone else in another time... another place, instead of this beautiful, mature woman in his embrace. Then the fleeting illusion was gone, as swiftly as it had appeared; as he looked down into her face and felt her body begin to move with, and against him as he pressed her down into the mattress,

110

legs tangled, and bedcovers askew. Arching her back, she pushed him deeper inside. Her long fingernails raked furrows down his back as they moved together. Nobody else existed but the two of them; nobody and nothing else mattered in the isolation of this anonymous room as their intense lovemaking blotted out her darker memories and deeper fears.

Much later, he lay on his back with his arms wrapped about her, encased in the warmth of their mutual afterglow. She traced a finger across his lips.

'Not bad for an old broad?'

He stared indignantly at her.

'Old Broad? I only make love to beautiful women… and you're the most beautiful so far.'

She smiled

'Good answer, Callaghan! You can come again.'

He grinned sleepily.

'I intend to… a little later on.'

Early the next morning. Gil Callaghan awoke needing to take a pee. Charlotte was still sound-asleep in his arms. Carefully, he extracted himself and went to the adjoining bathroom. Having given himself a quick wash and brush-up, he returned to find Charlotte lying on the bed in her full, naked glory. She smiled, and held out her arms to him.

'Good morning. I've put the "Do Not Disturb" sign on the door, honey. Come and disturb me.'

Two hours later; Gil Callaghan had sneaked back to his room to make it look as though someone had actually slept in it, and Charlotte was dressing when the club orderly came around knocking on doors and rousing the occupants. She put the finishing touches to her make-up and stepped out into the corridor. Gil Callaghan was just coming out of his room. For the benefit of the other people in the corridor, she walked up to him and said,

'Good morning, Staff Sergeant. Did you sleep well?'

He drew himself up… almost to attention.

'Very comfortably. Thank you, Ma'am. Were your quarters satisfactory?'

She nodded.

'Very satisfactory, thank you Staff Sergeant. Would you walk me down to breakfast?'

He nodded.

'My pleasure Ma'am.'

As she turned to walk with him; she glanced at him from under

lowered lashes and whispered.
    'Yes, it was… and for me.'

Chapter Eight.

Sunday, 23rd October 1960.
Hickam Air Force Base. Honolulu.
Oahu.
The Hawaiian Islands.
North Pacific Ocean.

Gil Callaghan and Charlotte walked across the ramp at Hickam towards the big, streamlined, silver, and white USAF Military Air Transport Service C121 Super Constellation. Callaghan grinned.

'We're in luck, Ma'am. She's one of the fleet that service U.S. Embassies around the world. She's transiting directly to Andrews. There'll be no stopping over at Travis Air Force Base this trip. It seems it's just the crew and us.'

Charlotte glanced at him.

'A direct flight? How long will that take?' he paused and glanced at his wristwatch.

'It'll take about sixteen and a half hours. She's due out in about twenty minutes, so we'll be coming into Andrews at about 02.30, tomorrow morning. I'm afraid we'll have to sleep in the seats... this bird doesn't have the luxuries of the Stratocruiser.'

'Charlotte smiled.

'Well, if last night was anything to go by... and if there were; in all probability, we wouldn't be doing too much sleep anyway!'

Callaghan grinned.

'You're probably right, Ma'am.'

He paused, and a thoughtful expression appeared on his face.

'What happens with us when we get back to Foggy Bottom?'

She smiled softly.

'Let's wait and see, shall we?... And I don't think you need to call me "Ma'am" any more... unless we have official company!'

113

Charlotte sat with Gil Callaghan in the otherwise empty cabin of the Constellation looking out of the window with rising consternation at the spectacle of the engine starts. She knew, from her flight in the Stratocruiser, that these radial engines blew smoke on start-up, but the display unfolding with the starting of the port engines was in a completely different league. The lengthy turning over of the propeller and the subsequent belching of smoke and long tails of flame from the exhaust pipes was disconcerting to say the least. The engine started whining, then spluttered and banged for some time until it picked up with a reassuring roar. Callaghan grinned.

'Don't worry. These birds are famous for this sort of thing. It's completely normal. With these engines, they can turn over the motors without having the spark plugs working. This is to get oil moving out of the bottom cylinders... see how many times the propeller turned over before the engine fired up? All that time it was sucking in fuel and not burning it.

When they finally turned on the mags, the spark plugs came live and the engine started. The smoke and flame are down to the engine pumping out all that unburnt fuel, as well as some oil burn-off that has collected in the lower cylinders. They don't call her the oily bird for nothing!'

Eventually, with all four engines running, and the whole fuselage vibrating gently; the pilot guided the Constellation away from the ramp out to the runway, ready for engine run-up. He braked to a standstill and ran the engines up to full power, one by one, then taxied onto the runway and lined up for takeoff. The thin whine of hydraulics penetrated the cabin as he set the flaps; the engine roar increased, and with a gentle jolt, the brakes were released and the big, streamlined airplane began rolling down the runway. The airplane accelerated quickly, past airport buildings and parked aircraft; the nose lifted, followed by a couple of jolts as the big airplane gained buoyancy and airspeed; and the runway receded as it rose smoothly with the engines roaring at full power, with long blue flames streaming from the exhausts. Climbing out over Mamala Bay away from the heat rising from the land, the airplane settled slightly as it sped out over the cooler ocean.

It took about forty minutes to reach the Constellation's cruising altitude of twenty thousand feet. Looking out of the cabin window, Charlotte gazed down on the Pacific. It resembled an unbroken azure-blue carpet, merging seamlessly with the sky. She looked around the spacious cabin interior. It included a full-size airline-style galley forward of the two washrooms and toilet cubicles, all of which were located at the rear of the cabin; two original sleeper berths on the port side, ahead of the galley area; and the first-class section in which they were sitting at the rear of the fuselage just behind the wings, was equipped with full size seats and large tables.

Callaghan grinned as he pointed to the sleeper berths.

'OK, so I was wrong. We won't have to sleep in the seats after all!'

Charlotte raised an eyebrow.

'Yes; it'll be one bunk each... so don't go getting any cute ideas about sharing on this trip. You'll just have to wait until we get back home.'

Callaghan made a sad face and thrust out his lower lip; then a slow smile spread across his face.

'When we get home?'

Charlotte gave him an admonishing stare.

'Down boy. Let's see what they have arranged for us at Foggy Bottom.'

5.25pm. Sunday, 23rd October 1960.
Western seaboard north of Monterey Bay.
California. USA.

Callaghan pointed out of the cabin window towards a thin, gray-green smudge on the horizon barely visible in the early evening light.

'Look! Out there; the good old US of A!'

Charlotte peered out across the wing in the direction that he had indicated. Sure enough; a distinct line had appeared on the distant horizon. She glanced at her wristwatch. Almost half past five. She felt her ears begin to block as the Constellation started its fifty-mile descent towards the western coastline of Northern California. Callaghan stood up.

'We should be coming in over the Santa Cruz Mountains just south of San José before too long. You should be able to see San Francisco Bay over to the north. Fancy a bite to eat and a coffee? I'll go see what I can rustle up in the galley.'

By the time Callaghan returned, they had crossed the coastline slightly farther north than he had supposed... at Año Nuevo Bay. As he handed her a plate of ham sandwiches and a cup of coffee, they were crossing the Santa Cruz Mountains and she noticed that the extensive sprawl of San José and San Francisco Bay were obscured by a pall of haze hanging over the suburbs like a great, off-white blanket. The Santa Clara valley opened up below sliced through with the thin line of US Highway 101 running down its length... a ribbon that sparkled and flashed as the sun caught the scurrying tiny automobiles of the commuters hurrying home.

The valley gave way to the heavily wooded sculpture of the lower slopes of the Sierra Nevada Mountains, which, in turn, faded to the snowy shoulders of the higher peaks as the Constellation sped over them at twenty thousand feet. There was a little turbulence rising from the mountains, but it wasn't a big deal. The Captain turned on the seat belt sign which remained illuminated for twenty or so minutes; however, what bumps there were, were not particularly uncomfortable.

The east slope of the steep Sierra Escarpment range fell away and the southern edge of the ragged, heart-shaped Great Basin Desert of Nevada began to spread out off to the left of their flight path. It was a harsh expanse of dry desert and high mountains between Utah's Wasatch Range... the western edge of the greater Rocky Mountains and the Sierra Nevada; extending into western Utah, and parts of Idaho, south-eastern Oregon, and Wyoming; Callaghan remarked that it covered roughly two hundred thousand square miles, almost one-fifth of the West. He said that he had seen aerial photographs taken at night, which showed the bright lights of Las Vegas, Reno, and Salt Lake City. In between them was a vast, black hole. That was the Great Basin; an immense emptiness in the heart of the West. He continued; saying that many considered this area to be little more than "fly-over" country... a dreary, dry, empty expanse of sagebrush, and nothing much else. Most people would be wrong. The Great Basin contained all manner of fascinating sights... recent volcanoes, earthquake activity and faults, deep trenches such as Death Valley, ancient, dried-up rivers, and fossil sand dunes; as well as canyons and badlands. The pity was; that up here at twenty thousand feet, it all looked brown; with odd patches of green, and snow on the highest mountain ridges.

Callaghan checked his watch... a quarter to seven. The few light clouds in the sky were just beginning to hint at pink and gold. He glanced out of the cabin window.

'We'll soon be crossing into Utah. You just might be able to see The Great Salt Lake over to the north. It'll be about a hundred miles away from our flight path. It just depends on how much cloud there is up there.'

Charlotte smiled.

'Maybe we'd be better if we settled down to get some sleep instead of sightseeing. If it's two-thirty in the morning when we arrive at

Andrews, then it's going to be a long day tomorrow. They'll want us to get up to Foggy Bottom right away for debriefing, and then there will be all the arrangements for accommodation and redeployment to deal with.'

Callaghan nodded.

'I suppose you're right. What's it to be, then? Sleeper seats or bunk?'

She smiled.

'Nice try, big boy! With those guys up front, it's "bunks" with an "S". There'll be plenty of time for fooling around when we get home.'

Callaghan grinned.

'Who said I was fooling around? I want us to be much more than just that.'

She smiled again.

'Good answer, Callaghan. Not bad... not bad at all.'

2 am. Monday, 24th October 1960.
Approaching the Appalachian Mountains,
West Virginia.
USA.

A gentle hand on her shoulder woke Charlotte with a start from a strange dream in which she was being pursued by someone... or something she could not see; through a labyrinth of narrow, shabbily varnished, wood-clad passages lit with flickering candle lamps, which resembled a mine shaft, but was not a mineshaft. The floor was planked; rising and falling without any logical progression. The passage was dark and twisting; the low roof... also clad in planks, was supported by large, rough-hewn timber beams. At intervals; withered old men dressed in shabby, turn-of the-century clothes, sat at grimy desks and tables continually shuffling reams of dog-eared, yellowing papers, and paying no attention to her passing. It was like something out of a Dickensian novel. What the hell it meant was anybody's guess.

Gil Callaghan stood by her bunk and smiled down at her.

'Good morning, Ma'am. It's time to get up. We're half an hour out of Andrews.'

The familiar drone of the airplane's engines allayed her sleepy anxiety, and gathering her thoughts, she gave Callaghan a quizzical look.

'We're very formal this morning, Callaghan.'

He nodded towards the galley aft of the sleeping bunk area and gave her a wry smile. Following his gaze, she saw that it was occupied by one of the crew members making coffee. She nodded,

Thank you, Staff Sergeant. Where are we?'

Callaghan glanced back at the crewman for confirmation of her question. The young airman paused from pouring the coffee,

'Good morning Ma'am; Good morning, Staff Sergeant. We're just passing Clarksburg, West Virginia, Ma'am. If you look out of the window, you'll see the lights of Pittsburgh, Pennsylvania out on the port quarter. Would you care for a coffee, whilst I'm making it?'

Charlotte smiled and nodded. Callaghan moved back to the galley to pour each of them a cup whilst the airman moved back along the fuselage to the flight deck with cups for the crew. She pulled back the cabin window curtain and gazed out across the port wing. In the distance, was a faint glow, lighting the few scattered clouds from below. Those must be the lights of Pittsburgh. At twenty thousand feet, dawn was beginning to break; a faint grey, merging into pink, pearly light was visible on the eastern horizon. Below; there was still darkness. There were few clouds in the area they were flying though; but there was little to see; and what there might have been was obscured by the gentle flare of the spears of pale blue flames emanating from the engines' exhausts and reflecting back from the underside of the wing.

As the airplane banked on its final heading she saw out of the cabin window that the vast carpet of darkness was sprinkled with a scattering of distant, faint lights from the far-flung townships across the immense, thinly populated tracts of West Virginia and to the north; Pennsylvania. Callaghan returned with the coffee. He smiled.

'Here; it's good coffee. Sorry about the formal wake-up, but I figured that it's bad manners to compromise a Captain's rank in front of enlisted airmen. Now I'll do it properly.'

He glanced along the fuselage. The airman had disappeared into the cockpit and closed the door. He knelt beside her bunk and made to kiss her. She pushed him back.

'God... No, Callaghan! I've got yuck mouth from breathing pressurised air all night. At least let me brush my teeth first! Besides which; how can you want to, with me looking like this?... all black, raccoon-eyes and Bride of Frankenstein hair?'

He grinned.

'That, baby, is what love is all about.'

The Constellation came in down the twenty-mile wide corridor between Washington DC and Baltimore with her engines throttled back, on inbound approach to Andrews Air Force Base. The floor of the cabin deck shuddered slightly as the undercarriage went down and locked in. There was a final short burst of power to lift them over the threshold, and hardly a bump as the wheels touched down, before the final roar of the propellers as the pilot selected reverse pitch. The Constellation slowed and turned off the main runway along the southern taxiway; coming to a standstill on the south ramp. The young airman came back down the fuselage aisle and opened the passenger door. The landing steps had already been brought up. Callaghan left the airplane first, followed by Charlotte. She noticed that the airplane parked well away from the main buildings. Two Air Police jeeps were drawn up alongside, with a group of officers waiting for them to embark from the airplane. Callaghan handed some documents to a white-helmeted officer wearing Captain's bars. The officer inspected and returned the documents with a salute.

There would be no customs inspection today. The immigration officers were already in the first police jeep which was slowly disappearing back towards the administration buildings to the north. The Air Police Captain accompanied Callaghan and Charlotte off the ramp and led them to a side entrance of the nearest hangar where two men were waiting. Both were wearing black suits, black ties, and black sunglasses even though it was only 3am in the morning. They really couldn't have done any more to advertise that they were spooks, if they had tried.

The taller of the two spoke.

'Captain Mckenna, Agent Callaghan; welcome home. Your ride to Foggy Bottom awaits.'

He motioned to a side door with all the wit and charm that went with the typical coldness of a spook. Their sparse luggage was brought round and they were taken to the side door and out to where a black Lincoln Continental was waiting, its engine purring and the blinds in the rear window pulled down.

As the car swept away towards the north gate of Andrews in the half-light of dawn; only a thin haze from the city softened the glare of the lights across the air base. The taller of the two spooks turned and spoke.

'We are to take you both direct to Foggy Bottom on the orders of the Director, Ma'am.'

Charlotte nodded.

'Thank you, Agent...?'

The man merely gave a thin smile and turned back in his seat.

At the north gate, the driver turned right and drove up to Pennsylvania Avenue, where he turned left for the drive up through the suburbs towards downtown Washington.

There was little traffic this early in the morning, and the driver made good time. As they came down to the long, sweeping "S" between the suburbs of Dupont Park and Randike Highlands, most of the houses on the outskirts still slept, while others appeared to be just waking, with lights coming on. Now, they were coming away from the suburbs and approaching Washington proper. The black Lincoln swept across John Philip Sousa Bridge... named after the famed conductor and composer of patriotic marches, spanning the Anacostia River. They would soon see the vast white dome of the Capitol Building through the trees lining the Avenue. Charlotte smiled to herself. This was the same route that Josie Pullen had taken all those years ago, when Charlotte had first arrived in the United States.

The Lincoln turned off Pennsylvania Avenue, past the imposing Library of Congress, and sped down Independence Avenue; with the massive Capitol building looming on the right through the trees. Just beyond the splendid Neo-Classical, Revival-style House of Representatives; the black Lincoln turned hard right onto 1st Street S, and accelerated up towards the substantial President James Abram Garfield statue. Behind his monument; the Capitol Building rose in splendid majesty across the wide, green expanse to the right of the road. The driver didn't slow, but continued at speed along to the extension of Pennsylvania Avenue, which merged with Constitution Avenue NW; and then turned left onto Constitution Avenue NW, proper. The broad Avenue was also lined with dramatic buildings that flashed past as the Lincoln accelerated through the early morning traffic. The buildings thinned out; to be replaced by open parkland.

Across to the right; in the distance; The White House came into view, while, to her left; the huge obelisk of The Washington Monument built to commemorate the first U.S. president, General George Washington rose grandly into the early-morning sky. A little farther on, they passed the Constitution gardens, and through the trees, could be seen the glitter of the reflecting pool and The Lincoln Memorial. The driver made a sharp turn to the right, into E 23rd Street NW, and drove half-way along the street; then turned into the drive of an imposing building complex at number 2430. There were no guards, no check-points... nothing. The car drove around to the grassed square in the centre of the compound and stopped outside a long, two storey building lined with Doric pillars along its entire frontage. The driver climbed out of the driving seat and opened the rear door for them. They were there.

The complex consisted of four buildings, including the Central Administration Building which had contained the office of William Donovan, the O.S.S. chief when Charlotte had arrived there for the first time in 1945 after her flight out of Germany. The North, Central, and South buildings didn't look any different to those she remembered.

Charlotte and Callaghan walked from the car up the wide flight of stone steps of the central building to the large entrance door surmounted by a towering white Doric pediment supported by pillars spaced across the front of the building. Inside the large, marble-floored entrance hall, a handsome young man with a military-style haircut; and wearing a dark civilian suit, stood from behind his polished reception desk, smiled amiably; and addressed her.

'Welcome home, Captain Mckenna; Agent Callaghan. Director Dulles will see you now.'

The Director of Central Intelligence occupied a modest office. There was nothing ostentatious about it... an ordinary desk, a few comfortable armchairs, and the obligatory flag... artistically draped as they always were; in the corner. Director Dulles also portrayed a modest appearance. Grey-haired, with a trim moustache, and wearing thin-rimmed spectacles with round lenses; behind which, his grey eyes held an avuncular twinkle... giving him the appearance of a friendly favourite uncle. He put down the pipe he was smoking; closed the thin file that he had been studying, which confirmed Charlotte Mckenna as being a brilliant covert operations officer; but also something of a maverick who constantly twisted the rules to her own ends; and invited them to sit. He opened a buff file on his desk and scanned the first page. He studied Charlotte over the top of his glasses.

'Your reports out of P'yŏngyang have been of significant advantage; both to us, and to the South Korean Intelligence Service. You are to be congratulated, Miss Mckenna.'

Charlotte was puzzled. Why did Dulles not use her rank title? This was the first time that anyone in the Company had used a civilian title when addressing her.

Dulles had noted her reaction and smiled in his unfailingly friendly manner.

'You may wonder why I did not address you as Captain. As of now; both you and Mr Callaghan no longer retain a quasi-military title. You are now Specialized Skills Officers and I am sending you on what may turn out to be one of the most significant operations of the entire cold war.'

Charlotte glanced at Callaghan, who gave an imperceptible shrug. Dulles continued.

'As you may be aware; the situation in Europe is becoming dangerous. Two years ago; the Soviet Premier Khrushchev delivered a speech in which he demanded that the Western powers of the United States, Great Britain, and France pull their forces out of West Berlin within six months. This ultimatum has developed into a crisis over the future of the city of Berlin. We are about to enter a Presidential election, and the incumbent President, Dwight D. Eisenhower, is not eligible to run again. All the signs are that the Democrats' nominated candidate, John F. Kennedy; the Senator from Massachusetts will win. If he does, I don't think he's the man to take crap from the Russians. I'm sending you into Berlin as a team. Berlin station will brief you when you arrive.'

He closed the folder and leaned back in his chair.

'I'm sorry that this is so sudden, but it is imperative you get into Berlin as soon as possible. Take a couple of days to unwind, and we'll send a car for you Thursday morning. I've arranged for an apartment to be prepared at the Riggs Street address for you. Now, Callaghan; would you mind waiting outside, whilst I complete my conversation with Miss Mckenna?'

Callaghan nodded, rose, and left the room. Dulles leaned forward.

'I was so sorry to hear about the loss of Max Segal, Charlotte. I know that you and he were significant to each other. I have Presidential agreement that he is to be interred at Arlington. It's the very least that a grateful nation can do for him.

Charlotte nodded sadly.

'Thank you, Director. He would have liked that... and I will always know where he is.'

The car arrived promptly outside the apartment complex on Riggs Street at six-thirty pm to take them to Andrews Air Force Base for their flight to Europe. The airplane was a Douglas C-118A Liftmaster ... the military variant of the DC-7 four-engined, prop airplane. It was a night flight full of all Army and Air Force ranks and dependents of all ages-wives, kids, and babies, flying to Frankfurt am Main, Germany; stopping at Gander Airport in Newfoundland, and Shannon in County Clare, Ireland for refuelling.

The airplane landed at Gander just after ten pm. The refuelling would take about half an hour. The futuristic terminal was filled with pretentious avant-garde art and furniture, but the coffee was good. The next leg of the track was across the Atlantic Ocean to Shannon. The Captain announced that there would be tailwinds of anything up to one hundred knots, and because of this; the Atlantic crossing would take something approaching five and a half hours, whereas, going in the opposite direction, it might take an east to west flight seven hours. They would probably be landing at Shannon at around 6am the following morning.

The Liftmaster taxied out to the runway and turned her nose into the south for the rush down the long north-south runway. With the engines roaring at full power she sped down the ten thousand feet of asphalt ribbon and soared into the blackness of the night sky, with blue flames gouting from the engine exhausts in exactly the same way that the Constellation had done during Charlotte's trans-Pacific flight.

Five hours later, the Liftmaster began its ten-mile descent into Ireland. As it crossed the coast, the clouds broke up revealing the dark mass of the Loop Head peninsula... the south-westerly tip of County Clare; with nothing but a lighthouse beam's penetrating gaze sweeping out and spearing through the darkness across the western approaches to the Shannon estuary. Slowly, the darkness began to be flecked with pinpoints of light from the scattered, dwellings; the swinging headlight beams of early-morning cars on the lanes and roads, and at last, in the distance, the blinking green-and-white identification beacon of Shannon airport.

The Seat belts and No Smoking signs flashed on and below; the bright red and gold of the approach lighting rushed beneath them. With a gentle bump and a squeal of rubber the Liftmaster touched down between the brilliant blue ground-lights which blurred past as the airplane rushed down the runway; slowing as the pilot braked and applied reverse pitch to the propellers. With the blue lights now drifting past; the airplane turned from the runway and trundled to the brightly-lit terminal.

Whilst they refuelled and checked the airplane, there was time for a quick bite to eat. Charlotte and Callaghan tried the Cod and chips. They were surprised to find that British and Irish chips were significantly thicker than the American-style French fries; and the fish was coated in a light, golden-fried batter. Salt and vinegar were sprinkled liberally over the meal which was eaten with a fork, although they noticed that many of the locals merely used their fingers.

With the meal consumed, they each ordered an "Irish Coffee"... hot coffee laced with Irish whisky and topped with half an inch of thick, fresh cream; and served in impressive, stemmed glass goblets with a small finger handle moulded to the stem. Following this, there was time to wander around the souvenir shop easily resisting the non-existent impulse to purchase any of the "Genuine Irish Trinkets" on display. Somehow, *"Connemara Marble Bead Rosaries," "Miniature Irish Bog-Oak Harps,"* and *"Genuine Brass Leprechauns"* didn't quite fit into what might be awaiting them in Berlin.

Their mild amusement at these tasteless, gimcrack artefacts was interrupted by an announcement over the loudspeakers in a thick Irish brogue, in which only the words "Frankfurt" and "Boarding" were intelligible; that their flight was ready to leave.

8.30 am. Tuesday, 25th October 1960.
Frankfurt Airbase.
Rheinisch Hessen.
Federal Republic of Germany

The Liftmaster touched down at Frankfurt in gusting rain. Charlotte and Callaghan were met by a local CIA operative who identified, and introduced himself as Vern Madsen. He explained that the connecting flight to Berlin was delayed by a storm front tracking up across the Hartz Mountains, and that he had arranged rooms for them on the Air Base. He said that there were three alternative methods by which they could get to Berlin… by flying, driving or taking the "duty train." The duty train was made up of two or three cars belonging to, and operated by the U.S. Army; attached to a German train. It ran from the Haupbahnhof in Frankfurt in the West to Berlin in the East. Both of these alternatives necessitated transit through the hundred-mile-long corridor in the Soviet Zone of the German Democratic Republic… which was not the brightest idea… considering who they were. Consequently, they would be flying. The accommodation was in the Air Force "Motel" on the base. Charlotte and Callaghan were given adjoining rooms furnished in the usual spartan military fashion. Food was available in the Officer's Club. After a half-decent rib-eye steak, there was little to do except wander around the base, for the rest of the day and explore the terminal building of the adjoining Flughafen Frankfurt am Main, the chief commercial airport for the greater Frankfurt area, which was situated on the north side of the complex.

After a few drinks in the Officer's Club, Charlotte and Callaghan decided that an early night might be a good idea in view of the lengthy trans-Atlantic flight they had experienced. The room allocated to Charlotte was cold. The window faced east, and already, the wintery chill that always swept across Europe from the Ural Mountains at this time of year was causing the temperatures across Germany and Poland to drop rapidly. She undressed and slipped naked, between the chilly sheets. Had Callaghan taken the hint? Would he come to her room when the motel had quietened down?

She waited, with the sheets and blankets pulled up to her chin for almost half an hour before she heard the soft click of the door handle being turned as Callaghan slipped quietly into her room. She sniffed.

'Damn you, Callaghan; you took your time.'

The bed dipped as Callaghan slipped under the covers beside her and wrapped her in his arms.

'Sorry, baby. There were two passengers chatting out in the corridor by your door. I thought they'd never leave. Shall I go and lock the door?'

'No, it's cold out there. If you move the blankets, you'll let in the cold air.'

He grinned, pulling her into his arms.

'I could always warm you up.'

She pulled him on top of her.

'Don't just talk about it, Callaghan... do it!'

He nodded, pulling her head back to kiss her gently on the lips, and then kissed his way down her body, taking a nipple in his mouth as she arched against him. His mouth continued its path down her body, swirling his tongue in her navel before hovering between her thighs. Her eyes fluttered open.

'Yes, Callaghan... oh, yes!'

She gasped out as he covered her with his mouth.

'Oh God.'

She ground her crutch against his mouth as his tongue circled her and she began to tremble with her arousal building. He slipped a finger into her, stroking gently as she tightened around him. She wound her fingers in his hair, trying to pull him up. Slipping his fingers deep inside her, he sucked her into his mouth, flicking with the tip of his tongue. Her orgasm broke instantly, washing over her like some unstoppable tidal wave crashing onto the shore.

He gently kissed his way back up her body to kiss her on her lips.

'I love you Charlotte Mckenna.'

He whispered as she rode the last lappings of the wave that had engulfed her, and her eyes fluttered open with a tiny sated smile upon her lips.

'Mmm'

She moaned; before wrapping her legs around his waist, and rolling him over so that she straddled his hips. She stroked him gently;

smiling as her touch hardened him against her belly. She settled herself over his hips and he could feel the wetness of her arousal against his lower belly as she leaned down to kiss him. Her hands guided him into her, as she sank onto him. She gave a sharp gasp of pleasure as she rocked against him.

'I love you too, Alex Callaghan.'

She whispered as she raised herself nearly off of him before sinking onto him again. He clasped her hips, holding her onto him as he pulled out of her almost completely before driving back into her as she bucked and, ground her hips against him in time with his thrusts. His pace quickened as her hips rose to meet his every thrust. He leaned forward, kissing and nibbling the skin of her throat, and she gasped with pleasure. They fucked each other as if it was their last night on Earth, as if they'd never feel the touch of another person again; as if the world was burning around them and they didn't care.

When they were both close, he clasped her hips tighter and began thrusting fiercely into her. The change angled them perfectly, and she came hard, clenching around him as he thrust twice more before coming deep inside her, as she came again. She wrapped her legs around his hips, keeping him inside of her, unwilling to release him. He lay on his back and wrapped his arms around her. She settled against him, her head on his chest, and her arms around his waist. He pulled the discarded sheets and blankets around them as they drifted into a warm, sated sleep.

Callaghan woke in the early hours as the predawn light crept through the curtain that was pulled across the window of the room. He was on his back, naked, and Charlotte lay on top of him with her head nestled in his arm, in more or less the position in which they'd fallen asleep. He felt the delicious softness of her breasts pressing against his chest and thought it would be so easy to wake her and start all over again, but he didn't move; she looked so peaceful, and he could feel her heartbeat gently pulsing on his chest. God, she was beautiful, and he was the luckiest man in the world.

After breakfast in the Officers' Club; an orderly came and asked them to get ready to take the courier flight to Tempelhof Air Base in Berlin. Their airplane was, as expected, one of the famous wartime "Gooney Birds," a Douglas DC-3 or in military terms, a C-47 Skytrain. The best deal on this particular flight would be cold, metal bucket seats and coffee from a thermos flask. Charlotte smiled. The last one of this type of airplane she had flown on was the Russian license-built version of the DC-3 Skytrain that the CIA had used for covert operations out of Osan Air base in South Korea, and in which she had been inserted into North Korea. It was just as noisy and uncomfortable as she remembered. Fortunately, the flight down the Berlin southern corridor would only take about one and three-quarter hours. She just hoped that the storm front which had delayed them had moved through by now.

The young Loadmaster... a first-term airman, by the look of him; advised them to remain buckled up for the flight. He explained that The Soviets were trying to institute new restrictions on flights approaching the city while allowing their fighters to buzz allied airplanes flying through approved access corridors. They were attempting to limit Western Allies traffic use of the Berlin corridors to altitudes of between two thousand, five hundred, and ten thousand feet. That was why they were flying in a Gooney; the jet and turbo-prop airplanes needed to use a higher altitude.

He said that, five months previously, Soviet fighter airplanes had forced down an American C-47 transport that had strayed off-course on a flight from Copenhagen to Hamburg. Although the airplane and its crew were released a few days later, the incident had really heightened the tension for pilots flying the Berlin routes.

The flight was uneventful... different, but uneventful. Approximately five to ten minutes before landing; as the airplane began its descent, the lakes around Potsdam, and the city, itself became visible just to the left. Several familiar landmarks in the city of Berlin came into view... the Funkturm... the large radio tower near the stadium built for the 1936 Olympics; the Brandenburg Gate... now a checkpoint between the British and Soviet Sectors. The final leg of the approach took them out over the East Berlin border. The massive Soviet monument in Treptower Park... half as high again as the Statue of Liberty, built to commemorate all Russian Troops lost in the Battle of Berlin towered in the distance as the Skytrain banked steeply over Marx-Engels Platz; the renamed square on the Museum Island in the middle of what had once been central Berlin; and that Charlotte had known as Der Schlossplatz; and turned south towards Tempelhof.

The final flight path into Tempelhof was flanked by the five-storey apartment blocks of the western fringe of Neukölln district. The approach was turbulent, and the Skytrain pilot descended very quickly... the so-called "Tempelhof landing"... whereby, due to the restricted runway length, airplanes touched down with a high-nose altitude and were held nose-high until the engines were throttled back.

This caused the wing to act as an airbrake and use of the wheel brakes was cut to a minimum.

From the air, the sprawling airport cut an oval-shaped basin out of the south-west suburbs of Berlin. The huge concrete apron in front of the immense terminal's long sweeping curve... eight storeys high, with at least three levels beneath ground; and laid out in the shape of an enormous Nazi eagle, with a wingspan of over a mile; merged with a broad, oval swathe of grass encircled by a wide taxiway. The enclosed grass was bisected by two runways running east to west, and the whole airport was surrounded by misty silhouettes of apartment blocks, factory chimneys, and ancient church steeples.

The Skytrain touched down on the southern runway and taxied right up to the building, halting beneath the huge, cantilevered canopy that ran the entire length of the massive, mile-long quadrant containing the hangars and the terminal facilities, and which sheltered the disembarking passengers from the weather. Charlotte and Callaghan descended portable stairs, which had been brought up to the airplane, to be met by a middle-aged man in a dark suit pretending to be invisible behind a pair of "Made in Saigon" mirrored lenses. He identified himself as Emerson Gilley from the Berlin Office, and pointed along the massive hardstanding beyond the Air France Caravelle jet and the BEA Viscount turboprop disgorging their passengers; towards a Pan American DC-6 surrounded by a crowd of journalists, and smiled.

'Great timing! They're all occupied by the arrival of the movie actress, Romy Schneider. We'll disappear through hangar five and miss the circus through customs controls to the reception hall. We have a car waiting outside.'

They walked across the concrete ramp to hangar two. Inside, leading off from the huge space it was an endless maze of dark halls, stairways, anonymous doors, and brief detours out into the other hangars, which used to house the fighters of the German Luftwaffe. There was an atmosphere here; a cold, ominous, spine-chilling feeling.

Gilley remarked that the SS troops had made a final stand at Tempelhof, during the last days of the Battle of Berlin. They offered stiff resistance to the Red Army troops in the labyrinthine Tempelhof structure. After two days of heavy fighting; two of the five layers of the underground redoubt under Tempelhof were cleared by the Red Army... and the remaining levels had been simply flooded in the end to drown the remaining defenders. There was thought to be literally tons of old explosives, munitions and booby traps still down there in the flooded labyrinths... not to mention the remains of those who were trapped and drowned. They would probably never be cleared, and had been sealed up by the American forces when they occupied the complex. These forsaken victims were said to haunt the halls and crevices of Tempelhof. Charlotte repressed a cold shudder, and quickly followed Gilley to the exit.

By the time they reached the hallway through the women's barracks in Hangar Two of the east wing they were breathing through their mouths, trying to keep the putrid air from entering their noses and making their stomachs heave. Gilley said it was a problem with the plumbing. Apparently, the old pipes just couldn't take it anymore and sewage was backing up into the women's showers.

Outside in the Platz der Luftbrücke, a black government-issue Chrysler sedan was waiting. Settling themselves in the rear seat, the car swept out onto Tempelhofer Damm and travelled south through the Tempelhof suburb, then turned right into Friedrich Karl Strasse. Charlotte was surprised. This street had been named Lothar Erdmann Strasse when she had last been in this area. How many more street names had been changed... and for what reason? The car took the south-western exit from the Platz into what was now called Attilastrasse. She shook her head quietly. This street had also had its name changed. She remembered it as being Kurt Eisner Strasse.

This part of Berlin had not been damaged by bombs to such an extent as other parts of Berlin, and it was still possible to get an impression of what Berlin's nineteenth-century architecture had looked like. When she had left in 1945, most of Berlin was little more than an expanse of ruins. Almost half of the city's buildings had been completely destroyed. Although much of Berlin's rubble of war had been cleared and most of the demolished buildings rebuilt; out here... save for the odd bomb site, it appeared to have changed very little since she had travelled to and from the old O.S.S. Berlin Operations Base in Föhrenweg back in the late Forties.

Emerson Gilley turned in his seat as the driver turned into Steglitz Damm.

'Not too far, now. We just have to cross through Dahlem via Albrechtstrasse, Grunewaldstrasse, and Königin-Luise-Strasse; then it's up Clayallee to the U.S. headquarters compound. That's where you and Agent Callaghan will be brought up to date with what's going on around here.'

Charlotte nodded. Clayallee?... She'd never heard of that one. Gilley smiled.

'You probably knew it as Kronprinzenallee, during your time at

BOB. They changed the name on June the First, 1949 in honour of the U.S. military governor of the American occupation zone in Germany... General Clay; the "father" of the Berlin Airlift.'

Chapter Nine

The Berlin Operations Base was located in the grounds of U.S. Army headquarters complex on the north-east corner of the Clayallee/Saargemünder Strasse junction. The huge, gated complex of two-storey stone buildings were built in 1938 as a barracks and administrative headquarters for "Luftgaukommando III" which coordinated air defence in the region stretching from Berlin to Frankfurt-Oder in the east, and Dresden in the south. In 1943, when the seven Luftwaffe air defence districts were consolidated into one central command, the compound became the headquarters for the air defence of the whole of Germany; reporting directly to Hermann Göring. In 1945, the U.S. Army confiscated the facility, which hadn't suffered too much damage in Allied bombing, and the military government, headed by Eisenhower, established itself there. Ten years later, the relatively new Central Intelligence Agency needed offices for its expanding Berlin operations based in Föhrenweg and had been allocated a building in the compound.

The driver turned the black Chrysler sedan off Clayallee at the entrance to the U.S. headquarters compound and stopped at the sentry station building on the left, behind the large entrance gates. Gilley flashed a security pass to the MP Corporal and was immediately admitted. The driver drove up the tree-lined driveway that led directly to the portal of the main headquarters building, and stopped outside. Gilley led them into the building past the reception desk and into the main hallway.

Head of Station's office in this grandiose Teutonic bastion was something of an anti-climax. It was a smallish room, sparsely furnished with utilitarian military furniture, and dominated by a large, plain, beechwood desk, behind which, a man in his mid-thirties; wearing black-framed, Buddy Holly-style spectacles and unassuming

131

civilian clothes, glanced up as Charlotte and Callaghan were shown into his presence. He gave them a thin smile.

'Welcome back to Berlin, Captain Mckenna. You'll find things are run a little differently these days to the way that Washburn ran BOB.'

He glanced at Callaghan.

'We won't need you, Staff Sergeant Callaghan. As of now, you are attached to the cypher section. Gilley will show you the way down.'

Callaghan glanced at Charlotte. He saw her face tighten imperceptibly, and watched; fascinated, as any trace of warmth in her eyes vanished... as though someone had suddenly thrown a light switch. Head of Station either didn't, or chose not to notice her sudden change of demeanour. He paused momentarily to draw breath, and then opened his mouth to continue his pronouncement.

Charlotte cut in. Her voice held a portentous, icy edge.

'Mr Murphy; as you are fully aware, we are not just two more pawns in your private chess tournament between CIA Station Berlin, and the KGB at Karlshorst.'

She knew his type. She had met far too many of them during her days in Washington... Yale men who imagined themselves to be real smooth operators. She regarded them all as pretentious, Ivy League assholes who justified their superiority complexes by conjuring up images of Uncle Sam and soaring eagles, or some shit like that; when they wanted to make a point.

David Murphy gave her a shocked look. No one in the CIA Berlin Station had ever been permitted to use his real name. None of his CIA officers were ever permitted to refer to CIA Berlin Station by any other name than Clayallee.

He was Head of Station, for Chrissakes. In his rigid, authoritarian empire, when he spoke, they all jumped; and this bloody woman was effectively ignoring him. Before he could say anything, Charlotte continued.

'I am attached to Berlin for a specific operation on the direct orders of Director Dulles. Mr Callaghan is my support officer for the Internal operation that I am instructed to expedite. This operation is on a rigid "need to know" collocation, and you do not need to know. All I require from you is logistic support.'

She stood up and leaned on Head of Station's desk.

'My team is not covert; we are low-profile, and wear civilian clothes so others cannot distinguish officers from NCOs, since as Special Operations Agents we all have the same authority in the field, but we don't disguise who and what we are. For this reason, we do not employ rank titles at any time, and I expect you, and your operatives to adhere to this protocol.

'Washington expects your complete cooperation, Mr Murphy. We shall relocate into the city tomorrow. For tonight, should you need to contact us; we shall be staying in the Dahlem Guest House. Good day to you, Sir.

She turned and stalked to the door, followed by Callaghan; leaving Head of Station, Berlin wondering what the hell had just blown in from Foggy Bottom.

Dahlem Guest House, Ihnestrasse 16, was located just across the road from the Officers and Civilian Club in the substantial white stone Harnack House at Ihnestrasse 19. The four-storey guest house, although post-war built, had been designed in quasi-Bauhaus style, with a frontage that curved into a full-length, ground to roof glass next to the entrance. After a trouble-free night in the comfortable reserved room and a substantial breakfast in the dining room; a car arrived to take them to the apartment that had been allocated.

The driver handed them a large manila envelope bearing the Company seal, and carrying the red-inked stamp: "Confidential." Charlotte opened it and studied the sheaf of close-typed papers. They contained information on Charlotte's and Callaghan's new Legends together with documents supporting them; relevant documents concerning their apartment, bank credentials; and a detailed briefing on their mission. She slipped the papers back into the envelope and smiled at Callaghan.

'Congratulations, "Herr Streckenbach." It seems we have been man and wife for three weeks!'

Callaghan was still looking a trifle bemused as the driver turned off the northern end of Clayallee and accelerated away up Hubertusbader Strasse that dog-legged east and then north through the Grunewald district. It was very noticeable that most of the bomb-damaged buildings out here had either been demolished or rebuilt. Berlin certainly had not wasted any time in the ensuing fourteen years since Charlotte had last been here, in re-inventing itself. What the eastern Soviet zone districts would be like was another matter. The Russians were not supposed to be very big on reconstructing the capital of their former mortal enemies. At Henrietta Platz, the driver skirted the Rosen Eck traffic island over the Stadt Autobahn bridge and accelerated up Kurfürstendamm.

Charlotte was surprised to see that there was no real sign of war damage anywhere along this broad Boulevard. It was lined with fashionable shops and cafes and thronged with people. The driver explained that in the middle to late 50's, the trend in Berlin was to tear down buildings damaged in the war and to build new. In the distance, the stark, ruined fang of the Kaiser-Wilhelm-Gedächtniskirche fire-blackened, main bell-tower spire now shared Breitscheidplatz with a towering slender rectangle of steelwork that rose almost as high as the original. The driver remarked that the old church was saved by public opinion, and the new structure was a bell tower that was being built. The car turned into Leibniz Strasse lined with a mix of traditional buildings interspersed with modern apartment blocks, and travelled north to Kant Strasse. It brought back memories to Charlotte; she had driven down this street as she escaped the final days of Berlin.

An old Schupo had advised her to take shelter in the Zoo flak tower; and when she refused, had told her to take this route out of the city. She wondered if he had managed to escape the final onslaught. She recognised the next landmark...the wide space of Savigny Platz. It was here that she had deceived the Hitler Jugend checkpoint by driving the Red Cross Sanitäts-Staffeln vehicle straight through with the Martin horn blaring and headlights blazing. She smiled quietly. She was young and stupidly brave back then.

The driver turned left immediately after Savigny Platz and drove to the end of Uhlandstrasse. He stopped outside an impressive, five-storey apartment block; turned, and handed Charlotte a key.

'Your apartment is on the third-floor, Ma'am; number twelve. Your car is in the allocated parking space over there.'

He pointed towards a. black Mercedes-Benz sedan parked on the opposite side of the street and smiled.

'It's a two-year-old, 220SE... six-cylinders and fuel-injected. "They" won't ever manage to catch you in that if you happen to get into a chase. The car keys are in the apartment. As far as the concierge is concerned, you are Herr und Frau Streckenbach, from Potsdam. You are in business as footwear agents and are opening up new market opportunities in the Soviet sector.'

The magnificent pre-war Prussian Altbau apartment block at Uhlandstrasse 192 was one of the survivors of the wartime bombing campaign. Prussian Altbau general courtyard design apartment blocks were separated by walls or fences from neighbouring courtyards, and their courtyards contained old trees, paved pathways, and beautifully tended decorative garden-beds. The apartment was reached from the entrance hall by a classical Viennese elevator, known in Germany and elsewhere as a Paternoster... an open-front continuously-moving chain of open compartments that moved slowly in a loop up and down inside a building without stopping. For those residents who preferred stairs; these flanked the paternoster's shaft. The concierge; a portly Berliner in his mid-sixties, welcomed them, and introduced himself as Herr Günsche. He gave them a quiet smile.

'Welkommen! I am officially the concierge; but also, I am the "Gatekeeper." You will not be disturbed by unwelcome guests; and your apartment will remain secure at all times.'

He turned to the paternoster.

'Could you make your own way up? I'm afraid my rheumatism is bad today. It's the Berlin weather. It is too cold and too damp; and on the few occasions that the sun does come out, you can barely see it through the smoke from the cheap coal everyone has to burn especially in East Berlin.

Fifteen years since the war ended, and it is still mostly a pile of rubble over there; and it's noisy, with four occupying armies; and something is going on every hour of the day and night, mostly things involving sirens. Fortunately, we don't get too much of that out here in Charlottenburg.'

The ride in the paternoster was strange. It needed a certain skill to step out whilst the cabinet was moving... albeit slowly. Apartment twelve was to the right. Charlotte slipped the key into the latch and opened the door.

The typical old Berlin apartment comprised four big rooms; each retaining the typical features of the late 19th century... high, stucco ceilings, wing-doors and original wooden cassette doors; and beautiful old solid oak parquetry flooring throughout. The main living area and bedroom had the original Prussian bow-top windows. The whole place was furnished with Bauhaus-style furniture which must have cost a fortune. Charlotte turned to Callaghan.

'Well, "Herr Streckenbach"; what do you think?'

Callaghan smiled.

'I think I'll be able to rough it here, "Frau Streckenbach." Let's go check out the bedroom!'

She arched an eyebrow.

'You know your trouble, Callaghan? You've got a one-track mind.'

He grinned.

So? Are you complaining?'

She turned, and walked towards the bedroom door, fully aware that Callaghan's gaze was locked onto her ass. She glanced back over her shoulder.

'Well? What are you still standing there for?'

Friday, 21st October 1960.
San Francisco International Airport.
California.
USA.

The Northwest Orient Airlines Constellation touched down at San Francisco International Airport at five minutes past six, Friday morning, after a fifteen-hour flight across the Pacific Ocean from Japan. Her mail cargo was transferred to the Customs shed where U.S. Customs Officer Douglas Conrad inspected every package for the chalk clearance marks and checked each label for evidence of contents. He gave the small package from Japan with the Korean Air freight label scarcely a second glance; the Japanese Customs blue chalk squiggle denoted that there was nothing suspicious about it. Japanese Customs checks were painstaking to the point of paranoia. The package was passed on down the Customs shed to be deposited in the secure cage awaiting the arrival of the next U.S. Postal Service truck.

Three hours later, the U.S. Postal Service truck stopped outside the elegant, bay windowed property at the top of Montgomery Street. The postman approached the front door of number 1120 and pressed the doorbell. A pretty, young oriental girl answered and accepted, and signed for the package he was delivering.

The girl closed the door and hurried to the room where an old oriental man was sitting with a book open on the table in front of him,

He looked up and smiled.

Well, daughter of my daughter's daughter; what have you there, my child?'

The girl bowed and proffered the package.

'The postman has just delivered it, honourable great-grandfather.'

The old man accepted the package and studied the labels. His lined and weathered face wrinkled into an amenable grin as he gazed at the Korean Air freight label.

'It is from your mother's sister, Su-Dae; little one. I have been anticipating its delivery.'

Chang Ho-Pyong; patriarch of the Chang criminal family of San Francisco, carefully unwrapped and opened the package. Reaching in amongst the shredded paper, his fingers closed over a smooth, cold object. Carefully, he lifted it out of its protective nest and held it up in his fingers.

The girl gasped.

'Great-grandfather; it is beautiful. What is it?'

The old man smiled benignly.

'It is a magical gem of great rarity and value; child. It is a flawless Garnet that has been brought out of the Homeland at great risk, to prevent it falling into the hands of an evil warlord. Its possession will be of great advantage to the family.'

Little Chang Soon-Ei stared, wide-eyed at the pigeon-egg-sized stone.

'A magical stone, great grandfather? What does it do?'

Chang Ho-Pyong held out the Garnet to her.

'This stone carries great reverence in Chinese beliefs, child. It is said to bestow immunity from harm or injury upon its wearer. It is also believed to attract the energy and influence of the Sun. The larger the gem, the greater is the attraction; and a Triad Dragon Lord will give great benevolence to one who presents such a stone to him.

Such beliefs also exist in out Homeland; but that is not the reason why we have possession of it. We shall use it to our advantage in the matter of manipulating the seats of power in this land of the round-eyed barbarians.'

9.15am. Saturday, 29th October 1960.
Berlin-Charlottenburg.
West Germany.

Callaghan turned the black, six-cylinder Mercedes-Benz sedan into Strasse des 17 Juni; crossed the Charlottenburger Brücke and accelerated through the partially refurbished porticoes of the Charlottenburger Tor flanking either side of the Strasse and headed down towards the Grosser Stern. The whole area of the Tiergarten presented a much more open impression than the last time Charlotte had driven down this particular Avenue into central Berlin. Most of the trees in the Tiergarten had been destroyed in the Soviet bombardment or chopped down for fuel by the surviving Berliners during those terrible days before, and after Berlin fell to the Russians The Tiergarten had been replanted after the war, but the Avenue lined with fifteen-year-old trees was nothing like the lush, towering tree-lined Boulevard that she remembered.

What was bizarre, was, that in the middle of what had been a virtual sea destruction; many of the elegant street lamps that had been designed by Albert Speer as part of Hitler's Grand design for his "Welthauptstadt Germania", and that had lined the broad Avenue, were for the most part, still standing and apparently undamaged... at least at the western end. Farther along; they had been replaced with modern lamp posts. The "Speerleuchten" were indeed elegant; designed as a slender pillar with a cruciform top bearing two opaque glass cylinders, topped with round ferruled covers. The glass cylinders appeared to be originals. How they had survived was one of war's ironies, when all around, most of Berlin had been pounded into rubble.

As Callaghan negotiated the Grosser Stern; Charlotte noted that the Siegessäule appeared to be virtually undamaged. The Statue of Victory... *"Goldelse"*... or, as the Berliners had nicknamed her... *"Golden Lizzie"* still stood shining in the sunlight almost sixty-seven metres above the roadway, and in the distance, the Brandenburger Tor loomed, apparently fully restored; topped by the Quadriga, which had been a shattered ruin when she had last seen it. The effect was somewhat marred by a substantial flagpole atop the Tor, from which, a large red flag fluttered ominously. This was supplemented by a complimentary flagpole in front of each of the Tor's flanking guard houses, from which another red flag fluttered.

A little farther on towards the Brandenburger Tor, they passed the enormous Soviet War Memorial flanked by two Russian T34 tanks mounted on plinths at either side of the entrance over to their left.

Callaghan glanced at Charlotte.

'What the hell? Are we in the Russian sector? I didn't see any signs.'

Charlotte smiled.

'No; this is still the British sector. The memorial was erected on Remembrance Day, 1945, in the hope the British would simply vacate their area and let the Soviets move their zone further into the west. Unfortunately, for them, it didn't work out that way, and so building it here put it beyond everyday reach for the Soviet Army. To be able to visit the memorial it was agreed that Red Army troops had free passage to the memorial on certain days of remembrance, and allowing a Soviet guard of honour to mount arms there. The border proper is at the Brandenburger Tor. Look! There's the warning sign coming up.'

Callaghan began to slow the Mercedes-Benz as they approached a sign attached to one of the lampposts. It proclaimed in large black letters...

Achtung!
Sie Verlassen nach
70m West-Berlin.

Which roughly translated, informed them that they would leave

West Berlin at a point seventy metres ahead... at the Brandenburger Tor itself.

Immediately in front of the west Brandenburger Tor was another sign standing peremptorily, and in splendid isolation; directly in their path. It proclaimed:

ACHTUNG!
Sie Verlassen jetze
WEST-BERLIN.

Beneath the central arch stood a grey-green uniformed Volkspolizist who raised his hand in the universal "Halt" sign. Callaghan pulled up, and flashed their passes. The young Volkspolizist saluted smartly, stepped back, and waved them on.

Beyond the Brandenburg Gate, East Berlin was another world. The vast boulevard of the Unter den Linden, still elegant, with young, re-planted Linden trees was largely deserted with wide, open spaces where the once-sumptuous buildings of Parisier Platz had stood. The Adlon had gone; great tracts of weeded wasteland had been left where substantially damaged buildings had been razed to the ground. The huge Soviet Embassy stood broodingly on one side of the wide thoroughfare. Farther along, the destruction the war had brought was still visible. Buildings stood derelict, next to empty spaces where others had been destroyed. Posters everywhere proclaimed, *"Build the Socialist Fatherland."*

Even out here; in what was once Berlin's most beautiful Boulevard, the dead hand of the Soviet zone was creating a dour transformation into an ugly, grey, concrete corpse of a once proud city. The intersecting streets of towering, two-tone, foggy grey concrete slabs stretched out along the wide boulevard of grey tarmac, almost empty; save for a few pedestrians, a scattering of cars and military vehicles; and the inevitable Volkspolizei, and uniformed Soviet soldiers. Occasionally, they passed a civilian who seemed to take more than a passing interest in the Mercedes-Benz. They were almost certainly Stasi... Ministry for State Security officers.

As they approached Marx-Engels Platz... the large, vacant space at the eastern end of Unter den Linden, where the old Imperial Palace had once stood; the decaying ruins of which had been demolished by the Communist authorities in the early fifties... Callaghan glanced at Charlotte.

'OK; so tell me. What the heck are we doing out here?... and where are we heading?'

Charlotte was silent for a moment.

'Just take the bridge to the right of the Cathedral. We're heading up through Alexanderplatz to a place in Prenzlauer Berg. I'm meeting a contact there. He sent me a message that he has uncovered something that could be very significant to our government.'

Callaghan raised an eyebrow.

'So, when were you planning to tell me this?

Charlotte smiled.

'Gil; what you don't know can't be beaten out of you. I've done this before… with the Gestapo; and the Stasi aren't all that different, by all accounts. They've taken the Gestapo's methods of extracting confessions from enemies of the state to new levels of sophistication. Torture is not just physical but psychological as well.'

Callaghan snorted.

'Bullshit! I'm no rookie spook, y'know. I can pay my way!'

Charlotte looked at him

'I know you can, Gil. I want you as a back-up I can rely on… not a dead hero or one who's been beaten to a pulp by these Commie bastards. You have to remember that East Germany really does deserve its reputation as being West Germany's evil twin.'

Callaghan said nothing and drove across the bridge into Karl Leibknecht Strasse which Charlotte remembered as being named Kaiser Wilhelm Strasse. She glanced at him.

'Oh, come on, Gil; don't be sniffy. We need to stay sharp. Take the next right into Spandauer Strasse, and turn left at the Rotes Rathaus.'

The Rotes Rathaus… the Red Town Hall; a distinct landmark in Berlin, appeared to be pristine. It had been heavily damaged by Allied bombing in World War II and rebuilt to the original plans in the early fifties. Many buildings along Rathausstrasse had survived; and many had been rebuilt. The Stadtbahn viaduct… the railway bridge leading out of Alexanderplatz Bahnhof had been repaired; but the front of the Alexanderplatz Bahnhof itself was still a gaping void, although the station had been partially re-roofed and appeared to be fully operational. Charlotte indicated that Callaghan should turn the Mercedes-Benz into the station car park. As he did so; the unobtrusive DKW saloon that had followed them from Marx-Engels Platz accelerated past, belching thick blue smoke from its straining two-stroke engine, while the two men inside turned their heads and gave the smart Mercedes-Benz cold stares in the best *"Knallharte"* tradition… the tough, almost violent quality that post-war Germany rewarded with admiring glances. As the DKW disappeared under the bridge into Alexanderplatz, Callaghan glanced at Charlotte.

'Commie spooks?'

She nodded. They were probably Stasi; just keeping an eye on these two "Wealthy West Germans." She pointed to a shabby Wartburg sedan parked at the far end of the station car park and told Callaghan to park up next to it. This was their ride into the Prenzlauer Berg district. Her contact had said this old wreck would invite less curiosity than their Mercedes-Benz. He was obviously of an excessively optimistic nature. The Wartburg was painted in a garishly obvious, bilious lime-green colour between the patches of rust, and its presence was almost impossible to ignore. Stepping out of the Mercedes-Benz, they hurried into the station, as though they were about to catch a train. The plan was that this would raise no suspicion from anyone who might be watching.

They waited for ten minutes on the draughty platform, then made their way quietly back out into the car park. The air was filled with the smell of burning coal; the odour of Communist totalitarianism. Perhaps it was just their imagination; but it was difficult to feel safe or comfortable in East Berlin. There was something threatening, menacing about the place; somehow enhanced by the pervasive, sulphurous odour of brown coal smoke… the cheap, peculiar sandy lignite used to heat most buildings in the Eastern Sector. No one seemed to be paying any attention to them as they reached the scruffy Wartburg. Callaghan moved towards the driver's side, but Charlotte caught his arm.

'Let me drive. I know the way; and a woman driving might make us look less suspicious.'

Callaghan nodded, and opened the driver's door for her. She reached up and felt under the sun visor. Her fingers touched a bunch of keys. As Callaghan climbed into the front passenger seat, she slipped the ignition key into the lock, turned the key, and the asthmatic three-cylinder, two-stroke engine burst into clattering life, belching out a huge cloud of blue smoke from the exhaust pipe which drifted lazily across the car park. Apprehensively, Callaghan glanced around. Nobody seemed to be taking the slightest notice, as Charlotte shoved the column gear stick into reverse and pulled out of the parking bay. Banging the column gearshift into first gear she drove out into Rathausstrasse, and turned left towards Alexanderplatz trailing a pretty cloud of blue smoke in time-honoured two-stroke fashion.

Once beyond the Stadtbahn viaduct, Alexanderplatz opened out before them. It bore no resemblance to the "Alex" that Charlotte remembered. The only recognisable pre-war structures were the Behrens-designed, eight-storey Alexanderhaus, and Berolinahaus flanking the entrance to the otherwise windswept wasteland. The whole of pre-war Alex had gone... the Herti department store on the corner of Alexanderstrasse, the brooding Polizeipräsidium opposite, on Dircksenstrasse; all gone. Even the spire of Georgenkirch, which had withstood the Allied bombing and the Soviet onslaught of Berlin, had been demolished. She swung the Wartburg around the oval traffic island in the middle of Alexanderplatz and accelerated away up Memhard Strasse into Münzstrasse. The damage out here was lessening. Prenzlauer Berg had not been as badly affected by the bombing and fighting in the Second World War as other parts of the city. The Soviets had fought their way into Berlin along Frankfurter Allee, which the Communists had renamed Stalin Allee some two kilometres to the east. Many of the old Scheunenviertel tenements...the turn of the century "Mietskasernen"... "Rental barracks" had been torn down.

Many had been bombed; and in their place, the ugly, grey. Stalinist "Zuckerbackerstil"... "Wedding cake style," low-cost, prefabricated concrete slab apartment blocks were being constructed. On the surviving Mietskasernen, the stucco facade ornamentation had been removed and replaced with the same flat, plaster exteriors as their post-war concrete neighbours. The jumbled wings and entire buildings had been demolished to dispel the permanent gloom of the narrow courtyards. This had exposed blank fire walls which had abutted onto adjoining properties; and seventy-foot-high rough brick walls stretching up to a hundred feet long along the property lines were common in this area. Everything was the same, smoke-stained, dingy grey-brown colour above narrow, stained, grey pavements.

It made Charlotte's skin crawl driving down the streets of East Berlin The drab sameness, the ugly council flats where the workers lived... all reminders of daily life under Communist rule. It was supposed to be their workers' paradise, but in truth it was a grey, unbeautiful excuse for a city where the ghosts of the monstrous Third Reich still lingered in the shadows of uninspiring, drab stucco blocks of flats, alongside ancient neglected, smoke-stained churches. The contrast between this place; and the colourful, vibrant West Berlin was stark.

Charlotte turned the Wartburg into Alte Schönhauser Strasse, and then turned left into Mulackstrasse and right into the short, narrow Rücker Strasse lined with original Mietskasernen. She stopped a little way inside the street and glanced at Callaghan.

'OK. This is it. Let's go, but let me do the talking.'

Callaghan nodded. The dank smell of crumbling bricks mixed with the unmistakable scent of cat piss wafted into the car as he opened the door and stepped out onto the grimy, narrow, pavement flagstones; shadowed by tenement buildings five, and six-storeys high closing in on the narrow, deep cobblestone street like two granite cliffs, linked only by dingy lines of washing stretching high above their heads. Cautiously, they approached what looked like a deserted Mietskaserne across the street. It was a desolate area, even by East Berlin standards. The shell of a house stood precariously on the corner of the block, rising out of the debris of its own wreckage. It was as though the bombs had fallen yesterday, not fifteen years earlier. An old iron gate led into a dim passageway that gave access to the first courtyard. The whole place looked as though it had been deserted since the end of the war; the windows were broken; the brickwork was crumbling, and it didn't look like there was much left of the roof.

A short flight of worn steps led to a massive weather-beaten hardwood door. Callaghan gave it a push and it moved, but not much. He put his shoulder to it and it opened a fraction more... enough for them to slip inside. Even with the door ajar it was almost pitch black, and they could feel that the floor was covered with debris... probably pieces of plaster from the ceiling and walls, some broken roof tiles, and God knows what else. Glass crunched under their feet as they took a few steps into the void. The place was goddamned eerie... anyone could be waiting in the shadows. Callaghan drew his SIG semi-automatic pistol and chambered a round. Charlotte glanced at him.

'You won't need that, Gil.'

A voice answered from the black void in front of them.

'Listen to the Lady. You are perfectly safe, and I am unarmed.'

A figure approached from the darkness, with his hands held out from his sides... palms forward. He spoke with a pronounced Russian accent.

'It's so nice to see you again, Nadia... or should I say, Charlotte?'

Callaghan glanced at her and slowly lowered his pistol. The man came closer. She gasped in complete surprise.

'Viktor? What the hell are you doing here?'

Viktor Malinovskii; who had been Second secretary at the Soviet Embassy in P'yŏngyang, North Korea when she was under deep cover as Colonel Nadia Tolenkanovna at the T17 sniper academy in P'yŏngyang; smiled amiably.

Callaghan slowly raised his pistol again, but she reached out her hand and pushed its muzzle down towards the ground.

Viktor Malinovskii smiled; a slow, knowing smile.

'Captain Charlotte Mckenna; Deep cover agent of the Central Intelligence Agency. We knew all along who you were and why you were really there. I was sorry to hear about Max Segal. He was very well thought of in Karlshorst, even after he had defected. That is why you were allowed to remain in the heart of the military administration of those crazy North Koreans. With the information we allowed you to pass back to Seoul; we both successfully kept the black channels open and probably averted a Third World War...'

He smiled.

'... and I did so enjoy the few brief times we were together.

Charlotte stared at him through the gloom.

'So, what do you want, Viktor?'

His smile faded, and he became serious.

'We have uncovered a most dangerous situation. It is my opinion that we are dealing with...'

His eyes held steadily on hers;

'... A matter of extremely high security, not only within the intelligence community; but on the highest levels of both our governments.'

Charlotte nodded. She had always suspected that Malinovskii was much more than an Embassy Second secretary.

'OK, Viktor tell me what you know.'

He hesitated and then pulled himself upright in his dark trenchcoat.

'There is a Cuban ghost buried in Berlin, on this side. He is a grave danger to both our sides.'

Charlotte stared hard at Viktor Malinovskii in the dim light.

'So what are the Stasi doing about it?' The East German Counterintelligence guys are usually extremely efficient.'

Malinovskii shrugged... a typically acquiescent, Russian shrug.

'They cannot reach him.'

Charlotte smiled.

'What about your people?'

Malinovskii shrugged again.

'If we could reach him, I wouldn't be asking for your help.'

Charlotte nodded.

'Quite a Ghost.'

Malinovskii's demeanour changed. His tone of voice became solemn.

'He is so much more dangerous than that. From what we have

learned, he is here to gather information and tradecraft in order to fulfil a specific assignment.'

Charlotte studied Malinovskii for a few moments.

'A specific assignment? For the Castro government?'

Malinovskii shook his head.

'No. For whoever is paying him.'

Charlotte was silent for a few moments as she absorbed the information. What the hell was a Cuban operative doing here, gathering intelligence and tradecraft... and from whom? Studying Malinovskii's expression for any faint sign of complicity or deception, she saw none.

'You don't know who's paying him?'

Now; Malinovskii paused. His eyes flickered from Charlotte to Callaghan. Then he spoke.

'We believe it is someone in the Kremlin. They couldn't risk using a Soviet for their purpose.'

The silence was deafening. Charlotte went cold.

Malinovskii spoke again.

'We made the approach. We have to trust you... and your Mr Dulles.'

Charlotte thought for a few moments, and then said,

'Viktor; you're talking about a Cuban operator buried in East Berlin and preparing some kind of a strike, and he's being paid to do it, possibly by someone inside the Kremlin. Is that right?'

Malinovskii nodded.

'Yes.'

This was deadly serious... especially at this particular stage of the Cold War, and especially here in Berlin. It was probably the most dangerous place in the world at this point in time. Two years previously, Soviet Premier Nikita Khrushchev had delivered a speech in which he demanded that the Western powers of the United States, Great Britain, and France pull their forces out of West Berlin within six months. This ultimatum had sparked an ongoing crisis over the future of the city of Berlin. President Dwight Eisenhower became determined not to give in to Soviet demands. Instead, the two sides opened a foreign minister's conference at Geneva in the summer of 1959 and made an attempt to negotiate a new agreement on Berlin. Khrushchev wanted the Western garrisons out of West Berlin as a precursor to reunifying the city, but Eisenhower believed that protecting the freedom of West Berlin required an ongoing U.S. presence.

Although Khrushchev and Eisenhower made some progress toward mutual understanding during talks at Camp David in the United States in 1959, but relations had since been badly damaged after the Soviet Union shot down an American U-2 spy plane snooping over Soviet territory last May. In the wake of this incident, there appeared to be little hope for any sort of accord. At that point, talks ceased, and the Soviet Premier appeared willing to wait for the U.S. Presidential elections to take place so he could begin anew with the incoming administration. It really wouldn't take very much for the tense situation to escalate out of control and a loose-cannon Cuban could so easily be just the catalyst that was needed.

Charlotte took a deep breath, and held Malinovskii's eyes in a steady, calm gaze; although her stomach was fluttering at the awful possibility of what he was about to reveal to her. Her voice was calm and steady.

'OK Viktor; who is his target?'

Malinovskii looked steadily at her, and then spoke.

'Senator John F. Kennedy.'

Charlotte shivered. Kennedy was tipped as favourite to be elected within a month as the New President of The United States. Kennedy seemed to have it all; looks, charm, intelligence, a sense of humour, power, and the Kennedy fortune. He was a man's man and a woman's man. He was also impatient, self-absorbed, a womanizer, an adulterer, physically unhealthy, dishonest, and extremely reckless; but he had the hearts and minds of the American people.

During the campaign, Kennedy charged that under Eisenhower and the Republicans the nation had fallen behind the Soviet Union in the Cold War, both militarily and economically, and that as President he would "get America moving again." He had also given support to the Civil Rights movement during his campaign speeches saying that discrimination stained America as it led the west's stance against the Soviet Union during the Cold War. He also said that a decent President could end unacceptable housing conditions by using federal power. His call of sympathy to Martin Luther King's wife, Coretta, when King was in prison was seized upon and well publicised by the Democrats. None of this had enamoured the young Massachusetts Senator to the many White Supremacist groups of America.

Charlotte glanced at Callaghan and then, back to Malinovskii.

'You are absolutely certain about this, Viktor?'

He nodded.

'Yes. The information was uncovered quite by accident, in the course of our normal intelligence activities. However, we are unable to take appropriate action, for obvious reasons, which is why you have been called upon. Unfortunately, you won't have much time to act. The Cuban is thought to have been here for several weeks, and is about to transfer to a secret training facility, which of course, is outside the inner German border.'

Charlotte studied Malinovskii.

That's it? Somebody has a plan to assassinate the man who is likely to become the future President of the United States? You have no other information… no clues, no leads, no hints… nothing except, there's a conspiracy somewhere out there?'

Malinovskii nodded.

'That's correct. This threat is believed by certain officials of the Communist Party of the Soviet Union to be some well-organised conspiracy on the part of some group or groups inside the United States… or somewhere close by in that part of the world. The suspicion is that it is being covertly funded by Kremlin black funds through an intermediary who has contracted this Cuban. They'll try to make it look like it was our side. … But it will be your side.'

Charlotte caught her breath.

'Jesus H. Christ, Viktor! You expect me to believe…'

He interrupted her and put his hand on her arm.

'No, Charlotte; I don't expect you to believe. I expect you to find out. You must get this information back to Alan Dulles. If they succeed, it could spark another World War. These are very dangerous people… fanatics. Promise me, if only for old time's sake, that you will not try to stop this by yourself. I don't want to have to arrange for you and your partner to be returned to West Berlin in pine boxes.'

Charlotte put her hand over his.

'I'm sorry; Viktor. I can't make you that promise. I must try to uncover more than you have told me. It's what I do.'

He nodded, almost sadly.

'I knew you'd say that. The only other thing I can tell you is that this plot does not come from First Secretary Khrushchev, or any members of the Presidium Central Committee. The KGB has conducted extensive investigations since we first heard of the conspiracy, but has uncovered nothing.'

He reached into his trenchcoat inside pocket and brought out a manila envelope which he handed to her. His face lost its serious expression, and he gave a slow smile.

'Knowing you as I do, *Milaya moya*; I knew you would need these. The envelope contains your identity documents. You are once again,

Colonel Nadia Tolenkanovna, KGB. Karlshorst. The other document names your partner as Major Sevastian Levkova; also of Karlshorst. All it needs is his photograph and this…'

He handed her a rubber stamp. She stared at him.

He grinned.

'Yes, it's real. Just don't let your Bureau use it too often. I must go now. Take great care, Charlotte. *"Do novyh vstrech!"*… Until we meet again; *"Do svidan'ya, Nadia"*… 'Goodbye, *Nadia*'

He turned, and slipped away into the darkness. Clutching the envelope and rubber stamp, she called softly into the pitch-black void of the passageway.

"Do svidan'ya, Viktor."

Chapter Ten.

Monday. 14th November, 1960.
Tauentzienstrasse, West Berlin.

Charlotte came out of the main entrance of the Kaufhaus des
Westens... the famous KaDeWe department store that was said to be
the West German equivalent of Harrods in London, where she had
been enjoying a few hours relaxation, shopping; and looked up the
street towards Breitscheidplatz and the gaunt spire of the Kaiser-
Wilhelm-Gedächtniskirche, in the hope that she could hail a taxi. She
and Callaghan had been searching almost continuously for any small
lead that might lead them to the Cuban operative who was supposedly
still in the city. This expedition was a small relaxation to try to inject
some sort of normality into the fraught and dangerous existence they
had both been keeping over the last couple of weeks... the systematic
searching of East Berlin for the slightest clue, without attracting the
attention of the Stasi. Callaghan had dropped her off earlier that day,
and then driven over to Clayallee to report in and send a signal to
Washington.

Burdened with several shopping bags and parcels, she spotted a
black Mercedes-Benz with a taxi sign on its roof approaching.
Flagging it down, she approached the driver's window and asked to be
taken to Uhlandstrasse, Charlottenburg. The driver nodded, and
opened his door... apparently to help his fare with her bags. As he
opened the rear door to allow her to get into the rear seat; suddenly, he
pushed her hard. Overbalancing; she fell across the rear seat and felt
handcuffs being snapped onto her wrists behind her back. A dark
fabric hood was pulled down over her head, and her legs were roughly
shoved into the car. She heard the doors slam and felt the car
accelerate away. After what seemed like hours, the car stopped and
someone else got into the front passenger seat. She felt the car begin

to move again, and mattered voices from somewhere in front of her. There was another long drive, and then, the car abruptly screeched to a halt. From the back seat, Charlotte heard one of the men grunt as he opened the car door. This was followed a moment later by his vice-like hands seizing her by the upper arm. A harsh voice yelled at her,

"Hinaus!"... "Out!"

She struggled to sit up, but obviously not quickly enough to suit her captor. As she managed to sit up, he violently yanked her by the arm. Now completely disoriented, she lost her balance and lurched forward. Because her hands were handcuffed behind her back, she was unable to break her fall and fell heavily on her left shoulder. The man ignored her cry and again roughly jerked her arm. He yelled to her,

"Steh auf, du Schlampe ungeschick"... "Get up, you clumsy bitch!"

Someone else, probably the driver, took her by the other arm and together the two men hoisted her to her feet. They began shoving her along over what felt like rough cobblestones. She was having difficulty maintaining her balance. It would have helped if she had been able to see, and her shoulder was hurting like hell. The hood they had jammed down over her head when they grabbed her was loosely fitted, but was causing her to have trouble breathing properly. After what seemed like miles, she felt her foot touch steps. They must be at the entrance of a building; although where, and what, was another story.

The two men shoved and dragged her up the steps and through a door. Inside, at the head of the steps, Charlotte, and the two men passed through a door. Once inside one of the men snapped,

"Informieren Sie Major Richter dass wir die Verhaftung gemacht haben"... "Inform Major Richter we have made the arrest."

She heard a third person begin to dial a telephone as they dragged her to a flight of steps that led downwards. Once at the bottom they turned left. It was much colder down here... wherever this was; and the whole place smelled like a latrine... the unpleasant odour of urine and God only knows what else. They walked along an echoing corridor and then stopped. She heard a jingling noise followed by first a soft click, and then the unmistakable squeal of rusty hinges as a door swung open. She was pulled forward and held firmly by the arms While one of them unlocked her handcuffs someone else removed her hood and for a fleeting moment, she was able to catch a glimpse of where she was. She stood in a long corridor; there were three men, and several steel doors. They were cells!... Prison cells!

She opened her mouth to say something, but was not given time to even form the first word before one of the men forcefully pressed his hands up against her shoulder blades and roughly pushed her into the stinking cell. She stumbled forward and heard a loud clang as the big steel door slammed shut behind her. The cell was now completely dark. There wasn't even a window.

Her shoulder was aching from the fall. She sat on the iron bedstead for a few minutes, whilst she tried to figure out what the hell was happening. Everyone was speaking in the thicker German accent that was prevalent in East Berlin. She could only be in one of two places... Stasi headquarters on Ruschestrasse, in Lichtenberg; or the Gedenkstätte Hohenschönhausen Stasi Remand Prison on Genslerstrasse; also in Lichtenberg. Because of the cobblestones, it was more likely to be the latter. This grim place had been a Soviet "special camp" set up after the end of the Second World War. It became the main Soviet prison in Germany for people awaiting trial. Thousands of political prisoners were held here at one time or another; including almost all of the GDR's best-known dissidents.

The snatch off the street had been a slick, professional job. It had to be the Stasi... but why? With the addition of the new identity that Viktor had arranged for her; her cover was impenetrable. What did they want? She decided that sitting here in the darkness was no way to find out. She moved to the door and began banging on the cold, rough metal with the flat of her hand. It probably wouldn't have any effect, but the sensation of slapping of her palm on the cold metal was focussing her thoughts. She heard heavy footsteps out in the corridor. They stopped outside her cell door. She heard the jingle of keys and the rasp of the lock and stepped back. The cell door banged open to reveal a large, heavy-set guard.

She opened her mouth to speak, but in the same instant, the guard drew back his arm and smacked her hard across the mouth with the back of his hand. He snapped.

"Gefangene werden nicht erlaubt zu sprechen!"... "Prisoners are not allowed to speak!"

He drew back his arm and punched her hard in the stomach. With the wind driven out of her; Charlotte collapsed on the filthy floor. The guard took two paces forward and kicked her hard in the ribs as she lay gasping on the floor of the cell. He laughed; a harsh, brutal laugh, that almost had sinister echoes of the Gestapo in it.

"Geben Sie mir nicht nicht mehr beunruhigen sich Weibchen!"... "Don't give me any more trouble, bitch."

He turned, and left the cell; slamming the door and leaving her gasping in pain and shivering on the cold concrete floor in complete darkness.

151

After what seemed like hours; keys jingled in the door lock again. An authoritarian voice outside in the corridor demanded sharply, in German...

"Was hier geschehen?"... 'What happened here?'

The reply was unintelligible. The door opened, and light from the corridor flooded into the cell. Charlotte painfully sat up in the bedstead and blinked at the doorway as she tried to adjust her eyesight to the glare. As her vision became slowly accustomed to the light, she saw a figure in a civilian suit standing in the doorway; flanked by two guards. He stepped forward and spoke in Russian;

'Nadia; are you alright? Have these stupid bastards harmed you?'

She recognised the voice. It was Viktor Malinovskii.

Quickly gathering her scrambled wits, she replied, also in Russian.

'No, Comrade. Not much. Just a few slaps.'

Viktor turned and glared at the two guards who shrank back, apprehensive of what might now be about to explode in their faces.

He spoke quietly. His voice was as cold as the Siberian Steppes... you could almost hear the chains rattling in the snow.

'Get me a proper physician and find us a warm room. The fools on your watch have falsely imprisoned and mistreated an officer of the Committee for State Security. She is a Colonel of the Second Chief Directorate, attached to Karlshorst. Now, find me the pig who did this to her.'

As one of the guards clattered away to carry out Malinovskii's orders, he put his arm around Charlotte and helped her out of the cell into the corridor. The other young guard helped to support her as they guided her to the stairs. The Watch Commander came rushing down from the front office and directed them to a warm, anonymous interview room where a pot of steaming coffee, cups, glasses and two bottles of vodka had been speedily placed on a table. Malinovskii helped Charlotte across to an examination bed and helped her up onto it. As she lay back, he studied her face. Bruised mouth and cheek; cut lip. As to what her other injuries might be, was for the physician to establish. He didn't like the way she had flinched as they had moved her from the cell in the basement. His thoughts were interrupted by a soft tap on the door. Malinovskii called out in German,

"Kommen!"... "Come in!"

The door opened and an oldish civilian entered. He carried one of the old-fashioned, "Gladstone bag" portmanteau Doctor's bag, which he placed carefully on the end of the examination bed. He smiled gently and encouragingly at his patient, and turned to Malinovskii.

'I am Doktor Lehrhardt. I have a practice in Lichtenberg. They said you needed my assistance.'

Malinovskii nodded.

'Yes, Herr Doktor. Could you please check over my associate? She has had a recent altercation with a guard in this pigsty, and I need to know the extent of any injuries she may have sustained.'

The old Doctor nodded and asked Malinovskii to leave the room. Turning to Charlotte, he asked that she removed her outer garments. As she did so, he studied her movements observing that she winced as she raised her left arm. He noticed the livid bruise gathering across her solar plexus from where the guard had punched her. Her facial injuries were superficial and would heal without scarring. What did worry him was the mottling around the ugly scrape along her right side. He looked down at her.

'Fraulein; I have to feel your side. You show trace evidence of a previous injury directly above this new one. Have you perhaps recently broken a rib?'

'Charlotte nodded.

'Yes Herr Doktor. I was in a car accident and broke three ribs; one of which punctured my lung.'

Otto Lehrhardt nodded.

'I must examine the injury site. I will be as careful as I can, but it will hurt you.'

She nodded. He gently laid his fingers over the injury site and began to probe.

Charlotte bit her lip. The stabs of pain were brief but sharp. At last the old Doctor looked at her.

'There is no recurrence of rib fracture, but the underlying tissue is badly bruised. You will be uncomfortable for quite a few days, and I would suggest that you refrain from any physical exertion for at least a week to ten days.'

She nodded.

'Thank you, Herr Doktor.'

Upstairs, Malinovskii was questioning the Watch Commander as to which of his guards first went down to the woman's cell.

The Watch Commander said it was Obergefreiter Munz. He had reported that there had been an accident. The woman had "slipped over" in the cell. The old Volkspolizist who had brought the Doctor caught Malinovskii's eye. He moved quietly towards the old Policeman who surreptitiously informed Malinovskii that this guard; Obergefreiter Gerhardt Munz had quite a reputation out on the streets.

He enjoyed hurting women. He had almost killed a couple of whores a few years previously, but nothing was ever proved. The old policeman said that in his opinion, Munz needed putting down in the same way you would have a savage dog put down... before he actually did kill some girl out in the dark, grey streets one night. Malinovskii nodded and thanked the old Volkspolizist.

The Watch Commander returned with Obergefreiter Munz, a hulking brute, who now stood sullen and arrogant before them. Stony-faced; Malinovskii said that Munz should show him where and how the accident had happened. With Munz leading the way; they disappeared down the steps into the basement. Two minutes later; the sound of a single, echoing gunshot shattered the silence. The Watch Commander and two of his men rushed down the steps and found Malinovskii nonchalantly replacing his Makarov pistol into its holster, and Munz sprawled across the floor of the empty cell with a bullet hole dead-centre between his eyes and most of the back of his head and brain splattered across the cell wall.

Malinovskii turned, and merely said that the guard had turned sharply and attempted to attack him. Perhaps, in view of the fact that this pig had also attempted a serious attack on a Soviet Officer... namely the female Colonel; it might be advantageous for the Stasi to clean up their own mess rather than have a couple of investigators pay them a visit from Karlshorst... unless, of course, the entire Gedenkstätte Hohenschönhausen Stasi prison detachment fancied a tour of duty out on the Polish Border. The Watch Commander swallowed hard and almost ran back upstairs to sign the release papers for the woman prisoner.

Viktor's car was parked up outside the main prison block. It was an old EMW 340... the East German version of the same-numbered BMW model. This particular example was finished in a particularly mundane shade of off-white. Malinovskii opened the passenger door for Charlotte and, walking around to the driver's side; opened the door and climbed into the bench seat alongside her. As he started the engine, he turned to her.

'I am so sorry about this; Charlotte. The idiots were only supposed to pick you up on the pretence of arresting you. I should have realised that the Stasi would overreact and fuck it all up.'

She smiled painfully.

'It's OK, Viktor. It wasn't your fault. Why did you want me picked up?'

He glanced at her as he turned out of the prison into Genslerstrasse;

and drove down towards Frankfurter Allee.

'There has been a major development. As you know, Kennedy has now been elected as President. Consequently; the Cuban's preparations have been brought forward. We are tracking several leads, and may run him to earth quite soon. It is quite possible that you and Callaghan will be called upon to retire him before very much longer.'

He paused, and jerked his thumb towards the back seat.

'Your equipment. Compliments of Karlshorst.'

She turned gingerly and saw a black leather satchel embossed with the KGB Sword-and-Shield emblem. Malinovskii smiled.

'It contains two ex-GDR, Makarov nine millimetre pistols with extra magazines and a pair of silencers. Ballistic investigation will prove that the demise of the Cuban was expedited by East German assassins. No one will believe that your government had any hand in this; You Americans would never use a Makarov... you much prefer your own domestic weapons. It has been decided by the Central Committee that this is now entirely your game. The Soviet Union cannot allow itself to even be suspected of any involvement in this situation. Therefore, Karlshorst has received a direct command that you are to be facilitated in any way you need. This is the first facilitation in compliance with that command. Informations will be provided as acquired by us and transferred by dead-letter drop in a mutually specified location.'

He glanced at her.

So; how are you feeling? Are you ready to return to West Berlin?

She nodded.

'I'm OK, Viktor... I've had worse... and yes; please take me back to the Tiergarten. I can walk from there; and Callaghan will be getting worried.'

Viktor Malinovskii nodded, and cut out into Frankfurter Allee; accelerating through the sparse traffic; and heading west towards Friedrichshain. The journey was uneventful. They were not followed and reached the Brandenburger Tor without incident. As he drove onto Strasse des 17 Juni, Malinovskii glanced at Charlotte.

'Where would you like me to drop you?'

She smiled.

'Down by the Charlottenburger Brücke would be fine, Viktor.'

He nodded.

'I could drop you outside your home if you like.'

She shook her head.

'It's better if you don't know the location, Viktor. It's not that I don't trust you... but what you don't know can't be gotten out of you.'

He grinned.

'Wise decision... but you always were the careful one.'

Stopping the car a little beyond the Charlottenburger Tor. He turned to her.

'So where will we arrange for the dead-letter drop location?'

She looked at him

'Do you have paper and pencil?'

He nodded, and brought out a small diary and a silver pencil. Opening the diary to the address page, she wrote a name and a telephone number. Handing them back to him, she smiled.

'This is my contact point, Viktor. Keep it safe.'

He nodded, and squeezed her arm as she got out of the car.

'Do svidan'ya, Charlotte.'

She closed the car door and leaned in through the window.

'Do svidan'ya, Viktor.'

As she walked away towards Charlottenburger Brücke, he opened the diary and read what she had written...

A single name: "Frau Streckenbach."

Beneath which, was a telephone number: Berlin 32-37-95. He nodded, watched for a gap in the traffic, and swung the car around; heading back towards the Brandenburger Tor.

On the other side of the Atlantic; far away from the tale of two cities that was Berlin; the Cold War was creeping closer to home. The United States had become alarmed by Castro's involvement in the overthrow of the U.S.-backed Cuban President Fulgencio Batista, and his relationship with Soviet First Secretary Khrushchev; and had implemented an economic blockade of the island.

As a response; Castro had agreed to provide the USSR with sugar in return for crude oil, fertilizers, and industrial goods. Relations were also established with other Marxist-Leninist governments, such as the Socialist Federal Republic of Yugoslavia, the People's Republic of Poland, and the People's Republic of China. The Cuban government had ordered the country's refineries... then controlled by U.S. petroleum corporations... to process this Soviet oil, but under pressure from the U.S. government, these companies refused. Castro responded by confiscating the refineries and nationalizing them under state control. In retaliation, the U.S. government cancelled its import of Cuban sugar, provoking Castro to nationalize most U.S.-owned assets on the island, including banks and sugar mills.

Added to this; relations between Cuba and the U.S. had been further strained following the explosion and sinking of a French vessel, the *Le*

Coubre, in Havana harbour in March. She had been carrying weapons purchased from Belgium, and the cause of the explosion was never determined; but Castro publicly accused the U.S. government... and the CIA, in particular; of sabotage. In March, the previous American President Eisenhower approved a document laying out a program of: "Covert action against the Castro Regime in Cuba to bring about the replacement of the regime with one more devoted to the true interests of the Cuban people and more acceptable to the U.S. in such a manner to avoid any appearance of U.S. intervention."

In August, Eisenhower approved a multi-million-dollar budget for the operation. By the end of October, most guerrilla infiltrations and supply drops directed by the CIA into Cuba had failed, and developments of further guerrilla strategies were replaced by plans to mount an initial amphibious assault, with a minimum of fifteen hundred men.

Now, ominous signals were being received from Washington by the Berlin operations base on Clayallee. Although Charlotte and Callaghan were working autonomously; Washington was advising all foreign stations that there was uncorroborated intelligence circulating Berlin concerning a foreign asset... of possibly Caribbean extraction; who was thought to be in the eastern sector undergoing training as part of a conspiracy. Against what, or whom this conspiracy was targeted was unclear, but it was apparent that the foreign asset was high value; which suggested that the suspected conspiracy was well-funded. In keeping with Agency protocols; a signal was sent out to all CIA operatives in the city. Charlotte received the sealed signal by courier on the morning of 16th November, whilst she and Callaghan were having breakfast.

She had briefed Callaghan on her meeting with Viktor Malinovskii concerning the Cuban operative, but had decided to wait for him to contact her as arranged, before she proceeded with any investigation. Now, she handed the signal across the kitchen table to Callaghan. He frowned as he read the close-typed words. At length, he looked up.

'D'you think this is the same thing?'

She shrugged.

'What else could it be? It's too damn close to be anything else. The problem is; that we can't tell if the asset is an operative for a hostile government, or a Cuban exile hired by the Mafia as a contract hit man. Don't forget, he could be contracted to anyone. Kennedy has upset enough people already, and he hasn't even been inaugurated yet!'

Callaghan shot her a quizzical look.

'Like who?'

Charlotte gave him a gentle, pitying look.
'Do keep up, Gil! Do I really have to spell it out?'
He nodded.
'Yes.'
She sat down and poured herself another cup of coffee.
'OK, first off; there's the Cuban Regime. There's no love lost between Washington and Havana, because the trade embargo has really hit them. After that, there are the Cane Sugar Refining Companies. Since Cuba cut off supplies and began trading with Khrushchev, their raw material costs have rocketed, and they are losing money. Next; you can add the crazy White Supremacists. Kennedy really pissed them off during his campaign speeches with regard to the Blacks. It was probably nothing more than vote-catching rhetoric, but those good ol' boys down south are too dumb to see the difference. Then again; it might simply be the Mafia. Kennedy has already hinted that he will make his brother Bobby, Attorney General, and it's common knowledge that he is down hard on organised crime.'

She glanced at the signal once again; then looked up at Callaghan.

'I think it's time for us to start sniffing around in East Berlin again... with or without the benefit of Viktor's intelligence.'

Friday, 18th November, 1960.
The White House.
Pennsylvania Avenue NW.
Washington DC.
USA.

CIA Director Allen Dulles and his Deputy Director for Plans Richard Bissell gave the initial briefing of the outline plans to overthrow Castro to President-elect John Kennedy. Having experience in actions such as the 1954 Guatemalan coup d'état, Dulles was confident that the CIA was capable of overthrowing the Cuban government as led by Prime Minister Fidel Castro since February 1959.

On 29th November; outgoing President Eisenhower met with the chiefs of the CIA, Defense, State, and Treasury departments to discuss the new concept. No objections were expressed, and Eisenhower approved the plans, with the intention of persuading John Kennedy of their merit. Kennedy was ambivalent; in spite of the CIA's alacrity to take swift action in Cuba, fearing the rise of a dangerous communist regime only ninety miles from American soil; Kennedy, however, was in two minds. While a successful invasion would topple Castro's anti-

American government, a failed mission could be disastrous for his image, both at home and abroad. After the CIA assured him that the "invasion force could be expected to achieve success," and that the United States would be only minimally implicated in the operation, Kennedy appeared to accept Eisenhower's decision.

On the 8th December, Bissell presented outline plans to the "Special Group" while declining to commit details to written records. Further development of the plans continued, and on the 4th January 1961, they consisted of an intention to carry out a "lodgement" by seven hundred and fifty men at an undisclosed site in Cuba, supported by considerable air power. On the 28th January, three days before his inauguration; President-elect Kennedy was briefed, together with all the major departments, on the latest plan which was now code-named *Operation Pluto*. It involved one thousand men to be landed in a ship-borne invasion about one hundred and seventy miles south-east of Havana. Kennedy authorized the active departments to continue, and to report their progress.

New Year's Eve, December 31st, 1960.
Georgievsky Hall, The Kremlin,
Moscow.
USSR.

As the clock struck midnight; Nikita Sergeyevich Khrushchev surveyed his New Year's Eve Gala guests thronging the magnificent multicoloured parquet floor in the sumptuous Georgievsky Hall of The Great Kremlin Palace on Red Square. He watched them as they drank and chatted amidst the carved and gilded furniture upholstered in watered silk of the same colour as the Decoration Ribbon of The Military Order of St. George; and admired the delicate relief work; the sculpted and gilt-bronze decorations adorning the snow-white walls and the vaulted ceiling.

He quietly mused on what these well-fed, louche apparatchiks were thinking as they gazed in wonder at the glittering, many-tiered openwork bronze chandeliers and wall lamps set all along the cornices; whilst they waited for him to deliver his much-anticipated New Year's Eve toast.

Although he exuded an outward aura of contentment and bonhomie; his thoughts were elsewhere. The Soviet Union had suffered her second straight failed harvest. He was failing miserably in his campaign to overtake U.S. living standards by 1970; not even meeting his people's basic needs. His advisers were telling him the chances of a workers' revolt were growing. Compounding this; his foreign policy of peaceful coexistence with the West, which in itself, was a contentious relinquishing of Stalin's conviction that eventual confrontation with the West was inevitable; had foundered spectacularly when a Soviet missile brought down an American U-2 spy plane over Soviet territory the previous May.

As if this was not enough to sour his enjoyment of the Gala proceedings; he was apprehensive about forthcoming Twenty-second Communist Party Congress in October, where he knew his enemies would be sharpening their knives behind his back. He had used just this gambit himself to purge his own adversaries, and he would need all his guile to avert the same fate himself.

Draining his Vodka flute, he faced the guests and commenced his speech. He informed the gathering that the American people, by voting for Kennedy against then-Vice President Richard Nixon, had cast their vote against their country's confrontational Cold War policies, and hoped the new U.S. President would be like a fresh wind blowing away the stale air between the USA and the USSR.

As his guests applauded, he neglected to say that through a number of intermediaries, he was already urgently seeking an early summit meeting with Kennedy in Berlin on other matters. If that didn't succeed, internal pressures from the Central Committee would push him towards a quasi-Stalinist-style confrontation.

Khrushchev was fully aware that The Soviet Union; born in blood at the dawn of the twentieth century and tempered by war, was gradually turning a corner into a modern era of prosperity. To do so, it must shed the poisonous legacy of Stalin and his Gulag. The unfortunate truth was that at this point in time, relations between the two Super Powers were as cold as the howling wind of the storm outside which was depositing a thick layer of snow on Red Square.

Nothing threatened Khrushchev more than the deteriorating situation in Berlin, through which; the massive emigration westward was stripping East Germany of its most capable professionals: Industrialists with their engineers, and technicians; physicians; teachers, lawyers and skilled workers. He knew that this irreverent city had become his Achilles' heel... the one place in the Soviet bloc where communism lay most vulnerable. It would soon become inevitable that the East German authorities would have no option but to stem this flow of defectors; and, as if he didn't have enough worries; Khrushchev had a particularly annoying thorn in his side.

Walter Ulbricht, former First secretary of the S.E.D... the Socialist Unity Party of Germany Central Committee, and an archetypal

Stalinist; had been named chairman of the newly-formed G.D.R. Council of State; and was therefore, effectively the supreme leader of the country. Since before Christmas he had been pressuring Khrushchev to stop the emigration outflow and resolve the status of Berlin. How this was to be undertaken was, as yet undecided; but the exodus of professionals had become so damaging to the political credibility and economic viability of East Germany that the re-securing of the German communist frontier was imperative.

Friday, January 20th, 1961.
Capitol Hill.
Washington, DC.
USA.

On a bitterly cold, snowy day; John Fitzgerald Kennedy was sworn in as the 35th President at noon on the newly-renovated east front of the United States Capitol Building.

Saturday, January 21st. 1961.
Berlin-Charlottenburg.
West Germany

07 45 am. In the streets below; everything was covered under a thick layer of snow and frost. The frozen, ice-cold winter of Berlin in January was an uncompromising behemoth blanketing over every last metre of city that it could it reach; carried by the north-eastern winds of a cold front from the depths of Russia that blew in unhampered, across the flat, northern European plains from the Ural Mountains. Charlotte gazed out of the window of the apartment on Uhlandstrasse across the rooftops of Charlottenburg towards the distant Tiergarten. The snow was falling quietly, gently, from the dirty, grey-cotton, cloud-choked sky billowing overhead.

She looked back to the thin sheet of paper she held. Old Herr Günsche, the concierge-cum "gatekeeper" had brought it to her twenty minutes previously. One of his network of "Lamplighters"... the people who carried out surveillance, cleared dead-letter drop boxes, and intercepted mail... had delivered it to him from the drop box arranged by Charlotte and Viktor Malinovskii two months previously; that was located at the Löwenbrücke... the Lions Bridge, in the south-western corner of the Grossen Tiergarten triangle, not far from the Neuer See lake. The dead-letter drop was in a small crack in one of the stone plinths that supported the leftmost of the two pairs of cast-

161

iron Lion sculptures guarding the little wooden bridge.

The note was brief, and came from Viktor Malinovskii. Charlotte and Callaghan were to meet a contact in Friedrichshain; at a disused garage in Böcklinstrasse, a little to the north-east of what was left of the Berlin Ostbahnhof marshalling yards. The contact; code-named *"Aquila"* was a trusted Stasi Captain... one of Malinovskii's informants; who had information concerning enquires that Malinovskii had ordered the Stasi to initiate with regard to any unidentified men of Cuban extraction in their sectors. Callaghan was wary. This could so easily be a trap.

Charlotte shook her head.

'No. Viktor is far too astute to be fooled by a Stasi double. We need to check this guy out; but if you're concerned; we'll take the Makarovs with us... that way; if he turns out to be dirty, we can deal with him and shift the blame back onto the Stasi, themselves.'

The streets were covered in a slight layer of snow as the flakes continued to fall from the light grey sky. The snow blowers had been out, and the Strasse des 17 Juni up to the Brandenburger Tor was reasonably clear. The Volkspolizist under the archway was huddled deep into his greatcoat and sheltering against one of the right-hand Doric pillars from the biting wind. He merely waved them through and pulled his greatcoat collar further up around his ears. Unter den linden was deserted. There were no snow blowers this side of the border, and the snow lay thickly on the roadway. A few workmen with large brooms were sweeping the pavements, but other than that, the blanket of snow was undisturbed. There were no tyre tracks along Unter den Linden; no vehicles had travelled east this morning... at least, not recently. The few vehicles... mainly cars... that were parked up along the Boulevard were covered in a thick layer of snow.

Marx Engels Platz was almost deserted; as was the drive up to Alexanderplatz. There would be no car swap today. Malinovskii had suggested that they stay with the black Mercedes-Benz. The Stasi used black Mercedes-Benzes; and such a car heading out towards Stasi Headquarters in Lichtenberg would get scarcely a second glance... albeit a frightened one. There were more people in Alexanderplatz, heavily wrapped up against the bitter wind with the scent of brown coal on it that was driving sleet across the asphalt as they scurried along the pavements, overshadowed by the gaunt skeletons of the construction tower cranes ghostly against the lowering dirty-grey clouds and thickening snow.

As they turned into Karl Marx Allee, Callaghan passed a side street and spotted a black Mercedes-Benz parked there. As soon as they drove past, it pulled out after them. He glanced into the rear-view mirror. It was one of the ubiquitous 190 models that were used widely as taxis. It might have been a taxi, but there was no sign on its roof. It was almost certainly a Stasi vehicle. Callaghan nudged Charlotte. She folded down the sun visor as though she was touching up her make up and watched the black car. It kept pace, about fifty yards behind. She folded the sun vizor back up and glanced at Callaghan.

'Just stay at this speed. They might just think we're one of theirs.'

He nodded and kept the Mercedes-Benz at a steady fifty Km/h. The trailing car stayed with them down the length of Karl Marx Allee past the rows of dreary, featureless buildings, all made from the same dirty oatmeal-coloured concrete softened by a thin coating of ice on their exposed surfaces. At Frankfurter Tor... the intersection of Karl-Marx-Allee and Frankfurter Allee; Callaghan indicated a right turn and drove into Boxhagener Strasse. Glancing into the rear-view mirror, he saw the other black Mercedes-Benz cruise past the turn and continue down Frankfurter Allee. He exhaled in relief.

'Good call, "Frau Streckenbach!" You were right. They thought we were one of theirs.'

At Wismar Platz, they took the right fork into the continuation of Boxhagener Strasse. Charlotte was watching the street signs.

'We should be close, now Gil... there! On the right!'

Böcklinstrasse, was flanked by the ruined site of a building that once stood at the corner, and now looked to have been demolished completely, leaving nothing but some of the frame and old piles of bricks. The street was narrow and particularly run down, having suffered a long period of neglect during the days of the GDR. Tumbles of concrete wreckage and twisted metal lay scattered across weed-infested vacant spaces that even two feet of snow couldn't really soften to the gaze. This part of East Berlin was like stepping back into a whole different era of shabby, run-down streets, bullet-ridden façades, chipped cobblestones; and rusty signs hung on blackened buildings. It was as if time had stood still here. Halfway down the street, an old BMW sedan was parked up outside what appeared to be a large pair of double doors in one of the few intact buildings that remained. Callaghan cautiously pulled in behind it and switched off the engine. He reached inside his coat and flicked off the safety of the Makarov silenced pistol... just in case; then they waited.

Five minutes later, the worn and paint-peeling garage doors were pulled slightly ajar, and a man stepped out onto the cracked pavement.

He glanced cautiously up and down Böcklinstrasse; then walked purposefully to the Mercedes-Benz. Callaghan wound down the driver's door window and studied the man. Looking past Callaghan, the man addressed Charlotte. He was tall and well-built; about thirty-five, and spoke with a perfect Berlin accent.

Frau Streckenbach? I am "Aquila." Please, let us go inside.'

He stepped back as Callaghan and Charlotte got out of the car and walked towards the garage doors. He stepped back to let them enter. Callaghan slipped his hand inside his coat and grasped the butt of the silenced Makarov. Aquila noticed this and smiled wryly.

'There is no need for you to be on your guard, Herr Streckenbach. Firearms will not be necessary.'

He followed them inside and closed the doors. The garage was in deep gloom, and deserted except for three chairs; and table, upon which was a bottle of Polish vodka and three tumblers. Aquila walked to the far wall and flicked a light switch. The single, bare light bulb hanging from the roof glowed wanly; dispelling a little of the gloom. Inviting Charlotte and Callaghan to sit; Aquila came to the table and pulled out his own Makarov, which he placed on the table. He smiled amiably.

There is no need for you to draw your weapons. In normal circumstances, we might well have met in the interrogation cells of the Hohenschöenhauser…'

This was the Stasi establishment a few blocks from their main Headquarters. It was also one of the few places in Lichtenberg where the KGB did not maintain a presence. Aquila poured three good measures of vodka into the tumblers and leant back in his chair.

'…However; these are not normal circumstances. It is time, as you say; to put our cards upon the table. I am not Stasi. I am a Major in the KGB, based at Karlshorst.'

He smiled.

It is not necessary for you to reach for those silenced Makarovs that Colonel Malinovskii supplied to you. I am instructed to take you to Karlshorst, where Comrade Kondrashev; Head of the Berlin Section has arranged for you to have full access to all the Stasi records concerning this case. There is no precedent for this level of cooperation, and it is unlikely that there ever will be again. Moscow is deeply concerned about this supposed conspiracy; as is Washington. Communications have been exchanged, and it is agreed that you will retain your personas as ordinary West German citizens; and, as far as the Stasi and the Volkspolizei are concerned; you will be treated as such.'

Callaghan glanced at Charlotte who sat calmly listening to the Russian. At length, she spoke,

'Thank you Major, for your candour. We appreciate your situation is an unusual one. Hopefully, this enterprise can be brought to a satisfactory conclusion within a reasonably short time.'

Aquila nodded.

'I hope so, too, Frau Streckenbach. If we fail and this supposed Cuban succeeds, then we will truly be stepping into the Valley of the Shadows.'

He drained his tumbler and poured himself another. Turning the glass in his hands, he gazed into its depths for a few moments and then, looked up.

'I must confess; I am not comfortable with this conspiracy theory. As yet, there has been precious little... if any, information unearthed by the Stasi about this Cuban. If they cannot trace him, then he is not in Berlin; and if he is not in Berlin, then we are truly chasing shadows. To ensure the people of East Germany remain submissive to Communist rule, the Stasi have their agents and informers everywhere. The population is constantly under surveillance, with telephone taps to West Berlin and West Germany. They have officers posted in every major industrial plant... in every school, university, and hospital.'

He continued.

'Without exception, one tenant in every apartment building is designated as a watchdog reporting to the area Volkspolizei. In turn, the police officer is the Stasi's man. If a relative or friend comes to stay overnight, it is reported. All denominations of churches have their informers, to the extent that even the Catholic confessionals are fitted with eavesdropping devices. Religion may well be frowned upon over here... but it does have its uses for information gathering.'

He smiled, and continued;

'You think your CIA and FBI are efficient? Their technicians have systematically bored holes in virtually every apartment and hotel wall to film suspects with special cameras fitted with listening equipment. Even bathrooms are monitored by the Stasi. Nothing is sacred, and like their predecessors, the Nazi Gestapo, the Stasi is another example of the sinister side of *Deutsche Gründlichkeit*... German thoroughness, to the extent that the communists' brutal oppression of the nation by means including murder as well as legal execution puts the Stasi leadership on a par with Hitler's gang.

East Berlin is a city based on lies and deceit, and you should trust no one or take them at face value. I cannot say for certain whether this Cuban exists. They should have uncovered something by now. Perhaps it is, as you say, "a wild goose chase"; but our two governments insist that we must apprehend this "Ghost" at all costs.'

He drained his tumbler, and scraped back his chair.

'It's time we proceeded to the Rezedentura. We'll go in my car. You can park your Mercedes out of sight in this garage.'

The ride to Karlshorst was a relatively direct and short one in spite of the fact that many of the pre-war streets that crossed Berlin were still impassable... a veritable tangle of dead-ends in a crumbling vista of dingy apartment blocks, run-down and abandoned factories and weed-choked, desolate bomb sites. The Rezedentura was located in a building within a compound and bound by four relatively intact streets: Bodenmaiser Weg, Zwieseler Strasse; Dewetalle, and Arberstrasse. On one side, the compound peeked slyly from behind its walled-fort; whilst on the other side, squatted the picture-perfect houses of the Russian officials in Berlin.

Aquila entered the compound through the main entrance on Zwieseler Strasse; flanked by two guard houses and drove onto the wide, cobblestone area fronting the cold and foreboding three-storey administration block built in an architectural style that was simple and almost featureless; a functional concrete building typical of the era of Soviet influence on its satellites.

The front of the building was dominated by six tall, plain columns supporting an equally plain Doric-style portico over the main entrance which still bore the plastered-over, ghostly outline of the carved stone Wehrmacht eagle... *"Die Heeresadler"* that had once adorned the portico. There were a number of high antenna masts on the roof, all connected by cables.

Once inside; the lower halves of the stairwell and walls throughout the building were painted in an unpleasant shade of mustard, topped by a dull, neutral grey. The upper floor corridors ran the entire length of the long building, lined on both sides with door after door, leading to nameless rooms and offices. As they passed one doorway, a uniformed KGB operative came out, and as Charlotte glanced inside she saw that the walls were padded, and what looked like traces of blood were evident on the floor beside an empty metal chair, to which handcuffs were attached.

Aquila led them to the far end of the corridor to an anonymous-looking door. Opening it, he invited them to enter. He closed the door behind them and snapped his fingers. Two large, uniformed KGB privates stepped forward from an adjoining room and took up positions flanking either side of the closed door with their AK-47 assault rifles held diagonally across their chests.

Chapter Eleven.

KGB Zentrale-Karlshorst.
Zweiseler Strasse,
Berlin-Lichtenberg.

The Karlshorst Rezidentura surveillance files collated by the Stasi that Charlotte and Callaghan were allowed to access were comprehensive... several boxes of files bulging with sheaves of close-typewritten, flimsy yellowing papers; but after three hours of extensive searching, revealed little that could be of any use with regard to the whereabouts or identity of any Cuban National who was a specific person of interest to the Stasi, or anyone else for that matter. They reported their findings to Aquila when he came to check on their progress. This appeared to be a dead-end.

He nodded.

'I didn't expect much else. The Stasi don't necessarily release all their information to us; but I can apply a certain amount of leverage. It means that we need to go over to their headquarters in Normannenstrasse. This, in itself is something of a challenge. They don't even like us visiting them; let alone taking two American agents with us. There is no way to know how they might react if they know who you are; so I shall inform them that you are two of our " illegal rezidents" based in West Berlin and under direct control of Karlshorst. That should placate them sufficiently for them to allow you to research any files that have so far, not been accessible to you.'

Aquila turned the BMW out into Tretskowallee and drove north through Friedrichsfelde to Frankfurter Allee; heading west, back towards Berlin-Lichtenberg. As he drove, he glanced at Charlotte in the front passenger seat beside him.

'When we reach the Stasi complex; let me do the talking. Just produce the passes I supplied and act dismissively towards them. That way, they will automatically assume that we are all KGB. It would be even better if you would speak German with a Soviet accent.'

Charlotte nodded.

That's not a problem. Would a standard Moscow accent be OK?'

Aquila grinned.

'It most certainly would! It would make them think you were out of the Lubyanka, and they'd probably crap themselves!'

Charlotte smiled.

'Kak rabotaet jetot zvuk?... How does this sound?'

Aquila grinned.

'Perfect! Just the right cold feeling to it. OK, here we are.'

He turned into Ruschestrasse, and drove along the street dominated by towering "Plattenbau" buildings... the German expression for a structure constructed of large, prefabricated concrete slabs; that ran the entire length of the right-hand side of Ruschestrasse They were huge and ugly; fourteen storeys of dismal grey concrete panels; with each panel pierced through with a plain-double paned window. Aquila nodded.

'And this is just the one side. The complex covers the entire square bounded by Frankfurter Allee, Ruschestrasse; Normannenstrasse, and Magdalenenstrasse. Building One, where the minister's office is located, is at the centre of the complex. The office of Markus Wolf, the head of the General Intelligence Administration, where we are heading; is in Building Fifteen.'

At the end of the main block, which didn't actually stretch the full length of Ruschestrasse, but was continued as a four-storey annex constructed in the same grim concrete panels; Aquila turned into an access road that led through a short tunnel under the annex, and stopped at the red and white pole barrier. A mean-looking guard wearing a grey-green uniform stepped forward and snapped his fingers officiously.

'Identification, please.'

He glanced at their identification cards, then peered into the interior of the car, and snapped contemptuously,

'What are you doing here? This is a restricted complex.'

Aquila looked him up and down.

'We are here to meet Herr Wolf; head of the General Intelligence Administration.'

The guard glanced at Callaghan in the back seat, and then fixed his insolent gaze on Charlotte.

'And who might you be?'

She gave him an icy stare and replied in gutter German, with an ominous Russian accent...

'Who I am is none of your fucking business, soldier.'

He stared at her as though he couldn't believe what he had just heard. His face reddened and he snapped.

'You can't talk to me like that...'

Charlotte interrupted his blustering rant in mid-flow. Changing smoothly from German to Russian, with a portentous, icy tone; and her cold blue eyes boring into him, she spoke quietly...

'Mne po figu. Mne nasrat', chto ty dumaesh'... 'It's all the same to me. I don't give a shit what you think.'

The guard started. This woman had to be important and influential to dare to speak to any member of the Ministerium für Staatssicherheit, in that tone of voice... and in Russian. He couldn't understand exactly what she had said... his grasp of Russian wasn't that good; but he certainly got the gist of it. The tone said to him that if he continued with this particular line of enquiry; at best, he would find himself on permanent cleaning out of the interrogation cells duty; and at worst; would end up freezing his nuts off with the Coastal Border Command up on the Barents Sea coast. Stepping smartly back; he raised the barrier and waved Aquila's BMW through into the central courtyard of the complex.

Aquila pulled into a parking space at the southern end of the central courtyard and switched off the engine. He turned in his seat and spoke quietly.

'When we get up to Markus Wolf's office, let me do the talking.'

He glanced around the courtyard. There were a few cars parked up there; mainly Ladas and the ominous black Mercedes-Benzes; but there were also several plain, off-white box vans. Pointing to the one with an incongruous sign painted on its side, which declared: *Obst und Gemüse*... Fruits and vegetables; his voice became circumspect.

'They are the new Barkas Stasi-Gefangentransporter... prisoner transport vans, which are mainly used to move prisoners between here and the Hohenschönhausen Remand Prison... but also to snatch suspects off the streets. They are disguised as bread or grocery delivery vans and hold up to six suspects or convicted prisoners in individual prisoner isolation cages that have no windows or light. It's part of the Stasi system of disorientation which makes the subsequent interrogations more effective. The prisoners don't even know what they are charged with; are kept in darkness, and have no clue where they are going; because the Stasi drive them around the streets of

Berlin for five or six hours to completely disorientate them before they actually arrive at the prison.'

Leaving the car, they walked across central Courtyard Five towards the Frankfurter Allee end of the complex; passing between the HVA... *Hauptverwaltung Aufklärung...* General Intelligence Administration Block Fifteen annex and the six-storey Building Seven... where the Stasi Department V, responsible for the internal surveillance of East Berlin citizens was based. Walking purposefully into into Courtyard Six, which was surrounded on three sides by the massive, grey cement, asbestos, and prefabricated concrete Building Fifteen, which incorporated three, adjoining, fourteen-storey blocks on the western corner of the complex, facing out onto Frankfurter Alee and Ruschestrasse; they were met by a sour-faced Oberfähnrich who conducted them along, wood-panelled, impersonal corridors, lined with anonymous office doors, to Markus Wolf's office suite. Behind these doors almost anything could be happening: interrogations, imprisonment; examinations, education, or simply, administration. Inlaid into the dark laminate, corridor floor at regular intervals were pale wood strips proclaiming in bright red, capital letters; the same, repetitious, chilling slogan:

"FEIND IST, WER ANDERS DENKT."

("THE ENEMY IS WHOEVER THINKS DIFFERENTLY.")

Which played a suitably paranoid counterpoint to prominent notices, also at regular intervals along the wall, which proclaimed:

"Staatssicherheit, Garant der SED-Diktatur."

"State security, Guarantor of the SED (Socialist Unity Party) Dictatorship"

The Oberfähnrich knocked on the door at the end of the corridor, and opened it; motioning that they should enter. The room was panelled in similar wood to the corridors. Behind a large light wood desk sat an athletic-looking man, aged about forty; with greying hair, a long, intelligent face, and penetrating brown eyes. He stood as they entered, and surveyed them with a wry smile. Tall, suave, and impeccably dressed; Wolf was the absolute antithesis of the colourless, vapid apparatchiks who ran East Germany.

Stepping out from behind the desk, he held out his hand to Aquila...
a hand with long, artistic fingers. He spoke, with an educated accent.

'Welcome, Stepan. It's good to see you. How may I be of assistance
to you, today?'

Aquila shook hands and smiled.

'You are looking well. Markus. We need a little information from
you if you don't mind.'

He turned to Charlotte and Callaghan.

'May I introduce you to my fellow investigators, Colonel Nadia
Tolenkanovna and Major Sevastian Levkova of the Second Chief
Directorate; attached to the Rezidentura, Karlshorst. They are seeking
information on a Cuban dissident who is alleged to be active in the
GDR. It is suspected that he may be involved in a well-organised
conspiracy. This is a matter of extremely high security, not only
within the intelligence community but on the highest levels of
government. If this conspiracy succeeds, it could spark another World
War.'

Wolf directed his gaze towards Charlotte.

'Comrade Colonel; what makes you think this Cuban is involved in
a conspiracy of this magnitude?'

She glanced at Aquila, who nodded imperceptibly.

'We have established that there is a Cuban operative buried on this
side of the border. He is a grave danger to both our sides. This threat
is believed by certain officials of the Communist Party of the Soviet
Union to be some well-organised conspiracy on the part of some
group or groups inside the United States... or somewhere close by in
that part of the world. The conspiracy involves the projected
assassination of the newly-inaugurated American President, John F.
Kennedy.

The suspicion is that the plot is being covertly funded by Kremlin
black funds through an intermediary who has contracted this Cuban.
They couldn't risk using a Soviet. The conspirators will try to make it
look as though the perpetrator was on our side; but it will be a home-
grown American plot.'

Wolf studied her for a few moments. He leaned forward across his
desk, and nodded.

'I agree, Comrade Colonel. If this conspiracy actually exists, then it
has severe implications for all of us. We have detailed files on over
five million East German citizens as well as all Foreign Nationals
within our borders. All phone calls to and from the West are
monitored, as is all mail. If this Cuban is within our borders, then rest
assured that we shall find him. I must, however, inform you that

Castro's regime in Cuba is particularly interested in receiving training from us. I have instructors working in Cuba, and Cuban communists receiving training in certain facilities located in the east. The intention is to set up the GDR system in Cuba. It is unlikely, but not impossible that one of the Cubans receiving training in East Germany is the one that you are seeking. I shall initiate an investigation into this possibility and notify Colonel Marisova here, of our findings at the earliest opportunity.'

Charlotte nodded.

'Thank you, Herr Wolf. Your assistance in this matter is greatly appreciated. Moscow Central is extremely concerned of the possible consequences if this Cuban manages to evade detection and initiates this perilous enterprise.'

Wolf smiled; an open charming smile.

'You are most welcome Comrade Colonel. I am only too pleased to be of assistance to you. It was a great pleasure to meet you.'

Charlotte returned his smile. She had astutely figured this charming, urbane spymaster out... as far as anyone might ever figure him out. He understood the attractions of the West and had a taste for life's luxuries, as well as an eye for beautiful women. For many men the Cold War was a game, and clearly, Markus Wolf was very good at the game.

Returning to the car; Callaghan nudged Charlotte.

'Jesus H. Christ! This place makes Foggy Bottom look like Goddamned college dormitory!... and, we've just met the guy they call "The Man Without a Face" because he's so damned good at avoiding being photographed! The Western intelligence agencies have only ever managed to get one grainy shot of him... and we've just spent twenty minutes close enough to see if he had a close shave this morning!

Charlotte smiled.

'True; but don't forget the First Commandment of Spookcraft... "Thou Shalt Not Get Caught"... and we really don't need to give the slightest intimation to these Stasi bastards that we are anything other than a pair of hard-nosed, intransigent investigators from Moscow Central. Our best course of action now, is to behave with complete arrogance towards them and follow Karlshorst's lead. We sit tight and wait for Colonel Marisova or Viktor to contact us.'

Callaghan nodded.

'Yeah, that sounds good to me. How does a Russian Major act towards these Commie Krauts?'

Charlotte smiled again.

173

'The same way that I behaved towards the North Koreans... and the Nazi's for that matter, when I was coming out of Berlin just before it fell to the Russians in '45... the cold, disdainful stare, and the "I really can't be bothered to carry on a conversation with a piece of shit like you" tone of voice.

You have to remember; all the foot soldiers of these totalitarian regimes... especially the East Germans; are a nation of natural slaves. They've always responded to the crack of the whip and the threat of the jackboot; to the shrill blast of the whistle and the hectoring shouts of their superiors. Treat them like something you've just stepped in on the sidewalk, and it will never cross their minds that you are anything other than what you appear to them to be.'

Tuesday, January 24th. 1961.
Chinatown, San Francisco.
California.
U.S.A.

Chang Ho-Pyong; patriarch of the Chang criminal family sat in the study of the elegant, bay windowed property number 1120; situated at the top of Montgomery Street in the Telegraph Hill district... the heart of Chinatown. He studied the pigeon-egg-sized, blood-red Garnet gemstone that had arrived from his granddaughter, Chang Su-Dae after being diverted by her from its scheduled flight to the United States as a result of an oversight by the Embassy in Seoul. Normally, such an item should have been despatched in a Diplomatic pouch, but it had been dealt with in the Embassy post room by a Korean, who had been planted there by Kim Jonghyun, mob boss of Seoul's notorious Yangeundongpa gang, who had arranged for him to be placed in the post room, specifically for the purpose of locating this gemstone. Kim Jonghyun had been tracking the Garnet gemstone for years, reasoning that since he had originally made a gift of the Garnet to the North Korean leader, Kim Il Sung; and therefore, there had been an inferred obligation, which had not been honoured by reason that the South had not fallen during the war; it was his right to repossess the gemstone. It was a potent bargaining chip in the shadowy, dangerous world of organised crime.

The Garnet carried significant reverence in Chinese beliefs as bestowing immunity to injury upon its wearer. It was also believed to attract the energy and influence of the Sun. The larger the gem, the greater the attraction; and a Triad Dragon Lord would bestow great favour and acceptance upon a rival mob boss offering such a prize.

Kim Jonghyun's Yangeundongpa gang was powerful in Seoul, but nowhere near as powerful as the Chinese Triads that were moving in. Such a gift as the Garnet gemstone to the right Dragon Lord would guarantee co-operation in criminal enterprises and ensure that the Yangeundongpa gang would retain face and dignity.

Chang Ho-Pyong had decided, quite autonomously, to adhere to the same protocol. The Chinatown Lai Ying gang; a supposed martial arts club headed by a Kung Fu Master who was actually a Triad *Straw Sandal;* was becoming a serious threat to Chang Ho-Pyong's operations. The Lai Ying gang members supposedly studied the martial arts, but drove away American-born young Chinese from Chinatown and "protected" the community from outsiders. This protection had evolved into gun trafficking, prostitution, drug money laundering; illegal gambling operation, arson, hire for murder, and assault. Lai Ying's Master would be a powerful ally for the Chang criminal family; who, as a matter of professional courtesy, had, up to now, concentrated their operations within the Korean community in the Bay Area of San Francisco. The Lai Ying gang members were beginning to prey upon this community. Some of the younger family members were already protesting that they should teach these Chinese *Geseki deul...* sons of bitches, a lesson they would not forget. The last thing that Chang Ho-Pyong wanted was all-out war... it was not conclusive to good business.

As undisputed patriarch of the Chang criminal family, his word was absolute law; but he still had his suspicions that sooner or later, one of the young hot-heads would do something really stupid. It was time to negotiate with the Lai Ying Master.

Chang Ho-Pyong sat and mused for a while. It would not be prudent to entrust this task to one of the young men of the "Family." They were impetuous; they lacked the coolness of mind normally associated with their Buddhist creed. They had been in America for too long and the ways of the Old country... "The Land of the Morning Calm" had been diminished by too many television shows and gangster movies. He would send his other granddaughter; Gabriella Chang.

Gabriella was a beautiful, American-born Korean, twenty-two-years-old; with dark, almond eyes, a pretty, retroussé nose; and rose-petal lips. She wore no more than a touch of make-up and did not need to, for she had that rosy-tinted skin on a pale, honey-gold background... the colours of a pale peach, which was quite common among Korean women. Her hair was black with dark-brown highlights. It fell in tumbling waves to her shoulders, with a soft fringe that ended an inch or so above her straight, fine eyebrows. Her teeth were even and white, and showed no more prominently between the lips than a Caucasian girl. She had a beautiful figure, equal to that of any of the chorus girls to be found in the elegant venues in the San Francisco Bay Area. Visually, she was beautifully delicate and feminine; but Gabriella Chang had a secret; and one that could prove lethal to any hot-shot Chinese street-gang punk who thought he could get lucky... or, perhaps, try to force himself upon her.

Gabriella Chang was a black-belt in the Korean Martial Art of Hapkido... a discipline that used the opponents' force against themselves. As if this was not enough; she also carried a wicked-looking spring cosh of Nazi Gestapo, World War Two vintage, which had probably been brought home by some G.I. as a war trophy. How it had come into the possession of Chang Ho-Pyong was another story, but suffice it to say that Gabriella was more than capable of using it in a way that its original owners would have been proud of.

Gabriella Chang turned her jet-black Porsche 356 cabriolet into California Street; the fifty-four blocks long, dead straight artery that split the city of San Francisco east to west from the San Francisco Bay waterfront to Lincoln Park in the far northwest corner of the city overlooking the Pacific Ocean, and accelerated up the hill in the direction of Nob Hill. Grandfather Chang Ho-Pyong said that the Lai Ying gang's headquarters was located behind the Chan Yang Garden restaurant just west of Sabin Place.

A little way past the Spring Street junction, glancing into the rear-view mirror, she noticed a customised Chevrolet Bel Air sedan slide out of an alley and begin to follow her. It had all the characteristics of being a Chinese street gang ride. She smiled. It was no more than she had expected. It just depended on what their intentions were.

The Chevy held back and kept pace with her speed. As she came to the Chan Yang Garden restaurant and pulled into the sidewalk curb, the Chevy pulled in about twenty feet behind. Gabriella scanned the restaurant. It was closed up. There was no bell push; at least, none she could see on the street frontage; but there was an alleyway alongside the building. Getting out of the Porsche; she walked around the corner into the alleyway. It was a crooked brick canyon; dark, and very narrow; with a thirty foot wall at the far end... just the sort of place to get trapped. She felt for the spring cosh and closed her slender fingers around the butt end. The dingy brick cliff-face to her left was solid and unbroken by any windows or doors, with a couple of grimy, overfilled dumpsters shoved up against its base; spilling garbage onto the squalid, cracked asphalt surface of the alleyway. Half-way along the right wall was a solitary, nondescript doorway set slightly back. That must be the place.

Carefully, she began making her way along the filthy alleyway, trying not to soil her expensive, Italian *"Bruno Magli"* heels. Suddenly, there was a squeal of tyres out on the street, as the Chevy pulled sharply across the entrance, effectively trapping her. Five Chinese "Dudes"... or what they imagined themselves to be; the epitome of Chinatown "Cool"... T-shirts, chinos, and excessively arrogant swagger; piled out of the car, and, spreading out across the alleyway, began to stroll towards her.

The leader of the group; a real tough guy wearing a pair of cheap, imitation Wayfarer sunglasses; laughed.

'Well! What do we have here? Looks like *dài dàng fù*... a Korean slut. Wanna make out, baby?'

Gabriella Chang began backing away along the alleyway. The five Chinese were laughing as they began moving forward. Judging by the bulges in their chinos, their idea was to turn this into a gang rape. The leader grinned. This would be good. This lone girl looked frightened, but defiant. He laughed again... a harsh, pitiless laugh.

'You can blow me first, baby; and then the troops can get their piece of ass.'

A thin black tube appeared in the girl's hand. She flicked her wrist; and with an evil click that echoed between the tall brick cliffs of the alleyway, the tube instantly extended into a baton... a flexible, spring baton with a vicious-looking ferrule at it tip. The Chinese hesitated; then the leader grinned.

'Stupid *mŭ gŏu!*... bitch! You were only going to get fucked. Now, you're gonna get cut up ... and fucked, for your insolence.'

He pulled a vicious-looking switchblade from his pocket and flicked it open. He gave an evil, toothy grin.

'Here it comes... it's Showtime, Bitch!'

Slowly, he began to advance on Gabriella; with his four buddies spread out behind him. She stood her ground with the mean-looking spring cosh held ready in her hand. When he was less than three feet from her and poised to strike; he grinned.

'It's gonna hurt...'

Gabriella gave him a cold, thin smile.

'You're certainly not wrong about that; asshole...'

And, with an almost balletic fluidity; she crouched, and slashed him across his knee-caps with the spring baton. With a sickening crack of shattering bone, he went down like a two-dollar whore; screaming and writing in agony on the filthy asphalt. His buddies faltered momentarily; then rushed at her.

Suddenly, the door opened behind them as a tall, distinguished-looking, middle-aged Chinese man stepped into the alleyway and spoke one word in Mandarin... a cold, commanding word...

'*Dāng!*... Stop!'

The four Chinese thugs froze. The man walked past them towards Gabriella, and as he did so; swiftly disarmed the writhing, whimpering leader, tossing the switchblade into the nearest dumpster. He stood in front of her; pointed at the spring cosh, and gave a thin smile.

'You may close that weapon, my dear. You will not need it again. May I introduce myself? I am Sebastian Lee; Master of the Li Ying Tong; and you are the granddaughter of the venerable Chang Ho-Pyong; I believe?'

Gabriella Chang nodded as she twisted the springs of the extended cosh and closed it.

Sebastian Lee nodded and turned to his five cowering pupils. He spoke in Mandarin; quietly, and without rancour, but the cold tone in his voice caused Gabriella to shiver imperceptibly.

'*Chīrén chī fú*... A fool suffers foolish fortune.'

He turned to her again.

'Forgive me; it is an ancient Chinese idiom that they will come to understand in its entirety. These fools are without honour, and bring shame upon their ancestors. They will be suitably chastised. Now; I understand that your grandfather wishes to take counsel with me?'

She nodded;

'Yes, Master Lee. The suggested venue is to be a neutral location of your choice for both parties, without subordinates from either side.'

Sebastian Lee smiled.

Your grandfather is a careful and honourable man. We will arrange this counsel and hopefully, reduce the danger and tension in what has become a difficult situation in Chinatown for both of our organisations.'

Gabriella Chang smiled;

'I will relay your reply to him, Master Lee. Your magnanimity in this difficult matter will certainly be rewarded.'

Lee nodded, and brushing past his five cringing "Dudes"; escorted her out to California Street to where her Porsche was parked up.

Two days later; in the North Beach neighbourhood of San Francisco known as Little Italy, which was slightly to the north of Chinatown;

two expensive automobiles approached each other from opposite ends of Vallejo Street and stopped outside the elegant and discreet Ristorante Césarina. An elderly Oriental gentleman climbed out of the large, imported British Jaguar Mark VIII, dove-grey, four-door sports sedan under the watchful gaze of his driver; who escorted the old man to the restaurant's entrance. A little way down the street, the gleaming black Lincoln Continental Limousine disgorged its black-suited driver who opened the rear door for a tall, distinguished-looking, middle-aged Chinese man, who strode across the sidewalk to the restaurant entrance, nodded at the old gentleman's driver, and entered the establishment. The two drivers returned to their respective automobiles and, getting in behind their steering wheels; watched each other with ill-concealed suspicion.

Inside the Ristorante Césarina; Chang Ho-Pyong and Sebastian Lee faced each other across a check-clothed table in an unobtrusive booth towards the rear of the dining area. Chang Ho-Pyong motioned to the discreetly hovering waiter and smiled at Sebastian Lee.

'Would you care for a proper American drink, Mr Lee? I fear that rice wine is probably not on their wine list.'

Sebastian Lee smiled at the old Korean gang boss.

Thank you Mr Chang; the lack of rice wine is of little consequence; for I much prefer a Kentucky sour mash Bourbon.'

Chang Ho-Pyong nodded approvingly.

'Bourbon is as American as Apple pie, Bald eagles and the Wild West, Mr Lee. I salute you in your embrace of our adopted land.'

He motioned to the waiter.

'Bring us a bottle of Old Crow Bourbon and two decent-sized glasses, if you please.'

Chang Ho-Pyong broke the foil seal on the bottle and pulled the cork. Pouring a good four fingers of the deep, golden liquid into each glass; he handed one to Sebastian Lee and gazed into the depths of his own glass. Then he looked up. His gaze was calm, but thoughtful. He spoke quietly.

'Mr Lee; I have asked for this meeting because I am concerned that a disquieting situation appears to be developing between my family and your organisation. It would seem that the younger members of my family and the youths of the Lai Ying club are nurturing a burgeoning animosity towards each other. My fear is that, unless we curtail this situation forthwith; we may be facing an all-out street war. This, of course would be extremely detrimental to our respective business interests in Chinatown.'

Sebastian Lee took a generous pull from his glass and nodded.

'I agree, Mr Chang. It has already become necessary for me to make an example of five Lai Ying members for just this sort of thing. They accosted your granddaughter outside my premises when she came to arrange this meeting. Please assure the young lady that they have been dealt with accordingly.'

He paused, and took another pull at his glass.

'I concur that we need to reach an accord in this matter. I suggest that we designate district boundaries for our activities. In this way we may exist in harmony with each other.'

Chang Ho-Pyong nodded and reached into his pocket. He brought out a small, velvet pouch and pushed it across the table to Sebastian Lee.

'Please accept this modest gift as a token of our accord. Its meaning and worth is more profound to you and your countrymen than it is to mine.'

Sebastian Lee released the pouch's drawstring and tipped the contents onto the table. The large, blood-red Garnet gemstone sparkled in the subdued lighting of the booth. He glanced up at Chang, who smiled benevolently.

'This is an artefact of great worth, Mr Chang. I am honoured by your generosity.'

Chang Ho-Pyong bowed his head imperceptibly.

'I am honoured that you consider it worthy of acceptance, Mr Lee.'

Pouring two more large measures of Bourbon; Sebastian Lee raised his glass.

'To our accord, and friendship, Mr Chang.'

Outside the Ristorante Césarina the two drivers were still engaged in attempting to stare each other down from behind the windshields of their respective automobiles. They were so immersed in their battle of wills that they failed to notice a dark-coloured Buick pull into the sidewalk some thirty yards behind them. Two men emerged and began strolling down Vallejo Street in the direction of the Ristorante Césarina. When they reached the rear of Chang's Jaguar, one man stopped and bent down as if to tie a shoelace. The other man walked past the entrance of the restaurant towards Lee's Lincoln. When he was alongside the driver's door, he reached into his jacket and pulled out a pack of cigarettes. He paused, and began searching for a match. The Lincoln's driver watched him suspiciously. The man shrugged, and turned to the driver's door, motioning that he should wind down the window. As he did so, the man smiled apologetically and asked if the driver had a match.

The Lincoln's driver shrugged, and reached for his Zippo. As he looked away momentarily; the stubby nose of a silenced pistol suddenly appeared in the man's hand. There was a dull "Phft!" as the silencer muffled the noise of the bullet and the driver was thrown across the front seats as it smashed into his face and blew his brains across the passenger-side window. Chang Ho-Pyong's horrified driver saw this and clawed for the pistol in his shoulder holster as the man with the shoelaces rose up alongside the passenger side of the Chang's Jaguar and pumped two shots from his silenced weapon into Ho-Pyong's driver's head; throwing him against the plush interior door panel as the top of his head exploded, hurling bloody debris against the leather and glass. Both men then entered Ristorante Césarina and walked quietly to the rear of the dining area. They each raised a silenced pistol and shot both Sebastian Lee and Chang Ho-Pyong dead in their booth, with headshots placed with surgical precision.

The silencers made whispers of the gunshots. The two men then calmly finished the dead men's drinks, picked up the Garnet gemstone, and casually strolled out of the restaurant.

Vinnie Culotta and Angelo Valachi; the two gunmen who had executed the mob bosses, Sebastian Lee and Chang Ho-Pyong in the Ristorante Césarina were making good time on Interstate 80 towards Sacramento. They were Mafia torpedoes out of Reno, Nevada, sent down to San Francisco by their crime family Consigliere: Joseph "Crazy Joe" DeCicco, to "whack" the two principal Asian criminal gang bosses in the city. The objective of this "hit" was to set the two Asian gangs at each other's throats, in order that the avenging attrition rate would be so far-reaching, that the Asian gangs' hold on the lucrative trade of prostitution and drug dealing, together with the extensive money-laundering; protection rackets, and gambling profits, would be effectively broken. The Lanza crime syndicate could then step in and run San Francisco. This was just one of the several city take-overs that La Cosa Nostra was planning. The ultimate goal was that organised crime across the United States would be syndicated solely by "The Commission"... the governing body of the American Mafia.

As the lights of Sacramento appeared in the distance; Vinnie Culotta tipped the Garnet gemstone into his palm and admired it as it reflected the light from the Buick's dashboard. His boss would be pleased with this gem... and with the successful method that they had employed in the hit. He might even promote both of them from being lowly "Soldati" to a much higher rank in the family... perhaps, even to "Made Man." This signified that they would then become untouchable in the criminal underworld and any harm brought to them would be met with retaliation from "The Family." He glanced across at Angelo Valachi and nodded contentedly. Only another two-and-a-half hours to Reno at a steady cruise speed; and then, the accolades of the family would be theirs.

San Francisco's finest didn't take very long to reach the Ristorante Césarina in Vallejo Street once the alarm had been raised... the Police Department Central Station was only four blocks down the street. Homicide detective Jack Reed scrutinised the scene of carnage in the cosy booth. Both victims had been shot in the forehead with a single bullet. Judging by the splatter of blood, bone fragments and brain matter that was plastered across a considerable area of the booth's walls; the gunmen had used hollow-cavity bullets... similar to the standard hollow-points, but with a much larger cavity in the tip of the bullet. These rounds didn't have much penetration...but they expanded rapidly upon impact; inflicting enormous damage; and by the look of the massive holes in the backs of the victims' heads; the rounds had been fired at a very close range. This observation was completely contradicted by the absence of any powder-burn stippling around the entrance wounds in the foreheads. Jack Reed nodded to himself. These killers had used silencers. This was a professional hit... and this was an ominous sign. Both victims were known to him. They were both Asian organised crime bosses. Might this be the beginning of all-out gang warfare?

His thoughts were interrupted by his partner, Charlie Ramirez, who came into the restaurant looking distinctly pale. He had been checking out the two dead drivers. He stared at the two bodies slumped in the booth and turned to Reed.

'The two stiffs outside in the automobiles; they were popped in just the same way, Jack. What in the hell is going down here?'

Jack Reed shook his head.

'Dunno, Charlie. This has all the marks of being a...'

He was interrupted by a howling siren and screeching brakes outside in the street. Blue and red reflected lights danced around the walls of the buildings across the street as a car door slammed, and the Precinct Captain hurried in through the door. He called out to Reed.

'What's the situation, Jack? I got a Code Two, Ten-Seventy-One as I was coming in.'

Reed jerked his thumb in the direction of the booth.

'Multiple homicide, Captain. Two here; and the two drivers outside.'

Captain Ed Delaney was fiftyish; short, square, and solid; a human bulldog running a little to jowl and paunch. Delaney wasn't a smart cop; but he was a wise, thirty-year veteran; and on these streets that was pretty damn rare. He walked over to the booth and peered inside. Slowly turning; he stared at Reed; grim-faced and silent. Then he spoke.

'Holy Mary, Mother of God! I thought I'd seen the end of this sort of killing when I was a rookie during the Tong wars of the thirties. Whatcha got so far?'

Reed shrugged.

'Not a lot, Captain. Two hit men; white, and cocky. After they executed the Chink and the Gook; they calmly finished off the victims' drinks and just strolled out. One of the waitresses saw a dark Buick... probably an Electra, zipping past the front of the restaurant just after the shooting. She caught a partial licence plate... blue on white... probably Nevada; starting with the letter "W"... and with the last three numbers "812." She said there was nothing else in the street.'

Delaney nodded.

'OK. Put out an APB to the Highway Patrol. Tell 'em these guys are armed and dangerous, and likely to be running up Interstate 80, heading east.'

Nevada Highway Patrol State trooper Herbie Jepson sat in his blue and white Pontiac Pursuit Special a few miles to the west of Reno, just inside the Nevada State Line; and parked up, hidden behind a large, free-standing billboard which bore a cartoon character of a dozing driver clutching a steering wheel, alongside a tombstone; and sternly cautioned errant drivers..."*Sleepy?... From Short Nap comes Long Nap.*" He had been here for about twenty-five minutes in response to the urgent telex from The San Francisco P.D. He was on the lookout for a dark, possibly blue, Buick Electra coming up Interstate 80 from the direction of Sacramento.

Herbie was bored and annoyed. Twenty minutes before the end of his shift, and the dispatcher had called him up and told him to stop this damned suspect auto on sight. Just to keep it interesting; he had added that the SFPD Homicide Division had also said that it contained two men, who were armed and dangerous. Great! Apart from fucking up his plans for the night, there was also the real chance that he could end up getting his head blown off.

Herbie's idea of "blown off," that night, was what he was hoping the pretty little blonde blackjack dealer at the Silver Dollar Casino whom he had been humping for the last few weeks, would have done for him in the back seat of the Pursuit Special if only he had been on the other side of Reno when the squawk came in.

It was a dark night with a waning moon. The distant mass of the mountains jutted into the starlit sky out to the right. In the distance, lightning was flashing, but there was no sign of rain. This was typical desert weather tonight... hot, dry, and windy. To the left, there was nothing except the endless shadow of the Tahoe National Park, and the gun-metal shimmer of the moon on the asphalt of Interstate 80. Herbie could see for miles back down the highway. The glow from the lights of Sacramento washed across the horizon; but there were no headlights anywhere to be seen. He glanced at his wristwatch. The big luminous minute hand was crawling round to eleven o'clock. He swore quietly. What a waste of fucking time. The suspects probably weren't even coming this way any time soon... if at all... and by now, he'd have had the panties off his pretty little blonde blackjack dealer and be well into getting it on with a really sweet piece of ass.

Morosely, he lit another Chesterfield and settled himself more comfortably in the driver's seat of the Pursuit Special. He glanced at his wristwatch again. The big luminous minute hand was just coming up to eleven-fifteen. Now the thunder was rumbling fitfully; delayed, and distant. Briefly, the lightning flashed again, far off, beyond the crouching shadow of the mountains. He took a deep drag from his cigarette and began fantasising about his little blonde. He grinned to himself; Oh man! She could suck dick like she was siphoning gas.

His boner-inspiring fantasy was rudely interrupted by headlights coming up the highway from the direction of Sacramento at quite a speed. Tossing the cigarette out of the window; Herbie Jepson fired up the motor, and prepared to hit the gas. A car flashed past... a dark car that looked like a Buick, judging by the shape of its tail lights. Herbie punched the gas pedal to the floor, and, with the rear tires squealing and spinning against the gravel, slewed the Pursuit Special out onto the highway. The Sonofabitch was moving fast; but not fast enough for Herbie's three-sixty-one cubic inch, Vee-eight motor pushing out three hundred and ten kick-ass horses. He switched on the lights and siren and accelerated after the dancing tail lights. The speedometer needle of the Pontiac was climbing past the eighty mark. He smiled grimly. Even if they weren't the suspects, he'd got them. A straightforward speeding citation would just round the night off nicely, and then he could go pick up his little blonde and get it into her; but, just in case; with one hand still on the wheel, he reached across for his new Mossberg pump-action shotgun, shoved the shoulder stock down onto the seat between his legs; and cycled the slide with a mean, ominous "Ka-chack." Now; if they were the suspects, he had six rounds of buckshot that he could slamfire into them.

Angelo Valachi glanced into the rear-view mirror and swore quietly. The flashing red light of the cop car was getting closer. He glanced at Vinnie Culotta.

'Well, whaddya wanna do now, Vinnie? Do we act cute... or give this dumbfuck the hard good-bye?'

Vinnie Culotta grinned.

'We'll pull over like we're good citizens; then, when he comes to the window, we'll take him down.'

Herbie Jepson was coming up fast behind the Buick, when he saw the right rear turn signal suddenly begin blinking, and the stop lamps light up, as the driver began pulling over onto the shoulder of the highway. He switched off the siren and pulled in behind the Buick; stopping some twenty feet back. Setting the parking brake but leaving the motor idling; he picked up the Mossberg; stepped out of the Pursuit Special; and began to walk towards the Buick. Angelo Valachi glanced in the side mirror and watched the cop walking slowly along his side of the car; rolling his window down as the cop approached; and feeling for the silenced pistol out of the cop's line of sight.

With the Mossberg held barrel to the sky and resting against his shoulder; but with his finger on the trigger... just in case; Jepson shone his flashlight into the car and looked Angelo Valachi up and down.

'Do you know why I pulled you over, Sir?'

Valachi looked at the cop guiltily.

'I guess I was doing a little over the speed limit, officer.'

Jepson nodded.

'Yep; you could say that. The speed limit here is only sixty-five miles an hour and I clocked you at well over ninety. Sir, I'm going to have to ask you to step out of the vehicle.'

It was the last thing he ever said.

Valachi and Culotta fired at the same time. The two bullets smacked into Herbie Jepson's chest and hurled him backwards. The Mossberg's barrel toppled over from its upright position as Jepson's almost dead finger jerked on the trigger by pure reflex. The twelve-gauge buckshot blast took Valachi full in the face and blew most of his head off, splattering Culotta with blood, brains, and bone fragments.

Vinnie Culotta sat, frozen in the passenger seat of the Buick; the interior of which, looked as though someone had tossed a bucket of slaughterhouse offal in through the window. For a few minutes he sat motionless, staring at the remains of Valachi's head; and totally shocked by what had just happened... then self-preservation kicked in. What the fuck should he do now? One dead cop; one dead partner with only half a head.

He forced his brain to think. Dump Valachi out on the highway along with the cop; high-tail it on to Reno, and hand over the gemstone and the details of the successful hit, and the death of Angelo Valachi to "Crazy Joe" DeCicco. After that it would sure as hell be time to get the fuck outta Dodge and go to ground somewhere he couldn't easily be found... like Las Vegas.

With the interior of the Buick spattered with the remains of Angelo Valachi's head; Vinnie Culotta decided that it would be a good idea to pull off Interstate 80 as soon as he possibly could. Cops tended to notice shit like a car drenched in blood barrelling up the highway late at night. Just to the north of the town of Truckee, he swung the car onto Highway 89 that ran north to Sierraville and accelerated away up the deserted asphalt ribbon. To the west; beyond the mountains, a bolt of lightning silently streaked the sky. Light rain began to spatter the Buick's windshield.

Two miles to the north, Vinnie Culotta turned onto the back road that led up past Prosser Creek reservoir and continued on past Stampede reservoir. He knew that this back road would be deserted and would eventually double back towards Reno. After he re-crossed Interstate 80 he could take the fire-roads through the Sunflower Mountain forest towards "Crazy Joe" DeCicco's imposing residence overlooking Virginia Lake in the suburbs of Reno.

Parking the Buick up at the side of the house; Vinnie Culotta walked around to the front door and reached for the doorknob. Opening the door, he stepped inside; and then, before he knew it, a gun was pressed to his temple and a big hand grabbed his shoulder. A hard voice with a pronounced Chicago accent rasped in his ear.

'Welcome home, Vinnie. We're havin' a house party, and you're the Star turn.'

Vinnie Culotta was roughly shoved into the living room. Four men were standing around; and sitting in an expensive leather recliner was the Mob Consigliere: Joseph "Crazy Joe" DeCicco smoking a fat Havana cigar. Two of the men grabbed Vinnie and roughly dropped him into a chair opposite DeCicco.

DeCicco tapped the ash from his cigar and studied Vinnie. Then he spoke.

'Hi, Vinnie. News travels fast. Now, we're gonna have a little session about how you've pretty well fucked up our plans for taking over San Francisco's business interests...'

Vinnie opened his mouth to protest, but before he could say a word; DeCicco leaned forward and slammed him hard in the nose with his fist. As blood spurted; "Crazy Joe" grinned.

'Damn! That smarts, don't it, Vinnie? Gettin' socked in the nose fucks you up real good. You got that pain shootin' up through your brain. Your eyes fill up with water. It ain't any kind of fun. But that's as good as it's ever gonna fuckin' get for you, and it won't ever get that good again. Whatsamatta? Can't breathe? Get used to it. We got a beef with you, Vinnie boy. You got yourself eyeballed when you hightailed it outta there after you whacked the Chink and the Gook in that shithole eatery. You wouldda gotten away with it, but you fuckheads had to go and take down some dumb cop out on the highway. Every fuckin' cop in Reno is runnin' around like their butts are on fire and they're fucking up business real good. Clipping that cop was right off the fuckin' record; and I don't believe even you could be that fuckin' stupid... your shithead buddy, Valachi; Yeah, I could believe it from that fuckin' "*mortadella*"; but you?'

Vinnie dripped blood over Crazy Joe's finest English Wilton, white carpet. He reached into his pocket and pulled out the little velvet pouch; handing it to DeCicco. Sniffing back the blood, he looked at his boss pleadingly.

'Valachi bought the Goddam farm, so I left him out there with his fuckin' head blown off. Shooting the cop was his idea. We took this from the Chink. We figured you might like it.'

Crazy Joe tipped the contents of the pouch into his palm. The big, blood-red Garnet sparkled in the light from the chandelier; and a bright spark glowed deep in its heart. DeCicco smiled.

'That's a pretty thing. You think it makes things OK between us now, you fuckin' "*Pucchiacha?*" A headless stiff who can lead the law straight back here...with a dead cop for company? And just to make it really peachy... the Chink and Gook Street gangs have begun rubbing out every soldier in Chinatown and the Bay area that they can chase down. It's "*Gira diment*" down there... and all because you and Valachi fucked up. No dice, Vinnie boy. You're a fuckin' busted flush.'

He turned to one of the men standing in the room.

'Frankie; take Vinnie here for a nice road trip.'

The man grabbed Vinnie by the collar and yanked him to his feet. With a swift, practised movement, he yanked the collar of Vinnie's jacket down, trapping his arms; and frog-marched him out of the room. DeCicco leaned back on his recliner, admiring the gemstone. Taking a long puff from his cigar he glanced at another of the men.

'Marty; go lose that Goddam heap of junk messing up my driveway. Vinnie won't be needing it any more.'

Two days later a delivery man was driving up from Reno on the road to Pyramid Lake when he spotted something pink sticking up out of the Black Rock Desert. Stopping his truck to check it out; he discovered that it was an arm; and the hand at the top of the arm was holding a busted flush of King, Queen, Nine, and Three of Hearts, with a Jack of Clubs, all neatly fanned out. The cops eventually arrived with spades and dug around for a while until they found the rest of the guy at the other end of the arm. He was buried with the back of his head blown off.

It was Vinnie Culotta.

Chapter Thirteen.

Thursday, January 26th. 1961.
Kampfgruppen der Arbeiterklasse Training Camp.
Schmerwitz Forest, Brandenburg.
East Germany.

Fernán Pasuali squinted with his left eye and stared down the scope of the East German DDR bolt action sniper rifle with his right; as he pulled the bolt back on the rifle chambering another round into the breech. He drew the stock of the gun firmly against his shoulder and aimed. The target sat square and dead centre in the cross hairs, almost three hundred metres down-range.

He breathed in, and squeezed the trigger as he exhaled; feeling the recoil kick hard against his shoulder, rocking him backwards slightly. Absorbing the rifle's recoil all morning had left his shoulder sore and badly bruised. His instructor lowered the spotting scope and grinned.

'OK, Pasuali; that's another in the black. We'll make a sniper of you yet. That's enough for today; collect up your spent casings and report to Oberfeldwebel Traugott for the tradecraft and infiltration session.'

Fernán Pasuali; a twenty-three-year-old post-graduate in Economics at The University of Havana had been studying at the Faculty when the Cuban Dictator Batista had ordered the university to be closed after the University students' federation attempted to kill him in an armed assault on the Cuban Presidential Palace on March 13th, 1957. Batista had managed to escape, although many students had been killed during the action. In the months that followed, the police executed many of the students who had led the failed coup but had completely missed Pasuali. Castro's regime re-opened the university in 1959 and banned student demonstrations and political affiliations. As a member of Castro's 26th July Movement; Pasuali had been approached by a Ministry of the Interior official and recruited for a "special assignment" that he was led to believe would enable him to become a champion of anti-imperialism, humanitarianism, socialism and environmentalism for the greater good of his homeland. Three months later; here he was, in a forest wilderness some seventy kilometres to the south-west of Berlin, being taught to become a covert assassin in a God-forsaken training camp of the *Kampfgruppen der Arbeiterklasse...* the Combat Groups of The Working Class; sick of the cold, German winter and grey skies, and longing for the warm climate and blue seas of his Caribbean home.

After the day's training and the evening meal; Pasuali was sitting on his bunk in the barracks, cleaning his sniper rifle and minding his own business when the door banged open and the barracks block bully, Truppführer Breuer; and two of his cronies swaggered in. Looming over Pasuali's bunk; Breuer sneered and nudged his pals.

'Fuck Me! That's all he ever does; creeping up the arses of his instructors.'

Shoving the sniper rifle out of Pasuali's hands; he stuck his gorilla-paw of a hand into Pasuali's chest and shoved him back on the bunk.

'I dunno what the fuck you think you're doing here with decent Germans; so why don't you just piss off back to coconut land, you Spic shit?'

Pasuali looked up at Breuer with a thin, dangerous smile on his face.

'You trying the old "Uber Alles" crap on me again, Breuer? It hasn't worked twice this century for you goose-stepping assholes; so what makes you think it will work with me now? You might be a born bully, recruit-chasing prick; but I really don't give a shit about you, or your arse-creeping harem.'

Breuer's face grew slowly scarlet with rage. His fists clenched at his sides, and his eyes glittered. Pasuali looked at him through narrowed eyes.

'Bully boys like you,'

He said, contemptuously,

'Always end up as losers. You know that? They always do. I've known a shit-load of your type. When I was with Che Guevara, fighting in the Escambray Mountains back home; there were several of 'em. Great loud-mouthed fuck-pigs that never knew when to stop.'

His thin smile faded.

'They're all pushing up daisies now... *"Requetemuerto"*... where they belong. They asked for it, and they got it... and so will you, in the end.'

Breuer snarled and lunged forward; his huge fist balled tightly, and raised to smash into Pasuali's face. Almost quicker than the eye could follow; Pasuali's right hand shot out with the knuckles locked straight, in the infamous Bear-claw, martial arts punch. His rigid front knuckles struck Breuer directly in the throat below his Adam's apple with such force that Breuer's neck broke with an audible crack. The big man's eyes rolled, and pinkish foam suddenly specked his lips. He lurched back clutching his throat and making a terrible, choking, gurgling noise. His glazed eyes were those of a man already dead, as he toppled backwards and hit the floor with a sickening crash. His heels drummed on the concrete for a few moments, and then he lay still.

Grün and Fritsch; Breuer's two sidekicks gaped at the motionless body. Pasuali eyed them steadily.

'You want some too, ladies? If not; then just piss off and let me get on with cleaning my weapon.'

They looked at him... then at each other; and ran out of the barracks without uttering a word.

Ten minutes later; two Military police Stabsgefreiters came rumbling into the barracks; hands on their Makarov holsters. They saw Pasuali still cleaning his rifle and paused. Pasuali looked up, and then continued to clean the weapon. The larger of the Stabsgefreiters bent down to the lifeless Breuer and felt the man's neck for a pulse. He didn't find one. He stood and walked over to Pasuali. Splay-legged, and with his hands upon his hips, he spoke.

'So what happened to this piece of shit, Pasuali?... as if I didn't fucking well know.'

Fernán Pasuali eyed the big Stabsgefreiter up and down.

'He slipped on the floor and fell down... and smacked his head on the edge of the bunk. It serves him fucking well right. That's what comes of galloping around in an unregimental manner.'

The big Stabsgefreiter nodded.

'Oh Yeah? That's not quite what his pals reported. Put down the rifle and stand up.'

Snapping the handcuffs on to Pasuali, he shrugged.

'Well, Pasuali; you're really up shit creek this time. You've killed the bastard... and a senior NCO at that. It's the glasshouse for you, my lad; and the Tribunal in the morning. If they're in a good mood, they'll just shoot you. If you try to be a smart-ass with them; it'll be a one-way trip to be shaved by the big razor at the Stasi prison in Berlin-Hohenschönhausen. Think yourself lucky. In the old days, it would have been a drumhead court-martial and an immediate fucking firing squad.'

The cell they put Pasuali in wasn't particularly uncomfortable. At least, the bed had a mattress even though it was stuffed with straw. He spent the rest of the day wondering just what they had in mind for him. Tribunal? He wasn't in the military... but in this Stalinist puppet regime, did that make any difference at all? He knew that someone was investing a considerable amount of time, money, and effort into his training. Would they now come and get him off the hook to protect their investment? He shrugged to himself. He would just have to wait and see. With this in mind; he settled into a more comfortable position on the lumpy mattress and watched the light fade through the iron bars of the cell window as dusk fell.

He awoke to voices echoing from the walls of the barracks and penetrating the cell. Heavy boots approached down the corridor. No military boot in the world has the ominous sound of the German jackboot. It was designed and built to imprint fear and horror into those who heard it. The Prussians had invented it; the Nazis had managed to evolve it to its pitiless perfection; and now, the Communist State used it to their intimidatory advantage.

The footsteps came to a halt just outside the cell. Heavy keys jingled as the cell door key was pushed home in the lock. It turned twice, and the heavy door flew open. The red enamelling of the Hammer and Compass cap badge gleamed warningly from the door opening. A tough face peered into the cell from under the shiny black peak of the stone-grey vizor cap.

'Fernán Pasuali? On your feet, and come with me.'

Pasuali stood up and put his arms out in front of himself.

The big Oberfeldwebel looked at him.

'What the fuck are you waiting for?'

Pasuali gave him a puzzled look.

'What about the manacles or handcuffs? Don't I get them before I'm hauled before the Tribunal?'

The Oberfeldwebel shook his head.

'No Tribunal today, pal. You're off to see the Kommandant.'

Pasuali looked even more puzzled.

'The Kommandant? What time is it?'

The Oberfeldwebel grabbed Pasuali by the shoulder and shoved him out into the corridor.

'Time to get your arse moving. Now come on.'

He glanced at his watch.

It's 08.05. Think yourself lucky you're not being hauled off to Tegel to be sat on a stool that's been polished to a high gloss by hundreds of trembling arseholes in one of their interrogation rooms.'

The Kommandant sat behind his ostentatious desk and gave Pasuali a bilious glare as he was marched into the office. He slowly opened a buff folder and studied the contents. At length, he spoke.

'Pasuali; the only reason that you are now still in the business of drawing breath is because you appear to have some very influential friends. If it was my decision; you would be staring down the wrong end of a firing squad right now. However...'

He gave Pasuali another choleric glare;

'... I have an order here from no less than The Kremlin that you are to be removed from this facility and transferred elsewhere. I have therefore decided to send you to the Prora barracks on the Baltic Island of Rügen. If nothing else; you will be out of the way up there where I can drop you out of sight in the old *Kraft durch Freude* resort which is now an army training barracks. You have twenty minutes to pack your kit and get your murderous arse off my camp. Dismissed!'

He closed the folder and tossed it aside with a contemptuous flourish that wouldn't have come amiss during the days of the Gestapo.

The Prora barracks on the Baltic Island of Rügen was some two hundred and seventy kilometres to the north-east of the Schmerwitz Forest training camp and took Pasuali and his escort almost six hours to arrive there by train. As usual, the train journey was overcrowded and slow, owing in part to the poor condition of most railway lines in the GDR; and the fact that the steam locomotive was somewhat asthmatic, and needed to stop every hour to replenish its water tanks.

Prora was exactly what Pasuali had imagined it to be... a concrete monster. Built as a colossal Nazi-planned tourist structure resort... *"Das KdF-Seebad Rügen"*; it had been converted into a sprawling military training barracks for use by the GDR. The Prora resort... the largest architectural project of the Third Reich, was to consist of two immense structures... the North complex... *"Der Nordflügel"*; and one to the South... *"Der Südflügel"*; each consisting of four, six-storey, residential blocks five hundred and fifty metres long; sub-divided into ten housing units; each with its own staircase building; and providing accommodation for twenty thousand Nazi holidaymakers in eleven thousand apartments; each of which, had a view of the sea. It was planned that the stay at the new resort would cost only Two Reichsmarks per day, and it would include all associated costs, such as taxes, beach chair; and swimsuit, towel, etc.

Between the two complexes would have been administration

buildings and a massive, open festival square with an assembly hall at one end. The housing sections were joined by community buildings and swimming halls. The complex included plans for several restaurants, cinemas, sport halls, and other entertainment sites; as well as housing for the permanent on-site staff; a rail station, and other necessary infrastructure... water works, an electrical substation, post office, etc. When completed, the complex would have stretched along the beach for almost five kilometres. A large quay was built at the seaside in the centre of the complex, with moorings for the KdF cruise ships "Robert Ley" and "Wilhelm Gustloff."

A total of five of these resorts had been planned for the Nazis to provide the ordinary working-class German people with affordable holidays in beautiful surroundings, allowing them to return to their everyday lives and the workplace refreshed and with renewed vigour... or at least; that was the utopian dream that would have been sold to them In reality; Prora was an intrinsic part of the Nazi propaganda programme, offering its people a sweetener for its less palatable policies. Ultimately, it would give its people the "strength" to deal with the impending war.

The entertainment would be pure propaganda, and daylight hours would have been taken up with a diet of Nazi-approved exercises, courses, and talks. This system would precisely adjust each holidaymaker's sleep, diet, entertainment, and beach time schedule down to a scientifically designed formula. With typically ruthless Nazi efficiency, the goal was to pack a three to four week holiday into just seven days. The intent was to extend the typical worker's limit of peak efficiency from the age of forty... as it was calculated in the 1930s... to the age of seventy... and beyond.

Each guest room was designed to be identical... small and narrow; five metres long by two and a half metres wide; and equipped with standard furniture... two beds, a built-in wardrobe and a small seating area next to a washbasin with hot and cold water. The concept was to oblige guests to join the collective areas located in every block. Individuality was not to be tolerated. Even the toilets and showers were communal, and located in the landside spurs adjoining the stairwells.

However; before the first tourists arrived, Hitler invaded Poland. Need for construction materials for the war effort halted the project. Work was scaled down at Prora and eventually abandoned; and the resort never actually functioned as such, although refugees from the bombing of Hamburg and other cities lived in the most-compete buildings during 1944-45. As the war progressed; the complex was also used as a training site for police and female signals auxiliaries, and as a military hospital.

Since 1956, the buildings had become a restricted military area housing several East German Army units; as well as soldiers from "socialist countries" such as Cuba, North Korea, Angola, and Mozambique. It was a perfect place for Pasuali to become just one more anonymous trainee.

Wednesday, February 8th, 1961.
Charlottenburg. West Berlin.

The situation concerning the tracking down of the supposed Cuban dissident was getting a lot more difficult for Charlotte and Callaghan. Up to this point in time; Aquila's intelligences had been consistent... if somewhat futile. With all of Wolf's informants at his disposal; nothing had been forthcoming with regard to the Cuban. It seemed that, if he existed; he had simply vanished.

Wolf had more to worry about than some ephemeral conspirator. During the early days of 1961, the GDR government was actively seeking a means of halting the emigration of its population to the West. The East German President Walter Ulbricht was attempting to persuade the Soviets that an immediate solution was necessary and that the only way to stop the exodus was to use force, and resolve the status of Berlin.

Khrushchev was not impressed. The four-power status of Berlin specified free travel between zones and specifically forbade the presence of German troops in Berlin. Ulbricht was taking a risk on the assumption that he would continue to be successful or in favour, but, just in case; was already stockpiling building materials for the erection of a permanent barrier that would cut Berlin in two, and permanently seal off East Germany in the event that Khrushchev wouldn't play ball with his aspirations.

Wolf was also in possession of information to the effect that U.S. President John F. Kennedy did not see eye to eye with the West German Chancellor, Konrad Adenauer on the West Berlin issue and German settlement. It appeared that Adenauer doubted Kennedy's resoluteness to hold firm on the German and Berlin questions. The Soviets were now trying to exploit this uncertainty to drive the wedge deeper between the Chancellor and new Kennedy administration.

Having spent the morning shopping in the KaDeWe department store on Tauentzienstrasse and generally relaxing; Charlotte and

Callaghan strolled back up to Breitscheidplatz, passing under the shadow of the ruined spire of the Kaiser-Wilhelm-Gedächtniskirche and crossing Joachimstaler Strasse turned into Kurfürstendamm. Callaghan glanced at his wristwatch and motioned with his hand towards the Café Kranzler across the street.

'It's almost four o'clock... *"Kaffee und Kuchen Zeit."* How about over there?'

He grinned.

'I think that's how it's pronounced!'

Charlotte nodded.

'Very good, Callaghan! Coffee and cake time. What a wonderful idea!'

Entering the Café Kranzler, they chose to take a table on the pavement under the red-and-white striped awning, and ordered coffee and *Schwarzwälder Kirschtörtchens*... Black Forest Cherry tart.

Café Kranzler was a great place to people watch, and let Berlin go rushing past. The weather was fine, the skies were blue, and the coffee was good. They were enjoying a second cup of coffee as they watched the world pass by, when a shadow fell across their table. Charlotte glanced up into the eyes of Viktor Malinovskii; who stood there gazing down at them with a preoccupied expression on his face. He touched the brim of his fedora to them.

'Good afternoon, my friends. Please forgive the intrusion; but our colleague in Lichtenberg has unearthed some interesting information concerning our "missing friend." Could you pay me a visit at the office this evening, when we can finalise the transaction?'

By this, he meant that he needed them to get to Karlshorst where this information could be passed on to them in completely safe surroundings, without any chance of the Stasi intercepting any details. Malinovskii didn't trust the Stasi, or anyone with the slightest connection to them. Aquila was tolerated because of his information-gathering usefulness; but Malinovskii didn't trust him any farther than he might have been able to throw him.

Charlotte nodded.

'That is very interesting, Viktor. We'll be there tonight.'

Malinovskii nodded and turned to leave. He touched the brim of his fedora again, and said,

'See you later. Enjoy the rest of the afternoon.'

He stepped out onto the pavement; blending with the passers-by; and was soon lost in the bustle of Ku'damm.

The trip into East Berlin was not quite as easy as it had been on their last visit. The Brandenburg Tor was alive with Volkspolizei, and once through the inner border; the military presence along Unter den Linden right up to Max Engels Platz was considerably larger than usual. Charlotte and Callaghan were also followed by two Stasi cars through Alexanderplatz and along Frankfurter Allee and Alt Friedrichsfelde as far as the junction with Am Tierpark. As soon as Callaghan turned right, the two Stasi cars peeled off and turned north. They knew that they were about to enter the Soviet restricted-zone around the Berlin-Karlshorst Rezidentura.

The first restricted-zone checkpoint was where Am Tierpark became Treskowallee. The checkpoint guard waved the Mercedes-Benz down and motioned to Callaghan for his pass. Callaghan wound down the window and flashed the Soviet pass that Viktor Malinovskii had provided. Charlotte merely waved her pass between two fingers. The young private stepped back smartly and raised the red and white striped pole, snapping smartly to attention as he did so. Callaghan accelerated away. So far... so good!

The next checkpoint was located on the corner of Kopenicker Allee and Rheinsteinstrasse, which led into Zwieseler Strasse; where the main entrance of the Rezidentura was located. Again; the passes seemed to intimidate the guards and the Mercedes was waved though with only a cursory glance and an immediate snapping to attention.

Callaghan cruised up Zwieseler Strasse and slowed to turn into the Rezidentura compound. As the Mercedes approached, an armed guard stepped out from the guardhouse on the left hand side of the tall steel gates and held his hand out. Callaghan wound down the window and flashed his pass. He spoke tersely to the guard using the Russian sentence that Charlotte had made him repeatedly practise all the way down Am Tierpark and Treskowallee until she was satisfied with his pronunciation...

"Polkovnik Tolenkanovna dl'a Polkovnika Malinovskiya. My ozhidayems'a"... 'Colonel Tolenkanovna for Colonel Malinovskii. We are expected.'

The guard snapped to attention and waved them through into the compound.

Callaghan ostentatiously parked up the black Mercedes-Benz directly in front of the main entrance; got out, and opened the passenger door for Charlotte. As she emerged from the car; a young *mladshij serzhant*... a junior sergeant; came running out of the building to meet them. Saluting smartly, he guided them up to the first floor and along a corridor painted in the unpleasant shade of mustard, topped by a dull, neutral grey, which appeared to be the standard paint scheme for the entire building. He paused at an anonymous door about half-way along the corridor and knocked. An authoritative voice replied from behind the door...

"*Vojdite!*"... 'Enter!'

The young junior sergeant opened the door and ushered Charlotte and Callaghan inside. Viktor Malinovskii; resplendent in his Colonel's uniform with broad red collar tabs and double red-striped shoulder boards bearing three gold stars, stood up from behind the large desk and came towards them hand outstretched in welcome. He smiled.

'Charlotte; Callaghan... welcome to my lair! Come! Sit down and make yourselves comfortable. There is much to discuss, and not much time to act upon it.'

Opening a folder embossed with the Stasi seal of the *"Schild und Schwert der Partei"*... the "Shield and Sword of the Party," resting on his desk; he began to read from the close-typed document.

'The Stasi have received a disciplinary report from the Kommandant of the KdA training camp located at Schmerwitz, concerning a Cuban national who was undergoing training there as a sniper. This individual was involved in a barrack-room altercation which resulted in the death of his assailant. The automatic penalty for this state of affairs is Court-martial, and handing over to the civil police to be charged with murder.

It would, however, appear that someone in The Kremlin has intervened; and as a consequence, the culpable individual has not been charged. This state of affairs is so unusual that alarm bells began sounding as soon as the report crossed the desk of the receiving officer at Normannenstrasse. Aquila passed the dossier to me.

The man is named as being one Fernán Pasuali; an activist with Castro's 26th July Movement; who may well have fought with Che Guevara during the guerrilla campaign that deposed the Batista regime during the Cuban Revolution. Preliminary investigations that we have carried out reveal nothing beyond what I have just told you; but, I think we have him, Charlotte. I think this man is our Ghost.'

Thursday, February 9th, 1961.
KdA Training Camp.
Schmerwitz Forest, Brandenburg.
East Germany.

Oberst der Volkspolizei, Gerhardt Schreiner; Kommandant of the Schmerwitz training camp sat behind his desk and quietly swore to himself. The camp had been like an ant's nest with a big boot shoved into it since the killing of the bullying Truppführer Breuer at the hands of the Cuban. The Stasi had been crawling all over the camp for more than a week now; interrogating and coercing "witnesses"... anyone that they might use to keep their records tidy. Now; on top of all this disruption, the SED hierarchy in East Berlin had tersely informed Schreiner that two investigators were travelling down from Karlshorst. That was all he needed; two KGB hard-asses sniffing around and digging up fuck knows what.

Up to this point; running the Kommandature of Schmerwitz had been a really easy deployment... "palmy days" as they called them... when you considered what the alternatives were; but now, it looked as though it was all about to turn to shit in front of his eyes... and all because of some Spic asshole who wasn't even in his Command.

His contemplation was disturbed by a knock on the door of his office. Schreiner looked up and snapped

"Kommen!"... 'Come!'

The door opened, and one of his Volkspolizei Instructor Feldwebels ushered a strikingly attractive woman and a tough-looking man into his office. He rose to greet them; but the woman produced a military pass and placed it on his desk. As he looked down to study it; she spoke.

'Comrade Kommandant Schreiner; we have no time for niceties. I am Colonel Nadia Tolenkanovna and this is Major Sevastian Levkova; both of the Second Chief Directorate; attached to the Rezidentura, Karlshorst. We are here to establish the true identity and objectives of the accused offender, Fernán Pasuali who is under training at this facility.'

Schreiner studied the two "investigators"; wondering which way he should proceed. The woman was very attractive; but her eyes were cold... as cold as ice. The man was big... at least two metres tall; with shoulders like a Hamburg docker. They both gave the impression of being typically intractable and dangerous, KGB Karlshorst hard-nuts. She was doing the talking; her companion stood silent; his blue-grey eyes... as cold and unfathomable as the Baltic Sea in winter; never left Schreiner's face.

Gerhardt Schreiner's mouth was suddenly very dry. Get this wrong... give the impression that he hadn't followed procedure to the letter; and he might well find himself incarcerated in the notorious Ministry of State Security secret labour camp "X", next to the Lichtenburg-Hohenschönhausen remand prison.

Attempting an indiscernible swallow; he found his voice, and addressed Charlotte...

'Comrade Colonel; I am afraid you are too late. I had Pasuali transferred to Prora barracks on the Baltic Island of Rügen, as a result of his proposed indictment to Court Martial being commuted on the instructions of none less than The Kremlin itself. He was transferred out on the 28th January. Had it been my decision; albeit Section 112 of the Criminal code specifies no less than ten years' imprisonment or life imprisonment for his offence; I would have advocated that he be shot on the spot.'

He leaned back in his chair; hoping that his insinuated tough attitude would placate the two investigators.

The woman glanced at her companion; who nodded imperceptibly. She studied Schreiner for a moment; then spoke. Her tone of voice gave him an involuntary shiver.

'Very well, Comrade Kommandant Schreiner. It appears that you have acted in accordance with your procedures. However…'

Schreiner's gut tightened as she paused; holding his eyes with her icy stare;

'… Should any sort of similar situation ever arise again; you would be well advised to inform Karlshorst prior to reporting to Normannenstrasse.'

Schreiner nodded avidly.

'Yes, Comrade Colonel. I will see that this requirement is added to Standing Orders.'

She nodded.

'Then our business is concluded, Comrade Kommandant. I bid you good day.'

As they left the building; Charlotte turned to Callaghan.

'Well, what do you think, Gil? Is this Pasuali the one we are looking for?'

Callaghan shrugged.

'This guy seems to be our best bet… in fact; he's our only bet so far. He sounds like a dangerous bastard… the kind of guy who could snap at any moment, but you'd never be able to predict when or why. Just the sort of crazy fanatic they'd get for this sort of job. I think we ought to drive up to this Prora place and see what we can dig up.'

Charlotte nodded.

'Yes; you're right. We'll go up there tomorrow. D'you want to drive?... or shall we catch a train?'

Callaghan grinned.

'Why be uncomfortable? We'll use the Merc'.

Next morning; they set out early. Strasse des 17. Juni was virtually deserted. The Brandenburger Tor was unguarded and Unter den Linden was silent and empty. Crossing a deserted Max Engels Platz, they crossed into Rathaus Strasse and drove up to Alexanderplatz. Callaghan continued along Königstrasse to Griefswalder Strasse, which led into what had been Berliner Allee but was now renamed Klement-Gottwald-Allee; and the suburb of Weissensee. Beyond Weissensee, the route led out through Malchow and Lindenberg onto the Berliner Ring at Schwanebeck.

As Callaghan turned onto the long ribbon of concrete, Charlotte glanced at him, and folded her map away.

'We can go straight up the Berlin-Stettin autobahn and turn off towards Prenzlau; which will take us up through Pasewalk and Greifswald to Stralsund. Then it's across the Rügen Causeway to the island.'

Turning onto the access road north, Callaghan accelerated to eighty km/h. The autobahn ran relatively flat and straight through farmland for the first five kilometres, and to the right, was a pleasant view of the old town of Bernau. Three and a half kilometres farther on, was the autobahn exit to the old town. Two kilometres farther, and the forests began to close in on either side of the carriageway. The autobahn was deserted except for the odd truck hauling one, or sometimes two trailers. Callaghan increased the speed of the car; staying in the outer lane at one hundred and ten km/h through the beautiful, undulating countryside dotted with lakes in the rich forests of northern Brandenburg.

Passing the exit to Wandlitz, the route curved to the north-east surrounded by beech forests stark against the winter morning sun. The next landmark was the small bridge over the upper end of the Obersee; a little to the west of Lanke. Just beyond, was the exit to the village. The autobahn straightened again for a lengthy run through the forest which was now becoming densely wooded with pine trees. Callaghan glanced at Charlotte. She was quiet... thoughtful. She had travelled this same route with Max all those years ago; when they were travelling out to the remains of Goring's Carinhall as they searched for clues as to the whereabouts of that damned Abaddon Stone. Choosing not to intrude on her thoughts; Callaghan smiled to himself and continued driving.

The autobahn was curving gently to the left. The forest seemed to be thinning slightly as they crossed the wide, Eberswälde valley. Out to the right was an airfield, occupied by aircraft emblazoned with the Soviet Red Star. This was Eberswalde-Finow; originally a Luftwaffe Base, and now taken over by a Soviet Bomber Regiment. Parked up along the hardstandings were a mixture of straight-wing, twin-jet Il-28s and swept-wing, twin --jet Jak-28s. There were also a couple of MiG-17 fighters across on the far side of the base.

Beyond Eberswälde, the autobahn rose slightly to cross the Finowkanal, and one and a half kilometres further on to the north; the Hohenzollernkanal. Out to the left, the edge of The Schorfheide, a vast wilderness that stretched from the old Polish frontier in the east almost to the shores of the Baltic in the north, marched away towards the horizon. They drove on through an open stretch of farmland and small woods which continued to flank the dead straight concrete ribbon for some twelve kilometres, until they came to the Kleiner Buckowsee on their left, and the Grosser Buckowsee on their right. Both lakes were partially obscured by stands of trees, and a little farther on were the entry and exit roads to Werbellinsee.

The Joachimsthal exit off the autobahn soon came into view. Charlotte glanced at the map. The large expanse of the Grimnitzsee appeared on the left and then, the forest closed in again. The autobahn now ran arrow-straight through the encroaching woodland for almost eleven kilometres. Callaghan pushed up the speed and the Mercedes-Benz settled down to a deep purr from its six-cylinder motor with the tyres hissing on the smooth concrete as it raced through the dark tunnel of the forest.

Ahead; the edge of the dense woodland began to appear. Suddenly, they were in bright morning sunlight as the autobahn crossed the open fields surrounding the little village of Steinhofen before it plunged back into the dense woodlands of Metzower forest, five kilometres farther on. This extended for almost twelve kilometres; until. Suddenly, the autobahn came back into open countryside at Heidehof.

Charlotte consulted her map again and glanced at Callaghan.

'OK. Gil; the turn-off on to the B198 is coming up on the left in nine kilometres. That'll take us up to Prenzlau; then we take the B109 through to Pasewalk and stay on it through Anklam and Greifswald to Stralsund. It's about twelve kilometres to Prenzlau, and then, another twenty-two kilometres to Pasewalk. Perhaps, we could stop and have a coffee there.'

Pasewalk was a pretty little town nestling in the rolling landscape of the northern Uckermark region of Brandenburg; and retaining considerable remains of its original medieval ramparts, gates, and towers. Charlotte and Callaghan found a little coffee-shop on the outskirts of the town. Callaghan parked up the Mercedes-Benz outside the coffee shop; and he and Charlotte went inside and took a table overlooking the street. As the waitress brought their coffee, they noticed an innocuous grey Opel Kapitän sedan cruise down the street and slow as it approached the parked Mercedes-Benz. Charlotte glanced at Callaghan and arched an eyebrow... plain-clothes Volkspolizei?... or Stasi?... or something else? As they watched; the grey Opel slowly moved on along the street and disappeared from view.

Callaghan looked at Charlotte. She gave a slight smile. This was no more than had been expected. They were probably the local Stasi. The clincher would be if the sedan returned within a few minutes. They continued to sip their coffee unconcernedly. Ten minutes passed; and then, a movement across the street attracted Charlotte's attention. There! The hood of the grey Opel sneaking into view from a side alley a little way down on the opposite side of the street. Slowly, it inched forward until the two occupants had a clear view of the coffee shop and the parked-up Mercedes-Benz. Unfortunately for them; if they could see the Mercedes-Benz... she could see them. Two thick-set men sat in the front seats. They both looked to be in their mid-twenties. The driver wore a drooping, Mexican-bandit-style moustache. His companion was clean-shaven. Both men wore their hair much longer than even plain-clothes Volkspolizei were permitted. The problem was; that they didn't behave like Stasi... real Stasi would never have exposed themselves to their target in the way these two were doing; so... who, or what were they?

Charlotte and Callaghan waited for another five minutes. The grey Opel didn't move. Dropping a few Ostmarks on the table; they rose and left the coffee house. As they stepped outside; they heard the thin, metallic grate of the Opel's starter motor echo across the street. Without looking round; they reached the Mercedes-Benz as the Opel began to creep forward towards the corner of the junction. Callaghan unlocked the doors and they both slipped into the front seats.

Callaghan turned in his seat and reached back to unlock the secret compartment under the rear seat, from which he pulled out an Uzi Submachine gun. He glanced at Charlotte as he pulled back the charging handle on the top of the weapon; but left the selector lever in the "safe" position. Now; if the need arose; all he had to do was flick the selector lever through its "semi" position to "automatic." In this position, all Callaghan needed to do was aim, hold the trigger back; and the weapon would fire until the magazine was empty. The magazine loaded in this particular Uzi held fifty, nine-millimetre rounds. He gave a cold grin.

'Just in case we need some real firepower.'

Charlotte started the motor; slipped the column gearshift into first, and pulled away from the kerb. Glancing into the rear-view mirror, she saw the grey Opel turn out from the alleyway and begin to follow them. She pulled out her Makarov nine-millimetre pistol and handed it to Callaghan. He chambered a round; flicked up the safety, and placed it in her lap. The railroad crossing on Bahnhofstrasse was open.

The grey Opel followed them out to the B109; hanging back as Charlotte paused at the junction. As she turned right; she glanced back. Yes; the Opel's right hand turn indicator was flashing. She accelerated the Mercedes-Benz away up the northern carriageway, watching the rear-view mirror as the grey Opel turned out from the junction and began following; about three hundred metres to the rear. Charlotte increased the Mercedes-Benz's speed on the long, straight Anklammer Chaussee that led north.

Callaghan was keeping watch in the passenger's sun visor vanity mirror. He glanced at her.

'Any ideas as to who they might be?'

She shook her head.

'Nope. We'll just keep ahead of them. This road is pretty open until we get to Jatznick… that's about seven kilometres ahead. Then there's a seven-kilometre run through a forest. That's the place they'll pick to try something. After that; its all open countryside again right up to Anklam.'

He raised his eyebrow.

'How d'you know that?'

She smiled.

'I was reading the map in the coffee house whilst you were watching them from the window!'

The road surface was average; but the advanced, fully independent suspension of the Mercedes soaked up the ruts and undulations. The pursuing Opel however, was wallowing and bouncing alarmingly as the driver tried to keep pace. Callaghan grinned.

'That Opel's handling like my old Ford Fairlane... and that was like driving a barge in jello! He's all over the highway. If we can get him to drive any faster he's sure to wreck.'

Charlotte grinned.

'OK, Hot-shot, let's do it!'

And shifted gear; then hit the gas pedal. The low grumble of the straight-six motor rose to a deep boom; and the Mercedes-Benz leapt forward as the speedometer needle began winding up past the ninety km/h mark and continued climbing. Ahead, the highway stretched dead-straight for three kilometres towards the small village of Belling. Callaghan glanced into the rear-view mirror. The Opel Kapitän was dropping back rapidly as Charlotte barrelled the powerful Mercedes-Benz over the uneven surface of the highway at over one hundred and thirty km/h.

Approaching Belling; she eased off the gas and dropped her speed down to the legal fifty km/h. Half-way through the village she passed a parked-up Volkspolizei Wartburg, and glanced in the rear-view mirror. The Opel was gaining distance quickly. With luck, he would be exceeding the speed limit when he passed the Volkspolizei and would get pulled over.

As they left the village, she glanced back again, and saw the Volkspolizei Wartburg pull out; blue roof beacon flashing; behind the speeding Opel. Ahead, beyond the approaching curve at the end of the village, the highway became arrow straight right up to the next place... Wilhemsthal. Here, the highway forked. With luck, the Opel would now be far enough back for their pursuers not to know which fork they would have taken. Smiling grimly; she floored the gas pedal again. The Mercedes surged forward, taking the curve with a long, rising whine.

There was no sign of the pursuing Opel as they passed through Wilhemsthal and the next little town... Jatznick. Beyond here; was dense woodland bordering the road as far as the next village... marked on the map as Heinrichsruh. Charlotte checked the Mercedes-Benz's dashboard instruments. Temperature and oil pressure were reading normal. The gas gauge was showing just over half a tank. As the woodland enveloped the highway, she glanced into the rear-view mirror... nothing but an empty, unfurling vista of highway between lines of trees that stretched away behind them like a green, narrow corridor.

Slowing to negotiate an ancient tractor trundling along towards the village; Charlotte checked the mirror again. The highway behind was deserted. It looked as though they had lost their pursuers. There was one more open section of the B109 as it crossed the flat expanse of fields that stretched up to the next large village of Ferdinandshof.

North of Heinrichsruh; the highway skirted around the eastern edge of Ferdinandshof and veered north-west on to a long, dead-straight stretch across open countryside; passing through a couple of tiny villages before it reached the little town of Ducherow. Out here it was wide open... perfect tank country; which is why the Russians had sent a spearhead of armour through here in 1945. It also afforded Charlotte and Callaghan a perfect view of the highway to the rear for several kilometres... and so far; there was no sign of the pursuing Opel Kapitän. Beyond Ducherow; keeping the Mercedes-Benz at a steady ninety; and without taking her eyes from the highway; Charlotte spoke.

'Well, Gil? Any thoughts on whom these guys might be?... For I sure as hell don't know.'

Callaghan shook his head.

'Not a clue... but it seems we've lost them... at least, for now. Where the hell did you learn to drive like this?'

She smiled.

'Firstly; in wartime Berlin; and later; a quick refresher in Washington at the MPDC Academy on pursuit, evasive, and tactical driving.'

Callaghan whistled softly between his teeth.

'Just as well. Take a look in the mirror.'

She saw a tiny black speck in the far distance. It must have been at least five kilometres back. She glanced at Callaghan, and her lips tightened.

He saw this, and shrugged.

'It's probably nothing. So there's another driver on the highway. It could be almost anyone. It doesn't mean that it's our friends... and besides which; they'd have to be real hot-shots to make up time like that... especially with a choice of roads to take back there where the road forked.'

Charlotte increased speed. The tiny black dot did not increase in size as she negotiated the dog-leg bend in the B109 as it skirted the tiny village of Neu Kosenow. A sign flashed past. They were now only six kilometres out from Anklam; and this was where they could be in trouble. According to the map; they would have to cross the Peene River... and there was only one road bridge; which meant that they would have to drive through the centre of the town. They would lose valuable time and distance with the low speed limit in the town... and this could easily prove to be a dangerous problem later on, if that black speck was their pursuers; when they were out in open country again.

Anklam was a country market town with narrow streets and a considerable amount of agricultural traffic. Threading their way through the slow-moving tractors, trailers and various farm implements took time... time for the suspicious grey Opel... if, indeed, it was following them... to gain a significant advantage in distance.

Once across the bridge; the road numbering changed to the B110 for two kilometres, before a left turn signposted Ziethen directed them back onto the B109... again signposted as Dorfstrasse. Charlotte accelerated the Mercedes-Benz back up to ninety. The highway ran north for almost six kilometres before it cut into another substantial woodland area. She glanced into the mirror for perhaps, the tenth time since they had crossed the river... and there; behind them, the black speck had now become a dot... too far away to recognise; but definitely gaining on them.

She swore quietly, and floored the gas pedal. If it was their pursuers; how the hell did they know the route that she and Callaghan were taking? It might be good guesswork; but that was so unlikely that this situation now had to change from being suspicious to sinister. Had there been a leak back in Berlin? It would not have been Malinovskii, or anyone at Karlshorst... the stakes were far too high for that. It could only be the bloody Stasi at Normannenstrasse. Was Markus Wolf playing some sort of double-cross? The Mercedes-Benz surged forwards again... ninety-five... one-hundred... one-hundred-and-ten km/h. The black dot began to gradually recede until it was, once again, merely a dark speck in the rear-view mirror.

Half a kilometre beyond Ziethen; the highway emerged from the trees into open countryside once more and curved into an almost dead straight line towards a wooded area some seven or so kilometres north. Charlotte checked the mirrors. There was now no sign of anyone following. She eased off the gas and the Mercedes-Benz settled down to a smooth cruise at seventy-five km/h.

As she passed a crossroads signposted Ramitzow-Salchow; ahead, in the distance she saw a blue, flashing light... some sort of emergency vehicle. She sighed. Just don't let it be an accident. Another hold-up could be dangerous if the grey Opel was still chasing them. As she approached whatever incident it was; there were four more cars stopped in line on the carriageway. Slowing; she pulled in behind them. The flashing blue light belonged to another green and white Volkspolizei Wartburg patrol car parked at the side of the highway. Parked up next to it was a lurid electric-blue Opel Kapitän with two men leaning against its side, nonchalantly smoking. This whole scenario smelt like an intercept.

Callaghan had the Uzi ready across his lap. She shook her head.

'No, Gil; put the Goddamned thing out of sight. The last thing we need is the Merc' to be damaged in a shoot-out.'

He nodded, and slipped the weapon under the passenger seat. Looking up; he glanced into the rear-view mirror. The grey Opel was coming up fast behind them. Glancing at Callaghan, she picked up her Makarov and flicked off the safety. The Opel pulled up alongside the Mercedes-Benz and the passenger... the man with the drooping Mexican moustache, held up a familiar, red-cloth covered, KGB identity card for her to see. It appeared to be genuine.

She rolled down her window; keeping her hand on the Makarov. The Mexican moustache gave a wry grin and spoke.

'Comrade Colonel Nadia Tolenkanovna? We had one hell of a job trying to catch you. You must have been trained at the Kiev Academy.'

Charlotte studied him. The ID appeared to be genuine, but then; there were good forgeries about. There was, however, one infallible check... Malinovskii's signature word that would always be used in circumstances requiring total verification of a person. This word had been agreed between Malinovskii and Charlotte during their briefing session at Karlshorst, and would be issued to his bona fide agents in the field that she would expect to deal with. She watched Mexican moustache for a few moments, and then spoke.

'What is the signature word, Comrade?'

He nodded thoughtfully.

'Very good, Comrade Colonel. The word is... *"Louise."*

Charlotte nodded. He was indeed out of Karlshorst... and had been briefed by Viktor Malinovskii. The signature word was, in fact, her middle name... a fact known only to her, and Malinovskii.

He passed the identification card across to her. Flipping open the gold-embossed cover, she studied the photograph and details. The card identified Mexican moustache as being Captain Makary Kravchek of the Third Chief Directorate; Karlshorst. The Third Chief Directorate handled military counter-intelligence and armed forces political surveillance. What the hell was going on? She handed the KGB identification document back to Kravchek, and gave him a wry smile.

'It's just as well you didn't catch us, Comrade Kravchek. You and your driver could easily have ended up getting shot. Now; what is this all about?'

Kravchek pointed to an industrial site a little way further on the right.

Let's pull in over there, and I'll explain what is happening.'

He rolled up his window, and the grey Opel pulled away. As

Charlotte followed she noticed that the other two men returned to the electric-blue Opel Kapitän; and pulled out behind her. The three cars turned into the wide parking area in front of the industrial buildings and everyone got out. Callaghan followed Charlotte with the Uzi held casually in his right hand; muzzle towards the ground. Kravchek grinned.

"Vsyo nishtyak!"... 'Everything is OK! You won't be needing that; Comrade Major Levkova.'

Charlotte studied Kravchek. She was very aware that the other two men and Kravchek's driver were standing behind them. Facing Kravchek, she spoke. Her voice was cold and authoritative.

'Very well, Comrade Captain; why did you need to stop us?'

Kravchek's voice became serious.

'We were instructed by Colonel Malinovskii to intercept you before you reached Prora; Comrade Colonel. A major conspiracy has been uncovered back in Berlin. Schreiner; Kommandant of the KdA Training Camp at Schmerwitz has been implicated in a wide-reaching plot to prevent you from apprehending the Cuban dissident, Pasuali. The traitor, Schreiner finally admitted under interrogation at Hohenschönhausen remand prison that he had received a substantial amount in Russian Gold Roubles; which had been deposited in a Swiss account as payment for causing Pasuali to disappear. He also implicated several Stasi officers based at Normannenstrasse. The Third Chief Directorate has established that this payment was initiated at Kremlin level, but then, the trail went cold.

Karlshorst is satisfied that there is a cell of ideological subversives active within the Prora framework that is concealing Pasuali from our investigation of the facility. It is entirely possible that you and Major Levkova would have walked into a trap.'

He motioned to the other three men.

'My driving companion is Captain Anton Gulin; also of Third Chief Directorate; Karlshorst. My associates...'

He pointed at the two men who had driven the electric-blue Opel Kapitän;

'... Are Spetsnaz GRU ghosts. We shall call them Comrade Black, and Comrade Brown... for obvious reasons. Colonel Malinovskii has deployed us as your protection officers.'

He turned to Gulin and pointed to the grey Opel.

'Anton; go and get the special magazines for the Colonel and the Major.'

Gulin nodded and walked to the trunk of the grey Opel. Opening it;

he rummaged around for a few moments, then returned with six Makarov magazines. He handed them to Kravchek; who passed them to Charlotte and Callaghan.

Charlotte glanced at the top of one of the magazine. It was loaded with very strange-looking rounds. She looked at Kravchek and raised an eyebrow.

He grinned.

'You won't have seen those before, Comrade Colonel. They're something special from the Moscow research centre that we use for covert assassinations. Some idiot research technician nicknamed the rounds *"Molotok Tora"*... "Thor's Hammer". These became known as *"Molos"*... and the name stuck. They are basically, hollow points, but with a radically reduced outer wall. They really are ferocious rounds. At close range they'll blow a hole the size of a dinner plate in someone; and at distance, the effect is like being hit by a truck. Nobody ever gets up again after being hit by one of these.'

He glanced at his watch.

'We'd better get moving, Colonel. You'd better reload your side arms with the *"Molo"* magazines before we start out. We really don't know what we might be running into at Prora.'

Chapter Fourteen.

9. 40am. Friday, February 10th, 1961.
Virginia Lake.
Reno. Nevada.
USA.

Crazy Joe" DeCicco sat in the study of his imposing residence overlooking Virginia Lake in the Reno suburbs, turning the spectacular Garnet gemstone in his fingers and watching the blood red shards of light reflecting the sunlight from its exquisitely cut facets, dancing across the walls. He smiled complacently to himself. This rock could easily be used to bribe his way into having considerable influence in Washington D.C.'s political circles by way of a certain corrupt Senator whom he had in his pocket. This particular Senator had clout in the higher levels of the various law enforcement agencies, and would be a useful asset for deflecting any unwanted attention from DeCicco's ventures centred on the several West-coast city take-overs that La Cosa Nostra was planning.

He nodded, and smiled to himself. The buzz was that the New First Lady had a fondness for expensive jewellery; and this beautiful red gemstone would certainly be appreciated. It also meant that influence might be brought to bear on the new President to persuade him to maybe think again about the appointment of his Goddam brother Bobby, as United States Attorney General; who was now laying all kinds of shit down on organised crime.

Playing with the gemstone so that the blood-red flares of reflected light played and flickered across the ceiling; DeCicco picked up the telephone and dialled the code and number for a line in Morningside, Washington D.C. Getting the connection; he leaned back in his big leather chair and spoke amiably into the mouthpiece.

211

'Buenos días, Therasia; it's Joe DeCicco. Is the Senator there?'

10. 15am. Friday, February 10th, 1961.
Chinatown, San Francisco.
California.
U.S.A.

Gabriella Chang sat at her grandfather's desk in the study of the elegant, bay windowed property at the top of Montgomery Street in the Telegraph Hill district of San Francisco and studied the louche Chinese man sitting in front of her. He was in his late twenties, and wore a Sears suit; the material of which was perhaps, a little too shiny to be in the elegant good taste that he obviously considered his appearance suggested. This was Dorian Lin; former acolyte of the late Sebastian Lee; and present Master of the Li Ying Tong.

Gabriella had assumed control of the Chang criminal family on the death of her grandfather, Chang Ho-Pyong; executed in company with Sebastian Lee by the Reno torpedoes, two weeks previously; and had initiated a meticulous search for the killers in and around San Francisco. She had also made an approach to the Li Ying Tong; and furnished them with an offer they really couldn't refuse. She had told the new Master, who now sat before her; that she was fully aware that they had no involvement in the killings; but that she was now going to give him two choices...

They would agree to join forces and share information on the killings, or, they would be deemed as being implicated by their lack of co-operation, and regarded as being without honour, and thus, lose considerable face, and bring shame upon their ancestors. The entire Chinese street gang enclave would be driven out of Chinatown and the Bay area and harassed wherever they went, by the several powerful Korean-American mobs in the United States with which the Chang family were affiliated. Gabriella hadn't made any threats; she merely laid out the probable outcome of Dorian Lin making the wrong decision.

Dorian Lin understood perfectly. The Chinese gangs might well be feared; but the Korean gangs were dreaded. When there was any sort of violence involving them; they always showed "The Blank Face"... impassive, unfathomable... deadly. You just couldn't figure out what they were about to do, or when it was coming. Jesus H. Christ!... and they said HIS troops were inscrutable! He studied this beautiful, American born, twenty-two-year-old Korean girl; with her dark, almond-shaped eyes, pretty, retroussé nose; and rose-petal lips; and inadvertently shivered.

Gabriella Chang noticed his ill-concealed discomfort and smiled to herself. These Chinese thought they were tough and intractable. The real truth was that they were babes in arms compared with the Korean syndicates. No matter; it was necessary to combine forces. Her ears on the street were getting the same story. Two Mob torpedoes out of Reno, Nevada had made the hit on her grandfather and Sebastian Lee; and now, Gabriella had formulated a plan of revenge. She would need Dorian Lin's muscle... at least; that's what she would tell him. In fact; the Tong muscle would be used as patsies, when and if, the bullets started flying.

The main plank of the plan was that Gabriella would hit the casino's of Reno; posing as a rich, good-time girl. She would attract the attention of the Mob and, work her way up the food chain as necessary, until she reached her target. She would then cut him out of the pack with the promise of oriental delights; and execute him when they were alone and undisturbed. She even had her victim's name... "Mad Joe" DeCicco.

Dorian Lin had little choice but to agree. Gabriella Chang was a dangerous, frightening woman. Her influence was far-reaching; and her power on the streets of Chinatown was now omnipotent. It was however; entirely possible that she would be rubbed out in the same manner as her grandfather; if she took on the Mob.

If this occurred; the Chang crime family would probably collapse... there was no one else to take her place. He would send her some foot soldiers that he deemed disposable; and then, when her plan fell apart, the Li Ying Tong could take over the streets of Chinatown without any opposition.

With this in mind; he made a suggestion that he considered would speed up the process. Why didn't Gabriella contact this "Mad Joe" DeCicco directly? She could lead him to believe that the Koreans had wiped the Chinese gangs off the streets, and that San Francisco was ready for the Mob to take control. Then she could entice him into a little "Coochie-Time" as part of a celebratory evening; and execute him at her leisure. Gabriella Chang considered this for a few minutes whilst Dorian Lin sat quietly and attentively. She nodded her approval. This course of action would certainly save time.

Dorian Lin smiled to himself. Stupid Bitch; so preoccupied with revenge that she couldn't anticipate the likely consequences. The Reno Mob would retaliate for the killing of their boss, and all Koreans street gang members would be killed on sight. The Mob would turn it into a hunting party all the way down the West Coast; and the Chinese Tongs could quietly take over the various city Chinatowns whilst the Mob were otherwise engaged in running down the Korean gangs.

9.45pm. Saturday, February 11th, 1961.
Harolds Club.
North Virginia Street,
Reno. Nevada.
USA.

The gleaming black Lincoln Continental Limousine whispered to a standstill outside the entrance of Harolds Club beneath the huge porcelain enamel steel tile mural depicting a wagon train of pioneers crossing the Great Plains, and featuring an illuminated waterfall and flickering campfire. Two young, tough-looking Chinese wearing Tuxedos jumped out and opened the rear door for a beautiful, young oriental girl wearing an exquisitely sexy, tight-fitting silk cheongsam slashed to her hip, to delicately alight from the limousine onto the sidewalk lit by the garish neon of the Casino's frontage. The liveried doorman stepped across the sidewalk to escort her inside with the two Chinese flanking her. As the party entered; one of the Chinese discreetly signalled to a Cadillac Eldorado Brougham that had pulled in a little way behind the Lincoln. Four more of Dorian Lin's troops alighted from the Cadillac and slipped unnoticed into the alleyway next to the casino.

Gabriella Chang entered the main gambling area flanked by her two elegantly attired "companions," and surveyed the scene. There was no way of reaching any other part of the casino without passing between the banks of slot machines and gambling tables. She had arranged to meet DeCicco in the famous "Covered Wagon Room." Whilst negotiating this beguiling snare to the altar of chance; always, somewhere, was the intoxicating silvery cascade of coins or occasionally the golden cry of "Jackpot!" ... at which point, the slot machine addicts would raise their gaze from the whirring tumblers and stare with dead eyes, like so many Pavlov's dogs, in the direction of the perfidious lure that promised all, but invariably brought them nothing.

It was the same at the crap tables; with the unending clatter of the beautifully crafted, duplicitous ivory dice; and the whisper of cards across the green baize of the blackjack tables. She paused momentarily at one of the roulette tables; listening to its seductive whirl and the counterpoint of the whizz of the little ivory ball around the tilted circular track as it embarked on the circular odyssey of its impersonal choice to grant or shatter dreams. She watched as the punters stared mesmerised at the little ball's journey; until it lost momentum and tumbled out of the track with a merry tinkling sound into one of the coloured and numbered pockets on the wheel.

The dealer's voice droned out impassively:

'Eight. Black. Low and Even;'

And slipped a big ivory plaque out of his rack. Hungry eyes watched its progress across the betting area of the table as he slid it in front of the winner. Once again, Gabriella was reminded of Dr Pavlov's dogs. The dealer then swept away all other losing bets with his rake, and the spectacle of greed began again.

The Covered Wagon Room decor was what could only be described as inelegant "Rustic cowboy"... obvious and vulgar; with novelty features such as "The Silver Dollar Bar." This was an elaborate, curved bar with silver dollars embedded in clear plastic as the bar top. The rail of the bar was a bright orange plastic and the silver dollars were backlit which gave the bar top an idiosyncratic visual depth. In the middle of the bar area was yet one more Roulette wheel and table.

At the back of the bar was a waterfall streaming down rocks and splashing into a pool, all surrounded by rustic scenery; and to the left; was a large wall map of Nevada featuring various historical occurrences painted at locations throughout the depiction of the State. The highways were depicted by tubes of translucent plastic and from time to time, internal lights turned them into a red streak emanating from Reno to each historical point.

Farther to the left there were two large photographic slides of Lake Tahoe, measuring at least twelve feet wide, and reaching from floor to ceiling. Each panel was backlit to replicate the lighting change for a daily cycle of dusk to dawn. Now; during the evening depiction, moonlight shone on the lake. The carpet was woven with covered wagon designs interspersed with *"Harolds Club hiway"* advertising. Gabriella smiled. It really was the absolute epitome of garish bad taste.

Sitting at the bar, flanked by two tough-looking, sharp-suited, lynx-eyed mobsters, was Crazy Joe DeCicco. As Gabriella entered, he looked up and motioned to his two men. They rose and approached her and her escorts. The two Chinese assumed the attitude of preparing to square up to the approaching threat. Gabriella gestured that they should stay where they were, and brushed past DeCicco's men. He grinned. This broad had guts.

He invited her to sit on the bar chair next to him and eyed her up and down. So this was the new boss of the Chang family… and judging by the expanse of thigh she was showing; she was also a sweet piece of ass. He smiled; a smile that he imagined was suave and irresistible to a beautiful young woman… but only appeared to Gabriella as being slimy and licentious. She smiled back; this was better than her best hopes. DeCicco, in spite of his lofty position in the Mob; was just another dirty old man. He spoke. His voice was soft and silky.

'So very pleased to meet you, Miss Chang. How about a drink before we go up to the suite. After we have conducted our business, we can take a bite in the restaurant and maybe take in a little entertainment in the Fun Room?'

This was the venue where the big-name entertainers performed, up on the seventh floor.

Gabriella nodded.

'Thank you. A bourbon on the rocks please.'

DeCicco grinned to himself. Bourbon… better and better! Not only would he get to buffalo her over the control of organised crime; he could easily slip her a Mickie… the taste of which would be masked by the bourbon… whilst they were upstairs; and then, when it had worked its magic, he would get to fuck her as well.

In the suite on the third floor, DeCicco began plying Gabriella with bourbon as he went through the motions of discussing the arrangements for sharing control of the streets of San Francisco. He smiled smugly to himself; slowly increase the quantity of bourbon, and then, when she was well on the way to getting smashed; slip in the Mickie.

Gabriella though; had DeCicco's number as soon as she met him in the Covered Wagon Room. She would play him along until he was certain she was drunk enough not to put up too much resistance to his advances; at which point, he would probably slip her the Mickie. She knew exactly what to expect. Years ago; her grandfather had introduced her to the effect of a "Mickie" in the safe, controlled environment of the house on Montgomery Street. He said that she needed to know the symptoms and effect; should anyone try to slip her one out on the streets. She discovered that, in about ten minutes, it would create a drunken-like effect which could last for anything up to eight hours, depending on the mix. It strengthened the effects of alcohol, causing loss of inhibition, sleepiness; relaxation; and, eventually... amnesia. Gabriella didn't need ten minutes... she didn't even need five.

As the negotiations continued, DeCicco was getting aroused. She didn't object when he placed his hand on her knee in a fatherly fashion... then slowly slipped it up along the slit in her cheongsam, stroking her thigh. Gabriella gently removed his hand. He was getting too close to the Walther PPK pistol loaded with soft-nosed, hollow point slugs, tucked into her stocking top and nestling against the inside of her right thigh. She murmured softly.

'Wait! You'll snag the silk with your signet ring. I'll go and slip out of it and then we can get down to the action.'

She eased herself out of his embrace, and sashayed to the bathroom, swinging her ass provocatively. At the door she paused and glanced back at DeCicco. The prominent bulge in his pants jutting out below his fat belly betrayed the fact that his guard was dropping fast. She smiled alluringly at him. When they started to think with their dicks, it was game over.

She entered the bathroom and closed the door behind her. Carefully, she slipped out of her cheongsam, and pulled the Walther from her stocking top; laying it on the marble top of the vanity unit that stretched across the entire length of the room. Now; how far should she go? She smiled. The more she displayed... the less vigilant DeCicco would become. OK; the whole shebang!

Slipping out of her bra and panties, she stood naked except for her black garter belt, sheer black stockings and strappy black Prada heels. She smiled to herself. More than enough to titillate; more than enough to put DeCicco off his guard. She studied her body in the full length mirror, and nodded. Firm breasts, tight nipples, flat toned stomach, showgirl shave... irresistible!

Gently tweaking her nipples to make them stand out a little more; she dabbed on a touch of Guerlain Shalimar Perfume to her throat and breasts; picked up the Walther; chambered a round; and flicked off the safety. Walking to the door, she held the gun in her right hand behind her back and opened the door; giving DeCicco an eyeful of her side view. She saw him run a pale tongue across his wet, red lips, as she stepped out into the light. DeCicco's eyes greedily devoured her exquisite nakedness; running down from her breasts to her crotch and back again; his hand trembling and almost slopping his drink. Her body was every sweaty fantasy he'd ever had; come to life... right there in front of him.

She began strutting towards him; hips thrust out, with a sensual undulation of her ass. When she was five feet from him she stopped and stood before him, legs spread and feet apart; with her left hand on her hip.

DeCicco was sweating now, with a huge bulge straining against the crotch of his pants. She picked up the fresh glass of bourbon that she knew was laced with the Mickie and drained it in one gulp. DeCicco's eyes glinted with satisfaction and he almost drooled in anticipation. She smiled; a gentle, welcoming smile; stretched out a long, slender, black stocking-encased leg and gently teased the growing wet patch in his pants where the head of his rigid dick was straining against the material; with the sole of her strappy black Prada. Her voice was low and inviting.

'Like what you see, baby? You getting a hankering to shoot, huh?... Me too!'

Her right hand came from behind her back; and the little Walther coughed as it jabbed out its blue and yellow tongue. The first shot hit DeCicco low in his bulging belly. He squealed and writhed. She smiled.

'That one was for Sebastian Lee. Damn! I bet that hurts... but obviously not nearly enough, judging by that sad-sack, shitty squeaking noise that you're making.'

The Walther coughed again. The second bullet ripped into DeCicco's testicles. Now, he did scream. She smiled again.

'And THAT was for my grandfather, you fat pig.'

She let him writhe and shriek for a few minutes just to let him know what pain was really like.

Glancing at the wall clock she figured that she had about four minutes before she began to feel the effect of the Mickie. Damn! And he was suffering so nicely! She sighed and moved forward until she was standing over him. She looked down. The oh-so-powerful Consigliere of the Reno Mob writhed and whimpered in front of her. She raised the Walther. The last thing he saw in his world of excruciating pain were her magnificent breasts jutting over him before she put a bullet through each of his eyes and blew the back of his head off. She then turned and picked up the ejected shell casings before walking rather unsteadily towards the bathroom as the Mickie began to wash over her.

She awoke in her own bed with a really yuck mouth and a vague headache; almost as though she had been boozing all night. She peered at the clock on the bedside table. It read 2.15. The sun was streaming into the room. Slowly, her head began to clear. It had to be the afternoon. She could remember little of what had happened the previous night. The last thing she remembered clearly was being in a sumptuous suite with that fat pig DeCicco. How she had gotten back here was a complete blank.

While she was struggling to remember anything, there was a soft knock on the door. Her young lieutenant, Jimmy Yoo entered carrying a tray upon which was set a coffee pot and cup. The aroma of freshly brewed coffee filled the room. He set the tray down on the bedside table and whilst he poured her a cup, he looked at her with genuine concern in his eyes.

'How are you feeling, Miss Chang?'

She sighed.

'A little woozy, Jimmy. What happened last night?... and how did I get back here?'

He smiled gently.

You executed DeCicco in a most satisfactory manner, Miss. Your two Chinese escorts rubbed out his bodyguards and dumped them in the room with their boss; and the back-up escorts went in through the back entrance and brought you out to their automobile. They then drove back here and brought you home; asleep, but unharmed.'

She nodded.

'And was I dressed, when I got back?'

He nodded.

'Yes Miss. The guys said you were only missing your heels when they picked you up.'

Gabriella gave a quiet sigh of relief. So she had managed to get dressed before the Mickie really kicked in, and the Chinese escorts, although she was grateful to them; hadn't managed to get an eyeful... but who had undressed her and put her to bed?

She looked at Jimmy Yoo.

'So who undressed me and put me to bed?'

Jimmy Yoo blushed and dropped his eyes from hers.

'There was no one else here, so I did it, Miss; but don't worry... I won't say anything; and besides which... I'm not hot on girls... I'm a fag.'

He hung his head; overcome with embarrassment and shame for his confession.

She sat up and reached her hand out to him. As she did so, she realised she was naked under the covers. The sheet slipped down exposing her breasts. She ignored it, Jimmy's feelings were so much more important than her modesty. She smiled gently and touched his face.

'There's nothing to be ashamed of, Jimmy. We can't choose the way we are, nor who we choose to love. Thank you for looking after me last night. I really am happy and relieved it was you and not one of Dorian Lin's men.'

Jimmy Yoo nodded,

'I am so relieved that you are not angry with me for being so presumptive as to prepare you for bed, last night, Miss. Will there be anything else that I can do for you?'

She shook her head.

'No thank you, Jimmy.'

He bowed slightly and left the bedroom.

As she sipped her coffee she was pondering Jimmy. He would make the perfect confidant; after all, being a fag meant that he empathised in a way that no straight man ever could. He was faithful and undemanding... and he cared about her. He and his friends would probably gossip in the same way that women did... and this could be very useful for both gathering and spreading word on the street.

Meanwhile, back in Reno; the Mob Caporegimes had sent out their crews to scour the city for the killers of their Consigliere, "Mad Joe" DeCicco. The killing had all the marks of a "message job." Being shot through the eyes meant "We're watching you!" What the hell this implied was a mystery to the Boss. Joe DeCicco was his trusted advisor and right-hand man. There were also witnesses who said that two Chinese dudes were seen with DeCicco's muscle in the Silver Dollar bar at Harolds Club. These two soldiers were found with DeCicco. They had both been shot through the mouth.... Another "message job"... but one that indicated that they had been marked as "rats."

The Boss of the Reno Mob... *Capo Famiglia* Big Frank Catelli hadn't ordered any of these killings. His suspicions centred on the San Francisco Chinese street gangs. This had all the signs of the little yellow sonsofbitches carving out the Bay area as their exclusive territory. Worse than that; they had left Joe DeCicco in such a mess that the family would have to give him a closed casket funeral. This was the worst insult imaginable. No one would be able to pay their last respects to him in the time-honoured tradition; or have the consolation of a proper sense of closure.

OK. They wanted to play rough; he'd show them what rough was. He picked up the telephone and dialled a San Francisco number... The Police Department Central Station; and asked to speak to the Chief.

The voice on the telephone was amicable.

Good morning Frank. How may I help you?'

Big Frank Catelli replied:

'Morning Brad. I've gotta problem, and I'm calling in a favour. I need to know when all the Chinks will be in their club on California Street. The bastards whacked Joe DeCicco last night, and there's a price to pay. I don't need any of your guys getting heroic about this. I wanna clean sweep when I give 'em the hard goodbye. *Capiche?*'

After a pause. The voice answered.

'OK, Frank my patrol officers say the next full meeting is at seven, tomorrow evening. I'll clear the street patrols... just make sure it's surgical; and see that your troops don't burn any innocent passers by.'

7pm. Sunday, February 12th, 1961.
California Street. Little Italy.
San Francisco.
USA.

The two Chevrolet Corvair Greenbrier Sportswagons cruised along California Street and stopped outside the closed-up Chan Yang Garden restaurant. Six men climbed out of each van and entered the dingy alleyway alongside the building. They were all carrying pump-action shotguns. As they walked down between the high, grimy brick walls; two of the men pulled out what appeared to be grenades; whilst a third carried a five gallon gasoline can.

Half-way along the right-hand wall was a solitary, nondescript doorway set slightly back into the brick cliff. The men fanned out in a semi-circle across the alleyway, and two of them opened up with their shotguns which were loaded with rifled twelve-gauge slugs; shattering the door to matchwood. The two men with grenades pulled the pins and tossed them inside; followed swiftly by the third man hurling the uncapped gasoline can inside after them. Two muffled explosions were heard; followed immediately by a huge "Whumph" as the gasoline exploded. Yells and screams came from inside, and figures... some with their clothes in flames, burst out of the black smoke belching from the shattered interior of the building. The men with the shotguns opened fire as the occupants tumbled out into the alleyway. The slaughter lasted no more than five minutes; by which time there were at least thirty bodies sprawled in the alleyway.

As the flames took hold of the building; the men shouldered their weapons and strolled back out into the street, climbed aboard their vehicles and unhurriedly drove away. There were no police anywhere to be seen; the Boss's orders had been successfully carried out, and the Li Ying Tong... including its new Master, Dorian Lin, had been wiped off the face of Chinatown.

Friday, February 10th, 1961.
Nordflügel 2, Seebad Prora.
Rügen Island.
North Germany.

The Cuban, Fernán Pasuali; now using the false identity of Ferdinand Poeschl; Stabsgefreiter in the Nationale Volksarmee; was studying the manual of his brand new, and as yet, experimental Soviet SVD sniper rifle. Both the weapon and its scope were still undergoing extensive field testing before being introduced as the standard squad support weapon throughout the Soviet Union and Warsaw Pact countries. An impressive weapon; with the scope, its range was thirteen hundred metres... more than enough for the assignment for which he had been hired. His concentration was disturbed by a sharp knock on the door of his room on the fifth floor of block two of the North wing of the Prora complex. Opening the door; he was confronted by the duty Gefreiter, who handed him a sealed signals envelope.

Closing the door; Pasuali ripped open the envelope and unfolded the thin signals sheet. It was coded, and took a while to decipher; but its contents were specific and concise. Berlin KGB had penetrated the veil of secrecy surrounding the conspiracy in which Pasuali was embroiled. At least two Karlshorst investigators were on their way to Prora to detain him. His anonymity had been blown wide open. Somehow, they had managed to put a name to him, and several arrests had already been made in Berlin among his co-conspirators. The plug had now been pulled on the whole operation at Prora, and he should get out of there as fast as he could by whatever means possible. Contact would be made again at a later date. The assignment was, as of now, on hold.

Pasuali swore volubly.

'Fucking Hell!'...

How had they managed to find him up here in this God-forsaken, ex-Nazi shithole; buried away among almost ten thousand goose-stepping assholes? No matter; the prime importance now was to evade these KGB investigators. There was no way of knowing how close they were...or even if they had yet arrived at Prora. Nonetheless, it was time to high-tail it out of here. Swiftly packing the most basic of requirements, he shouldered the sniper rifle and stepped out into the corridor. It was deserted. Even if the KGB had actually arrived; it

222

would take them a while to reach his room. The corridors alone were almost one and a half kilometres in length; and they would have to negotiate four flights of stairs to reach his level.

Pasuali was thinking on his feet as he hurried down the seemingly endless fifth-floor corridor of North block... Nordflügel 2. He was moving north; towards the main administrative area. The Soviets had started to demolish parts of the Prora northern housing blocks at some point in their occupation; and the remaining structures had been used by the Nationale Volksarmee, the police, fire-fighters and Red Cross; house fighting and civil protection squads; and by the 40th Parachute Battalion as a practice site for urban combat training; and large sections of the buildings had been blown up. The shell of Nordflügel 3 was structurally intact but minus all its windows and outer walls; and Nordflügel 4 was partially demolished.

It was reasonable to assume that the KGB would enter the accommodation block through the administration building on the south corner of Nordflügel 1 and systematically work their way through the ten housing units of Nordflügels 1 and 2... the two habitable blocks; when they discovered he was not in his allocated apartment.

If he used the top floor of Nordflügel 3 and stayed in the centre of the building; it was almost impossible for anyone to observe him unless they too, were on the same floor. The only problem would be whether the stairwells would be intact at either end of the block. Nordflügel 4 would not be a problem. There was so much demolition debris on that site, he could move under cover from one end to the other. The only possible problem there would be just how stable the remaining standing ruins were.

Up here on the northern end of Nordflügel 2... which was pretty much unused due to its proximity to the battered Nordflügel 3; Pasuali realised what a stunningly creepy place this really was. There were sudden shadows to hide in, and long, open stretches that gave an awful feeling of being totally exposed. The dark shadows of its history stalked this place; the ghosts that whispered through abandoned corridors, slammed doors, and moaned through the cracks in the steel-reinforced concrete... the spectres of fanatical Nazi dreamers... the egotistic architects and the cynical planners of the Third Reich's sinister, insidious scheme of social engineering; the construction workers, the victims of war; the bombed-out refugees from places like Hamburg, Rostock and Berlin; the displaced and the homeless refugees who had fled from the east; and the Russian prisoners of war and Eastern European forced labour workers who had been incarcerated in this megalomanic edifice. Quickly, he moved on along the deserted corridor towards the northernmost stairwell. The entire block was silent. Such troops as were quartered there were all out on manoeuvres somewhere in the three hundred hectares that the *"Sperrgebiet"*… the prohibited military area, covered.

The north end stairwell was intact; although all the windows had been blown out. Carefully, Pasuali descended to ground level and paused at the exit doorway. The gaunt, brownish-grey, ferro-concrete skeleton of Nordflügel 3 towered before him across forty metres of open, exposed concrete that delineated the foundation of one of the four of the ten planned seaside Community buildings which had actually been started before the project was wound down. The concrete road that ran parallel to the rear of the accommodation blocks was deserted. It was silent at this end of the complex. The whole area was silent. Still as the grave, and twice as sinister… no sound at all save for the wind whispering through the lattice of reinforced concrete and hard-burnt bricks.

Pasuali stood in the doorway of the stairwell, and, ostensibly to anyone who might be observing him; casually adjusted his equipment. In fact; he was carefully scanning the immediate vicinity for any signs of movement. Seemingly satisfied with the positions of his ammunition belts and pack; he emerged from the towering shadow of Nordflügel 2 and walked across the open foundation towards the concrete roadway. The sheltering tree line was twenty metres to his left; and his objective… a spot midway between the permanent on-site staff housing blocks and the original site where the large-scale garage would have been constructed was close to two hundred and sixty metres to the north. At this point, a disused roadway veered off into the wooded area.

He had previously checked this area out as a likely escape route and knew that it was just over half a kilometre through the densely pine-wooded area to the roadway and rail track that spanned a fifty-metre wide, open cut through the woods. Beyond that point; it was a straightforward slog of six hundred metres through the sandy, calcareous grassland, salt marshes; and reed beds full of rising damp and mosquitoes, to the wash margin of the Jasmunder Bodden lagoon. As he made his way carefully through the trees; Pasuali was working out the route he would take. The best way would be to follow the lagoon's wash line to the north. The shallow cliff would provide cover as he followed the edge of the lagoon up to the little town of Leitzow where he could cross the causeway onto the main part of the island.

Faintly, in the distance to the north; he could hear the popping of small arms fire. They were playing war games out on the training area south of Staphel... he could easily skirt around them.

As he came out of the trees at the site of the old garages; he saw three Russian GAZ 69 four-wheel-drive light trucks parked up on the concrete hardstanding. Pasuali smiled. Hot-wire one of these and he wouldn't have to traipse through five kilometres of stinking, rotten sea-kale and God knows what else, around the edge of the lagoon. He paused at the tree line and scanned the area. There was no one around and all was silent except for the thin backdrop of birdsong. Nonchalantly shouldering the sniper rifle; Pasuali strolled across the sparse, scrubby grass strip towards the hardstanding and approached the nearer of the trucks. He laid his hand on the hood. It was warm... the vehicles hadn't been here long; these vehicles were probably the transports of the poor bastards playing soldiers up in the smelly marshes at the northern reaches of the training grounds. He glanced into the cab. The key was in the ignition... but, why shouldn't it be? After all; they were in the middle of a restricted military zone... it wasn't as though anyone was going to just stroll in and steal the damn thing.

A final glance around to make sure there was no one about; and Pasuali climbed into the driving seat; laid the sniper rifle beside him and turned the ignition key. The fuel gauge needle flicked up to three-quarters tank. He pulled the starter knob and the engine clattered roughly into life. Pasuali winced. It sounded as though someone had strapped a bag of nails to the crankshaft... but he knew this was quite normal. These engines were as tough as old boots, in spite of the terrible pre-ignition from the laughably low octane gasoline that was available; and which would have wrecked any normal engine.

Banging the big, floor-mounted gear lever into first; Pasuali booted the accelerator pedal and sent the GAZ bouncing off the hardstanding as he headed for the entrance road of the Prora complex. Approaching the security barrier; Pasuali slowed as one of the guards emerged and watched the GAZ coming down the road. These guys checked everything coming in... but would they check vehicles leaving the complex? Pasuali changed up into second gear and braced himself ready to floor the accelerator. The guard indicated that he should stop. Leaning in through the passenger window; the guard asked where he was heading. Pasuali nodded towards the SVD sniper rifle.

'Just heading down to the old firing range to calibrate the scope on that bad boy.'

The guard nodded.

'Well, be careful. There's a new bunch of recruits pissing about out there, somewhere... and we all know what they're like!'

Pasuali grinned.

'Yeah; I'll be careful. We don't want them shitting their pants at the sound of a few close, high-velocity slugs, do we?'

The guard laughed.

'Too damn right!'

And waving an acknowledgement; he stepped back and raised the red and white pole. He gave Pasuali a friendly wave as the GAZ pulled away and accelerated down the long road across the sandy heath that passed through the southern sector of the training area and led down to the junction with the B196 at the little settlement of Kluptow. From here, Pasuali could drive up to Bergen and then, head down the B96 to Stralsund by way of the small town of Samtens. Once across the bridge, he would be home-free; the whole of Brandenburg province would be open for him to lose himself and wait to be contacted again.

As he was approaching the tiny village of Lubkow; about two kilometres from the complex; he saw three vehicles approaching from the opposite direction... two Opel Kapitäns and a Mercedes-Benz. The lead Opel flashed its headlamps, and the passenger put his arm out of the window and flagged Pasuali down. As the Opel slowed; Pasuali saw that all three cars bore Berlin Licence plates. Dammit! They were probably the KGB investigators. He decided that he needed to be very careful as to how he behaved and how he answered any questions.

A big man got out of the passenger door; walked across to Pasuali's vehicle, and stuck his head into the GAZ's interior. He made an unconvincing attempt to appear friendly.

'Is this the road to Prora Barracks?'

Pasuali nodded.

'Yes, comrade it's about two kilometres up to the security gates.'

The man nodded; grunted something that might have been construed as a "thank you," and returned to the leading Opel Kapitän. As they drove on; Pasuali saw that both of the Opels contained two tough looking men and the Mercedes-Benz contained a man and a woman.

Pasuali drove the rest of the way down to Kluptow with one eye on the road and the other in the rear-view mirror. No one was following, but he breathed a sigh of relief as he turned onto the B196 and accelerated away in the direction of Bergen.

The road across the heath was long and boringly straight. Callaghan had to keep the Mercedes-Benz at a steady eighty km/h to keep up with Makary Kravchek's grey Opel. His driver Ilya Zykov; was obviously a bit of a hot-shot. The lurid electric-blue Opel Kapitän containing the two Spetsnaz GRU ghosts..."Comrade Black," and "Comrade Brown"... stayed close behind. Callaghan was slightly concerned about this. If the convoy had to brake suddenly; the two Spetsnaz Comrades would probably end up in the back seat of the Mercedes-Benz. Suddenly, the grey Opel's stop lights flashed as the convoy reached a large signboard at the side of the road, upon which was painted in capital letters a foot high...

VERBOTENER ZUGANG: MILITÄRISCHE ZONE.

Entry Forbidden: Military Zone.

A hundred metres ahead; the red and white pole of the security post barred their way. The grey Opel drew up outside the guard post and a sentry bent down and spoke to the driver. The familiar, red-cloth covered, KGB identity card was waved under the young sentry's nose and a few words were exchanged. The sentry saluted; stepped back, and raised the pole; allowing the convoy to proceed. The road continued into the pine woods for only another kilometre before it narrowed to a mere track, and they managed to get a good first view of the vast, grey-brown stone Behemoth; an immense, Teutonic monolith crouching beyond the trees; six storeys high, and stretching along the windswept coastline in one spectacularly ugly, unending arc for almost five kilometres. The immense scale of the place made the huge arc of Tempelhofer Airport back in Berlin pale into insignificance... and that building was truly enormous.

This place was a particularly striking example of the Third Reich "Intimidatory" architectural style on a grandiose scale. It simply stretched away as far as the eye could see; the massive, identical accommodation blocks pierced through with thousands of identical windows in uniform ranks marching along each floor. The whole impression of the building was eerie and disturbingly unavoidable. Charlotte sighed. How the hell they were supposed to find one man in this gargantuan, characterless, concrete labyrinth made the only epithet that came to mind... the proverbial "Needle in a haystack"... seem as straightforward as a walk in the park.

Beyond the trees; the road crossed the concrete roadway that ran the length of the complex. Callaghan followed the lead Opel across to where a wide expanse of empty ground stretched between the north and south blocks. This was the area where the proposed, but never built, Festival hall would have stood. Getting out of the Mercedes-Benz; Charlotte looked around. It was literally impossible to take in the scale of this gigantic structure. The five surviving blocks were both chillingly prescient and terrifyingly huge.

The sheer scale of Prora; the quiet massiveness of the almost endless housing blocks rising like a grey, ghostly phalanx along the misty coastline was overwhelming. The Nazis typically employed architecture of colossal dimensions to overawe, and make the individual feel small and unimportant... and with Prora; even by the ambitious standards of Nazi monumentalism; they had succeeded beyond their wildest aspirations.

This eerie relic of Germany's Nazi past was downright sinister. The way in which this "Sieg Heil and Jackboot-polish" leviathan had been built into the strip of land separating the Jasmunder Bodden from the Baltic Sea and surrounded by forests and dunes, made it impossible to take it all in at once.

Prora had originally consisted of eight identical, rectangular six-storey buildings, three of which were now in ruins, curving around the bay in a neat arc. Each building was sub-divided into four, half-kilometre-long blocks; studded with extensions projecting out from the western aspect of the housing blocks; each of which contained a staircase, elevator, staff rooms, showers and toilets; washing chambers, and the sideboards and chutes for garbage and dirty linen.

Flanked by the KGB muscle; Charlotte and Callaghan walked across to the reception building attached to Südflügel 1... the most northerly block of the intact southern complex. On each side of the central square, two large reception areas had been planned in grandiose style; but only the southern one had been completed.

The completed Reception building was a three storey structure with a curved end wall; the only complete *Empfangsgebäude...* Reception building, that defined the south line of the central square; and was attached to an incomplete, colonnaded section that stretched between the main blocks of the north and south complexes and extended to the foundation base of the so called *Gemeinschaftshäus...* community house; which, if built; would have contained the kitchen/restaurant complex and would mirror the Reception building in its design; whilst overlooking the quay. During the time the NVA occupied the complex; the Reception building had been home to the officer's club; and now, was the domain of a corpulent Stabsfeldwebel with a face which bore a remarkable resemblance to that of a pig. He sat arrogantly behind large desk strewn with files and rubber stamps.

Stabsfeldwebel Otto Bächer eyed these "civilian" newcomers up as though they were something he'd just stepped in on the pavement. His little piggy eyes glittered and he opened his mouth to speak. Before he could utter a word; Makary Kravchek shoved the red KGB identity card under his nose. Bächer paled and jumped to his feet; his mind whirling.

What the fuck did these KGB hard-asses want? Kravchek answered his unspoken question.

'We are here to carry out an investigation concerning a dissident Cuban we believe to be deployed in this establishment. He is masquerading as an accredited German soldier under an assumed name. We wish to examine all records relating to Cuban Nationals undergoing training here.'

Bächer looked Kravchek up and down; a slim smile slowly spread across his pudgy features. His voice was condescending.

'I regret that I cannot possibly permit you to examine any files without the proper authorisation.'

Kravchek nodded.

'And what might the proper authorisation be, Herr Stabsfeldwebel?'

Bächer gave him an oily smile.

'Signed authorisation from Colonel-General Hoffmann at The Ministry of National Defence in Strausberg.'

Kravchek waited for him to finish blustering, and then spoke in perfect German. His voice was quiet... cold, sinister, and foreboding.

'Well; it's just not our day is it?'

He leaned conspiratorially across the desk to Bächer and smiled... the smile of a predator sizing up its victim. Lowering his voice, he spoke; as if to share a confidence with the now-sweating Stabsfeldwebel.

'Of course; you couldn't possibly know that I come from the Ukraine; and it's even less likely that you are aware that I am Jewish.'

Basher paled, and his left eye began to twitch almost uncontrollably. Kravchek continued in a quiet, almost friendly tone.

'I don't suppose that if I checked our records, I might find that you served in the SS during the war, Stabsfeldwebel?... or perhaps, you would prefer me to address you as SS Sturmscharführer? It really does have a superior ring to it; don't you think?

I imagine that you were a young, impressionable trooper with the swastikas shining in your eyes, in one of the Einsatzgruppen? You were having a little fun in Babi Yar ravine outside Kiev, perhaps? Or Kamenets-Podolsk? Or Volhynia? Or maybe you were enjoying yourself in Auschwitz-Birkenau? You might even have helped out in turning my family into piles of ashes and pieces of cheap soap.'

Bächer's face was chalky white... almost blue. Beads of perspiration stood out on his forehead. What he'd kept a secret for fifteen long years had been guessed, almost to the letter, by this KGB Untermensch piece of shit. Bächer had indeed, been Einsatzgruppe... operating with an Einsatzkommando unit of Einsatzgruppe "C", to be precise. They had murdered and pillaged their way across the southern Ukraine in '43. Bächer had gained quite a reputation back then, of employing an objective duplicity towards the kommando's victims. As they were rounded up; he would be sent in to assuage their fears with solicitous assertions that they were being resettled. He had once been congratulated by no less than his Einsatzkommando boss... SS-Standartenführer Böhme, for his impressive subterfuge of quelling dissent by permitting one Jewish family to celebrate the *Khaddish* before taking them away and forcing them to hang themselves in each other's presence. If any of this came out... especially in KGB circles; they would have him away into a Soviet Labour camp in Siberia faster than a monkey picking fleas off its bollocks.

Even if this scruffy KGB asshole didn't shoot his mouth off in the wrong place; the woman's stare was enough to shrivel a man's nuts. That look she was giving him had GDR-Military Prison, Schwedt written all over it. What was she? Stasi? Quickly; Bächer forgot all about "proper authorisation" and grabbed at the deep filing cabinet behind his chair. Riffling through the files, he withdrew a slender folder and opened it. Turning to Kravchek; he forced a pleasant smile and spoke... although his voice was now minus its officious tone...

'We have twenty Cubans at the complex, Comrade. They have all been here for three months.'

Charlotte glanced at Kravchek and imperceptibly shook her head. Their Cuban would have been here for less than a week. Stepping forward, she rested her cold blue gaze upon Bächer.

'How many personnel are undergoing sniper training at the establishment, Stabsfeldwebel?'

Bächer felt his guts tighten up under her gaze. He leapt at the filing cabinet again and frantically dipped into the files. He shuffled through them with trembling fingers and withdrew an even thinner folder. He didn't even open it; he handed it straight to her. Flipping it open; she scanned the typed page. It contained only three names. Two had been at the complex for more than two months; but one... Ferdinand Poeschl; Stabsgefreiter in the Nationale Volksarmee, had been here for only a week.

Charlotte turned back to Bächer and handed him the folder.

'Where are Stabsgefreiter Poeschl's quarters located?'

Bächer smiled nervously, and consulted what appeared to be an overly complex table towards the back of the file. He ran his pudgy, blunt finger down the close-typed table, and jabbed at an entry.

'North wing Two, level five. Section D, room 73.'

Charlotte nodded.

'Thank you, Stabsfeldwebel.'

She turned to her companions.

'OK boys; let's go see this guy.'

Chapter Fifteen.

Outside the reception building; the two Spetsnaz ghosts slipped away to cover this southern stairwell spur of North wing 2, whilst Kravchek and Gulin headed for the stairwell spur at the northern end of the block. The decision was, that Charlotte and Callaghan would enter north wing 1 and use the building as cover whilst they made their way up to North wing 2, in case Poeschl was watching out for them.

Cautiously; Callaghan opened the doors to the North Wing 1 building and stepped into the empty corridor coated with faded, oppressive paintwork... dull grey above a bilious green; peeling like sunburned skin from the damp concrete. A series of dim, cold, locked doors interrupted the vast plane of the right-hand wall; and each door was totally identical but for the cheap, plastic numbers and occasional random nameplates. There were no sounds coming from behind any of them.

In the distance, a separator wall projected into the corridor; marking one of the joining points in each of the block's five sections. The corridor ran along the landward side of the building, and each section appeared to contain seven rooms. This meant that they needed to traverse the entire length of North wing 1... a distance of well over half a kilometre of corridor before they even reached North wing 2. Charlotte looked at Callaghan and gave a sigh. This was going to be neither quick, nor easy.

They cautiously picked their way through the wind-blown debris that was strewn along the long, dank corridor as a result of several windows being broken. The whole place appeared to be deserted, with a creepy counterpoint of unexplained echoes and the continuous sound of dripping water. The long corridor was oppressive and boring; with dark shadows where the section dividing walls intruded into the corridor. The ridged stone tiles cladding the floor were cracked and

232

broken.

Along the vastness of the echoing corridor of this long-deserted building where Soviet troops had once walked; inexplicable noises echoed through its empty labyrinth studded with locked doors; occasionally interspersed with the sheer, vertigo-inducing drops of the dank and dripping stairwells smelling of mould. The cheerless, suffocating, and oppressive interior, and regimented row of seemingly endless identical grimy windows with their sills coated in a thick layer of dust and grime to their left, made for a chill, uncanny journey with shadows of hazy echoes of their footsteps resonating eerily from the rough walls.

Charlotte glanced at Callaghan.

'This really is one of the weirdest places I've ever been in, Gil. It's got an atmosphere that is really unsettling... almost as though the very walls have soaked up the fear and brutality; the despair and desperation of the thousands of young recruits that have gone through training in this place. The sooner we're out of here, the better, as far as I'm concerned.'

It really was an unnerving experience walking through the first of the mausoleum-like, silent spaces; the so-called "collective area" central hall... a wide, echoing space; twice the width of the corridor; and supported by large, square, free-standing pillars along its thirty-metre length. The wall opposite the windows was furnished with several double doorways and square apertures that might well have once been designed as serving hatches. Presumably, this area had been constructed to be a communal eating area... or something similar.

Beyond the large exit doors, the corridor continued along the second wing; through another "collective area," and on along another long, dank corridor to the end of the building. To reach the southern end of North wing Two, they had to cross the open, concrete foundation slab of an unbuilt community building a distance of close to one hundred and twenty metres. The two Spetsnaz ghosts were waiting for them outside the stairwell spur. Charlotte looked at them.

'Any movement, comrades?'

The taller of the two men silently shook his head.

'Quiet as the grave, Comrade Colonel. We'll let you get up to the fifth level and then come up to cover your backs.'

Charlotte nodded.

'Spasibo.'

Charlotte and Callaghan entered the south stairwell and began to ascend the stairs to the fifth level. The impression of openness was impressive. The banisters around the staircase weren't enclosed by brickwork, and the stair flights formed a kind of balcony on each successive floor so that the floor below could be seen from above, or below. The entire stairwell was pierced with deep windows that flooded the entire area with light. At the top of the fourth flight of stairs the balcony ended abruptly and became a solid wall once again. Here, they paused and listened... silence! The communal washrooms were to their left. A closed double door to their right led into the corridor of the fifth floor.

Here; the wall colour changed to dove-grey above a pale blue. The first door on the left was numbered 718. With seven rooms per section; this meant that Stabsgefreiter Poeschl's quarters would be located just this side of the third stairwell. This wing appeared to be... or to have recently been occupied. The entire structure was in much better condition than the semi-derelict wing that they had just negotiated. As to whether any of the rooms were actually in use was irrelevant. All the doors were closed and locked; and the ridged stone tiles on the floor were clean and polished; but the same oppressive silence permeated the entire wing.

Passing the entrance doors to the first stairwell spur; it was about forty-five metres to the next one. Beyond here it looked to be a shorter distance to the third stairwell... perhaps thirty-six metres. This was where they would find Poeschl's room... provided their calculation of the ascending room numbers was correct. Callaghan glanced at Charlotte. She nodded, and they drew their weapons from the holsters and aimed them ahead in unison; systematically covering each door as they passed them. Stealthily; so as not to let their footsteps echo on the stone tiles, and staying close to the wall, they moved down the corridor towards the next stairwell spur.

No sounds came from behind any of the doors. The deathly quiet atmosphere and the lack of any signs of life was enough to make anyone edgy; but they didn't have that luxury. This Cuban, according to Viktor Malinovskii; was the quintessential assassin. Charlotte and Callaghan needed to be fully vigilant and resolute for the next few minutes. Inexorably, the room numbers rose as they continued past the second stairwell... 726, 727, 728... There! Poeschl's room was the last one before the section dividing wall. Pausing; they both screwed the silencers into the Makarovs and cocked the weapons. Charlotte slipped past the closed door of room 732 and pressed herself against the corridor wall as Callaghan crept noiselessly up to the door; held his breath and put his ear to the keyhole. Dead silence!

Charlotte took up her position on the opposite side of the door with her Makarov held in the stable, double-hand grip, with the silenced muzzle of the weapon pointed towards the ceiling. Callaghan aimed his Makarov half-way up the door, and, shielded by the corridor wall, reached out and grasped the door handle. Turning it gradually, he inched the door open and then gave it a hard kick; bracing himself into the firing position as he did so. The door swung open to reveal a completely empty room.

From the general disorder, it was evident that the room's occupant had left in a hurry. The bedspread was rumpled as though a valise had been hurriedly packed upon it; there were no personal effects anywhere to be seen. The wardrobe was empty, save for a single, freshly pressed Stabsgefreiter's uniform... with a name-tag still attached... Poeschl. F.

Charlotte turned to Callaghan.

'Damn! We've missed him. How in hell did he know we were coming for him?'

She was interrupted by the sound of someone running up the stairs in the adjacent stairwell spur. Swiftly; they both ran into the corridor and stood; weapons aimed at the doorway. Makary Kravchek burst into the corridor and stopped dead as he saw two ominous black eyes of the silencers pointing at him. He threw out his hands in front of him.

'Whoa! They've just telephoned in that a GAZ has been taken from where it was parked up, and the sentry at the security gate says that Poeschl drove out about twenty minutes ago; saying that he was going out to the old range to calibrate the scope on his sniper rifle. The *Svoloch* has, as you Americans say; "Flown the coop"... and he's armed with one of the new SVD sniper rifles. They're good for a kill at thirteen hundred metres; so we are going to need to be careful from here on in.'

Charlotte nodded.

'How did he know that we were coming for him?'

Kravchek gave a snort of contempt.

'That fat *Svoloch*, Bächer down in reception somehow managed to get a message to him. It seems that there is a group of dissident activists in this complex. Bächer has been arrested, and we're sending in a team of investigators to clean out the others. It would appear that they are knee-deep in this conspiracy that you and Colonel Malinovskii are investigating.'

He gave an apologetic smile.

'This guy is good. He gave us all the slip; so we'd better get moving if we are going to have any chance of intercepting him before he disappears into Berlin again.'

Charlotte nodded again.

'It's no fault of yours, Captain. This man is a trained assassin and has managed to avoid the KGB and the Stasi for months. No matter; we'll get him... we have to. You cannot possibly know what is likely to happen if we fail.'

Kravchek took a deep breath and held her gaze with a solemn stare.

Oh, yes, Comrade Colonel... I know exactly what will happen... Armageddon.'

5.40pm, Friday, February 10th, 1961.
Vorpommern-Rügen district,
North Germany.

Forty-year-old Wachtmeister Wendel Trommler sat in his parked-up green and white Opel Kapitän Volkspolizei patrol car at the side of the B194 highway just outside the town of Steinhagen, at the Grimmen/Richtenberg junction; ten kilometres south of Stralsund. It had been a good day; the sun was shining; nothing much had happened, and he was making up his notebook before he headed back towards the Frankendamm headquarters in Stralsund. After signing off; he would head down to the local Bierkeller with some of the lads and have a few steins whilst admiring the waitresses. There was one in particular that he fancied... a big, pneumatic blonde named Jutte... and boy! She "jutted" in all the right places. He smiled to himself. That was a good quip! He'd see if he could slip that one in later during the drinking session. It would raise a laugh amongst the lads; and Jutte had a great sense of humour. If he could get her laughing, he might just get lucky with her.

His thoughts were interrupted by the tinny crackle of the car's radio. It was an all-patrol broadcast to be on the lookout for a GAZ army four-wheel-drive light truck coming from the direction of Rügen's Prora barracks. The truck had been reported stolen and was thought to be driven by a deserter who was identified as being one Ferdinand Poeschl; with the rank of Stabsgefreiter in the Nationale Volksarmee. Due caution should be applied as it was confirmed that this man was in possession of a firearm.

Wachtmeister Trommler sighed, and tossed his notebook onto the passenger seat. Damn! That was all he needed. The Nationale Volksarmee didn't have any sense of humour at all when it came to deserters. If the suspected fugitive came this way; all that Trommler had to look forward to were several hours of mindless paperwork and a long drive in an asthmatic Volkspolizei Barkas Kleinbus up to the barracks to return the prisoner, who really wouldn't want to go back there. He pulled out his Sauer pistol from its holster and flicked off the safety; but left the cocking/decocking lever alone. Now; all he needed to do if the fugitive appeared; was to flick this lever down and the weapon was ready. Putting the Sauer down next to his notebook, he wound down the door window; reached into the glove box and pulled out a pack of "*Josma*" cigarettes; lit one, and settled himself for a long wait.

Fernán Pasuali was planning his escape route as he barrelled the heavy GAZ down the B194 keeping the speed up to its maximum ninety km/h. Judging by the way this old tub was drinking fuel, he would be lucky to get much farther south than Neubrandenburg... and that was at least a hundred kilometres short of Berlin. He could always slow down; but how much farther would that get him? Probably no more than a few extra kilometres. Well, fuck it! He'd keep going, and grab another vehicle at the first opportunity.

Wachtmeister Trommler was just beginning to get bored, when he heard the first, faint high-pitched howl of what was unmistakeably an army vehicle coming from the direction of the little village of Seemühl; some two and a half kilometres away to the north-east. He flicked on the blue flashing beacon on the roof of the Opel; opened the driver's door and stepped out into the road. The high-pitched howl was getting louder... Damn! He'd left his pistol on the passenger seat. Quickly he retrieved it as the army vehicle came into view, about five hundred metres up the road. It was a GAZ, and it was moving fast.

Trommler stepped out into the road and raised his hand. The howl of the oncoming truck rose in pitch as the driver changed up a gear. Trommler made ready to jump out of the way if the bloody driver accelerated instead of slowing down; but the vehicle slowed, and obediently came to a standstill just in front of where he was standing. Trommler stepped forward towards the driver who was fairly young... in his late twenties; and had dark hair and eyes...a typically Bavarian "Alpine Race" stereotype. Trommler looked closely at him. Something was not quite right, here. The man's hair was too long. Nationale Volksarmee soldiers' hair was always clipped close to the head.

With his hand on the butt of his pistol, Trommler spoke authoritatively,

'Ferdinand Poeschl; switch off the motor and step out of the vehicle. You are under arrest for...'

He didn't get any further. A silenced pistol appeared from its concealment below the driver's window and thudded twice. Wachtmeister Trommler was hurled backwards against his patrol car as the shots tore into him. His body bounced off the hood and lay sprawled by the roadside. Pasuali climbed out of the GAZ, walked casually across to the motionless body, and spat at it. He grinned.

'Fucking Moron!…'

And coldly fired another shot into the Wachtmeister's head. He then transferred his rifle and valise to the patrol car; climbed in and switched off the flashing blue beacon. Starting the motor; he jammed the column gear change lever into first; and swung out onto the highway, showering Trommler's corpse with dirt and gravel as the rear tyres spun, and then squealed as they gained traction on the asphalt.

Meanwhile; Charlotte and Callaghan, and their KGB "protection officers" were in hot pursuit. The two Opel Kapitäns were equipped with flashing blue beacons magnetically attached to their roofs with cables plugged into power sockets installed in the dashboards. Callaghan had to rely on the Mercedes-Benz's headlamps on full beam. The convoy was just coming off the Rügen Causeway and, with headlamps blazing and blue beacon flashing; Kravchek and Gulin were approaching the built-up area of Stralsund at close to one hundred and forty km/h. Callaghan saw the grey Opel's stop lights blaze as Gulin braked hard to bring the careening vehicle down to a reasonable speed, and stabbed at the brake pedal.

The big drum brakes hauled the Mercedes-Benz's speed down rapidly as the Opel leaned into the left-hand corner that led out through the industrialised part of the town and on down to the south. The Opel's stop lights flared again as Gulin braked at a crossroads. His right turn indicator winked, and he turned out as a battered IFA truck laden with hay bales, and towing two similarly laden trailers along the adjoining road from the left, grunted to a halt in compliance with the Opel's flashing blue beacon, allowing the three cars to cut out in front of it. Hauling down on the Mercedes-Benz's steering wheel to make the right turn; Callaghan briefly raised his hand in acknowledgement to the startled lorry driver, then straightened the car up and punched the gas pedal. The road ran straight for just over one kilometre and ended at a "T" junction with the B194. This time; Gulin drove straight out across the highway and stopped, blocking all traffic in order that the other two cars turn out from the junction without delay.

Callaghan now took the lead and accelerated up to one hundred and forty km/h. This was below the Opel Kapitän's top speed and would allow Gulin... who had proved himself to be a real hot-shot driver, to catch up without blowing up. The second Opel containing the two Spetsnaz ghosts was following twenty metres behind; and sure enough; within five minutes, a second flashing blue light appeared in Callaghan's rear-view mirror way back down the highway. As they approached the small village of Negast; Gulin overtook them and resumed the lead. Three and a half kilometres ahead down the dead-straight highway they saw a rash of blue lights and began to slow down. Three Volkspolizei cars and an ambulance were parked up; and in the centre of the gaggle of vehicles was a GAZ army truck and what could only have been a body covered by a blanket. A Volkspolizist armed with a mean-looking StG44 assault rifle stood in the middle of the highway and waved them down.

Kravchek alighted from the Opel; flashed his KGB identity card, and said something to the Vopo, who turned and hurried away to a group of Volkspolizei gathered around the GAZ. He returned with an Oberwachtmeister, who was obviously in charge. Charlotte opened the car door and stepped out onto the worn asphalt. Joining the two men, she flashed her identity card and was soon engaged in intense conversation with them.

As Callaghan watched; the Oberwachtmeister saluted her and she turned to return to the car. Getting in, he could see from her expression that this was not a good situation. She turned to him; her tone of voice was solemn.

'It's Poeschl all right. He's killed a Volkspolizei Wachtmeister and stolen his patrol car. We're in a totally different ball game now. This guy has nothing to lose now. The order has gone out to shoot him on sight...which now makes him lethal... a loose cannon. They think he took the B194 down towards Demmin. It looks as though he's heading back to Berlin... and if he gets there... we've probably lost him for good. The trouble is, that we have no idea what he looks like; and whether Poeschl is an alias...I'm pretty certain that it must be; it doesn't sound very Cuban to me.'

2.30pm. Wednesday, February 15th, 1961.
2131. Eastshore Drive,
Virginia Lake.
Reno. Nevada.
USA.

"Crazy Joe" DeCicco's imposing residence overlooking Virginia Lake in the suburbs of Reno had been unoccupied since his assassination; but was frequently checked out by the Reno Mob's soldiers. Today, it was the turn of Nicky Agosto; a smart-ass young triggerman, who imagined himself to be a dead ringer for Tony Curtis; and had a penchant for twenty-dollar haircuts, sharp Italian suits; heavy gold jewellery, and big-breasted blondes. He was sitting out on the sun terrace, sipping a Tom Collins and admiring the spectacular breasts of his *"Comare"*... a gorgeous, blonde, air-head bimbo wearing a miniscule bikini, who was frolicking in the huge swimming pool. Her name was Rochelle and she was the sort of babe that every self-respecting wise guy should own. Not only did she fit his "Italian Stallion" image... she was stacked; and she popped Purple Hearts like they were M&M's Chocolate Candies. When she did that... hot-ass didn't even come close; her motor ran like she was lapping the whole Goddam field in the Daytona 500.

He took another slug of his Tom Collins and glanced at his flashy, rose gold Omega Constellation wristwatch... a "payment in kind" from an old Jewish jeweller who hadn't kept up with his protection fees. He slouched back into his sun recliner. Give Rochelle another twenty minutes, then split, get her home, break out the Purple Hearts; and when she was revved up; let her ride the rod a while; and then, fuck the ass off her.

His fantasy was interrupted by the chimes of the front doorbell. Irritably he stood up and walked back through the house. Glancing out of the window, he saw a black Porsche parked in the driveway. Who the fuck was this? Flipping up the retaining strap of his shoulder holster containing a big, kick-ass Colt 45; he opened the door to be faced by a pretty, young Asian girl and a slim, effeminate-looking Asian man. He looked them up and down and snapped,

'Yeah? Whaddya want?'

The girl smiled.

'Good afternoon. We have been asked to come and evaluate this property on behalf of the executors of the estate of the late Mr Joseph DeCicco. I am Veronica Lin of Bennett Realty Associates; and this is my assistant surveyor, James Yuang. May we come in?'

Nicky Agosto glowered at her.

'Don't know nuthin' 'bout that. Get lost!'

The girl smiled sweetly.

'Wrong answer, asshole.'

Her hand came from behind her back, holding a silenced Walther PPK pistol. Before Agosto realised what was happening; there was a dull "Phft!" and he was hurled backwards into the hallway with a neat hole punched between his eyebrows. He was dead before his body hit the highly polished parquet floor. The girl stepped over the body and motioned her colleague towards the rear of the building.

Pretty, dumb Rochelle was still splashing around in the pool when she heard a polite cough. Looking up, she saw a young, Asian man wearing a sharp suit, standing by the edge of the pool. She stood up, and waved, with a bright, sexy smile that froze as he raised a silenced pistol and pointed it at her. Her eyes widened in terror and she opened her mouth to scream for Nicky. She didn't get the chance. The pistol coughed, and the slug smacked home between her spectacularly pneumatic breasts. The impact hurled her backwards into the water where she slowly drifted away towards the far side of the pool, with a thin trill of blood tracing her passage across the azure surface of the water.

It took a little over two hours for Gabriella Chang and Jimmy Yoo; her trusted lieutenant and bodyguard, to search through DeCicco's large, and ostentatiously furnished residence. Following the assassination of her grandfather and Sebastian Lee; Gabriella Chang had made an inconspicuous visit to the Ristorante Césarina in Vallejo Street, San Francisco; the place where the executions had taken place; and spoken discreetly with the staff.

The waitress who had been working that particular evening told her that the two killers had picked up a small velvet bag from the table where the victims had been sitting. Gabriella had seen her grandfather place such a pouch... which contained the large Garnet that he intended to present to Sebastian Lee, in his coat pocket before he had left for the arranged meeting.

It was reasonable to assume that this gemstone had been taken to the man who had organised the killings... and that man was "Mad Joe" DeCicco. Gabriella was determined to retrieve this gemstone; which was the reason why she was here. DeCicco's address in Reno had been easy to ascertain; it had also been expected that there would be someone there, even though she had successfully executed DeCicco herself; but, the killing of the girl in the pool was distasteful. She turned to Jimmy Yoo.

'Was it really necessary to kill the girl, Jimmy? After all; she was just that asshole's squeeze.'

Jimmy Yoo nodded solemnly.

'Yes, Miss Chang. It is my duty to protect you from all things at all times; and she would have undoubtedly been able to give the cops incriminating information.'

Gabriella nodded.

'Yes, Jimmy; I suppose you're right; but it doesn't make me feel any better. Now, let's find this damned gemstone and get the hell out of here.'

Jimmy Yoo eventually discovered the pouch containing the gemstone tucked away in an ornate bedside cabinet in one of the guest bedrooms. In the same concealed drawer, he also found several thousand dollars in high-denomination notes, and two thin, black hardcover notebooks with elastic band closures, filled with the names and addresses of the Reno, and San Francisco Mobs' contacts and associates. Leaving the money where it was; he removed the pouch and notebooks and brought them to Gabriella. He told her of the money, but said that it was better to leave it where it was; because the Reno cops always went to town on robberies where fatalities had occurred. If they found that no money or valuables... like Agosto's expensive gold watch and jewellery, had been taken; they were just as likely to decide that this was a Mob slaying... perhaps an *"Omertá"*...code of silence killing.

Gabriella turned to leave, but Jimmy Yoo returned to Agosto's sprawled body and bent down towards it. Gabriella paused.

'What are you doing, Jimmy?'

He looked up.

'I'm just going to move this *"Pabajay"*... Loser, to a more believable position; maybe a sun lounger, or even in the pool with the girl.'

Gabriella stared at him.

'But what about the blood?'

Jimmy Yoo smiled.

'The only blood is that which you can see, Miss Chang. I took the liberty of loading a low-power shell into the top of your Walther's clip. The slug stayed in his head... so no splatter.'

He grabbed Agosto's corpse, and with a strength that belied his effeminate appearance, hauled it outside onto the sun terrace. Heaving it into the sun lounger; he then carefully knocked the Tom Collins glass down from the table, where it shattered on the tiles. To all appearances, it now looked as though Agosto had been shot where he would be found. Returning to the hallway; he carefully took a tissue from his pocket; cleaned up all traces of blood from the parquet floor, and, walking to the cloakroom, flushed the bloody tissue down the toilet. He then left the house.

Gabriella had already started the Porsche and was waiting for him. He climbed in, and they drove out through the gates into Lakeside

Drive; where she stopped the car. Getting out; he opened the trunk and removed a realtor's sale board which he attached to the gates. Returning to the car, he got in, and Gabriella accelerated away towards downtown Reno, where eventually, they would join the slip road onto Interstate 80.

6.35pm, Friday, February 10th, 1961.
Mecklenburg-Vorpommern district,
North Germany.

Fernán Pasuali first spotted the distant flashing blue light in his rear view mirror as he came on to the five kilometre straight that ran down along the edge of the Keetzseen forest; south of Neustrelitz and Lindenberg. He knew exactly what they were... Volkspolizei; or maybe something even worse... and here he was; in a stolen police car that could be seen halfway across Brandenburg Province; and just to make it interesting; he was getting low on gas. He gave a wry grin. OK let's give the bastards a run for their money. Stamping on the gas pedal, he sent the Opel hurtling down the long straight.

The overheating Opel finally ran out of gas just as Pasuali came out from the forest into open country some four kilometres north of the next town... Alt-Lüdersdorf. As the motor spluttered and faded, he gave the gas pedal one last vicious jab and steered the car to the side of the highway. Now What? He scanned the surrounding area. A line of low trees and a hedgerow lined the eastern edge of the highway. Out to his left were open fields; but, about two hundred metres distant, standing in isolation in the middle of the first field were two clumps of trees.

He nodded to himself. A perfect place for a sniping hide. Anyone out on the road would have no idea where shots were coming from; and by the time they'd realised that it was probably from one of the tree clumps across the field; they would all be dead, anyway. Picking up his rifle and valise; he hurried across the highway and walked out into the field; making sure he only stepped on stones or clumps of grass and weeds, in order that he wouldn't leave any tell-tale footprints in the rich, dun-coloured soil.

Settling into a comfortable position under cover of the nearer of the two stands of trees; Pasuali unslung the SVD rifle, and settled into his firing position. The light was still good; even though it was well past sunset. He squinted through the scope and sighted on the abandoned Volkspolizei Opel out on the road. Ratcheting in the adjustment screws to two hundred metres, he centred the scope crosshairs on the

243

blue beacon lamp housing. Perfect! Now he was zeroed in for accurate head shots. He made himself comfortable and went over the SVD rifle with minute care.

Twenty minutes later; he heard the sound of motors echoing from the forest. The first car appeared... a grey Opel Kapitän with a flashing blue beacon on its roof. Pasuali flicked off the safety and aimed at the slowing vehicle. As he did so, a second car appeared... a black Mercedes-Benz; which was followed by a lurid blue Opel; also with a flashing blue beacon. All three vehicles stopped close to the abandoned Volkspolizei car. The passenger door of the first Opel opened and a man climbed out. Pasuali trained the scope on him and his eyes narrowed as he recognised the distant figure. Kravchek... Captain Makary Kravchek, KGB; of the Third Chief Directorate; Karlshorst. The other guy in the car would be KGB as well.

Pasuali's finger tightened on the trigger. Wait! See who else was out there on the road. Two men were getting out of the blue Opel and walking towards Kravchek... KGB?... no; they were more interested in scanning the surrounding countryside. They were certainly Russian; but their actions suggested they were military. The occupants of the Mercedes-Benz were getting out and moving towards the abandoned car... a man and a girl. They appeared to be civilians... but, with the KGB you could never tell.

Through the scope, he could see that Kravchek and his buddy were carrying AKM Assault rifles. The other two men were armed with much shorter weapons. These appeared to be compact sub-machine guns... most likely the new Czech Skorpions. If that were true, then these two men were Spetsnaz. The couple from the Mercedes-Benz appeared to be unarmed. Centring the crosshairs on Kravchek's head, he squeezed the trigger. The SVD shuddered against his shoulder and Kravchek fell; a bright plume of blood spurting from his right temple as his buddy spun around and raised his AKM in the general direction from where he imagined the shot had come. Pasuali squeezed the trigger again and the man was thrown backwards across the Volkspolizei car's hood with half of his face blown away.

The couple from the Mercedes-Benz had ducked behind the car; but the other two men were running forward as they opened up with their weapons; roaring and flaming on full automatic fire. Pasuali heard the crash of the bullets among the treetops above him, and fixed the crosshairs on the man to the right. He squeezed the trigger. The man's legs buckled, but his momentum still carried him forward. He crashed into the ditch at the side of the road as his clenched finger went on firing the gun aimlessly up towards the darkening sky until the magazine finally emptied itself.

The second man dived behind the body of his companion and began firing accurately into the clump of trees where Pasuali had concealed himself. There was no way of knowing if the man had spotted him, or whether he had seen the muzzle flashes from the SVD. No matter; he was getting too damned close with his bursts. Bullets were chopping into the trees and spattering Pasuali with slivers of wood. He fired again. The corpse of the first man jerked. Damn! Too low! The second man rose and ran for cover behind his car; firing as he did so. Pasuali swore volubly. Fuck this!

He flicked the gas regulator; rose, and squeezed the trigger. The man had almost reached the safety of the blue Opel when Pasuali's final rapid shots caught him; tearing open his chest and spinning him around like a marionette puppet with tangled strings. As he crashed to the ground, Pasuali sighted the scope on the black Mercedes-Benz. Nothing moved. Ejecting the spent magazine and clicking in a fresh one; he emerged from the trees and began walking towards the road.

Crouching behind the cover of the Mercedes-Benz; Charlotte and Callaghan saw the figure emerge from the clump of trees and begin walking purposefully across the field towards them. He was far beyond the range of their Makarovs which had an effective range of no more than fifty metres. The assault rifles of Kravchek and Gulin were out of reach on the road... as were the Skorpions of the two Spetsnaz men. Charlotte glanced at Callaghan.

'You stay there; I'll move to the front of the car. We'll split his aim, and then one of us can get him. Remember, we want him alive.'

Callaghan nodded.

'OK, but for Chrissakes, keep low. This bastard is good.'

She nodded, and keeping low, moved to the relative safety of the left front fender, where she drew her Makarov and chambered one of the vicious *"Molo"* rounds.

The sniper was now less than one hundred metres distant. He was walking unconcernedly across the last few metres of the open field towards a farm track that bordered the adjoining strip of land between the field and the road. Charlotte glanced at Callaghan. He was crouched with his pistol ready. She looked back at the man. Suddenly; he did something totally unexpected. He lifted his rifle and ejected the magazine; then, holding the weapon above his head, walked calmly into the middle of the road and stopped, facing them. Charlotte and Callaghan stood up; aiming their pistols at him. She called out, coldly,

'Put the rifle down, and raise your hands slowly.'

The man obeyed. Callaghan moved out from behind the Mercedes-Benz and kicked the rifle away. The man gave a wry grin, and spoke in perfect English...

'That's no way to treat one of the Soviet's new, experimental rifles.'

Keeping him covered; Charlotte stepped out into the road. Who the hell was this guy?... one of the "off-the-books" contract cowboys who got a hard-on looking at the pictures in American Rifleman Magazine? OK. Stay sharp. One false move; and she'd blow a Goddam great hole in him. She looked him up and down. Her voice had a hard edge to it.

'Cut the smart-ass remarks, Pasuali. You're under arrest for conspiracy to murder.'

Pasuali shrugged.

'As you wish; Captain Mckenna. Don't look so surprised. I was given access to detailed files on all our operatives and assets in Germany before I came out on this mission.'

Charlotte stared at him.

'Detailed files? Mission? Start talking Pasuali; and can the bullshit.'

Callaghan moved to Pasuali and frisked him. There were no concealed weapons on him. Callaghan nodded.

'OK, wise guy. You can put your hands down. Now start talking.'

Pasuali relaxed slightly. He looked at Callaghan and then, at Charlotte.

'I know that you are fully familiar with Colonel Malinovskii's conspiracy investigation. He was correct about the identity of the Cuban assassin, Fernán Pasuali; and I was sent in to take his place after our people targeted him over eighteen months ago in a brothel in Prenzlauer Berg. He was taken to a safe house in Stralau where it was made to look as though he had been beaten up by the brothel's enforcers; and he was then dumped off the Straulauer Brücke into the Spree with his throat cut.'

Charlotte studied him intently.

'Ok; so you're another "Ghost"... but who are you working for? Stasi?... BND?.. MAD?... BfV?

These last three were the Federal German Intelligence Agencies.

He grinned.

'Not even close! I'm out of the Miami office.'

Charlotte studied him.

'So, you'll be familiar with the Miami Head of Station then?'

He grinned.

'Better than that. I was detached to Miami by Jim Noel, the Station chief in Havana, when Bob Reynolds; who is now Miami Station chief, was still the Caribbean Desk Chief.'

Charlotte paused, and lowered her Makarov. Only another member of "The Firm"... however implausible; could possibly know that Reynolds had been the CIA's Caribbean Desk Chief before he became the Miami Head of Station.

'So who the hell are you?... and how long have you been out here?'

Pasuali glanced up and down the road.

'Let's get in the car and get the hell outta here. When we're rolling, I'll fill you in on everything that I am at liberty to tell you. Deal?'

Charlotte nodded.

'Deal.'

She turned to Callaghan, who was watching Pasuali closely for any suspicious movement. When he saw none, he lowered his pistol and opened the rear door of the Mercedes-Benz for Pasuali to get into the back seat. He then got in beside him whilst Charlotte slipped into the driving seat; started the car; switched on the headlamps, and pulled out from behind the grey Opel; steering carefully around the sprawled corpses of Kravchek and Gulin. She accelerated the car up to eighty km/h; and then, glancing into the rear-view mirror; spoke.

'OK. So start talking.'

He nodded.

'My name is Tony Garcia and I'm with Special Ops. I've been here for almost two years now. I was flown over from Opa-locka on a clandestine Southern Air Transport Herc' and parachuted in. My mission was to check out the intelligence that the Soviets were leaking to us. Someone high up in their Command was running scared about this conspiracy and what it might lead to.

To cut a long story short; I discovered that there was nothing to trace beyond Pasuali. It was all an elaborate subterfuge originating from back in the good old U.S.of A. Pasuali was a wild goose set up for both us and the Russians to chase. The Cold war paranoia did the rest. As far as I have been able to establish positively; is that there IS a conspiracy to assassinate someone and pass the blame on to the other side. Who it is; I don't know... but the conspiracy is real, and already in place.'

Charlotte nodded.

'That's what Malinovskii told me. The target he mentioned is John F, Kennedy.'

Garcia stared at her reflection in the rear-view mirror; then said, very quietly...

'Jesus H. Christ! So we'll blame the Russians and escalate the Cold

War. We've gotta get back and warn them; it's all beginning to make sense. The East German State Council chairman, Ulbricht is already pressuring Khrushchev to divide Berlin and East Germany from the west, permanently; and something like this conspiracy... if it succeeds; could tip us over into a Third World War.'

The run down the Berlin-Stettin Autobahn was uneventful. As Charlotte turned onto the Berliner Ring at Schwanebeck, Callaghan leaned forward.

'Are you going to tell Malinovskii anything?'

She glanced at Callaghan in the rear-view mirror as she turned the Mercedes-Benz onto the exit road for Lindenberg and Malchow; slowing the car to below the sixty km/h speed limit.

'I shall just inform him that Pasuali has been eliminated, and that we found no further evidence pointing to any co-conspirators. If he is still unconvinced; then the KGB can conduct their own internal investigations to sort their side of this mess out.'

Callaghan nodded.

'Good move. What about Murphy at Clayallee?'

She gave a small, disdainful huff.

'Screw Murphy! We're completely autonomous as far as the Berlin Station is concerned.'

She glanced at Garcia.

So; are you going to come out with us?... Or are you going to stay in Berlin?'

He shrugged.

'I'm done here. I figure it's time to head home; and having just retired those two KGB goons and their buddies; I guess I've outstayed my welcome in the backyard of the Wandlitz Warriors.'

Charlotte smiled. Garcia's use of the "Wandlitz Warriors" quip was a reference to the fact that most of the GDR hierarchy lived, far removed from the general population; in an exclusive and expensive secure housing zone... *Die Waldsiedlung*; a forest settlement twenty-five kilometres north of Berlin; and close to the town of Wandlitz.

Chapter Sixteen.

8.20pm, Friday, February 10th, 1961.
Weissensee District, Pankow.
East Berlin.

Approaching Klement-Gottwald-Allee; Charlotte eased the Mercedes-Benz's speed down to below the fifty-six km/h speed limit through the unlit East Berlin streets. The last thing they needed was to attract the attention of some overzealous young Volkspolizist. She and Callaghan had the KGB identity documents; but Garcia had no identification at all... that was standard procedure for Special Ops guys... members of the unit normally did not carry any objects or clothing that would associate them with the United States government. If they were compromised during a mission, they were on their own. The government of the United States would deny all knowledge of their existence.

As they turned into Griefswalder Strasse; an unmarked EMW 340 sedan pulled out of a side road and began to follow them. Above the dim street lamps that were now infrequently spaced along the merging of Griefswalder Strasse and the beginning of Königstrasse which led down to Alexanderplatz; the sky was black, The moon had yet to rise, and there was no movement in the streets; these were the dead hours in East Berlin. She glanced into the rear-view mirror. The feeble, yellow beams of the following car's six-volt headlamps were unmistakeable. They were probably Volkspolizei... the Stasi tended to use black Mercedes-Benzes.

Callaghan glanced back.

'We're being followed. Who d'you think they are?'

'They're most likely Volkspolizei attracted by the car. I figure they're trying to spook us into breaking the speed limit. They like to get their hands on Western Marks,'

She commented wryly; as she crossed the Prenzlauer Berg/Am Friedrichshain junction with the red just flicking to green. Fifty metres into Neue Königstrasse, she saw a car standing on the far side of Linienstrasse, an old, dark-coloured Mercedes-Benz. She couldn't be sure whether there was anyone sitting in it or not, but it was pretty certain there would be. In the rear-view mirror the dim yellow headlamps were much closer. This smelled like an intercept.

She accelerated slightly and drove as far as the second intersection at Gerlach Strasse; then turned north to come into Alexanderplatz from the direction of Prenzlauer Strasse; just in case there was a third car waiting there. Half a block later, the old Mercedes Benz was in the mirror. At the next street the Mercedes and the EMW were both there; taking up positions at a distance and keeping pace. Charlotte swore under her breath. Damn! Now that they were staying on her tail they wouldn't waste any time. Alexanderplatz was coming up fast and it was going to be very difficult to make a switch in that big, open space.

A switch is a manoeuvre that is easy to describe and usually, almost impossible to pull off. If you were being followed; whether on foot, or as now, in a vehicle; the idea is to suddenly vanish and then reappear on the tail of your pursuer. She'd practised it several times at the MPDC Academy back in Washington; but that had been on wide, American roads... not the backstreets of East Berlin.

Successfully negotiating Alexanderplatz; Charlotte sped down Rathaus Strasse; heading for Max Engels Platz. Two blocks from the Rotes Rathaus; she picked up two more suspicious cars making calculated loops around the side streets as the other two stayed on her tail. There was no chance of making a successful switch now. They would also have to make their move soon; for beyond Max Engels Platz, and once over the Spree Bridge; the Unter den Linden opened up for the one and a half kilometre dead straight dash down to the Brandenburger Tor and the safety of the British sector of West Berlin.

The two cars began to close in and make rushes as she slewed the Mercedes-Benz through Marx Engels Platz. First the EMW, and then the old Mercedes bumped her rear bumper; swinging the rear of the Mercedes-Benz against the kerb, whilst another of the cars came from in front with its headlights on full beam; blinding her momentarily and forcing her into a swerve. A truck loomed at out of the Friedrichstrasse junction and the EMW behind struck her rear bumper again; trying to push her forward against her brakes with the wheels locked and the tyres squealing over the surface as the truck grazed across the front end of the Mercedes-Benz smashing out a headlamp.

There was a slow-motion impression of the driver yelling and shaking his fist, as she floored the gas pedal, and the Mercedes-Benz surged forward again.

There was no way of knowing if they were trying to wreck her or whether this was just chance that the truck had happened to be in the right place at the wrong time. Charlotte guessed that they were trying to get the car stopped, and that was when they would close in and make the kill if that was their intention. It was pretty damned obvious that they were not Volkspolizei... so who were they? Stasi? KGB? Who were they after? It had to be Garcia; so, was this the rogue Kremlin connection?... or even more sinisterly...the Russian Mafia?

Callaghan had his Makarov out, and threw it to Garcia. He grabbed the Uzi and yanked back the charging handle. Charlotte concentrated on the driving. The wide boulevard of the Unter den Linden had become a stone and concrete channel cut through the city. The moon was rising; its light shimmered like silk through the naked branches of the young Linden trees lining the boulevard, strobing disconcertingly across the shadows between the street lights. A line of clouds marched across the moon and the kaleidoscope of the street's perspective was broken into a semblance of order... the dim street lights, headlamps blazing in the rear-view mirror, and the distant, welcoming glow of West Berlin beyond the shadowy edifice of the Brandenburger Tor.

Charlotte glanced at the speedometer; ninety km/h, and the EMW was still there and gaining on her. Suddenly, it swung away as it drew alongside; then swerved sharply in. The impact pushed the Mercedes-Benz sideways towards the edge of the carriageway. Charlotte hit the brakes and wrenched at the wheel to avoid hitting the kerb and rolling the car over. She was deafened by the sudden, tearing bark of the Uzi as Callaghan opened up at the car that was swerving away; going very fast towards the central promenade, before braking hard and slamming against one of the Linden trees. Callaghan continued to pump a burst of bullets into the car as it bounced off and overturned; scraping across the carriageway on its roof; throwing out a great shower of sparks. Charlotte swerved around the wreck and glimpsed in the glare of her remaining headlamp, someone tearing at the door as the fuel tank went up in a great, burgeoning burst of orange light.

In the distance; Charlotte could see figures milling around the roadways under the shadowy bulk of the Brandenburger Tor. She cursed under her breath. Oh, shit! They were Volkspolizei, setting up a road block as a result of their hearing the gunfire echoing up Unter den Linden, and seeing the exploding fuel tank of the EMW that had been pursuing and trying to force her to stop. Now what?

She made a spit-second decision; and, barely reducing speed; heaved down on the steering wheel and sent the Mercedes-Benz slewing and lurching to the left, into Wilhelmstrasse. The car skidded across the worn asphalt; fish-tailing viciously; but, with the application of a series of rapid opposite locks, and a little judicious Rally driver-style heel and toeing on the gas and brake pedals, she had the Mercedes-Benz under control within fifty metres.

Glancing into the rear-view mirror; Charlotte noted that no headlights were following the speeding Mercedes-Benz from Unter den Linden. As she sped down Wilhelmstrasse, she noted that it bore little resemblance to what she remembered. The Reichs Chancellery had been completely demolished; and the entire area around what had been Voss Strasse was an empty, shadowy wasteland; except for one surviving building in the entire length of the street.

One the opposite side; there were almost no buildings at all along the Wilhelmstrasse from Unter den Linden to the Leipziger Strasse. The only recognisable building was the huge edifice of Göring's Reich Air Ministry a little farther down on the right; where she intended to turn into Leipziger Strasse, and emerge through Leipziger Platz into Potsdamer Platz; then cut up Bellevue Allee to Kemper Platz. From there; she intended to follow Tiergarten Strasse as far as Stüler Strasse; and Budapester Strasse down to Breitscheidplatz; and on into the Ku'damm. The first problem would be getting through the sector boundary. The streets that crossed the border were under surveillance by the Volkspolizei; and vehicular traffic was checked. Time to bluff it out. Turning into Leipziger Strasse; Charlotte accelerated towards the huge lattice structure of the illuminated neon sign proclaiming *"Die Freie Berliner Presse Meldet"*... "The Free Berlin Press Announces"... erected on the western sector of the Potsdamer Platz in front of the Esplanade.

The whole area was an empty wasteland. The only buildings remaining of those that had once lined Leipziger Strasse and Leipziger Platz were the Air Ministry Annex and the Preussischen Herrenhaus. Even the huge Wertheim department store which had covered most of the northern side of the street had disappeared. Nothing remained of Leipziger Platz, except for the octagonal roadways flanked by piles of rubble. Directly ahead; in the glare of her one remaining headlamp, she saw the big sign which proclaimed in large letters...

ENDE
DES DEMOKRATISCHEN SEKTORS VON GROSSE-BERLIN
IN 19m ENTFERNUNG

There were no guards at the end of Leipziger Platz. Crossing the invisible sector border; Charlotte swung the Mercedes-Benz into Potsdamer Platz over the luminous white line painted across the cobblestones at the extreme end of Leipziger Platz which marked the sector boundary. She breathed a sigh of relief. They'd made it.

Only two buildings in the immediate vicinity of Potsdamer Platz still stood. One was complete, and relatively undamaged... the Weinhaus Huth; the other was a half-ruined shell. The Weinhaus Huth's steel skeleton had enabled the building to withstand the shelling and bombing of the war virtually undamaged, and it now stood out starkly amid a vast, totally desolate wasteland. A short distance away in Bellevue Strasse stood the blasted hulk of the former Hotel Esplanade. Where the Weinhaus Rheingold and the Café Josty had once stood were blackened piles of rubble. Even the ten-storey, ultra-modern office building, Columbus Haus had been demolished. Almost all of the buildings around Potsdamer Platz had been turned to rubble by air raids and heavy artillery bombardment during the last years of the war, as a result of being in close proximity to a major target area... Hitler's Reich Chancellery, just one block away in Voss Strasse; and many other Nazi government buildings in the immediate vicinity.

Charlotte remembered the devastation that she had seen of this once-geographical centre of the city, and heart of Berlin's nightlife, during her escape from the city in March, 1945. Then, it had been a nightmarish landscape of skeletal, shattered walls teetering over towering mounds of rubble; strewn with the detritus of war... wrecked vehicles, mangled corpses, and discarded weapons scattered amongst the torn up tramlines and shell craters. Since then, Potsdamer Platz had been more or less left to rot, as one by one, the ruined buildings were cleared away, with neither the Soviets nor the Allies having the will to repair or replace them. Now, in the light cast by the indifferent street lamps, it seemed that there was hardly a building left standing between here and the Tiergarten, almost half a kilometre to the north.

Turning left into Bellevue Strasse; other than the fragmentary remains of the Hotel Esplanade and piles of rubble, there was nothing except waist-high weeds and half-tidied wastes of empty bombed space stretching away to what, in Charlotte's previous memories of Berlin, had been called Skagerrak Platz; but was now renamed Kemperplatz. Once, the impressive Rolandbrunnen fountain had stood here on a traffic island; but now, Kemperplatz was nothing more than a road junction. Turning left again; she drove into what had once been

Tiergartenstrasse. During the final days of the Battle of Berlin; the swanky urban villas lining the southern side of the road had been almost erased to their foundations and had never had been re-built. Tiergartenstrasse was amongst the most heavily damaged areas in Berlin; due in no small part to the Red Army's assault which broke through the outer lines of Berlin's defences, and gradually pushed the defending German forces into the core of the city around the Tiergarten and zoo. There had been so little left, that the northern side of Tiergartenstrasse had been eventually integrated into the Tiergarten Park. It was in the ruins of one of the now-vanished villas that Charlotte had first met Max when he had been a young Russian Major commanding a combat group during the fighting; and she had been disguised as a German nurse.

She smiled softly to herself. Max... her Max; Major Maksim Siegel. She remembered that first moment as though it was yesterday. She still missed him, after all these years. He'd died too soon; but that was the risk they all took when they chose to play the spook game... and, even though they were far too few... they had known the days.

Her thoughts were interrupted by Garcia.

'Captain Mckenna, Ma'am; I have to report in. Can you drop me off at the Kaiser Wilhelm church? I've got a safe room just off Tauentzien Strasse; and the sooner I'm away; the safer you'll be. They'll be looking for me now.'

Charlotte glanced into the rear-view mirror.

'Why don't you come and lay low with us while I arrange an extraction? We'll get a flight out of Tegel within a day or so.'

He shook his head.

'Thanks, but I still have one more assignment to complete; then I'll make my own way out.'

Charlotte nodded, as she turned into Budapester Strasse with the jagged spire of the Kaiser-Wilhelm-Gedächtniskirche towering like a blackened fang into the night sky.

'OK; your choice.'

It was raining hard when Charlotte and Callaghan arrived back at Uhlandstrasse 192. As she locked the car she noticed that there was an odd smell in the air. For a second she could not place it, then realised that it was a smell that she remembered from the burning city; those last days before it fell to the Russian onslaught. Surely she must be imagining it. She had heard people say that, when it rained in Berlin; even after all these years, you could still smell traces of the burning... a chilling echo of how it had smelled after the years of countless bombings, and during the final Soviet assault. She had thought that it was just talk... but now, as the cold rain hissed against the wet sidewalk; she smelled it again... faint, and indeterminate; like a ghost of the nightmare that had prowled the fear-stained streets during Berlin's *Götterdämmerung*... the fiery twilight of Hitler's *Drittes Reich*. She shivered, and ran across the road to the entrance of their apartment block.

They were met by the concierge, Herr Günsche who welcomed them back. He said that there had been no calls or visitors since they had departed. Charlotte nodded, and, as Callaghan moved towards the slowly revolving Paternoster, she quietly took Herr Günsche to one side.

'Herr Günsche; I need to use the telephone. Is it a secure line?'

He nodded.

'Yes, Frau Streckenbach. The "Firm's" technicians check it every week as a matter of course... considering the business that the residents are engaged in. It was checked yesterday. You just dial zero-two-two before the required number to activate the scrambler.'

She smiled.

'Thank you, Herr Günsche.'

He nodded and went back into his apartment. Callaghan said that he would go on up to the apartment and start making coffee. She nodded, and picked up the telephone handset.

As Callaghan disappeared in the Paternoster, she dialled zero-two-two, and heard a soft double click in the earpiece. She then dialled a Wilmersdorf district number, and asked to be connected with a Major Gilmore. After a slight pause, a voice with a distinctive Boston accent came on the line.

'Gilmore here. How may I help you?'

She spoke quietly.

'Hi, Carey; it's Charlotte. We have a compromised project. We are working "off the books," and Uncle doesn't need to know. We're in the black at the moment, but I can't tell for how long. We need a pick-up from the Uhland Bierkeller and a ride home.'

This spook-talk meant that the operation she had been working on was blown, but, as yet; her identity was unknown to the opposition. She needed to be collected from the Uhlandstrasse address for a flight out of Berlin as soon as possible; and that the Berlin Operating Base was not to be informed of her departure.

Major Carey Gilmore was stationed at the U.S. Army Security Agency, Special Operations Unit based at *"Der Teufelsberg"*... "The Devils Mountain"... an artificial hill built to the north of Berlin's

Grunewald forest from the bombing rubble remaining of the city's buildings destroyed during the war. There was a listening station on the Teufelsberg that could forward a signal back to Washington to arrange for Charlotte and Callaghan's extraction. Gilmore was an old friend from her Washington days; and could be relied upon to make the necessary arrangements. The soft, Boston accent came back down the line…

'OK Charlotte; sit tight. I'll get a car out to you in the morning.'

She breathed a sigh of relief.

'Thank you, Carey. Goodnight.'

The faint sound of tyres squealing and car doors closing roused Charlotte from her light sleep. Callaghan was fast asleep and snoring gently; he always did after they had made love. Rubbing the sleep from her eyes she glanced at the luminous hands of the little travelling alarm clock on the bedside table… Two, thirty-five. It was probably just a taxi bringing someone home from a night out in the clubs on Ku'damm. Nevertheless, she slipped out of bed and peered through the curtains at the street below. It wasn't a taxi, and they weren't night clubbers.

A big BMW 502 saloon had stopped outside. The driver had the engine running, the headlamps off; and the windshield wipers sweeping the rain away from his view of the street. Two men were crossing the deserted street and heading towards the entrance door of the apartment block. This looked all wrong… and deadly dangerous to her; particularly as they had turned up between two and four o'clock in the morning… the death hours. Quickly, she roused Callaghan and fetched the Makarov pistols from the main living area. Getting back into bed beside Callaghan; she handed him his pistol and silencer. He gave her a puzzled glance and was about to say something. She pressed a finger to his lips and whispered,

'I think we have visitors. Stay sharp, baby.'

Screwing the silencers into the pistols, they sat up in bed and waited; straining their ears for any sound that might confirm her suspicions. The apartment block was silent, except for the dull, perpetual grumble of the Paternoster. Callaghan slipped out of bed and crept to the door of the apartment. If there were intruders, they would probably use the stairs… and, characteristically for an old, pre-war Prussian Altbau apartment block; the stairs creaked. Listening carefully at the door, he heard a faint commotion down in the lobby. The stairwell shaft was open, and rose to the upper floors beside the enclosure for the paternoster. It was a natural echo chamber. He heard

256

old Herr Günsche's raised voice… and then, the flat, unmistakeable sound of a silenced pistol being fired… followed by a dull thud… as though someone had dropped a sack of potatoes on to the lobby floor.

Callaghan darted silently back to the bedroom, and in a low voice told Charlotte to get into the bathroom. She nodded, and slipped out of bed; chambering a round in her Makarov as she did so. Callaghan dragged back the bed covers and arranged the pillows and bolster pillow into the shape of two bodies. Tossing the bed covers back over them, he quickly adjusted them so that, in the darkened room, it would give the intruders an impression that there were two people sleeping in the bed. He then chambered a round in his Makarov and crept into the far corner of the room where he was shielded from the bedroom door by the heavy, Bauhaus-style wardrobe.

The stair treads on the flight up from the second floor creaked softly. He could just detect the sound of stealthy footsteps up the stairs that stopped just outside the door of the apartment; and readied himself; raising the Makarov in the stable, two-handed grip. He heard a muffled whisper… so; there were at least two of them. The floor creaked softly as their "visitors" crossed the living room and approached the bedroom door. Again… he heard muffled whispers and sneaking footsteps right outside the door. Callaghan held his breath… the doorknob began to slowly rotate, and the door began to open. It moved slowly, almost too slowly to be real. One of the hinges keened softly in protest from age and wear. Callaghan could see a shadow looming in the thin crack of light coming in from the landing. The blunt snout of a silenced pistol slid menacingly into his line of sight, and silently tracked across towards the bed and its "sleeping couple." The door continued to open and two figures crept into the bedroom. The second figure raised another silenced pistol, and in unison, the shadowy forms each fired two quick shots into the mounds under the bed covers.

Callaghan stepped out and fired; hitting the first man in the chest and throwing him bodily against the second executioner. Even with the restricting effect of the silencer, the ferocious *"Molo"* slug tore a huge hole in the first man's back; splattering the second man; which gave Callaghan a split-second to fire again. His shot slammed into the other man's forehead, causing his head to literally explode like a ripe watermelon dropped from a second-floor window onto a concrete sidewalk.

Callaghan reached across and flicked on the lights. He stared at the blood spatter on the once-pristine walls, and then, at the pool of blood seeping into the joints of the polished parquet floor. The two shattered corpses lay where they had fallen. Who the fuck were these guys? As he bent to frisk them for any identification... any clue as to whom they worked for; Charlotte came out from the bathroom. Her eyes widened.

'Holy shit, Callaghan. Who are these two?'

He held up an International driver's licence.

'Ukrainians... most likely, Russian Mafia. Get dressed, baby. Time to get the fuck outta here.'

She nodded and turned towards the bed; pulling back the covers. The bullet holes in the pillows and bolster pillow were in the approximate position of where a sleeping couple's heads would have been. She turned back to Callaghan.

'All the signs of a professional hit. What about the driver?'

Callaghan stood up more quickly than he had intended.

'Shit! I'd forgotten about him in all the excitement.'

Charlotte moved to the window.

'Turn out the lights, Gil.'

He flicked the switch, and she cautiously moved the curtain a little way from the wall.

'There's no one in the car... he must be coming up to check the place out.'

Callaghan stepped back into the shadow of the wardrobe. The sound of someone coming up the stairs carried along the landing. He motioned to Charlotte.

'Back into the bathroom and lie down in the tub... just in case the bastard manages to squeeze off a few rounds.'

His tone brooked no argument.

She nodded; and gathering up her clothes, disappeared into the bathroom and closed the door.

The floorboards betrayed the drivers approach. He came into the apartment cautiously. Callaghan followed his stealthy footsteps as the man crossed the parquet floor of the living room. He was wearing rubber soles... they squeaked slightly on the polished wood. At the doorway of the darkened bedroom, the footsteps stopped; and an urgent whisper penetrated the darkness...

'Mikhail... vse horosho?'...'Mikhail... everything OK?'

Callaghan stepped out of the shadows.

'Nikakoj mudak ... eto ne!'... 'No, asshole... it's not!'

The man spun around. He had no gun. Callaghan stepped forward and hit him hard across the jaw with the Makarov. The man went down like he'd been put to bed with a shovel. Quickly, Callaghan went

258

through his pockets, and grabbed the ignition keys to the car in the street. The Mercedes-Benz, with its busted headlamp, was now too easily identifiable. Calling out to Charlotte, he threw on his clothes, and started to gather up anything that could be used to identify who had been staying in the apartment. This safe house was now blown wide open, and the West Berlin Police had no sense of humour at all when it came to bodies... especially bodies with gunshots like these.

Charlotte emerged from the bathroom dressed and ready to go. She glanced at the third body; then at Callaghan.

'Dead?'

He shook his head.

'No, just out for the count. He wasn't armed. You ready? We'll take their car and head straight out to your buddy at "The Devils Mountain." No point in sending a car in the morning now. This place is blown, and we don't know if there are any more of these bastards... or why they're targeting us.'

She nodded.

'OK, let's go.'

Old Herr Günsche, the concierge was sprawled in the lobby with a neat bullet hole in his forehead. Carefully stepping over him, Callaghan cautiously opened the entrance door a little way and scanned the street. It was deserted; and the Russians' BMW was double-parked; effectively blocking the street between the lines of parked-up cars. None of the buildings in the immediate vicinity had any lights showing. Quickly and quietly, Callaghan and Charlotte slipped out of the apartment building and got into the car. Callaghan shoved in the ignition key and started the motor. The Vee-eight rumbled into life; he shoved the column gear shift into first and drove away down Uhlandstrasse towards Kant Strasse. Charlotte glanced at him.

'Will we be all right in this car, Gil?'

'He nodded.

'Yeah; this is an expensive car; the sort that the Berlin high-rollers drive. The cops will just think we're heading home after a night on the town... and those cunning bastards made sure it has West Berlin licence plates. We're heading out to the swanky district... the Grunewald. Any traffic cops we happen on won't give us a second glance. Relax! Just act as though you are the successful West Berlin businessman's beautiful blonde wife... "Frau Streckenbach!"

9. 25 am. Monday, March 13th,

Washington Street.
Russian Hill, San Francisco.
California.
USA.

The eyes behind the goggles of the figure in black racing leathers astride the stationary, imported English, Norton Dominator motorcycle were as cold as ice as they stared at the little black Porsche parked up outside the Han Mi Korean restaurant in Codman Place in the Russian Hill district of downtown San Francisco. The rider was parked-up across from the entrance to the short, dead-end side-street off Washington Street. He had been waiting in the vicinity for almost twenty minutes, having tailed the little black Porsche across from Montgomery Street in Chinatown; and had noted that it was being driven by a pretty, Asian girl. Target confirmed!

When she parked up outside the Han Mi Korean restaurant in the little dead-end side-street; he had waited for ten minutes; and when she didn't reappear; had slipped down the quiet street and attached a little present under the floor below the driver's seat of the Porsche. His contract required him to confirm the kill; so he walked back to his Norton; sat astride it, and lit a Chesterfield whilst he settled down to watch the girls go by.

Ten minutes later, he heard the Porsche's door slam and the starter motor whine. The grunt of the flat-four-cylinder motor firing up, echoed down the street, followed almost instantaneously by a huge fireball which erupted from inside the Porsche as the bomb detonated; vaporizing half the car and blasting a skin-searing shock-wave of wind reeking with the stinking mixture of gasoline and the sweet sickly odour of incinerated flesh out across the street with the crack-thump of the explosion, which rocked the heavy motorcycle beneath him.

As pandemonium broke out among the passers-by, the rider engaged gear and carefully accelerated away so as not to leave any skid marks. Within half a mile, he was doing sixty; weaving the big, 600 cc motorcycle through the traffic as the billowing mushroom of black smoke rose over Codman Place and was caught by the prevailing wind that began to drift it out over San Francisco Bay.

When San Francisco's Finest arrived; the fire department had already brought the fire under control. The damage to the frontage of the Han Mi Korean restaurant was extensive; but there was nothing to identify the driver, except for a few charred body parts. There were red traces on the road, on the sidewalks; and against the walls of the surrounding buildings; and there were glittering, dripping shreds high up in the telegraph wires strung across the street. Everything else had simply vaporised. The occupants of the restaurant had been removed, depending on their injuries; to hospitals across the city. The cops recognised the licence plate, which had been driven into the brickwork of the wall opposite the restaurant, as belonging to the Porsche that was owned by Gabriella Chang; the new boss of the Korean criminal syndicate operating out of Montgomery Street in Chinatown. Reasonably, they assumed that she had been the driver; and gave an early press release to that effect.

As he headed out through Pacific Heights towards the Golden Gate Bridge, the motorcycle rider, Salvatore DeLuca... freelance hit man contracted by the Reno Mob, was feeling pleased with himself. The Chang hit had gone like clockwork. The bomb he used was the old tried and trusted Composition B... a mixture of RDX and TNT that was used as the main explosive filling in land mines, hand grenades, sticky bombs and various other munitions. Easily available, and capable of being moulded into any shape; it was detonated by a simple pencil fuse. The bomb under the black Porsche had only needed the addition of a battery and mercury switch. The whole package had weighed a little over one pound; and the results were exactly as he had planned... complete destruction, and no real collateral damage... save for the restaurant; and that was probably full of the Asian bitch's associates.

He prided himself on efficiency... value for bucks; and the Reno boss, Big Frank Catelli had certainly gotten his ten-G's-worth with this one. Ahead; there was an opening in the traffic as it wound in regimented lines up to the bridge. He kicked up a gear and twisted the throttle grip open. The big Norton Dominator leapt forwards with a deep boom from its big, twin exhausts as he weaved his way through the ponderous, chrome-laden town automobiles carrying their fat business cargos up to Santa Rosa and beyond. Damn! These limeys sure as hell knew how to build motorcycles.

Leaning the Norton over into the slight curve at the north end of the bridge; he wound the throttle open and, as he sent the machine thundering up the concrete ribbon of the Redwood Highway towards the Waldo Tunnel, the wind pulled his face into a frozen grin; fluttering his cheeks as the speedometer crept up towards the ninety mark.

Twenty minutes after the explosion; the Fire department were still damping down the smouldering debris of what had once been the little black Porsche, and washing the human remains off the walls of the surrounding buildings in Codman Place. Two Highways department officials were peering into the ten-inch-deep crater that had been scoured out of the road surface by the force of the explosion; and the cops were crawling all over the scene. No one took any notice of the brand-new Ford Thunderbird parked a little way up Washington Street; or the two tough-looking Asian men leaning against its side. Nor did they see the slim Asian girl slip out of the ornamental gate of number 1040 Washington Street and slide into the rear seat.

Unobtrusively, the T-bird pulled away from the kerb and turned into Powell Street; heading north towards Broadway. Salvatore DeLuca would not have been so pleased with himself had he known who was in the rear seat. It had not been Gabriella Chang in the little black Porsche. It had been her close friend and trusted lieutenant, Jimmy Yoo. Gabriella had been in the back office of the Han Mi Korean restaurant engaged in checking the books; and Jimmy had offered to go out and gas up the Porsche for her.

Gabriella sat quietly in the rear of the T-bird as her driver sped up Powell Street. Her demeanour was composed and serene; but her thoughts were ice-cold and deadly. Poor, sweet Jimmy. He hadn't deserved to die like that. Now, the round-eye gangsters would know what real terror was. Now they would learn to fear the shadows.

Safely back at Montgomery Street; Gabriella made several telephone calls to West Coast numbers; followed by a long distance, International call to her sister, Chang Su-Dae; the Korean Air hostess. Su-Dae... known to the American side of her family as Suzie; was, if at all possible; even deadlier than Gabriella. She had served in the South Korean Army Special Commando before she became an air hostess.

Gabriella spoke to her sister for almost an hour, explaining the situation surrounding the San Francisco family. Suzie responded that she would catch the next flight out of Seoul. Gabriella replaced the telephone handset, and began to make arrangements for the interment of what was left of Jimmy Yoo; as seven thousand miles, and fifteen hours flight time away; the inevitable destruction of the Reno Mob boss, Big Frank Catelli, and his entire organisation began to gather pace. The Chang sisters; supported by the Korean West Coast syndicates, were now hell-bent on revenge; which would result in the annihilation of the Reno Mob to the last man.

10 am. Wednesday, March 15th,
Montgomery Street.
Chinatown, San Francisco.
California.
USA.

Gabriella and Suzie Chang sat around the table in the large kitchen of Montgomery Street, planning how they would proceed with the annihilation of Big Frank Catelli and his Reno crew.

The table was covered with U.S. Geographical Survey maps. The two small notebooks that Gabriella had removed from DeCicco's house were proving to be a gold-mine of information for targeting the Reno Mob members. The only problem was weaponry. Hand guns and shotguns would just not cut the mustard with the business in hand.

Suzie smiled

'Munitions and ordnance are not a problem, Sis. My contacts back home can get us anything we want.'

Gabriella raised an eyebrow.

'Doubtless; but getting them into the country is going to be a problem. US Customs are tough.'

Suzie smiled.

'You think? Remember; we were shipping heavy stuff into our guys across the North Korean border. It's easy. You just need to have the correct set-up.'

Gabriella studied her sister.

'So what's the set-up?'

Suzie gave her an enigmatic smile.

'Just leave that to me. Now; what d'you think we'll need?'

Gabriella began counting off their requirements on her elegantly manicured, slender fingers.

'Well; we'll need machine guns, explosives, ammo...'

Suzie nodded

'OK. I get the picture. None of that will be a problem to my contacts... and the best part is; that it will all be Soviet ordnance... then the Russian mafia will get the blame!'

2pm. Wednesday, March 15th,
Royal Air Force Station Brize Norton,
West Oxfordshire.
South East England.
United Kingdom.

The 1614th Support Squadron Convair T29, twin-engined airplane turned in over the small Oxfordshire village of Bampton as the pilot joined the circuit of the Strategic Air Command Station, Brize Norton... a former Royal Air Force Bomber Station nestling on a wide plateau in the gentle, green heartland of England. The T29 was based at Rhein-Main Air Base, Germany, and had been deployed to collect two U.S. government personnel from Royal Air Force Station Gatow in West Berlin. The flight had been pretty straightforward. There were no incidents in the Berlin corridor, and weather had been good across the North Sea.

The T-29 airplane was developed for the Air Force as a flying classroom used to train navigators; but this one was used to ferry government officials and intelligence staff... both British and American; between Great Britain and West Germany. The pilot, Major Gregg Dawes; made this flight on average, three times a week, and was very familiar with Brize Norton. His orders said that there would be a Boeing C-137 Stratoliner on station, waiting to fly his two special passengers to Andrews AFB. There was no mention as to who or what they were... the attractive blonde woman and her tough-looking companion wore civilian clothes... but, they smelled like spooks.

Gregg Dawes was used to ferrying UK/USA intelligence community officers... the British Government Communications Headquarters was only about twenty-five miles away at Cheltenham; but spooks? He'd only ever had to carry CIA on one occasion. They normally flew out from the Royal Air Force station at Northolt, just outside London. These two must be really important... or have equally important intelligence to get this VIP treatment. He gave a wry grin as he lined up on finals. Probably not a good idea to screw up this landing! As he came in for touchdown, he saw that most of the hardstandings were occupied by B47 Stratojets belonging to the 3920th Strategic Wing on Reflex Alert duty... the American defence strategy of the Stratojets being kept on full alert status ready for instant takeoff to inflict massive retaliation against Russia if the Soviet Union started a war. The Cold War was certainly chilly here! Across on the northern side of the airbase, he saw the Boeing C-137 Stratoliner; sitting incongruously alone amongst the rakish, streamlined B47s.

Having safely touched down; Gregg Dawes taxied the T29 across to the adjacent hardstanding and shut down. Before the propellers had windmilled to a standstill, an Air Police sedan had arrived. An airstair was quickly brought up; the passenger door opened; and his passengers were escorted to the waiting sedan. They were then whisked away to the big Boeing. Dawes shrugged. OK... Thanks!... not even so much as a goodbye!

He busied himself with his cockpit checks and then stepped out onto the airstair. The Stratoliner was tracking down the taxiway to the eastern runway 26 threshold. She turned, and rolled on to the main runway. As Dawes watched; the turbojets spooled up with a rising scream, and, in a haze of black smoke; she began her take-off run. Halfway down the main runway, her nose lifted, and, trailing four murky black fingers of burnt fuel from her jets; she pitched up to a fifty-degree climb-out; heading out across the English countryside for home; some four-thousand miles to the west.

Dawes grinned. Smelly and noisy!... but, how much longer would piston-engined ships like his T29 be operational? He glanced over his shoulder at her. Stable, forgiving, and a joy to fly; but the future was in those Kerosene-burning, flying blowlamps! So much for progress! He closed the passenger door, turned, and walked down the airstair; heading across the concrete towards the Officers club for a cup of coffee.

Friday, March 17th, 1961.
CIA Headquarters.
2430, 23rd E Street NW.
Washington D.C.
USA.

Foggy Bottom was a hive of activity when Charlotte and Callaghan arrived. As they entered the compound their car was stopped and checked by armed Marine guards on the gate. This, in itself was most unusual. The gates were usually left open and unattended. Inside the large, marble-floored entrance hall, at the reception desk in the Central Administration Building which contained the office of the Director; their identity documents were scrutinised by a tough-looking Marine Master Sergeant before they were escorted up to the Director's office.

Alan Dulles sat behind his desk and glanced up as they entered his office. He smiled, and closed a file marked "Zapata" that he had been studying.

'Welcome back, Charlotte... Agent Callaghan. How was Berlin?'
She studied him for a moment.

'Good and bad, Director. West Berlin is good; but, there are rumours that Ulbricht is pressing Khrushchev to allow him to permanently divide the city, because too many East Berliners are fleeing to the West. The assignment we were sent in on was a fake. We did, however discover that there is a conspiracy against the President; and it appears to be home-grown.'

Dulles sat up.

'Conspiracy against the President? We knew of a Cuban under training over there. It came through the black channels from our opposite number; but there was no mention of the President being involved. You'd better tell me everything you know.'

Charlotte relayed the whole story to him; leaving nothing out... the KGB and Stasi contacts; the Cuban, Pasuali; Tony Garcia; and the attempted hit on them at the Charlottenburg safe house... by unknown killers.

Dulles was silent for a while. Then he fixed her with a steady stare.

'Cuban, you say?

He tapped the folder on his desk.

'OK Charlotte. What I am about to tell you is not to be repeated outside this office. Yesterday, I had a meeting with The President, during which, the Deputy Director for Plans, Richard Bissell, and I presented him with three alternative plans for the Cuban operation which was conceived by Eisenhower during his presidency to prevent Cuba from becoming permanently established as a part of the Communist Bloc. The first option is a modification of the Trinidad Plan, which involves an amphibious/airborne assault to seize a beachhead contiguous to terrain suitable for guerrilla operations; but had been rejected by the President in its original form as too spectacular... too much like a World War II invasion.

The second plan targets an area on the northeast coast of Cuba, and the third, the so-called Zapata Plan...'

He tapped the folder again;

'... Is an invasion at the *Bahia de Cochinos*...The Bay of Pigs; an inlet of the Gulf of Cazones on the southern coast of Cuba. The President has ordered modifications of the Zapata Plan to make it appear more of an inside, guerrilla-type operation... and then, he'll think about it.'

He leaned back in his chair.

'In view of what you have told me concerning Berlin; I have another assignment for both of you. Whilst you were over there a report came in that the package you wanted to be sent from our Station in Seoul went astray. Both our guys and the FBI were tasked to investigate its disappearance. Investigations by the Criminal Investigation Bureau of the Tokyo Police subsequently proved that a Japanese Customs officer Kenichi Saito had intercepted the package at Haneda Airport. He admitted that he had switched address labels on the instructions of an air hostess on the Korean Air flight that was carrying the package. For whatever reason the package had been sent by a commercial carrier to Japan, rather than in a Diplomatic Pouch.

It was discovered during the investigation that this air hostess... a certain Chang Su-Dae, was related to the San Francisco Korean Chang crime family; and the switched address was in San Francisco... an address known to be associated with the very same Korean Chang criminal family. Since then, we have reports that all hell has broken loose around San Francisco; and also, around Reno, Nevada. According to the FBI, they figure it's a gang war between the Korean crime family and the Mob. Perhaps this package has something to do with it. You're being booked on a domestic flight from Washington National Airport to San Francisco. Get over there; liaise with the FBI, and see what you come up with. Meantime; I'll have this conspiracy checked out.'

As they left Dulles' office, Charlotte turned to Callaghan She was very pale.

'Oh shit, Gil! I have a horrible feeling that the trouble that the Director mentioned around San Francisco and Reno is down to that fucking Abaddon Stone again. I don't think I'm ever going to be free of it.'

Callaghan put his arm around her and gave her shoulders a hug.

'It's OK, baby. If it is what you think; then we'll face it together... just like we always have.'

She gave him a little smile.

'That's why I love you, Callaghan.'

He grinned.

'I know; and that's why I love you, Mckenna.'

Chapter Seventeen.

Saturday, March 19th, 1961
San Francisco International Airport.
San Francisco.
California.
USA.

The United Airlines DC8 jet landed at San Francisco International Airport at 2pm. A black Chevrolet Biscayne four door sedan was waiting on the apron in front of the terminal building. As Charlotte and Callaghan came down the passenger stairway; the two men standing beside the Chevy stepped forward and flashed their FBI Department of Justice badges. The taller one spoke first.

'Agents Mckenna and Callaghan? We've been expecting you. I'm Walker...'

He waved in the direction of the other man;

'... and this is Boyce. We're taking you down to the San Francisco Divisional office where Supervisory Special Agent Mayfield will fill you in on our investigation.'

The ride into downtown Fan Francisco took a little over twenty minutes. Supervisory Special Agent Mayfield's office was on the fourth floor. Mayfield was middle-aged; six-foot, and about one hundred and ninety pounds. He had a shrewd face, with a mouth that wore a wry smile. His eyes were quick and perceptive. The still-dark hair was brushed neatly to the right of a high forehead; and he wore a reasonably respectable three piece suit. Mayfield gave the impression that he was an "old-school" sort of investigator... a sort of modern-day Eliot Ness; whose idea of investigative work did not involve a hundred and fifty-watt lamp in your face, and a set of brass knuckles. Closing the door to his office, he invited them to sit, and opened a file on his desk.

'Washington has informed us that you reported a conspiracy that you had uncovered in Berlin recently, and this could tie in with an investigation we are involved with here, on the West coast. To fill you in; last year, we uncovered a trail that suggested that there was a huge conspiracy involving various politicians who were cosying up to the Mob, stretching right up to the top. It centred on an accusation made by a guy named Roberts at the University of Wisconsin, who had developed a process for creating synthetic rubies and had been suckered by the Hughes Research Laboratories in Malibu to handing them over; that the Hughes guys had effectively stolen them. This was some time after Howard Hughes disappeared... Roberts also alleged that he had been kidnapped by the Mob; and that they were going to screw the government over these rubies, unless the Feds laid off their business interests. Where it gets interesting; is that we've also had The Pentagon on our backs. They are keen to get their hands on these synthetic rubies. It's something to do with a machine they call a laser that is being developed. Apparently, it emits a weird light unknown in nature. We're talking weapons here; maybe some kind of Death ray... real "Flash Gordon" stuff;... which is why the CIA has jumped in.'

He looked up and studied Charlotte.

'Where you come in, is the package you had sent back from Seoul that was intercepted. They figure that, if these rubies are in the hands of the Mob; then this gemstone that was in the package might well be an alternative... and is an easier target to recover. We figure that the Korean crime family up in Chinatown have it; and might hand it over if we can put the frighteners on them with hints of deportation or putting the hard squeeze on their business operations around the city.'

2.50pm, Friday, April 7th, 1961.
Santa Clara County,
California.
USA.

The dark grey Chevrolet panel van sped down Highway 101 towards the town of Gilroy; keeping within the speed limits. Gabriella and Suzie Chang were not in the business of getting pulled over by some enthusiastic California Highway Patrol cop this trip. They were heading out beyond Salinas to rendezvous with a shipment that was being brought in by one of Suzie's contacts. The ordnance that Suzie had arranged to be delivered for the Chang family's war with the Reno Mob was being flown in from Mexico.

Once through Salinas; the route to the pick-up point was down the

Monterey-Salinas highway as far as the San Benancio turnoff just beyond a place named Torro Park. Once beyond San Benancio; it was about four and a half miles down to the yield sign at the junction with Corral de Tierra road, where they should turn right. Two miles along this road; and they should turn left onto Underwood road which led up to a disused homestead and the landing site.

Underwood road followed a narrow valley between the wooded slopes of the surrounding hills. The road began to climb as they moved farther away from the main highway. There were no houses... nothing except for trees. This was the perfect place. Almost five miles along Underwood Road, as they turned a sharp dog-leg corner; the homestead suddenly appeared from behind the trees to their right. It didn't look as though it had been inhabited for years. The barns were rusting; fences had rotted and fallen; and the house was missing half of its shingled roof.

Suzie glanced at Gabriella.

'Jeez! What a dump, Sis. It couldn't be more perfect!'

Gabriella nodded and glanced at her Rolex.

'When is he due?'

Suzie smiled.

'Don't worry, Sis. He'll be here. What time have you?'

Gabriella scanned the skies. She didn't see anything save for a couple of con-trails tracing their ribbons across the azure skies; heading north. She glanced at her Rolex again.

'Twenty past three.'

Suzie smiled.

'We made good time. He's due at three-thirty.'

She reached into her purse and brought out a pack of Winston cigarettes and lit one. As she wound down the window to blow out the smoke; faintly, out to the south; in the distance... but getting louder all the while; came the distinctive snarl of an airplane engine. Suzie listened for a moment and then smiled.

'That's him. No mistaking that sound.'

She started the van's motor and reversed back to the dog-leg bend. She then turned the van off the metalled roadway and began to follow a grassy farm track out into the fields to the south of the homestead, across to a large flat area, where she stopped on the edge of a long flat open field.

The snarling growl of the approaching airplane was getting much louder now. It sounded just like the little yellow training airplanes that Gabriella remembered seeing as a child; as they flew out from

Alameda Naval Air Station into the skies over San Francisco Bay. Low, over the trees came a high-wing, tubby airplane. Sounding like an irate buzz-saw; it banked around to the east; flew along the tree line, turned and came in to land. The pilot throttled back as he touched down and the angry buzz-saw noise diminished and became a deep, grumbling *"buhlup-buhlup-buhlup-buhlup"* noise as the airplane slowed with its propeller idling. The pilot turned at the end of the field and came back to where the van was parked. Leaving the motor running they saw the pilot leave his seat and move back into the fuselage where he opened the port side door. Suzie drove the van forward; turned, and reversed up to the airplane; stopping behind the trailing edge of the port wing. Climbing out; she opened the rear doors and called to the pilot.

'Hi, Tyler. Still flying the old Norseman then? Dammit, I'd have thought you could have afforded a half-decent ship by now!'

Tyler Clark; a six-foot, Texan; built like a Bay City quarterback; and carrying a sawn-down, twelve gauge, double-barrelled shotgun in a custom-made holster on his hip; had been a Mustang pilot during the Korean War; and, after the armistice negotiations of '53-'54; had become a modern-day buccaneer. He would smuggle anything... no questions asked. The only commodity he refused to carry were girls, who were being supplied for prostitution. He had met Suzie, and formed a working relationship with her when Seoul was being overrun for the second time by the North Koreans. He had flown her out from Kimpo; hidden away in the bomb bay of a B26 bomber he was ordered to fly out to the south to prevent it from falling into the enemy's hands. Since then; they had done business together on several occasions.

Clarke grinned.

'Don't go bad-mouthing my old lady, Suzie-babe. She the best Goddam ship on God's good earth for this kinda job. Short take-off and landing, gentle handling; good cargo space, and tough as a brick-built Shithouse!'

Suzie grinned.

'OK, Tyler; don't go getting riled. What are you hauling for me?'

He jerked his thumb at the stack of wooden packing cases.

'Five barrels of Ammonium Nitrate fertiliser; a hundred pounds of C4 plastique; four cases of Russian AK-47 Kalashnikov assault rifles with ten thousand rounds of ammo; and five cases of Russian RGD-5 hand grenades. Somebody must have really pissed you, babe!'

Suzie nodded.

'Damn right... and in spades! Now let's get this into the Chevy

271

before the Feds wonder where that noisy old bitch disappeared to.'

Tyler Clark grinned.

'No sweat there, Suzie-babe. They got no idea I'm here. I came up over the border through the Ensenada gap across the Ojos Negros valley. There's fuck-all down there but prairie dogs and tumbleweed; and I stayed below the peaks all the way.'

Suzie nodded,

'OK, Tyler but don't be too much of a smart-ass. The Feds out this way have no sense of humour at all when it comes to gun-running over the border. Now let's get this lot unloaded and you can be outta here.'

With the transfer finished. Tyler Clark slammed the fuselage door and, getting back into the cockpit; waved to the girls; turned the Norseman, and taxied back to the far end of the field. Turning again; he set the flaps and shoved the throttle forward. With a crescendo of noise; the Norseman rushed across the uneven field and rose ponderously into the air. With their ears singing from the harsh buzz-saw noise of the airplane taking off; Suzie and Gabriella carefully brought the van back to the metalled surface of Underwood road. As they headed back down towards the Highway Suzie glanced at Gabriella.

'Well, Sis? Will this be enough to sort out our problem with the Reno Mob?'

Gabriella nodded.

'Yeah, Suzie; I figure that'll do the job.'

Friday, April 14th, 1961.
Black Warrior Peak Ranch,
Washoe County.
Nevada.
USA.

Big Frank Catelli was getting worried. He had lost ten of the family within the last two weeks. Four had been shot down as they did the rounds of downtown Reno on the protection money runs. There they were; minding their own business; just doing a little intimidation and coercion; and they had been whacked from passing autos in a hail of automatic gunfire. Nobody had seen anything... nobody knew anything. No money had been taken; they had simply been blown away.

Two days later; three of his Caporegimes had been fried when a petrol bomb or some other sort of incendiary followed by a couple of hand grenades had been tossed through the door of the little hole-in-the-wall Italian Bistro on West Fourth Street that they used as a planning base. The cops, as usual, didn't have a clue and didn't really care.

A particularly damaging incident had occurred only three days ago. Big Frank Catelli's Underboss, Donnie Corallo and his latest showgirl squeeze met with a very nasty accident as they were coming back down Highway 395 from Carson City. Just south of Lake Washoe, Corallo's Chevy Corvette convertible was in a head-on collision with a Peterbilt eighteen-wheeler, semi-trailer. Corallo was driving with the power convertible top down; and was enjoying a little oral stimulation from the girl... or, at least; that's what they figured at the autopsy; due to the fact that Corallo's dick was missing from his corpse and had been discovered inside the remains of the girl's head. They guessed that the impact had caused the girl's jaws to snap shut whilst she was blowing him.

The Corvette had disintegrated like an eggshell, and the remains were dragged for almost a quarter-mile back down the highway before the gas tank exploded and incinerated the mangled remnants of Corallo and his squeeze. The driver of the semi-trailer said that a dark-coloured panel van that Corallo was overtaking seemed to drift out towards the centre-line of the highway and had pushed the Corvette directly into his path.

"Capo Bastone" Corallo's demise really pissed Big Frank. From what was left after the cops scraped the remains off the highway; it meant that there would have to be another closed casket funeral; in just the same way that his Consigliere, "Crazy Joe" DeCicco had to be buried, a little over two months previously. Big Frank figured that this was another deliberate slap in the face for the Family. A closed casket service was the worst insult that could be made against the Family hierarchy; and now it had been done twice. It was time to stop fucking around and Goddam-well do something about it.

Big Frank ordered the Reno crews to attend a meeting at the Mob ranch under Black Warrior Peak, close to Pyramid Lake, to figure out a plan. The ranch was remote; there were no neighbours for at least fifteen miles in any direction; and he decided that this place would be as safe as any. No one could approach the within two miles without being observed. The crews duly gathered on the evening of the 14th. Big Frank had arranged the food and booze from trusted sources.

The meeting attendees were given free choice of cuisine... why not? Big Frank could afford it. Consequently, French, Italian, and Chinese was ordered and brought out from Reno in the relevant company's delivery vans. Each van was carefully checked at the gate, three miles down the property access road. Big Frank was satisfied. Nothing but a Goddam air attack would get through to this meeting.

Forty of the Family's best soldiers were at the meeting. The atmosphere was relaxed; and a suitable plan of action looked as though it would be agreed. The discussion was interrupted by the arrival of the food, and the assembly moved to the big, glass-fronted dining room for the meal. As they were being served by waiters brought in by the delivery vans; one of the soldiers from the Sun Valley crew happened to glance up; and saw a delivery van roll into view outside the dining room... the Chinese cuisine van.

Gianni Nardi; Caporegime of the Spanish Springs crew, waved his fork towards the window and mumbled through a mouthful of Tagliatelle;

'Look! That Goddam Chink seems to be lost. He's going the wrong fuckin' wa...'

He never finished the sentence. At that moment, a huge explosion rocked the building as two hundred pounds of gasoline-soaked Ammonium nitrate fertiliser detonated beneath the false floor of the Chevrolet step-van. The vehicle simply disintegrated; and the detonation blew in the large wall to ceiling windows of the ranch house. The flying glass and hot metal mixed with ten pounds of hardware nails packed into the side panel of the van were lethal The searing heat when the violent blast hit, tore apart those unfortunate enough to have been seated on the window side of the table; whilst those facing them caught the full impact of the shockwave and the shrapnel; which killed several of them outright. Big Frank Catelli seated at the head of the table was just out of the main force of the blast; but was caught in the blast concussion, picked up, and thrown violently across the room into the wall.

As a huge mushroom of smoke rose over the devastated ranch house; the Mob soldiers on the gate leapt into their four-wheel-drive station wagon and hightailed it up the three-mile access road towards the building as fast as they could. They were watching the house so intently with disbelief as the roof sagged and began to collapse, that they completely missed the solitary figure on a small trail bike without lights, that had been concealed from the front gate guards by being suspended under the delivery van; speeding away across the sprawling corral to the right of the wrecked building.

Big Frank Catelli came to in a hospital bed; completely swathed in bandages; with a right arm that wouldn't move because of a smashed shoulder blade from where he had been hurled against the wall by the tremendous blast of the explosion. Apart from that; other than bruises and contusions; he had suffered no permanent damage. His one surviving Caporegime; Rudy Tramunti, who had sat at his boss's bedside for five days; told him that eighteen of his soldiers had been killed outright in the explosion; twelve had died later of their injuries; and six more... including Catelli's lieutenant and son-in-law, Marco Ferrante; would never be of any use, other than maybe, for book-keeping, ever again.

Big Frank was silent for a while whilst he took this in. Thirty-six soldiers down... almost three-quarters of his entire Reno Family... and Marco... his only daughter Francesca's husband; whom he was grooming to become Boss of the family when the time came for him to retire.

He looked at Rudy Tramunti; then spat out...

'Who did this to us Rudy? Who will die for this fuckin' iniquity?'

Rudy Tramunti hesitated; fearful of the venom in his boss's eyes and voice.

The cops found two bodies that they think were the Chinese delivery guys in the desert just up aways from Wadsworth. Seems the delivery van was hijacked before it reached the ranch. My guess would be that it's the little yellow sonsofbitches giving us payback for you ordering a piece of work to be done on that Chang bitch down in 'Frisco a month ago.'

Big Frank nodded.

'Yeah; I'll buy that. Rudy; take a crew down there and straighten the bitch and her little yellow fuckers out once and for all. Put 'em all away. I don't care how you do it... just get it done. *Capiche?*'

Tramunti nodded.

'OK, Boss. I'll round up Ritchie the Zip and Little Tony, and we'll go down and put it to bed.'

2.30pm, Friday, April 21st, 1961.
Montgomery Street.

Chinatown, San Francisco.
California.
USA.

The black Pontiac Catalina cruised up Montgomery Street and turned at the top of the hill. It slowly crept back down the street and stopped outside number 1120. The driver kept the motor running whilst two men got out and opened the trunk. The first man lifted out a pump-action shotgun and walked unconcernedly to the front of the property. He then put two shots into the front door; shattering the three-quarter-length glass panel. The second man walked from the Pontiac's trunk carrying a jerrycan. He placed it on the sidewalk and pulled two grenades from his coat pockets; pulled the pins, and tossed them through the shattered glass panel into the house. Bending down, he flipped the cap on the jerrycan and threw that into the house as well. Both men then turned and ran back to the car; got in, and, with a squeal of tyres the Pontiac took off down Montgomery Street. The ensuing explosion blew out the remains of the front door and engulfed the lower floors of the building in flames.

In the passenger seat; Ritchie the Zip pulled out a pack of Pall Mall cigarettes; lit one and grinned.

'Well; that's fucked them! You coulda blown me a bigger hole, Tony. It was Goddam tight to get the gas can through!'

Little Tony snorted.

'Always moaning. You couldn't throw a fuckin' tantrum!'

Rudy Tramunti cut in.

Can it, you guys. Just relax and act natural. The whole Goddam SFPD will be here soon. So let's haul ass and get outta here.'

When the San Francisco Fire department finally managed to get the inferno that had once been 1120 Montgomery Street under control, they discovered three bodies... a woman whom they estimated was in her twenties; and two young girls aged between ten, and twelve. Identification was difficult, but the medical examiner estimated that all three were Asian, and had died through smoke inhalation.

The FBI turned up and rummaged through the wreckage. There wasn't much to see. The torchmen had done a proper job. There was so much debris it was difficult to find anywhere safe to step. All they found was the jerrycan; split wide open down its seam and punctured with what looked like shrapnel. Supervisory Special Agent Sam Mayfield had seen this before at the killings in California Street, two and a half months previously. Then, it had been the burning out and slaughter of the Li Ying Tong. It was the same damn MO... gasoline and hand grenades. He called for the jerrycan to be bagged and tagged and sent to the Forensic Services Division. They might get lucky and find a print, but it was a long shot. The fire hoses had seen to that.

Sam Mayfield walked over to the medical examiner's unmarked panel van and glanced at the three body bags. He knew all too well who had lived at this address. The two smaller ones were easy. They contained Gabriella Chang's nieces. Was she in the larger one? It seemed likely, but due to the fire; only dental records would confirm this. He shook his head. If it wasn't Gabriella... he gave a quiet shiver. He knew what would happen. Gabriella Chang with her tail up... as it most certainly would be with the killing of her little nieces; was not something he wanted to spend any time at all thinking about.

6.40 am, Saturday, April 22nd, 1961.
2004 Washington St.
Pacific Heights.
San Francisco.
California.
USA.

The insistent ring of the phone had a certain sense of desperation to it. Charlotte carefully extricated herself from the warmth and comfort of the still-sleeping Callaghan's arms and picked up the receiver. Sleepily, she spoke into the mouthpiece.

'Hello?'

It was long-distance... Washington The voice on the other end of the line was terse.

'Charlotte? This is KUCLUB.'

This was the cryptonym for the CIA Office of Communications. Something damn serious must have occurred for them to be making contact over an unsecured line. The voice said that she and Callaghan were directed to continue their investigation with all haste. ZAPATA... launched five days previously had failed; and Washington was in uproar with GPIDEAL about to take responsibility.

This cryptonymous message meant that the Bay of Pigs invasion of Cuba had been a disaster and the President was preparing to take the blame. Consequently there would now be a massive witch-hunt within the Company, with The Pentagon snapping at their heels. The acquisition of Charlotte's target gemstone was now vital to placate the Hawks across the Potomac. Charlotte replaced the telephone receiver. Callaghan stirred. She looked over at his face and smiled;

277

'Sorry the phone woke you.'

He gave a sleepy grin.

'Actually, babe; the bed got cold when you moved. That's what woke me.'

He scratched at his tousled hair.

'Something important?'

She nodded.

'It was Washington. The words "shit" and "fan" spring most readily to mind. They've completely screwed up the Cuban job. The home team wiped the floor with them, and Kennedy is going to "The Hill" to put his hands up. That means everybody is about to go on a top-dollar, fall guy hunt. We have to find Gabriella Chang and the gemstone pretty damn quick before the Director and The Pentagon get embroiled in a major dick-measuring contest.'

Callaghan sat up in bed, grinning broadly. She frowned at him.

'It's not funny, Callaghan.'

He bravely attempted a serious expression… and failed, hopelessly.

'I know it's not, babe… but you have such a way with words.'

He chuckled to himself…

'Dick-measuring contest… that's a classic!'

The apartment on the fifth floor of the elegant, white stone, seven-storey apartment building at 2002 Washington Street overlooking Lafayette Park; had been a CIA safe house for several years; and was used as a base by out-of-town agents when it was not being used for its normal purpose.

Charlotte and Callaghan showered; grabbed a swift breakfast; and began to plan over several cups of coffee. The first place to begin their investigations would surely be the burned-out property in Montgomery Street. Perhaps someone had seen something. It was doubtful that anyone would give out any information; the SFPD and FBI had already tried; but any lead... any lead at all might be helpful. The San Francisco Office had provided Charlotte and Callaghan with a totally obtrusive ride... working on the simple principle that anyone who was a government agent would never be seen dead in such an eye-catching automobile. It was a two-tone blue, 1956 DeSoto Firedome Seville; modified with a four-on-the-floor Hurst-Campbell stick shift instead of the standard two-speed, Torqueflight push-button automatic transmission; and fitted with a much more powerful, 345 Hemi Vee-eight from a DeSoto Adventurer with a dual Carter four-barrel carb. The mechanic who dropped it off said, that in the right hands; this outwardly luxurious family cruiser would hit one hundred and forty miles per hour.

The two mile drive along Washington Street into Chinatown took twenty minutes through the morning traffic. At the intersection of Washington and Montgomery; by the Bank of America; Callaghan turned left and headed up towards, and crossed Broadway into the northernmost section of Montgomery Street. Driving up the steep slope to the end of the street; Callaghan pulled into the kerb. Setting the parking brake; he and Charlotte left the DeSoto and began walking back down the street to the burned out shell of number 1120. The once-attractive town house was gutted. Anyone in there wouldn't have stood a chance. There was nothing here that the Forensic Services Division guys wouldn't have uncovered. Charlotte glanced back up the street. So, what now? Door-to-door enquiries?

A movement at the top of the street caught her eye. A group of young Asian men were gathering around the parked-up DeSoto... and they didn't give the impression that they were just admiring the ride.

Callaghan saw them too. His hand slipped, almost involuntarily into his jacket towards his shoulder holster. Charlotte caught his arm.

'Leave this to me, Gil; just watch my back.'

She turned, and strolled up the street towards the group; who were lolling against the side of the DeSoto; watching her approach with hostile indifference. She stopped in front of them; and smiled.

'Good Morning...'

One of them gave her an intimidatory stare; and snapped, in gutter Korean...

'Yeah? What the fuck do you want?'

She smiled; and replied amiably in perfect Korean...

'I'm looking for information...'

She saw their faces harden. They knew something. She continued.

'I'm trying to find Gabriella Chang...'

Their body language showed that they were becoming truculent and threatening. Her smile faded and she slipped off her jacket. They could not fail to notice the Colt M.32 automatic in the neat shoulder holster under her left arm. They could also not fail to notice the tattoo of two dragons curling over each other; on her upper arm. The punks' attitude faded as swiftly as morning mist out on the Bay. They knew what this was; the mark of *Ssang Yong Pa*... The Double Dragon *Geondal*... Korean Mafia. She spoke again. Her voice was soft... soft enough to make the punks' stomachs knot in apprehension.

'I can be either a benevolent friend... or your worst fucking nightmare. The choice is entirely yours.'

279

One of the punks... the obvious leader; bowed imperceptibly to her and switched to English.

'Honourable Mistress; There is little to tell of this. Gabriella was not here when the fire happened. Her sister Suzie and the two young nieces died in this place. Old Han Hyang-Soon who lives across the street, heard gunshots; but, he is an ancient; and by the time he had reached the window to observe; the fire was raging. He did see a black automobile speeding away down the street. He said that he thought it was a Plymouth; perhaps a Catalina; but his eyesight is not as it once was. All this was told to the cops.

Charlotte nodded.

'Thank you. Your cooperation will be noted; and I promise your business endeavours will not be interfered with in this area.

She bowed imperceptibly and turned, to walk back down the street.

The punk called after her.

'Honourable Mistress; how are you called?'

She turned and smiled enigmatically;

'I am *"Hin-saek Gu-kwa"*... The White Chrysanthemum.'

The boy paled noticeably. He knew exactly what this meant. It had been whispered on street corners for years, of the existence of a position in the *Geondal* structure that bore this name. In Korean custom; the white chrysanthemum was symbolic of death and was only ever used for funerals. She was a *Geondal* assassin! No one would ever choose to be called by that name unless they were exactly that.

He nervously stepped forward.

'Honourable Mistress; It is said that Gabriella moved to the south of the city... somewhere in the Mission-Bayview area.

Charlotte nodded.

"Kamsahamnida"... 'Thank you.'

Then turned, and beckoned Callaghan to join her.

He came up the street just as she imagined he would. Shoulders squared; intimidatory; and with a purposeful stride. The punks moved back as he came around the side of the De Soto and opened the door for Charlotte to get in. He then walked around to the driver's door, got in, and fired up the big Hemi. Punching the gas pedal, he sent the car booming off down the hill; with the rasp of the big, twin exhausts bouncing off the buildings back and forth across the street.

As they turned into Broadway, he glanced at Charlotte.

'Where the hell did you get that tattoo? It wasn't there last night.'

She smiled.

'Like it? It's just a little something I drew on this morning with my eyebrow pencil and lip liner whilst you were shaving. Seemed to work though… that poor kid nearly crapped himself when he saw it. It'll come off easily with makeup remover; but I'll keep it for a while whilst we're moseying around the Korean areas. It might come in useful again.'

Callaghan grinned.

'Sneaky! What does it mean, anyway?'

She smiled.

'It's the tattoo of the Double Dragon Mob. Their turf is Gwangju, the sixth largest city in South Korea. When confronted by other mobs, they show their tattoos to help identify themselves. The tattoo can also be used as a warning to the public. There's no reason to suppose that those kids possibly suspected that I was anything other than what I led them to believe… a Mob torpedo; allied to the West coast Korean syndicates.'

Callaghan stared at her.

So; you're telling me we're undercover again?'

She nodded.

'That's the way it rocks, baby; and you're my bad-ass backup as far as they're concerned. Now; let's get on down to the southeast side and see what we can dig up.'

Monday, April 24th, 1961.
FBI Divisional Office.
Federal Office Building.
San Francisco.
California.
USA.

Supervisory Special Agent Sam Mayfield sat with Charlotte and Callaghan in his office, and pushed a file across the top of his desk to her. Opening it; she was confronted by a street photograph of a pretty, Asian girl. Mayfield spoke.

'Meet Gabriella Chang. She's the boss of the Korean Chang crime family that used to be resident in Montgomery Street. The property was torched last Friday. Three bodies were found inside… two female children and a female woman. We thought at first, that it was Gabriella Chang; but, dental comparison has proved it was not. Our Reno office has been reporting absolute bloody mayhem centred on the Reno Mob. Fire and grenade bombings; a delivery van bomb; and a very suspicious auto accident involving the death of their underboss.

We're pretty sure that this is a war between the Chang family and

281

the Reno Mob; caused by the killing of the Chang family patriarch in the city, three months ago. That hit had all the hallmarks of a Mob execution.

You know you don't have any domestic jurisdiction; that's down to us; but I need you, in your capacity of CIA agents, to put the frighteners on her; using whatever "National Security" shit you can come up with. If this goes on much longer; they're gonna start killing innocent people... and that ain't gonna happen on my watch if I can help it. I'm giving you full access to my field agents and any resources you need. The Secret Service is beginning to sniff around; so Washington has an interest. I have no idea why; but I figure there must be something in this "Death Ray" crap. We need to find out what happened to this gemstone that went missing... my gut tells me that's what they're really after. Perhaps Gabriella Chang is the key to this.'

Charlotte glanced at Callaghan; and then back at Sam Mayfield. What she and Callaghan had learned up in Montgomery Street would stay with them for now. She didn't need the FBI blundering about and scaring off any leads. She nodded.

'You could well be right, Agent Mayfield. So, where do we start? Where d'you think this Chang woman is likely to be?'

Sam Mayfield shrugged.

'I've had an APB out with the SFPD since Friday; but, so far... zilch! They tell me you speak Korean. Check out Chinatown and what's left of the Chang family soldiers. You might have more luck than my guys and gals. All they get is a dumb, polite silence.'

Charlotte smiled.

'Yes; that's what's called "showing the blank face" in Korea. They're damn good at that. Ok, Agent Mayfield; we'll see what we can do.'

Sam Mayfield nodded.

'Ok; but for Chrissakes be careful. Knowing that her two nieces have been killed; I figure Gabriella is gonna go for broke from here on in... and she was fuckin' dangerous and detached at the best of times; cold, calculating, and methodical. Now; she's going to be nothing less than deadly... a ruthless, efficient killing machine. In her mind; she'll have nothing left to lose.'

Charlotte glanced at Callaghan. He gave no clue as to what his thoughts were. She turned her gaze back to Sam Mayfield.

'Have we any idea where she might be now? Obviously she won't be at the Montgomery Street address.'

Sam Mayfield shrugged.

'I have no idea. I'm heading down to city hall to try to get a federal warrant issued on the grounds of reasonable suspicion and probable cause in regard to these hits. If I get one; I can put the squeeze on her Bankers and Lawyers to give me her new address. My main worry is; that she is staying with someone. If that's the case; we won't find her until she makes her next hit.'

Friday, April 28th, 1961.
The Mapes Hotel.
10 N. Virginia St,
Reno.
Nevada.
USA.

Big Frank Catelli and five of his boys strolled into the twelve-storey Mapes Hotel at the corner of Virginia Street and East First Street in downtown Reno. He was heading for the Sky Room at the top of the hotel for a little "chat" over unpaid protection money with the manager. The Sky Room was a beautifully appointed top-floor dining, dancing, drinking, and gambling room surrounded by large windows providing a gorgeous view of the Washoe Valley. Big Frank intended to show the bum a gorgeous view of the Washoe Valley... but from the outside of one of the windows.

The party headed across the expansive lobby to the elevators. One of Frank's soldiers pressed the call button, whilst the others scanned the lobby with cold, reptilian stares. No one bothered to take any notice of the pretty Asian maid as she picked up the reception desk telephone and dialled a number.

Gabriella Chang; looking very sexy in her maid's uniform, quietly told her accomplice up in the elevator machine room that the target was about to get into elevator two; and he should wait for her signal... three telephone rings, before he acted. She then replaced the receiver and slipped away to an upper floor.

As Big Frank's party waited for the elevator; one of his old buddies came across and invited him for a drink. As they were talking; the elevator arrived. Big Frank told his boys to go on up and introduce themselves. He would follow on up when he had finished talking.

On the third floor; Gabriella was watching the indicator arrow for elevator two advancing around its semi-circular dial plate. As the arrow reached floor ten; she picked up the corridor service telephone. The arrow crept around to eleven... she dialled the number and let the phone ring three times; then replaced the receiver and hurried to the stairs. A dull thump shook the building as her accomplice detonated a quarter-pound C4 charge at the top of the elevator shaft, which severed the cables suspending the car of elevator two and its connected counterweight. As both began to fall; the safety bolts fitted to the car activated... and then, snapped off at the point at which they had been partially cut through; sending the elevator car plunging uncontrollably down the shaft.

The Reno police engineer calculated that the elevator car was doing close on eighty miles per hour when it collided with the fallen counterweight which sheared through the floor of the car, moments before it finally hit the basement floor. When they managed to scrape the corpses of the five occupants out of the wreckage, the medical examiner discovered that not one of them was above three feet tall. The impact had splintered their legs like kindling and rammed the shattered bones up into their abdominal cavities. He estimated that none of them had taken much less than seven or eight minutes to die. It had not been a pleasant way to go.

Sitting in the rear seat of the gleaming black Thunderbird as it cruised calmly out beyond Reno's city limits, and headed south for Interstate 80; Gabriella Chang was fuming. After they had dropped the elevator, she had slipped into the room she had reserved, and changed out of the maid's uniform into a black, Givenchy silk shantung sheath dress, her Prada heels; a black wide brim picture hat, and, to complete the ensemble; a pair of Wayfarer sunglasses. She stepped out into the corridor; looking every inch, the sexy, sophisticated socialite.

Her accomplice had escaped down the fire stairs and now waited for her in the reception lobby, dressed immaculately as her chauffeur. As he guided her through the throng of hotel gusts gawking down the elevator shaft at the mangled wreckage; she had been taken aback to recognise Big Frank Catelli standing at the reception desk, white-faced and shocked. Quickly, her "chauffeur" had guided her outside to the waiting automobile; put her in, and driven away. As they crossed the State Line, Gabriella leaned forward.

'How did we miss the fat pig, Marty? The plan was perfect.'

Marty Ryom glanced into the rear-view mirror.

'The Fates decided that it was not his time to die, Madam. Do not distress yourself. His time will come.'

Chapter Eighteen.

2.20 pm, Friday, April 28th, 1961.
SFPD Potrero Station.
2300 Third Street,
Dogpatch Neighbourhood,
San Francisco.
California.
USA.

Callaghan turned the DeSoto off Twentieth Street in the Dogpatch Neighbourhood located on the eastern side of the city, adjacent to the waterfront of San Francisco Bay, and drove into the yard behind the SFPD Potrero Station on the corner of Third and Twentieth Streets. He pulled in behind two parked-up Ford Galaxie black-and-whites, switched off the motor, and glanced at Charlotte.

'Hell, babe; I wish you hadn't left your piece at home. From what I've seen as we came in; this looks like a real shithole neighbourhood.'

She smiled briefly.

'Dammit, Gil; I can't wear a jacket if I want them to see the tattoo; which means that a concealed carry is out of the question... besides which; the word will be on the streets by now that a *Geondal* bitch is coming to town. That, in itself, should be more than enough to spook the local low-life.'

Potrero Station was a two-storey, white stucco, Mission Revival-style building with a tile hipped roof. Inside; for a police station, it was very cramped. After showing their identification, they were shown upstairs to the office of the station Captain.

Neil Halloran was fiftyish; built like a longshoreman, with a broad Irish face, steel-grey hair and piercing green... almost turquoise eyes. He had an almost fatherly aura about him; but as he grasped her hand in a firm handshake; Charlotte sensed that he had learned his trade on the mean, violent streets that made up the nine-block neighbourhood that went by the name of Dogpatch. This was not a man to take liberties with. He invited them both to sit and asked what he could do for them. Charlotte studied this tough old cop and decided to lay it all out for him.

'We are down here to try to locate an American-Korean girl named Gabriella Chang. She is the head of the Chang criminal family up in Chinatown, and is believed to be carrying out a sustained series of killings of members of the Reno Mafia in retaliation for the targeting of her family members and associates. We need to find her quickly, before she herself is killed.

She is in possession, or knows the whereabouts of an item that Washington has instructed us to recover. We need your help, Captain. If we fail; then the FBI and the Secret Service will be all over this neighbourhood like a rash. We can go in without the bullshit and shields. All we need from your boys are eyes and ears on the streets; and for you to let them know that we are working the area.'

Halloran listened; and when she had finished; studied her thoughtfully. He spoke with a faint Irish brogue.

'Yeah; I can do that for you; but, I must caution you; this neighbourhood is not like the rest of the city. It's probably the most run down and violent place in the entire Bay area. It has become increasingly segregated from the rest of San Francisco; and is mainly Black-American, blue-collar workers and other racial minorities. Since the end of the War, the neighbourhood has declined as jobs have dried up at the shipyard, the slaughterhouses, and various other industries such as Western Sugar Refinery and Tubbs Cordage Company, who have closed up shop and moved overseas. Those are some damn mean streets out there.'

He paused and held her gaze.

'Are you carrying?'

She shook her head.

'No; but Mr Callaghan is armed.'

She showed him her right arm.

'This is the mark of the Korean "Double Dragon" Mafia; and I speak fluent Korean. The design is only drawn on with makeup; but a swift glance at it is enough to make anyone where we're going; very nervous indeed.'

Halloran nodded. This lady had balls.

'OK, Agent Mckenna; I'll brief the guys at the next roll call. Until then; I suggest you don't start snooping around until they're all tuned

286

in to you being here. Go cruise the neighbourhood for a day or so; get familiar with the place, and I'll clue you in on any word out on the streets in a couple of days.'

Charlotte nodded;

'OK, Captain; I guess the place to start is where the Koreans live and work. Where would that be?'

Halloran stood up; walked across to a large-scale map on the wall; and pointed to an area slightly to the east of Dogpatch.

'Most of them are in the Potrero Hill neighbourhood, around here; and pushing out towards the Mission district. You'll also find some of them down on the Central Waterfront, down here. You'll need to be cute; the streets you'll be working are predominantly Black; and the smaller ethnic groups tend to isolate themselves.'

Charlotte stood up;

'Well, thank you, Captain. We'll go take a ride around, and be in touch in a couple of days.'

Halloran smiled.

'OK Ma'am; but just remember the first rule of policing these streets… Don't go sticking your neck out.'

As Charlotte and Callaghan reached the door, she turned, and smiled.

'Good advice, Captain; but it's what I do!'

7.30 am, Sunday, April 30th, 1961
810 Kansas Street,
Potrero Hill,
San Francisco.
California.
USA.

Gabriella Chang put down the thin, black hardcover notebook with elastic band closures, which was one of the two notebooks Jimmy Yoo had found at the residence of the very late Reno crime family Consigliere: Joseph "Crazy Joe" DeCicco. It was filled with the names and addresses of the Reno, and San Francisco Mobs' contacts and associates. Turning to a street map of Reno, she traced down the index pages until she found the address she was searching for. So; Big Frank Catelli lived on Basque Lane in southwest Reno, on what must have been a million-dollar, gated country estate. She smiled grimly. Time to take a little road trip.

Fourteen blocks west of Potrero Police Station; rookie patrol officer Mervin Nicholson was just turning into Kansas Street from off

287

Twentieth Street when he saw an almost new, black Ford Thunderbird pull out of the ground floor garage of number 810. He was rather surprised to see an automobile of this sort in this area. Most vehicles around here were beat-up old wrecks. A young Asian man climbed out and walked back to close the garage doors; as the pretty Asian girl in the passenger seat wearing a stylish trench coat glanced at the young officer and smiled.

Nicholson returned her smile and continued on his beat. He had perhaps gone ten feet, when, with a squeal of tyres, the Thunderbird pulled out and accelerated away; heading north for the city. Nicholson turned, and took a note of the licence plate. Why? It was just hunch; but it was strange, seeing such an automobile in such an area.

As the Thunderbird crossed Twentieth Street; Marty Ryom glanced into the rear-view mirror and saw that the young cop had paused and was watching the Thunderbird disappear over the rise. He glanced at Gabriella.

'D'you think that Sonofabitch made us?'

She shook her head.

'No... Why should he? He was probably just drooling over the wheels. They aren't looking for us, and we aren't known in this part of town.'

Marty Ryom grunted.

'I don't like it. He was showing too much damn interest.'

She smiled.

'You worry too much, Marty. He'll figure that we're just another couple of slants who've made good with the American Dream!'

The journey up to Reno was uneventful. Four miles inside the city limits, Marty Ryom turned the Thunderbird off Interstate 80 into West Fourth Street. Gabriella was studying the road map. She jabbed her finger at the page.

'Fourth to your right in about a mile, Marty. Mayberry Drive.'

Marty nodded and dropped the Thunderbird's speed down. Turning into Mayberry Drive, he further reduced speed to the legal thirty miles per hour. They didn't want any keen cops pulling them over at this stage of the game. Gabriella consulted the road map again.

'OK; fourth to your right; Juniper Hill Road, in two miles.'

As they approached the turn-off to Juniper Hill Road; Marty spotted the nose of a black-and-white Reno PD squad car slow at the junction with its left-turn signal blinking. He swore volubly.

'Shit! That's all we need!'

Gabriella spoke quietly.

'Just drive on. We'll turn around and come back when he's gone.'

Marty drove on past Juniper Hill Road as the cop waited. Gabriella glanced at the black-and-white and gave the young cop a fleeting smile. She pulled down the sun vizor as if to touch up her makeup, and watched, in the vanity mirror as the black-and-white pulled out and moved off along Mayberry Drive in the opposite direction.

Marty turned in at the next left-hand junction leading into a residential development. Turning the Thunderbird around; he cruised back to the junction with Mayberry drive, and pulled out; retracing their steps to Juniper Hill Road. Turning in; he followed the road for almost a mile up to the Basque Lane junction. There were few houses around here. This was looking good for what Gabriella had in mind. It was just a question of whether the Mafia Boss, Catelli was home.

Basque lane was a dead end street a little over three-quarters of a mile in length, and dotted with a few examples of high-value real estate. Catelli's residence was half-way along the lane. Marty approached slowly, and stopped a little way beyond the sweeping driveway. The property was large and ostentatious; flanked with neat, white-painted, corral-style fencing. Even from the lane they could hear the sounds of music and laughter. Catelli was at home... and judging by the sounds being made; he was throwing a pool party.

Marty glanced at Gabriella. She nodded. Snicking the Thunderbird into gear; he drove quietly on along the lane; turned, and came back; stopping behind the large laurel hedge that bordered the edge of the property and effectively concealed the house from the lane. Leaving the motor running with the parking brake set; he got out and went to the trunk. Opening it; he pulled out an AK-47 Assault rifle and a short-barrelled, twelve-gauge, pump-action Remington shotgun, which he handed to Gabriella.

Marty picked up the two, forty-round Bulgarian magazines taped top-to-bottom, and back to back for a swift "eject-flip-reload" action, from the trunk of the T-Bird and clicked them into the magazine well. He firmly slapped the bottom of the magazine to ensure it was fully seated, before pulling back the charging handle and allowing the assault rifle's bolt to snap back forward with a metallic "Cha-Clack" sound; stripping a live round from the magazine and seating it into the chamber.

He usually kept his weapons on full-auto, only shifting to semi-auto when he decided that he had something to prove... or somewhere where a full auto burst would bring the cops in too quickly. This AK-47 was currently set to Semi. He flicked it up to Auto. This was no time to be fucking around with precision shit. This was back to the good old, bad old days; this was the all-or-nothing days. This was the killing time.

His thoughts were interrupted by Gabriella cycling the slide on the Remington with a mean "Ka-chack" as she chambered a shell. Marty smiled. Since Jimmy Yoo's unfortunate demise; he had become Gabriella's armourer... and this Remington was loaded with something that was particularly nasty... fail-safe... but nasty.

He had loaded the shotgun with "Federal" cartridge company, twelve-gauge' "Hi-Power Shotgun Shells." These held a special, antimony-rich, hard shot... and it was deer-hunter-sized buckshot. Together; these two characteristics combined to give Gabriella the fire-power of a much longer-barrelled weapon. She glanced at Marty.

'OK. Let's do this. Remember; Catelli is mine. You take out the rest.'

Marty glanced at her.

'Yeah; but I've never seen the guy. What does he look like?'

Gabriella gave him a cold smile.

'He's a big fat bastard; bald head, tinted shades; a mean-looking Sonofabitch.'

Marty nodded

'OK. He's yours. Let's go blow these pieces of shit away.'

Entering the property; they quietly made their way up into the woodland that obscured the house from the lane, and headed in the direction from where the music and general hubbub of noise; punctuated by raucous laughter and splashing, was coming from.

At the edge of the tree line; an empty, well-manicured lawn stretched to a large, and ostentatious swimming pool, in which, a naked pool party was in full swing. The guests seemed to be almost entirely composed of big breasted girls and gold medallion-dripping mobsters being waited on by white-coated waiters. Over by the terrace; several sun-loungers were occupied by naked, tanned couples in various states of sexual romping; and at least six couples were humping each other in the pool.

Catelli was nowhere in sight. Gabriella touched Marty's arm.

'Hold it, Marty. Wait until the Sonofabitch shows himself.'

He nodded.

'So, how d'you wanna play this?'

She smiled coldly.

'When he shows; spray the whole Goddam scene... but don't target him. In the panic, I'll go in and pop a couple into his fat gut in such a way that the pig will suffer in agony for hours before he finally dies.

He ordered the killing of grandfather, my nieces and my sister... and tried to kill me. Now; payback time has come.'

Five minutes later; with the party getting more rowdy by the minute; a grossly overweight, almost naked man came out of the house into the sunshine. He walked past the copulating couples on the sun loungers to the edge of the flagged terrace facing the pool, and, completely ignoring them; stood, watching the naked girls in the water. He was about five feet eight; aged about sixty; with slicked-back, greying hair clinging to his balding head. His belly was vast, and sagged over a tiny strip of black material covering his crotch. A mat of black hair covered his drooping breasts, shoulder blades; arms and legs. He wore a grey moustache that bristled over a wide, cruel mouth with thick, wet, crimson lips. His eyes were concealed behind sunglasses; and he wore the obligatory, heavy gold medallion and chain and a large gold wrist-watch on a gold bracelet.

He moved back towards one of the unoccupied sun loungers, wiping his hands down his fat backsides; then lay back among the cushions, and snapped his fingers at two heavily breasted blondes who resembled cheap, East Fourth Street whores; were wearing a lot of gold jewellery, and were laughing and chattering together. They wiggled across to his sun lounger and began to stroke and caress him; rubbing their breasts against his corpulent flesh, as one of the blondes slipped her red-taloned fingers under the tiny strip of black material and began to knead and caress him.

Gabriella nodded to Marty.

'OK; That's Catelli. I'm going to go take him down now, whilst he's occupied. Give me five seconds to get clear and then, do it.'

She handed the Remington to Marty; slipped out of her trenchcoat, and handed it to him. His eyes widened. Beneath the coat, she was naked; except for a tiny G-string. She held out her hand and he returned the shotgun to her. She stepped out from the trees with the shotgun concealed behind her back; and sashayed across the lawn towards the terrace. No one took much notice of one more gorgeous, naked girl as she approached the terrace. The couples on the sun loungers were too engrossed in their sexual antics to even glance up as her shadow fell across them.

Big Frank Catelli was getting nicely aroused by the two blondes, with his engorged member straining at the tiny strip of black material as the red-taloned fingers expertly squeezed, and stroked him. It would soon be time for a two-whore fuck-sandwich on his king-sized bed. A shadow fell across him, and he lazily glanced up at a pair of beautiful breasts below a gorgeous Asian face. He grinned licentiously. Three would be even better... then he froze, as the dispassionate black eye of a shotgun muzzle suddenly appeared from behind her back. He opened his mouth to scream... and his world exploded. The first shot ripped into his huge, fleshy paunch; the second into his groin... taking half the blonde's head with it. The slim figure vanished from the sight of his bulging eyes as his world dissolved into a maelstrom of pain... and faintly, above his screams, he heard the loud, roaring boom of a machine gun, and shrieks as the hail of bullets began tearing into his guests.

Marty heard the deep boom of Gabriella's shotgun and stepped out onto the lawn. Naked figures were scattering in all directions. He couldn't see her. He raised the assault rifle and squeezed the trigger. The AK-47 bucked in his grasp as it roared its hammering burst of full auto fire; with the smell of burnt gunpowder filling the air, and a steady stream of spent brass casings spewing from the side ejection port onto the lush, manicured lawn. Traversing the target, he watched the stream of lead punching holes through sun-tanned flesh, ripping ragged wounds through muscles and internal organs, shattering bones; exploding out of backs, creating tearing messy, ragged exit wounds. Blood splattered the sun loungers and walls, bits of flesh, and bone fragments exploded across the terrace; staining the expensive Italian flagstones, and turning the aquamarine waters of the pool into a swirling, red soup.

Emptying the magazine in one continuous burst; he pushed the magazine release lever forward; pulled out the spent magazine; flipped it over and shoved in the full one. Pulling back the charging lever; he opened up again on anything that showed the slightest signs of movement. Gabriella had said to kill them all; and that was exactly what he would do. He only stopped when the bolt clicked home on an empty chamber. Surveying the scene of absolute bloody carnage, he saw no movement; except... a naked figure walking unsteadily from behind the wall protecting the entrance to the house.

He saw that it was Gabriella; the shotgun held loosely in one hand, and blood seeping from between the fingers of her other hand which was pressed tightly against her stomach. Dropping the assault rifle, he ran to her. Her face was white, and her breathing was shallow and panting. He stared at her hand, and then slowly... gently lifted it away. The bullet hole was below and slightly to the right of her navel. Its edges were purple. He let her put her hand back and apprehensively looked around her side. There was blood all down her back; welling from a big ragged hole just below her ribcage. Grabbing

292

his handkerchief, he looked into her eyes; eyes that were dark with pain and shock.

'This is going to hurt, but I must try to stop some of the bleeding... what happened?'

Her voice was almost a whisper.

'One of his fucking goons wasn't quite dead, and managed to get a shot off.'

Gently balling the handkerchief against the awful hole in her back; he managed to get her to the trees and helped her to slip her trenchcoat on.

'I've gotta get you to an emergency room. Right now.'

She shook her head.

'No, Marty; just get me home.'

Marty's four-hour drive down Interstate 80 was a nightmare of gut-wrenching apprehension and panic. Gabriella was deathly pale, and continually drifting in and out of unconsciousness. Just south of Verdi he was picked up by a Nevada State Patrol blue and white that followed him all the way down Interstate 80 to the State Line, before it turned off the highway and parked up behind a large billboard.

By the time he reached the approach to the Golden Gate Bridge, her condition had worsened considerably. Marty made a snap decision. Even though Gabriella had said that he should take her straight home; the only way that she might stand a chance would be if he took her straight to a trusted Chinese physician down in Bayview.

Twenty minutes later, he pulled into the kerb halfway along Fitzgerald Avenue and carefully lifted Gabriella out of the T-Bird. He was horrified at the amount of blood on the passenger seat. He carried her up three flights of stairs as quickly as he could to the room on the third floor that the physician, Doctor Leong used as a surgery.

Old Doctor Leong; a native Chinese-American; had been a combat surgeon during the Korean War. If anyone could do something for Gabriella... it would be him. He was well-versed in the "Patch 'em up with no questions asked" treatment that was frequently sought after on the mean and vicious streets around here. He pointed to an old leather examination couch in the room and told Marty to gently lay her on it. He then carefully opened her trench coat and studied the wound. By now; a blue-black halo of bruising extending out for about an inch surrounded the bullet puncture wound. Charlie Leong nodded.

'Forty-five calibre at close range. Turn her gently and let me see the exit wound ... if there is one.'

Marty snorted.

'There is one, Doc. It's the size of a Goddam tennis ball.'

Charlie Leong stared at the awful hole in her back. He looked up at Marty.

'When did this happen?'

Marty tore his eyes away from Gabriella's chalky-white face; all damp with sweat.

'About four and a half hours ago.'

Charlie Leong shook his head sadly.

'I am sorry Marty; but this is almost certainly a death wound. The slug must have been a hollow point to have done this to her. She has suffered massive internal damage. It is a wonder that she has not succumbed to shock already.'

Marty stared at him.

'But, she cannot die. She is Gabriella... the *Bo-sseu*... the Boss of the Chang syndicate. You must do something.'

Charlie Leong shook his head.

'There is nothing I can do, except alleviate her pain with Opium. I fear that she is setting her feet upon the pathway of her journey over the mountains to "The Otherworld." even as we speak.'

As a consequence of massive internal haemorrhaging and extensive internal abdominal injuries; Gabriella Chang drifted in and out of consciousness all that evening and died in Charlie Leong's arms in the small hours of the following morning.

A distraught Marty Ryom drove down to the Central waterfront, racked with guilt and remorse for, in his mind; his failure to protect Gabriella by not confirming that all of Catelli's pool party were, indeed, dead; parked the T-Bird up on pier 70; and blew his brains out at around three o'clock in the morning.

The Reno police didn't discover the carnage at Basque lane until several hours after the shootings. The local residents had thought that the gunshots were fireworks being let off at Big Frank Catelli's party. They found thirty-six corpses strewn around the pool and terrace area; both male and female; eighty spent, seven-point-six-two millimetre brass casings marked with Russian Headstamp codes scattered on the lawn; and an AK-47 assault rifle; also stamped with Russian Manufacturer and proof markings.

Catelli was discovered at the side of the property; still alive; but with horrendous injuries to his abdomen and groin. He was rushed to Saint Mary's Hospital barely clinging to life. It was already too late. The antimony buckshot pellets were toxic... and deeply embedded in his intestines. Even if he had not succumbed to his injuries; the surgeons remarked that Catelli's gut and genitals resembled chopped liver, and, even if they could have done something; there was little doubt that he would have been condemned to spending the rest of his life as a eunuch, eating and defecating through tubes. As it was; Big Frank Catelli died on the operating table at around eight-thirty that evening.

9 am, Tuesday, May 2nd, 1961.
810 Kansas Street,
Potrero Hill,
San Francisco.
California.
USA.

Two SFPD black-and-whites and Sam Mayfield's black Chevy Bel Air sedan were already parked up outside number 810 as Callaghan turned the DeSoto into Kansas Street. He groaned.

'Oh, shit! That's all we need... the FBI blundering around, and muddying the pond!'

The young patrolman had reported in the sighting of the black T-Bird; and a licence check had revealed that it belonged to Gabriella Chang. Captain Neil Halloran at the Potrero Station had called them up at the Washington street number and given them the information. He had quietly suggested that they get down there fast, as he was about to call the FBI in accordance with his instructions.

Callaghan pulled in beside the black Chevy, and turned to Charlotte.

OK, babe; so what are we looking for?'

Charlotte shrugged.

'I have no idea; but, whatever it is... it certainly won't be the gemstone. That will be tucked away somewhere safe. I guess we search for something that will lead us to it.'

The apartment on the second floor that had been rented out in the name of Ryom; and occupied, according to the old lady on the first floor to a "nice young Asian couple" who were quiet tenants, and had paid a month's rent in advance; was an architecturally interesting, but decoratively bland, typical Potrero Hill rental. Sam Mayfield's boys had already carried out an extensive search... pulling out drawers, lifting mattresses and carpets... all the usual tricks; but had come up empty.

As Charlotte and Callaghan entered; he turned, and gave them a sardonic grin.

'Great! The cavalry's here! Maybe you can do better than us. We've done this joint over with a Goddam nit comb and turned up zilch! We'll leave you to it and get back to the office. Goddam waste of resources if you want my opinion.'

Charlotte nodded.

'OK. We'll see. Have a good day!'

Sam Mayfield grunted and jerked his thumb to his guys to leave.

Alone in the apartment; Charlotte turned to Callaghan.

'Right. We need to be cute about this. We're looking for anything that seems out of place. Any thing that doesn't fit the whole impression of the place. Koreans have an empathy with their surroundings. Everything fits in their environment; both at work and at home. OK; this Gabriella Chang is half-American... but this inherent tendency for order and harmony is deep-seated; and I imagine she is still guided by it.'

The first hour's searching was fruitless. Just as Sam Mayfield had said; the whole damn place was clean. There was nothing that revealed even the identities of the apartment's tenants. Charlotte leaned against the kitchen sink and surveyed her surroundings. She sighed. There was absolutely nothing there. Dammit! She called to Callaghan.

'D'you want a cup of coffee before we call it a day?'

His voice came back from the bedroom.

'Yeah... OK. Make mine cream and no sugar.'

She walked across to the wall shelf and reached for the coffee jar. As she lifted it from where it was resting it emitted a thin, dull clunk. Cautiously, she lifted the lid and peered inside. Nestling amongst the ground coffee beans was a little green-jade pillbox. She pulled it out; blew on it to clear the coffee dust from its surface; and lifted the lid. It contained a luggage locker key and a small fold of paper. She called out for Callaghan as she dropped the key into her hand and began to carefully unfold the thin, almost translucent paper square.

As Callaghan came into the kitchen she was smoothing out the paper. Drawn on it was what appeared to be a maze as seen from above; except there were no entry or exit points in the diagram.

Callaghan peered over her shoulder, and laughed.

'I thought you'd found something. It's just a kid's puzzle!'

She shook her head.

'No; it's much more subtle than that. The diagram appears to be made up of *Hangungmal* characters. Those are the Korean language symbols... like Chinese or Japanese... and there's this left luggage locker key. This is it, Gil. All I have to do is translate it!'

With a fresh pot of coffee; Charlotte sat at the table and began to transcribe the characters that made up the maze. The subtle construction of the interlocking lines was masterful... and complex. At length; after transliteration, her copy read...

"Nam-jjok me-in ho-rim-ni-da. Oen-jjok-ttoen ju-yo haeng-im-ni-da. Sa-mul-ham."

Translated literally; this now read:

"To the South is the main hall. The top left row. Locker."

The enigmatic locker key bore a stamped design of three letter "T"s on one side and the number "76B" on the reverse. It was definitely a left luggage locker key... but, to which rail or bus station did it belong?

Reaching for the San Francisco Street guide, she studied the index. There! It could only be that one... if the letters on the key referred to the name; and were not a manufacturer's mark. The Transbay Transit Terminal was on the corner of First and Mission Streets; less than three miles away; and had been built as the terminal for East Bay commuter trains using the newly opened Bay Bridge. At the time, trucks and trains used the lower deck of the Bay Bridge, and automobiles operated in both directions on the upper deck. In 1958, the lower deck of the Bay Bridge was converted to automobile traffic only, the train system was dismantled; and by 1959 the Transbay Terminal had been converted into a bus-only facility. It was the perfect place to stash something safely.

Charlotte replaced the locker key in the jade pillbox and slipped it, and the maze design, together with her notebook containing the translation into her purse, and turned to Callaghan.

'OK, Gil; let's leave this place to the cops and get across to this Transbay Terminal. I'm certain that we'll find something there.'

The drive across town took twenty minutes. Callaghan parked the DeSoto up in the Terminal plaza, and they walked across to the massive. drab gray concrete building; an eight hundred and seventy foot-long, flat slab with a two hundred and thirty foot-long central pavilion occupying three blocks of Mission Street, which had been designed in Bauhaus Moderne style and had not withstood the passing years very well. It had become a dingy, depressing place; fairy quiet, except for the infrequent Greyhound arrivals, and during the afternoon rush hours when one bus bound for the East Bay left every thirty seconds, normally carrying a full load of passengers; but, now there were no more than a handful of travellers waiting for their buses. There were, however quite a few drunks and deadbeats wandering around.

Charlotte walked down the granite mausoleum of the long, pillared, main waiting room; her footsteps echoing hollowly. The ranks of luggage lockers were grimy and dented; and many had been broken open. Callaghan followed a few paces behind. Towards the far end of the left-hand row of lockers, she found number 76B. The lock was intact.

Callaghan stood back watching the far end of the wide corridor between the lines of lockers as she slipped the key into the lock and turned it. The metal door swung open smoothly, to reveal a Pan Am cabin bag. Lifting it out; she ran the zipper fastener round to open it and peeked inside. It contained what looked to be about twenty thousand Dollars in hundred bills, and a thin white envelope. She squeezed the envelope and felt a hard object... another key!

Slipping the strap of the cabin bag over her shoulder; Charlotte closed and locked the locker, leaving the key in the lock. They then walked back to the exit, with Callaghan a little way behind and keeping a wary watchfulness on anyone who approached too closely, or showed more than a passing interest in Charlotte, or the bag that she was carrying.

Safely back in the DeSoto, Charlotte unzipped the bag and showed Callaghan the contents. He whistled softly through his teeth.

'Wow! There must be close on twenty Gs in there. Nest Egg?... or Escape money?'

She shook her head.

'I have no idea. This is what interests me...'

She pulled out the envelope; tore it open, and removed a key. It looked very different from a normal house key. The teeth had a square profile, unlike normal keys. She glanced at Callaghan.

'A Bank safe deposit box key, maybe?'

He nodded.

'Could be. But apart from that engraved number: 2619; how the heck are we going to find out which bank it belongs to?'

She smiled quietly.

'I might just have an answer to that one. The office will have a locksmith on the books. He can probably tell what brand it is; and then we can trace through the banks by elimination... if we strike lucky and it's an unusual brand of safes, and safe deposit boxes.'

Back at the CIA safe house apartment at 2002 Washington Street; Charlotte made a telephone call to the local office. Twenty minutes later, the doorbell rang. Opening the door, she was confronted by a man in his mid-forties, wearing blue coveralls and carrying a plain tool bag. He identified himself as Brody Schaeffer; attached to the Technical section of the SFPD Planning Division, and was here to identify a certain key in her possession. She smiled.

'Hi! I'm Charlotte and this is Callaghan. We have a key that was in the possession of a fugitive suspect, and would like to know what it unlocks.'

Brody Schaeffer nodded.

'Well, I'll give to my best shot; but unless it's a distinctive pattern it's gonna be a hit and miss guess.'

Charlotte gave him a rueful grin.

'OK; come and sit down, and take a look at it. Would you like a cup of coffee?'

Schaeffer nodded.

'Thanks. Cream and no sugar, please.'

She handed him the key and went to make coffee whilst he studied it.'

When she returned, he was smiling.

'You're lucky. It's a "LeFebure" safe deposit box key; that's about fifteen years old. Most of the city Banks changed over to "Diebold" brand boxes after LeFebure was taken over by Mosler and then, later, by Diebold.'

He pulled a slim black notebook from his tool bag and flipped through the pages. He looked up.

'There are only two banks still using LeFebure boxes... The Federal Reserve Bank on Sansome Street; and the Hibernia Bank on McAllister. My guess would be that this key belongs to the Federal Reserve.'

Charlotte smiled and nodded.

'Thank you very much.'

Schaeffer handed the key back to her, and closed the notebook.

'Don't get too much of a buzz just yet. You'll need a Federal Warrant before you can get to see what the box that this key fits, will contain. The way it works, is that a customer comes into the branch, walks up to the guy who looks after the boxes and says something like: "I'd like to get in my box please." He'll ask them their name, and then pull their card. They'll sign an entry slip, and he will compare the signature on the slip with the signature on the card. The box number is on the card.

He takes them into the vault, gets their key from them, inserts their key and his into the box, and opens the door. The boxes are actually long plastic containers behind the metal doors. He then hands the whole plastic container to the customer, and directs them to one of the privacy booths. Without a signature you won't get access... hence the need for a Warrant. Even then, you might have trouble; so be prepared to use the National Security Act if you have to.'

Chapter Nineteen.

10.30 am, Thursday, May 4th, 1961.
Federal Reserve Bank of San Francisco,
400. Sansome Street.
Union Square - Financial District.
San Francisco.
California.
USA.

Callaghan parked up outside the Federal Reserve Bank of San Francisco Building, at Sansome Street, and turned to Charlotte.

'How do you want to play this?'

She looked at him.

'First off; I guess we try the softly-softly approach with the Bank Manager. If he follows the Bank protocols, we hit him with the Warrant. If that fails; we play the National Security card.'

Together, the walked up the sweeping, steps that ran the whole frontage of the building, and crossed the paved area beneath the Ionic colonnade. Inside; Charlotte approached the lobby guard and asked for the Manager. Disdainfully, he looked her up and down.

'You have an appointment?'

She returned the favour by looking him up and down with an equal measure of disdain.

'No. This is Federal Business.'

The guard almost sneered... almost; until he saw Callaghan; big, broad, and forbidding; step up closer to her. His hand darted to the telephone on his table, and he quickly dialled a number. Within a couple of minutes, a young clerk came hurrying across the floor and invited them to follow him.

The Manager's office was on the second floor. Charlotte and Callaghan were ushered into the presence of the Manager... a portly, sleek, and urbane individual in his fifties; wearing rimless spectacles, and wearing a bespoke three-piece, chalk-strip suit that must have cost the thick end of five Gs. He stood, smiled benignly, and extended his hand to Charlotte; then invited her to sit. He spoke with a cultured Southern Californian accent.

'Good morning. I am Clifford C. Scott; Manager of the Federal Reserve Bank of San Francisco. How may I be of assistance, Madam?'

Charlotte reached into her purse and withdrew the key; laying it on the wide, polished surface of his desk in front of him. Studying him carefully; she spoke.

'This key has been seized from the possessions of a fugitive suspect. It has been identified as, in all probability; being the key to a safe deposit box in your vaults. We would like to inspect the contents of the box that corresponds with this key.'

Clifford C. Scott smiled condescendingly.

'Then I am afraid your visit will prove fruitless. The Bank Charter protocols with regard to safe deposit boxes require that only the depositor or an accredited signatory is permitted access to the said box.'

Charlotte nodded.

'I am aware of that; which is why I have a Federal Warrant issued by The Superior Court of The City and County of San Francisco, authorising me to seize any such evidence that the said box pertaining to this key, contains.'

Clifford C. Scott stared at her; and then, at the warrant she placed in front of him. He read it slowly; then looked up and shook his head. Before he could say a word; Charlotte snapped her fingers at Callaghan; who crossed the room and stood by the door; arms folded and immobile; creating an obstruction for anyone who might try to enter.

She looked back at Scott.

'Very well, Mr. Scott. I must inform you that you are now very close to being in contravention of the National Security Act of 1947, with regard to wilful obstruction of an investigation concerning a matter of National Security.'

Clifford C. Scott's face slowly turned pink, and he spluttered,

'Who the hell are you?'

Holding his eyes with her cold, blue gaze; Charlotte produced her CIA Identification card and laid it on the desk next to the warrant. He stared at it, and slowly, his face changed from pink to white. She watched him for a few moments; and then continued.

'If you choose to cooperate with me; all this will go away.

Otherwise, I really don't think that you would do particularly well with a ten-to-fifteen in somewhere like San Quentin, Mr Clifford.'

Ten minutes later; Charlotte and Callaghan were standing in the vault waiting for the clerk in charge to turn both his, and the suspect key in the two key slots of the door numbered 2619; halfway along the bank of identical doors lining the far wall of the vault. Along the other three walls were hundreds of safe deposit boxes containing who knows what?... priceless jewellery? A fortune in diamonds and other precious stones? Sheaves of thousand-Dollar bills, or Security Bonds? No matter; box 2619 was the only one that mattered. The thin oblong door swung open silently on its precision hinges. The clerk pulled the long, metal box out of the wall and invited them to follow him to a privacy cubicle across the vault which could be closed with a heavy curtain. He placed the box on a small examining table within the cubicle; stepped outside, and pulled the curtain across.

Charlotte lifted the lid. The only things inside, were a silenced Walther PPK pistol and a little black pouch with a tightly-pulled drawstring around its open end. She picked up the pouch and placed it on the table beside her. Leaving the Walther in the box, she closed the lid and glanced at Callaghan. His face was impassive... no curiosity; no anticipation... just a steady gaze at the pouch. That was odd; after everything that they had been through. She dismissed the thought and carefully loosed the drawstring; then upturned the pouch. The object inside slipped out onto the table and lay there; its cut facets reflecting the light against the walls of the cubicle like streaks of blood.

Charlotte stared at it as it lay there; this malevolent artefact that she had been pursuing across three Continents for almost as long as she could remember... and perhaps, if there was any truth in these things that so many people down the years had said or felt about her; that she was the reincarnation of "The Golden Child"... the Warrior Maid whose name was mentioned so many times within the pages of the ancient volumes discovered at Tunguska in the wastes of Siberia, and that she had painstakingly translated during her expedition in 1937 on the instructions of Reichsführer-SS Heinrich Himmler; when she had been known by her real identity of Fräulein Doktor Karyn Helle von Seringen; Deputy Researcher for the Deutsches Ahnenerbe Institute for Linguistic study, at Berlin-Dahlem; for so much longer than that.

If the legend of "The Golden Child" held the smallest grain of truth, and was to be believed; she might well have been inextricably bound to this malignant gemstone; perhaps, even back to the beginnings of time itself. The Abaddon Stone... "The Destroyer of Worlds," lay there; a tiny blood-red spark flaring deep in its heart... as if infused with a chilling smugness or perhaps, malignant pleasure that this convoluted odyssey of hunt and evade; stretching back across the years, had now come, it seemed, full circle. Staring at this Garnet gemstone laying quietly on the surface of the table; she suddenly shivered... as if, at that same moment; a grey goose had flown over her grave.

Callaghan seemed not to notice. He was staring at the gemstone; and although it might just have been a trick of the reflected light spearing from the cut facets; as she glanced up at him, for a fleeting moment, the pupils of his eyes seemed to glow red. She shivered again and carefully replaced the gemstone in the little pouch, then placed it in her purse. She glanced again at Callaghan. Whatever she thought that she might have seen was not there now. He picked up the box, and smiled.

'Is that it? Is that really what all this fuss has been about?'

She nodded;

'Yes, Gil. This is the Abaddon Stone. It's evil, and has brought so much death and misery to so many people. I had hoped that it would have been locked away forever by now; but, seeing as they couldn't even do that one small thing; now, I have to destroy it forever.'

He stared at her.

'But, what about our mission? What about the Pentagon? Don't they want it as a possible alternative to the synthetic rubies for designing this "Death Ray" that they're talking about?'

She gave him a hard look.

'Yes; and that's why they're not going to get their hands on it. I don't want to talk about it any more. Let's just get out of here.'

Callaghan was quiet on the journey back to the Washington Street apartment. Charlotte tried several times, to strike up a conversation; but without much success. She assumed that this was down to her decision to defy Washington, and the Pentagon in particular; with regard to this evil gemstone now nestling in her purse. She was confused about his sudden change in attitude. They had often talked about what should happen if, and when she finally managed to get her hands on the gemstone. She had explained in detail what it was said to be capable of; and what it was alleged to be. She had recounted in detail, her Siberian journey; the discovery of the sealed artefact; and what had ensued when it had finally been released from its confinement in Nazi Germany. He had seemed to understand; he had never questioned her intent... until now.

She studied him as he turned the DeSoto into Washington Street. This man whom she loved; this man who had declared his love for her; was now reticent and cold. She sighed. Whatever was bothering him would have to be brought out into the open... quickly; if their relationship was to get back onto an even footing. They needed to have a serious discussion... right now.

Inside the apartment; she confronted him.

'Gil; sit down. We need to talk.'

She sat on the sofa next to him, and studied his morose expression. Taking a deep breath. She began.

'I have no idea why you have suddenly become like this, Gil. You always knew that if I found this Goddam Abaddon Stone; my intention was either to destroy it, or make sure that it was locked away in some place where it could no longer do any harm. If the Pentagon hawks get their hands on it; there is no knowing what they might unleash. The whole situation since the Bay of Pigs fiasco has become a major embarrassment for Kennedy; and he and his brother seem to be getting obsessed over toppling the Castro regime.

Castro; and by association... the Russians, are really pissed; and think that we might try again. It's possible that the Russians will try to install nuclear weapons on Cuban soil... and that could lead to a nuclear confrontation between us and them. I for one, don't much fancy mushroom clouds for breakfast. That is why I have to do what I have to do.'

Callaghan was quiet... no argument; no opposition to her stance. He shrugged, and said, quite simply,

'OK... your decision.'

He stood up and glanced at his wristwatch.

'I'm hungry. D'you fancy some lunch?'

She nodded and began to get up from the sofa.

'Yeah, fine. I'll go make something.'

He put a hand on her shoulder to prevent her from standing.

'No; stay there. I'll do it. How about a cheese omelette with hash browns?'

She smiled up at him.

'Yes, thank you. That will be fine.'

He smiled. The old, easy smile that she had come to love.

'It's the least I can do after being so grouchy.'

In the kitchen, Callaghan began to prepare the meal He checked the big General Electric Refrigerator... plenty of eggs and a fair-sized block of cheese. Taking the block, he began grating the cheese into a bowl, whilst the omelette and Hash brown skillets were warming on the stove. Breaking four eggs into another bowl; he began whisking them with a fork. Dropping as mall square of butter into the skillet; he added the grated cheese; and whisked the mixture again.

Turning the Hash browns, he poured the omelette mix into the skillet... then carefully pulled a small pill bottle from his pocket. Shaking out three of the anonymous white pills that it contained; he placed them into the bowl of a dessert spoon and crushed them down with the back of the bowl of another spoon. He then sprinkled them onto the cooking omelette. With a spatula, he turned the omelette and cooked the other side. Arranging the hash browns on a warm plate; he turned out the omelette and picked up a knife and fork. He then carried the completed plate in to Charlotte.

She looked up.

'Mmm! That smells good. I wasn't aware that you're a cook as well!'

Callaghan smiled, and handed her the plate. She cut into the omelette and tasted it.

'That's a really good omelette, Gil.'

He nodded.

'I figured that you might like it. I'll go make mine now. Enjoy!'

He turned and walked back to the kitchen as she settled down to the last meal that she would ever eat. The pills that Callaghan had crushed into the mix were a particularly powerful and fast-acting Pentobarbital. There would be no suspicion... she would feel no symptoms. She would simply fall asleep; and then, he could complete his mission. Ten minutes later; she had finished her meal and he was half-way through his; when she turned to him.

'God! I'm bushed! I think I'll have a lie-down.'

He nodded.

'It's been a hell of a busy few days. Go get some sleep.'

'She made to get up from the sofa and wobbled; then slumped back among the cushions. He put down his plate and moved across to her.

'Steady, babe! I'll carry you.'

He picked her up and walked to the bedroom; where he laid her on the bed. She put her arms sleepily around his neck.

'My White Knight!'

He smiled, and tucked her in.

'I'll just go do the dishes and then I'll be back. Sleep tight!'

He left her for another ten minutes; then crept back into the bedroom. Gently, he nudged her... no response. He bent over her and put his mouth close to her ear.

'Are you asleep, babe?'

There was no response. She was in a deep sleep. He turned, and walked to the bathroom; where he closed the flue plate on the storage water heater, and fired it up. He then came back into the bedroom carrying a face cloth that he had soaked under the basin faucet. Standing by the bed, he studied Charlotte. She was out cold; her breathing was deep and rhythmical. He removed a small eye dropper bottle from his pocket and, holding the wet face cloth over his nose and mouth; unscrewed the top and drew a little of the clear liquid into the glass pipette.

He then reached over, and squeezed the rubber bladder... dropping four drops of the liquid on the pillow next to her nose and mouth. Stepping back sharply; he replaced the glass pipette and hurried out into the living area; closing the door behind him. He sat in an armchair, and sighed heavily. The eye dropper bottle contained an infusion of highly concentrated hydrogen cyanide. As it vaporised, she would inhale the extremely high concentrations of the poisonous fumes in the air; and there would be no time for symptoms to develop. In her heavily drugged state, she would simply stop breathing. It would be difficult to differentiate the effects of cyanide and carbon monoxide poisoning. The classic symptoms of poisoning with either of them were very similar.... hence the little trick with the flue plate of the storage water heater. Whoever found her would think that it was a tragic accident.

He sat for some time with his head in his hands. He didn't feel good about what he had just done. He had loved her; but she was so stubborn. Perhaps, that's why he had loved her. If only she'd listened; and agreed to take the fucking gemstone back to Washington. He shrugged and got up out of the chair. Walking across the living area, he paused, and opened the door an inch or so. There was no almond smell. Carefully he stepped into the bedroom, and walked over to the bed. She looked as though she was asleep... but she wasn't breathing. He laid his fingers on her throat. There was no pulse. He sighed heavily, then bent down and kissed her gently on her still-warm forehead. With tears in his eyes, he whispered,

'Sorry, babe; but it's a matter of National Security.'

He pulled the covers up around her and reached for her purse. His fingers touched the little black bag, and he pulled it out; slipping it into his pocket. With one last sad look, he left her there; walked to the front door of the apartment, and stepped out into the corridor. He took the lift down to street level, walked across to the parked-up DeSoto; fired it up, and drove away; heading south for San Francisco International Airport.

4 pm, Thursday, May 4th, 1961.
Washington National Airport.
Arlington County,
Virginia
USA.

Two men in dark suits and sunglasses were waiting for Callaghan as he came through the airside gate into the lounge of Washington National Airport. The taller of the two stepped forward.

'Callaghan? We have a car waiting.'

A black Lincoln Continental fitted with dark privacy glass was waiting outside the white terminal building. The two men, who smelled like Secret Service, opened the rear door or Callaghan to get in. Sitting in the rear seat was a large man aged about fifty; with short, white hair cut in a military style. The two men climbed into the front seat and raised the power partition. As the car moved out from the parking bay, the man turned to Callaghan.

'OK, Callaghan, What's the deal? You have the artefact?'

Callaghan looked at the man.

'Perhaps; but who are you?'

The man smiled softly.

'Just answer the question, Callaghan. I am Colonel Laumer.'

'Callaghan nodded. He had never heard the name; but he had never had any dealings with the Pentagon. He pulled the little pouch from his pocket and passed it to Laumer; who tipped the gemstone into his hand. Perhaps, it was a reflection; but, as Callaghan saw a complacent smile spread across Laumer's jowly face; just for a moment, it seemed that the man's pupils glowed red. It was really weird, and slightly unnerving.

Laumer slipped the gemstone back into the little pouch and turned to Callaghan.

'The woman has been dealt with?'

Callaghan nodded.

'Yes; it will look like an accident when they discover her.'

Laumer gave a chilling chuckle.

'At last! The Golden Child has embraced her doom!'

Callaghan stared at him. An awful, cold feeling touched him between the shoulder blades.

'The Golden Child? Who's that? Charlotte Mckenna had the gemstone. She'd been chasing it for years…'

Laumer laughed.

'You have no idea, Callaghan. Her real name was Karyn Helle von Seringen... or at least; it was, in this existence. In truth; we know that she was once Kathalyn Seregon; Guardian of The Light; far back in the Age of the Beginnings. The Golden Child has been a bane to the mighty art that we have wrought since the beginnings of time; and now, she is no more.'

Callaghan stared at Laumer; aghast.

'What the hell are you talking about, Laumer?'

Laumer grinned... almost giggled.

'I speak of the great design that, even now, wreathes about the pygmies whom you would call your government. The time of The Dark Lord is almost upon you; The Night of the Shadows Rising is poised to engulf you all.'

Callaghan shook his head trying to clear this crazy talk, but, in the back of his mind; something that Charlotte had said was prodding at his conscience... The Abaddon Stone... "The Destroyer of Worlds."

He stared at Laumer.

'What the hell are you ranting about? This is fucking rubbish. Dark Lord? Shadows Rising? The Pentagon instructed that this Garnet was to be secured for this "Laser" project.'

Laumer giggled again; an unnerving, almost feminine giggle.

'Callaghan; that was what you were told to believe. You will never comprehend what is about to eclipse your puerile existences. You were merely the vessel by which we could acquire the artefact. Now; just sit back and enjoy the ride.'

Callaghan's body was pulled out of the Potomac River, three days later. He had been shot twice in the head.

~ ~ ~ ~ ~ ~ ~ ~ ~ ~

Lightning Source UK Ltd.
Milton Keynes UK
UKOW041147171212

203761UK00002B/332/P